GLADYS

GLADYS OF HARLECH

L. M. SPOONER

With an introduction by
Rita Singer

WELSH WOMEN'S CLASSICS

First published by Charles. J Skeet, London in 1858
First published by Honno in 2017
'Ailsa Craig', Heol y Cawl, Dinas Powys, Wales, CF64 4AH

1 2 3 4 5 6 7 8 9 10

ISBN: 978-1-909983-54-0 print
ISBN:978-1-909983-55-7 ebook

Published with the financial support of the Welsh Books Council.
Cover painting: 'An Arrival' by Edmund Blair Leighton, 1916, from the Cardiff City Hall collection
Photo © Rob Watkins

Introduction

RITA SINGER

It is the year 1485. A young Welsh noblewoman sits in a mountain cave somewhere near Harlech, secretly sewing a standard to be worn in battle against the tyrant usurper currently sitting on the throne. She embroiders the white and green banner with a red dragon. Having finished her task, she asks her uncle to deliver the banner into the hands of their last hope and prophesied liberator upon his imminent return from exile in France. This hoped-for son of prophecy is, of course, Henry Tudor, Earl of Richmond, campaigning on the side of the House of Lancaster against the Yorkist King Richard III of England. The young Welsh noblewoman answers to the name Gladys and she is the granddaughter of the former Welsh keeper of Harlech Castle, ap Dafydd ap Jevan.[1] As the last of her noble lineage, young Gladys has dedicated her life to restoring her people's freedom and regaining ownership of her castle and lands. In this pursuit of Welsh liberty, she ultimately sacrifices her love for the noble English-born Ethelred Conyers and lives out her days in single maidenhood, keeping watch over her people from the battlements of Harlech Castle.

Tracing the literary output of Gladys's creator, Louisa Matilda Spooner (1820-1886), is difficult if not downright impossible. In 1858, she anonymously published her first novel, *Gladys of Harlech, or: The Sacrifice*.[2] Only a year later in an issue of the *Freemason's Quarterly*, her London-based publisher Charles J. Skeet announced the imminent release of '"Rich and Poor" by the author of "Gladys of Harlech"', but no such book seems ever to have appeared.[3] Instead, Spooner had changed publishing houses. Writing now for T. Cautley Newby, the other two of her known works carry the titles *Country Landlords* (1860) and *The Welsh Heiress* (1868), and identify the author only by her initials or in abbreviated form as 'L. M. Spooner'. To complicate matters further, for decades, *Gladys of Harlech* was attributed to one of her contemporaries, the better known writer Anne Beale (1816-1900) because she, too, published a 'Gladys novel', *Gladys the Reaper* (1860). Many of these hurdles which obstruct attempts to trace Spooner's literary output arise from the paucity of available information on her personal life. Little is known about her, except that she was the fifth of ten children of Elizabeth Spooner, née Easton, and 'the railway engineer and manager James Spooner, who came to Wales from Birmingham to work for north Wales slate-quarry owner Samuel Holland' and supervised the development of the Ffestiniog Railway.[4] Spooner was born and grew up in Merionethshire; she never married and, after the death of her father, moved in with her older brother Charles Easton Spooner, also a railway engineer, and his family.[5] Despite the scant information about her life, Spooner's novels reflect some of her family background. Her stories are largely set in her native Merionethshire and her protagonists hail from the nobility and gentrified classes in Wales. Likewise, her English family background provides a certain double vision of community life in north-west Wales and influences the social and political outlook in her portrayal of Welsh-language culture.

Gladys of Harlech is a product of the economic and political changes that took place during the 1850s and 1860s. The Welsh middle classes in particular profited from these developments, gaining equally in class and national confidence and subsequently pushing depictions of Welsh culture into Anglophone domains, such as the popular historical and social novel. Despite its medieval setting, Spooner's novel echoes these changes and illustrates the broadening definition of what it meant to be confidently Welsh in Victorian Britain. *Gladys of Harlech* reflects the ideals of readers for whom Welshness and Britishness represented no contradiction and who yearned for a positive representation of their lives in contemporary literature, as is evident in a favourable, if somewhat biased, review in the *Cambrian Journal*:

> Until the last few years we had no books of fiction, illustrative of Welsh manners and customs, that a genuine Cymro could for a moment tolerate [...]. Of late, however, (within the last ten years,) there has been a great reaction in this respect. Works of fiction are rapidly multiplying, and read with avidity by the Welsh population. [...] In the English language, too, we are beginning to have novels of the right stamp. [...] [T]he style of the authoress of *Gladys of Harlech* is simple and chaste, and the subject of her tale is pleasingly worked up [...]. [T]he true spirit of patriotism [...] penetrates [...] *Gladys of Harlech*, and gives life and vigour [...], which is refreshing to contemplate.[6]

Rewriting History

Gladys of Harlech is set in the fifteenth century and chiefly follows the Wars of the Roses between 1455 and 1485. The novel portrays the involvement of the Welsh nobility in the power struggle between the houses of York and Lancaster that plunged England and Wales into a series of armed conflicts. These conflicts ended with the eventual restoration of peace following the ascension of the Welsh Tudors to the English throne. The conflict originated much earlier in 1399 with the deposition of King Richard II, from the House of York, by his Lancastrian cousin Bolingbroke, the later Henry IV. Owing to Henry V's premature death (he had died of dysentery caught during a military campaign in France), King Henry VI had been raised under carefully chosen tutelage until he was old enough to rule on his own. However, he lacked his father's military authority and his grandfather's political zeal. Easily swayed in his opinions by his court advisors and his French wife, Margaret of Anjou, who effectively took over at court, Henry VI's rule was characterised by favouritism and political unpredictability. Over time, he also began to show signs of mental instability which frequently resulted in his total retreat from public life. These combined factors alienated the House of York and their allies, resulting in the open outbreak of hostilities in 1455 while Henry VI was suffering from an episode of mental illness. After the Yorkists won their first major battle at Towton in 1461, Edward IV was crowned while Henry escaped into Scottish exile. From there, the deposed king and his queen attempted to regain the crown in a number of poorly financed campaigns. These attempts resulted in Henry's eventual capture and imprisonment in the Tower of London in 1465, Margaret's flight to France and a last stand of the Lancastrian forces in a seven-year long siege of Harlech Castle. In 1471, with the decisive defeat of the Lancastrian forces in the Battle of Tewkesbury and the death of Prince Edward, Henry and Margaret's son, Edward IV cemented his supremacy for the time being. While Edward's rule initially returned tentative political and economic stability to England and Wales, in the late 1470s he fell out with his brother, George of Clarence, while his other brother, Richard of York, gained increasingly in power. After Edward's sudden death in 1483 and the subsequent disappearance of his son and heir in the Tower of London, the kingdom plunged once more into political turmoil as Richard of York ascended to the throne of England as Richard III. Opposition to Richard's rule formed early on in his reign, most prominently from the party of the rebelling Duke of Buckingham. After Buckingham's defeat in 1483, many of his former supporters fled to France. Among them was Henry Tudor, who laid tenuous claim to the throne of England by tracing his ancestry back to Edward III through his mother, Margaret Beaufort, Edward's great-great-granddaughter. In August 1485, Henry Tudor set out from France with the plan to land in his native Pembrokeshire. Relying on his Welsh ancestry through his grandfather Owain Tudur's line, Henry hoped to rally natural allies under the Dragon banner and gather more troops about him on his way to England and there engage Richard III in battle. The confrontation eventually took place in the Battle of Bosworth Field, where Richard III was killed and the Plantagenet dynasty came to an end. Conscious of his feeble claim to the English crown, Henry Tudor married Elizabeth of York, Edward IV's daughter, and effectively united the Lancastrian and Yorkist lines, thus ending the Wars of the Roses.[7]

With this broad historical dimension at the heart of the novel, Spooner appropriates old Tudor propaganda, which famously portrayed King Richard III as the ultimate villain, in order to place the Welsh nobility at the heart of British history. Owing to its medieval background, *Gladys of Harlech* takes the form of a classic romance. The plot focuses on the transformation of Wales from an oppressed to a ruling nation together with the emergence of modern Britain as the product not of English heroism but Welsh intervention. And it is this Welsh agency which, ultimately, results in the country's liberation from 'the Saxon yoke', i.e. Edward I's establishment of English rule over conquered Wales with the Statute of Rhuddlan from 1284.[8]

In addition to relating the key events of the Wars of the Roses, *Gladys of Harlech* fuses stories from the *Mabinogion* with Arthurian legends in order to create an alternative founding myth for the united kingdoms of England and Wales. The novel creates a Wales that is steeped in ancient '[t]raditions, not well-vouched history' by, for example, touching on the fate of the fabled princess Branwen.[9] These epic tales subsequently connect with the historically verified Wars of the Roses with the help of one of the novel's most interesting characters, the fictional Dewines, a female equivalent of the Arthurian Merlin. This soothsaying witch continues Merlin's vision of the combating white and red dragons as she prophesies Henry Tudor's reign under the banner of the Red Dragon, which is conveniently provided by the heroine Gladys (474-5, 525). Henry Tudor's historically verified ascent to the English throne after defeating Richard III's troops in the Battle of Bosworth thus turns entirely fantastic. Embedding the Dewines's prophecy in the historical novel forces the reader to rethink and re-evaluate Wales's right to rule. Rewriting British history as an epic tale thus defused the image of a politically impotent Wales, problematic as such historical revisionism was in the actual mid nineteenth century, given the political and social realities of England's relation to Wales during that period. Within the framework of the Wars of the Roses and the ascent of the Tudors, the novel rewrites history from a Welsh point of view as it is now England that is subjected to the rule of a Welsh monarch (525). For its Victorian readership, *Gladys of Harlech* followed in the footsteps of Tudor propaganda in its portrayal of Henry's prophesied reign 'which liberated the Welsh from colonialism, introduced them as junior partners into the merchant capitalism of the sixteenth century, at the price of the expulsion of their language from the state and official life'.[10]

Love on both Sides of the Anglo-Welsh Border

Set during an extended time of national disturbances, the matrimonial alliances between the fictional Welsh and English lovers portrayed in *Gladys of Harlech* are destined to fail as a result of tribal warfare and societal pressure. The love story of the heroine Gladys and Ethelred Conyers gathers momentum only belatedly in the second half of the novel. Against Ethelred's persistent pleading and her uncle's eventual acquiescence with the match, Gladys sacrifices her personal happiness so that she may uphold her function as guardian of the land. Gladys points out from the outset of her relationship with Ethelred that any amicable contact with him signifies much more to her people than social interaction:

I cannot accept of any sympathy, or be under any obligation to a Saxon, one of that race who are the persecutors of our land, our common foes. Alas! even my having any intercourse with you, (did my people know it,) would lower me in their eyes. (267)

In her role as the heiress of Harlech, Gladys stands in a symbiotic connection with the Welsh people as her body becomes public property. In front of her people, she is no longer Gladys, but at one and the same time the mother of the land *and* the community's 'own mountain child' (524). In contrast, the Saxon Ethelred does not stand in any symbiotic connection, neither with the land he owns nor the people in the surroundings of Criccieth. Therefore, he retains his autonomy in the private and in the public sphere, even though the Welsh see in him 'publicly, not privately, the enem[y] of this wild land' (251). Similarly, the marriage vow establishes a public declaration that ensures the recognition of their union before state and church. Thus, Gladys unknowingly and tragically follows in the footsteps of her parents. She may declare her love for Ethelred in private, but cannot repeat it in public. Even with the restoration of her ownership of Harlech and Henry Tudor's dedication of a charter that restores the legal rights to the people of Wales (521-2), Gladys's union with Ethelred ultimately has to remain unfulfilled because English law violates the Welsh sense of homeland which can only be guaranteed through the ownership of the land by the native nobility.

Hiraeth for the Homeland

In *Gladys of Harlech*, Spooner systematically ties landscape, geography and architecture to the emotions of her protagonists. The eviction of Gladys and her family from their ancestral home results in their experiencing *hiraeth*, a sensation of loss not only of place but also of selfhood. The surrender of Harlech after a long siege causes a rift between Dafydd ap Jevan's entire family and the territory to which they are attached historically and emotionally as they are forced into a state of exile – even though they remain in their homeland. Early on in the novel, the castle symbolises the family spirit and moral values of the keepers in its monumental architecture:

> It was a noted site from the earliest ages. The conquerors of the world had a fortress here, upon the wreck of which another was built by the Briton Maelgwyn Gwynedd. Upon this, the present building was founded by Edward I. [...] The face of the rock, steep as the walls which crowned it, [was] almost indistinguishable from the dark grey masonry [...]. (22)

Although the fortress had changed possession frequently and was as often rebuilt, it still blends in harmoniously with its surroundings, rooting the keepers and their families in the place, affording them a ruling gaze over the 'crags and hills [that] rose one beyond another in *noble* perspective' (23; emphasis added). Harlech Castle provides protection for its stewards who, in turn, cast their protective gaze from the battlements. In doing so, they impose an order on the surrounding land: the ordered space within their view provides their people with a home behind whose border lies chaotic and uninhabitable wasteland. Even the name of the castle manifests the encasement of the Welsh nobility in the architecture for '[i]n proof of the fact, what means Harlech but "the fair rock"' (23). Consequently, the loss of Harlech and retreat of Gladys's family into exile violates the principle of unity between the Welsh and their homes. With their expulsion from the castle and the loss of political power, Gladys's clan are divided from the externalised, architectural proof of the legitimacy of their rule. Owing to their identification as the rulers of the land, their division from the ancestral home produces an all-consuming state of longing in the entire clan to regain the castle as the external realisation of their honour and strength. However, while painful for the aristocratic Gladys and her family, their exile among the mountains has the benefit of reducing the hierarchical distance between themselves and the peasantry, a division which had previously been visible in the forbidding castle walls. At length, Dafydd rediscovers himself as a result of tilling the ground to feed his family and he is now related to his peasants on a more equal footing: 'He now appeared like a parent watching over his numerous offspring, rather than the renowned chieftain over the man of his clan' (109).

Despite this newly-found connection with the people they formerly ruled, the clan is consumed by *hiraeth* for Harlech. Gladys's quest to regain possession of the castle and simultaneously restore her people's rights proves her true status as political leader. However, before she can regain possession of Harlech, Gladys has to flee the country and match her inner exile with the actual exile of Henry Tudor. With the help of her devoted uncle Kynfin, she follows the

foretold king into France and there presents him with the
Dewines's prophecy of his kingship. France presents itself to
Gladys as a 'land of enchantment' (377) which matches her
supernatural message. Consequently, she successfully extracts
a promise from the exiled future king to restore her people's
freedom together with her ownership of Harlech.

Just as Harlech Castle embodies the spirit of its Welsh
keepers, so does Henry Tudor's new but crowded residence,
Windsor Castle, figure his: its many corridors and chambers
resemble the complexity of the state in which Wales and
England are united by his rule. In contrast to the identification
of Harlech's architectural qualities, Windsor is entirely
described in terms of fashion, envy and flamboyancy. The
moral substance that is contained in the architecture of
Harlech is missing from the royal court which is instead
defined by courtly insincerity. Not sharing their superficiality,
Gladys feels isolated from 'the fawning parasites of the court,
the flattering insincerity of the courtiers and the perpetual
dissipation around her' (508-9), suffering again from *hiraeth*
just as she did during her captivity under Gilbert Stacey. This
notion of Windsor, and by extension the new Tudor king, as
lacking moral substance is summed up by the Dewines's
insight that 'Henry VII, monarch of that name, is no longer
Henry of Richmond'(504) because he has sacrificed his
Welshness by tying his name to England. Gladys is only able
to return to Harlech, 'the place of her repose'(509), after
repeated requests to King Henry VII to grant the promised
Charter that restores the freedom of her people. At last on the
return to her ancestral home, Gladys reclaims her identity as
noble protector of the Welsh soil and its people.

In a move similar to Sir Walter Scott's retelling of the

Jacobite Rebellion from a Scottish point of view in his *Waverley* novels, Louisa Matilda Spooner subverts Victorian interpretations of a seminal period in the history of the British Isles by examining the Wars of the Roses with Welsh eyes. Furthermore, her perspective is woman-centred, and her female characters are not confined to the polite atmosphere of the drawing room. Whereas Queen Margaret and the Dewines face their enemies on the battlefields or on their side-lines, Gladys acts more as the political agent behind the scenes and on an international playing field. Admittedly, the gender dynamics in Spooner's medieval Wales and England still reflect many of the social constraints faced by the novel's female Victorian readership. Consequently, the female protagonists' actions directly relate to their comparatively more powerful male family members and each of their paths end in compromises. Margaret is spared execution only because she is a female Plantagenet, but not before having lost her son, her husband and her crown; the Dewines succeeds in her revenge for her daughter's rape, but has to surrender her identity as Bridget of Windsor together with her wealth; and Gladys succeeds in the proclamation of a Welsh charter and regains possession of Harlech, but has to sacrifice her love for the English-born Ethelred. However, despite the strict confines of a deeply patriarchal society, they strive for self-determination and political agency and so leave a lasting mark on the wider political and national landscape of Wales and England. The novel squarely re-assesses the rise of the Tudor dynasty as the source of a national founding myth of a modern Britain in which both women and the Welsh could take the lead in affairs of state and redeem, at least in part, their former subjugations.

Notes

1   Here and throughout the following novel, the text's original
    anglicized spelling of Welsh names has been retained: 'Jevan' is an
    anglicisation of the name 'Ieuan'. As an 'Errata slip' appended to the
    original text explained (with regard to such names as 'Kynfin'), 'In
    the Welsh names occurring throughout these pages, the English K has
    been adopted in place of the Welsh C, in order to aid the English
    pronunciation.' The footnotes appended to the 1858 text have also all
    been retained in this edition. Additionally, the names 'Maelgwyn' and
    'Maud' were incorrectly typeset as 'Maclgwyn' and 'Mavil' in parts I
    and II of the original novel. They have been corrected in this edition.

2   In a detailed family tree for the Spooner family, D. H. W. presents the
    years 1820-86; the date of death is further corroborated in a public
    notice placed in the *London Gazette* in 1887 by Spooner's solicitors
    who state the day of her death as 5 December 1886. See D. H. W.,
    'Family Tree of the Swinton Spooners', *Ffestiniog Railway Magazine*
    77 (1977): 21.

    Freemason's Quarterly (1859), 327.

    D. H. W., 21; Jane Aaron, *Nineteenth-Century Women's Writing in
    Wales: Nation, Gender and Identity* (Cardiff: University of Wales
    Press, 2007), 115.

    Aaron, 115; Bloxham and Son, 'Louisa Matilda Spooner, Deceased.'
    The London Gazette [London] 28 June 1887: 3516.

6   'Reviews', *The Cambrian Journal* (June 1858): 158-60 (158-9).

7   For a more detailed discussion of the Wars of the Roses and their
    origin in the deposition of Richard II in 1399, see Dan. Jones, *The
    Hollow Crown: The Wars of the Roses and the Rise of the Tudors*
    (London: Faber, 2014).

    John Davies, *A History of Wales* (1990; rev. edn., London: Penguin,
    2007), 226

    Anon. [Louisa Matilda Spooner], *Gladys of Harlech; or, The
    Sacrifice*, 3 vols. (London: Charles J. Skeet, 1858), 39;
    parenthetically cited page references to *Gladys of Harlech* are to this
    Honno edition.

10 Gwyn A. Williams, *The Welsh in Their History* (London: Croom
    Helm, 1982), 18.

GLADYS OF HARLECH;
AN HISTORICAL ROMANCE

"High on a rock, where ocean's waves are spread,
Fair Bronwen's tower erects its stately head—
Since known by Collwyn, then by Lear's name,
A fairer structure ne'er was known to fame."

IN THREE VOLUMES.

VOL. I

GLADYS OF HARLECH;
OR,
THE SACRIFICE

TO THE READER

Two centuries had elapsed after Wales had bent under the Saxon yoke. The people still lamented their country's subjection, and the wrongs inflicted upon them by the victors. Their princes, their bards, and warrior forefathers, all had perished. The country groaned under the oppressive exactions of the stranger; and its inhabitants beheld with the most painful anxiety continual encroachments upon their rights and liberties. Broken-hearted, despairing, the natives of the soil had ceased to struggle for their emancipation. Their wonted energy was extinguished; their former resolution had disappeared; and, sunk in despondency, they dragged out an existence at variance altogether with their former brave and patriotic character.

At such a disastrous period the present narrative commences, originating in a strong love of country on the author's part, and a wish to extend a knowledge of its mountain lands, characteristics, traditions, prejudices, and superstitions, at a remarkable period of our island history.

The Cambro-Britons, in those disturbed times, were not wanting in high-minded heroic men. The names of many such have been handed down in history, bright examples of admiration for their bravery and love of country. The subject is somewhat new. The difference noted in language, manners, and modes of thinking in the two countries, under an adherence to simplicity of style, in unison with the rude period to which the narrative relates, is essentially necessary.

There is no necessity for farther remark, or for any trespass upon the reader's historical recollections, from the very general character of the incidents related.

CHAPTER I

A Retrospect—The Sons of Harlech

PASSING over the period when Henry VI, while yet in his cradle, was proclaimed King of England, and proceeding to the year 1431, rendered memorable by the heroism of the renowned Joan of Arc, and the maledictions against the Duke of Bedford on account of her cruel fate, he being then regent in France, while Humphrey, Duke of Gloucester, managed the public affairs at home—passing over that period which simply indicates the date of the commencement of the present narrative, we travel at once to North Wales.

The massy walls of proud Harlech, that impregnable fortress, had long been a name familiar to the English soldiery. During the succeeding Wars of the rival Roses, it bravely resisted the repeated attacks of the Yorkists, while kept by that valiant Cambrian chief Dafydd ap Jevan ap Einion. At the present period the brow of that chieftain had scarcely been shaded with the sober hue of manhood. His father was the warden, a grey-headed old man, sitting in the spacious hall of the castle, in conversation with Grono ap Meredyth, who had arrived but a few hours before with a small, but chosen body of soldiers, upon their march into South Wales. They were warmly discussing the prevalent topic of the day, which was the war then carrying on in France. Dafydd, the young son of Harlech, who had already manifested a strong predilection for warlike affairs, was standing at the further end of the hall, feathering some arrows. Attracted by the subject on which his father and uncle were conversing, he desisted from his occupation, approached his relatives, and stood listening attentively to the topic on which they were engaged.

'You are on a recruiting expedition then?' said Dafydd, during a pause in Grono's conversation. He had been expatiating upon the campaign in France, and remarking upon the impossibility of our generals effecting any important operations with the slender amount of military strength of which they could, by every exertion, avail themselves.

'Yes, my good kinsman,' replied Grono, removing the tape which bound up a packet of papers which he held in his hand, 'I trow, you will perceive the urgency of my present mission, when you know the contents of these letters from Lord Talbot and John Fitzalan. They contain the strictest orders from the Duke of Bedford to lose not a moment in embarking troops from Wales.'

'What you, my uncle! Are you going to obey this Saxon mandate?' interrupted Dafydd, with an expression of countenance between incredulity and anger—'Can you, my uncle, be a voluntary ally to these English, the oppressors of our country! We should rather, this moment, be in arms against them, demanding justice for our country's wrongs— demanding, did I say?—conquering it! Have we not the heroic Joan of Arc for an example? Shall a woman shame us? When I reflect on her deeds, I feel my heart on fire. Emulation kindles in my breast to strike a blow in like manner against the common enemy. Would to heaven I had the same power to lead armies to victory—to strike mortal terror into the common foe; then never, never would I rest contented until we were free from the shackles which enslave us, until we were once more the free children of a free soil. You, my uncle, have a spirit not dead to the lamentations of our country. Remain at home, I entreat; combat here for our country's emancipation. Let us dare for freedom as our patriot fathers dared; and if we pour out our blood, let it be shed in a good and noble cause.'

The father startled at the bold language of his son, watched with a melancholy, yet admiring smile, his glowing cheek and ardent eyes, and thus addressed him in reply:—

'Ochan! Ochan! (alas! alas!) my brave boy! you have forgotten that our day of glory has passed away. Our warriors, where are they? Sealed in the sleep of death. Their swords rust in their scabbards, and with their unstrung bows hang idly in our halls. We cannot muster armies to enter the list with the countless legions of the Saxon. England is now a mighty nation, against which, to raise an insurrection would be madness. Listen to the counsel of age, my brave and patriotic boy. I have trod the weary pilgrimage of life, for long, long years, and experience tells me,—bitter experience too,—that we have no resource but to sustain our misfortunes with manly fortitude.'

'Must I then infer from the meaning of your words, my father, that we are to live and die serfs in our own land?' said Dafydd emphatically; 'are we reduced to this at last? Must our country expend its best blood in the cause of our oppressors?'

'It were more politic, nay, in some respects more just, to consider the cause our own,' interrupted Grono. 'Be not surprised, Dafydd, my lad, but it is necessary you should be undeceived upon this point. Our blood flows in the veins of the proudest aristocracy of England. The offspring of our noble kinsman, Owen Tudor, is closely allied to our young monarch, and the royal family. Two of the principal commanders now employed against the French, Talbot, and Fitzalan, Earl of Arundel, are both direct descendants from our countrymen, and the latter, we are all well aware, is a near connection of our own. I am ready to admit, independently of all this, and of my admiration of your patriotic spirit, that you are in error in supposing the position of the Welsh is such as it was formerly. England and Wales now constitute a single kingdom, united where they were once separate.'

'Not in heart—not in heart,' murmured Dafydd; 'where characters are so opposite, there can be no unison.'

'No unison in sentiment or feeling,' observed Grono, 'for we are forced to acknowledge that a yoke binds us to a foreign power. We are a conquered people. We must, as good Christians, patiently submit to circumstances over which we have not the smallest control. It was ordained above that this powerful nation should rule over us, and therefore our duty is obedience. Were I now to refuse sending auxiliaries to the Duke of Bedford, I should cast a stigma equally upon my countrymen and myself. No, my noble-spirited lad, this cannot be. Calm your impetuosity, and reflect upon my words. You will then, I trow, be ready to agree with me that it is better to embrace with eagerness so fair an opportunity for our own distinction on the battlefield, than to rise in arms against England. Let us show the world that Cambria, though conquered, still preserves its warrior heart.'

As Grono delivered with simplicity and earnestness the latter part of this address, young Dafydd's intelligent countenance changed its expression. Fixing his inquiring gaze upon his uncle, he stood silent for some moments, and then addressed him:—

'I have to thank you my good uncle, for having instilled new thoughts into my mind. I had flattered myself that I was becoming a man—I now see I am still but a child.'

Here he started up, and covering his eyes with his hand, quitted the presence of his father and uncle with a hurried step. Some hours elapsed before he sought again the company of his kinsman, and then he addressed him:—

'My brave and good uncle, I honour the sentiments which you recently expressed to me so clearly. I regret that, in ignorance of their justice, I was led astray in my views. Do not censure mutable opinions, when I make the acknowledgment to you that new feelings and fresh hopes of a different nature pervade my mind. I would fain have the benefit of your example in my inexperience, and entreat that you will permit me to accompany you to the field of arms in France. I condemned, it is true, the step you were taking; I saw not its good policy until you enlightened me. Fate has decided that I cannot take up arms for the benefit of our native land, and the restoration of its freedom—be it so. Only allow me to serve her in another way. Let me wield the sword or battle-axe, to redeem her renown in the ranks of war—that renown overshadowed by the power of the oppressor, but never stained with dishonour. I will stimulate our countrymen to gather glorious laurels in the battlefield, and win from the young sovereign who commands us, the reward every patriotic spirit desires; the revocation of the cruel and oppressive charter, which King Edward, with heartless vengeance, directed against our own Cambria and her rights. Would not such an act be a worthy offering to our country, the weal of which is the sovereign wish of my heart?'

'Noble-spirited boy!' exclaimed Grono, 'right proud shall

I be to present to Lord Talbot a young warrior so promising;—but hold, what are the opinions of your venerable father upon the subject? We must previously obtain his consent to your design.'

'My father,' said the youthful Dafydd, at the same moment turning his expressive countenance upon his father, and fixing his eyes anxiously upon him—'My father, I know, will not thwart my wishes, for he too has his country's good uppermost in his heart. He will be the first to rejoice, if I can in any manner promote its welfare.'

'Right, my brave boy,' replied the old man; as he spoke a nervous twitching shaking every line of his thin, furrowed face; 'Heaven only knows how much it will cost me to part with the stay of my declining years—my son, my only son; but it is the call of duty; thou shalt go.'

Again and again young Dafydd repeated his grateful acknowledgments; then pressing his father's hand in silence, quitted the hall. It was not long afterwards that with Grono, he made preparations for his departure; the object of his uncle's march into South Wales had been accomplished. That chief with his youthful companion then set out to join the English army in France.

Dafydd soon became a favourite with his comrades in arms, and that not only with those of his own subordinate military rank, but with officers far superior in rank and age. It was impossible for any to be insensible to the generous and fearless character of one who, so young in years, promised to become a distinguished character in his future career.

Fitzalan of Arundel had ever cherished a latent partiality for the inhabitants of the principality of Wales; and regarding Dafydd as a kinsman, showed a peculiar attention to him, until death deprived the youth of his friendship and patronage. Not that had Dafydd been less fortunate in his outset in life, his own merits and conduct upon all occasions would not have obtained success, but that it had hastened the acknowledgment of his merits to start under such auspices. Indeed, soon after his joining the army, his feats of arms were the subject of conversation, passing from camp to camp. Many a brave foe man sunk under his powerful arm; and as he thus distinguished himself, all the world became eager to ascertain who the young soldier was, and from whence he came.

Lord Talbot, at first a silent observer of the carriage of the young Welshman, pronounced him to be possessed of great military talent. He assigned to him repeatedly the post of honour as well as of danger, considering him equal to the most difficult duties, and reposing in him great confidence. At Montargis, the Earl of Arundel delivered to him the command of that fortress, during his own absence upon other duties; and through the wise and courageous conduct of Dafydd, 'the French troops,' as is observed by an historian of the events of that time, 'discovering that they were neither able to force the castle nor retain the town, retired, amidst the triumphant shouts of their opponents.'

But the success of the young hero did not terminate here. New laurels were gathered upon each revolving day, and he became unconsciously the object of general admiration. In Normandy, above all, he greatly distinguished himself during the insurrection in that province; on his conduct upon this occasion high encomiums were lavished. In a secret conference with the Earl of Arundel and Lord Willoughby, he prepared to attack the French during the night. His proposition, after some consideration, was accepted, and he was permitted to carry it into effect. The English in consequence gained a complete victory, and recovered the Vexin, Caen, and Lillebonne. In a conversation with Lord Talbot, the Earl of Arundel said:

'We have to thank the doughty young Cambrian and his men for this glorious advantage. Their courage and bravery in overcoming all obstacles were never surpassed.'

Time lapsed and bore away the events of that contest. The death of the Earl of Arundel and the Duke of Bedford took place. Dafydd returned to England. He was received at Court with the highest honours; and the British monarch expressed his desire to show some signal mark of his favour to one who had so nobly merited the distinction. This was speedily communicated to the object of the royal regard, when, to the astonishment of the gay and ambitious courtiers, the young hero with the warmest expressions of gratitude, requested to be permitted to decline any advancement or personal advantage.

'As to myself, most Gracious Sovereign,' observed Dafydd, 'I prefer being allowed to remain as I am; but not that I undervalue the goodness of which your Majesty has so kindly indicated to me the distinguished proof, in the acknowledgment of my humble services. If your Highness will permit me, I would venture to ask the favour of the transfer of your royal generosity to my unfortunate country, sorely oppressed by laws which are foreign to her people, their manners and customs. Gross injustice, too, is perpetrated on our borders, which it well-nigh demands more than human fortitude to endure. Be not, my Royal Master, displeased with the boldness of my petition. Sympathy for my suffering country has extorted the utterance of this my request. May it please Heaven to direct the kindness of your royal heart to the sufferings of my countrymen, your loyal subjects, that your Highness may order impartial justice in our behalf; and that the ignominious laws with which King Edward ruled us may be mitigated. This boon is all that either my fellow-countrymen or myself would solicit of your Highness in return for our services in the French war. The favour would be one of charity as well as justice, did your Highness but know the extent of our sufferings. Charity secures Heaven's blessing for crowns as well as subjects.'

'Your entreaty is noble,' replied the monarch; 'the worthiest subjects are those who disregard their own interests to serve their country. I accord you the consideration of your request. Our council shall be immediately summoned; and justice shall be done to my Welsh subjects without loss of time.'

With this promise, Dafydd withdrew from the royal presence; and almost immediately afterwards left the gay and brilliant court, impatient to reach his quiet home and fastnesses among the mountains of his own romantic land. Some years had elapsed from the time he quitted Wales until his return; and the meeting between the old Warden of Harlech and his son was proportionally touching. The hoary sire had almost persuaded himself he should see his son no more; to find him return, and under circumstances so auspicious, was almost too much for his timeworn frame to sustain. His ideas were confused when he heard the shouts and acclamations which, rending the air on all sides, echoed again from cliff and hollow, as Dafydd drew near the ancient walls of the castle, causing unwonted tumult. Tears started into the eyes of the venerable man, and rolled down his cheeks, deeply engraved by the hand of time, as he was told that the confusion around arose from the welcome the inhabitants of Harlech were giving to his beloved son upon returning to his native soil.

The set form and now manly figure of the young hero strikingly contrasted with the figure of the stripling, who had quitted home so suddenly to enter upon the arduous duties of a foreign campaign. Friends of his early youth crowded around him. They gazed upon his altered and noble bearing, they admired his handsome countenance now in pride of manhood's expression; they exhibited feelings of the most enthusiastic admiration, and then blended their voices in one simultaneous shout of praise, and imploration of blessings upon the son of their chief.

Happy were those times for Harlech. That grey massy fortress once more resounded, as it had done in years long past, with cheerfulness and revelry. Every countenance beamed with joy, every heart was happy, as it soon afterwards gathered to the castle to participate in the nuptials of the young returned chieftain. It was but a few months previous to the war that Dafydd had been betrothed to Maret, the fair heiress of the elder branch of the house of Tudor. He had not long been welcomed to his paternal home, before his thoughts turned towards her to whom his heart was given, and he had repaired to her father's home to demand her for his bride.

Other incidents of less domestic importance succeeded these memorable events. The aged warden of the castle, the hoary-headed Jevan, had become day by day more feeble, and then slept with his fathers. Dafydd was now the father of a young family, which introduced him to the cares and interests it involves. He took an undisguised pride in his offspring, and as they advanced in years, instilled into their minds the soundest principles of the faith he professed, of which both himself and their mother were preeminent examples. Thus there was every prospect of their becoming in future years worthy scions of a time-honoured race. Within the massive walls of Harlech castle all was peace and unity of feeling, so that the home of Dafydd might have been not only an object of envy in feudal times, but that of the indulgence and luxury of a later age. The hearty welcome which met him upon his return from the wild sports of the woods and mountains, or from any act of public service or local duty, was of the liveliest and heartiest character. A bright hearth, blazing logs, and sweet smiles ever met him in the hall, when the season was the most austere. The winning manners of his children deeply impressed his heart with paternal affection, and spread over it as well as on those around that indescribable charm which is perhaps the nearest to happiness on earth that mortal men are permitted to experience.

It is not to be credited that Dafydd was insensible to the blessings so copiously showered down upon him. On the contrary his high principles, yet humble spirit, continually overflowed with fresh feelings of gratitude to the Giver of all good.

It is painful to turn from similar scenes of domestic love and tranquillity to those of an opposite character—to discontent, jealousy and bloodshed in all their baleful aspects.

After Dafydd quitted the English court to return home, great changes took place, where pomp and brilliancy had been so conspicuous before. The deaths of Gloucester, and of the great Cardinal Beaufort, with the heinous murder of the unfortunate Duke of Suffolk, were events of the most startling importance to the people of England, and indeed to the world at large. The first cloud which gathered on the horizon, and portended an approaching storm, was the rebellion in Kent, where the insurgents were led by an Irishman of disreputable character, the notorious Jack Cade, who boldly declared himself to be of the house of Marche. He was suspected to have received secret encouragement from the Duke of York, in Ireland. By this outbreak, dangerous and unforeseen, great consternation overspread England. Notwithstanding the final overthrow of Cade, and the death of that insurgent himself, there was much danger to be apprehended from the influence and discontented spirit, which had prompted such an insurrection.

CHAPTER II

The Invasion—The Beleaguered Castle

WHEN the Duke of York received intelligence of Cade's ill success, then unknown to the King, he made preparations for leaving Ireland, the term of his governorship having just expired. 'The field now lies open before me,' thought the ambitious Duke, 'my powerful enemy Suffolk is dead; Cade's enterprise, as my fondest hopes prognosticated, has paved the way for the house of Marche. If so feeble a branch of our august family could raise such a rebellion, what may not be expected from the prince royal and sole heir?'

Animated with feverish dreams of regal pomp and military glory, the Duke shortly afterwards sailed from Dublin, with the intention of landing upon the Welsh coast. There, to his dismay and disappointment, instead of meeting with zealous partisans, as he expected, a hostile force stood in array against him.

Through some private source the chieftain of Harlech had gained information of the intended landing of the Duke of York, and of the cautious measures he was taking to prevent the King from hearing of his proceedings. Dafydd, with his usual forethought and discretion, seeing how detrimental such a step would prove to the nation, sent off with all speed to acquaint his royal master with the important fact.

Henry and his ministers, truly indebted to Ap Jevan for the timely intelligence, dispatched Jasper, the son of Owen Tudor, with commands to their trusty friend, once the young hero of the French war, to raise all the forces he could muster, and to go in person and secure the coast from invasion.

Ap Jevan thus appeared in the character of a military commander for the first time in his own country. Many years had passed since he first bore arms, and under what different circumstances! True, the freshness of youth was gone, but it was exchanged for the glow of a father's pride, as he marched at the head of his strong and fearless band, supported by his twin sons, Tudor and Kynfin, one on each side, high-spirited youths, who had entered upon their sixteenth year.

As they pressed on with eagerness to gain the Mona coast, Dafydd had the gratification of seeing his little army increase in number at every step. When they reached the Menai Strait he thought it advisable to form his men into battalions; appointing his uncle Meredyth and Jasper Tudor to take the command of the troops selected for the protection of the coast further to the north, Dafydd himself and his sons guarding the Mona Isle.

These arrangements were made with surprising rapidity, for time and circumstance alike pressed. The Duke's fleet was soon afterwards seen within the horizon. Dafydd, encouraging his men, with the spirit of a brave soldier, succeeded in bringing them up just in time to present a very formidable front to the Duke, who, observing them from seaward, appeared embarrassed and disconcerted becoming at a loss what measure to adopt. The moments which followed his observation of the Welsh troops were intensely interesting. The little fleet came hovering near the coast, and drew off again in another direction. Then, quick as thought, it tacked and wore again, till Night spread her sable mantle over sea and land, hiding from the belligerents the manoeuvres of each other.

It was a dark calm night, and Dafydd having given orders that his men should repose, with an anxious mind and in deep thought turned to the solitary beach, pacing it undisturbed and alone. Often were his eyes riveted upon the sails, just discernible in the dim expanse before him, ever and anon varying in their shape like wandering apparitions of the night. Not a sound was heard save the ripple of the waves, their monotonous murmuring accompanying the fast receding tide upon the sandy beach.

When the morning dawned a stiff breeze blew off the shore, and long lines of red streaks in the heavens portended stormy weather.

The Duke of York, like Dafydd, was a silent observer of the same scene from seaward, and it was with undisguised apprehension that he watched the changing sky. Scarcely had the early morn ripened into day, when a boat was lowered from his vessel, bearing a flag of truce, followed by a messenger sent to demand an interview with the Welsh chief. Dafydd, with his accustomed courtesy, received the messenger in his tent, and a prolonged interview took place.

The stipulations which were thus conveyed from the Duke were decidedly disapproved by the Welsh commander. He grew impatient at last, and unceremoniously broke up the discussion, dismissing the envoy with this simple but noble reply:—

'Go, tell his Grace that the Welsh chief scorns a bribe; tell him that he wears but one sword, which shall hew down every man who attempts a landing upon these shores without the King's permission.'

The Duke, exasperated at the bold reply, and vowing vengeance against the audacious Welshman, promptly ordered his pilot to steer for the land. In vain he tried to disembark his troops, they were repelled with redoubled slaughter at every fresh attempt. The numerous dead and dying around him showed the necessity of abandoning his purpose. He gave up the contest in despair, and quitting the Mona island, sought a haven further to the north. Here again his endeavours were frustrated by the gallant veteran, Ap Meredyth, and by Jasper ap Owen.

At these repeated discomfitures, the Duke of York, mortified and overwhelmed with the anxiety arising from his hazardous position, sailed from the coast; his little fleet, as it disappeared from the horizon, leaving its opponents highly gratified with the thoughts that they had succeeded in driving it back to its old quarters. But too soon they were undeceived. Scarcely had the following day's sun reached its meridian, when the unexpected news arrived that the Duke of York on the previous night had landed at a fishing village adjacent to the English coast, and was then on his march to the Metropolis; and further that he was surrounded by zealous partisans, many of whom were Welsh, who had assisted him in landing.

This was a severe blow to Dafydd's loyal heart. Ap Meredyth and Jasper ap Owen joined him shortly afterwards, and all condemned their countrymen for having aided the rebel Duke. With disappointment on every countenance, the troops were disbanded, returning to their homes to watch with increasing anxiety the dangers which overshadowed the country.

The sudden arrival of the Duke of York in London, with

four thousand men, occasioned great consternation. The quarrel between the Duke of Somerset and the Earl of Warwick, the first battle of the Roses, the political interference of Queen Margaret, the melancholy indisposition of the King, the birth of Prince Edward, and finally the instalment of the Duke of York as protector of the realm during the King's malady, were events of vital importance to the entire kingdom. One and all felt that there was a terrific storm approaching, while none knew how to avert its effects. It was not till Henry's restoration to health that civil war let loose its tigers throughout England's fertile land. Nor until that period did the pent-up feelings of the populace burst forth like an angry torrent, scattering before it desolation and death.

The Duke of York no sooner found himself deprived of his high office, and outwitted by the Queen, than his dormant ambition was reawakened. He once more became possessed with the idea that he was the rightful heir to the English throne, and made a vow he would never rest till England had acknowledged him her sovereign, let what might be the consequences; nor would he delay to contend openly for his rights. With these excited views, he retired to Wigmore Castle, and there by bribes, and other illicit means, he soon succeeded in gathering around him an augmentation of force which amounted to a potent army.

The brilliant promises which the Duke held out to the wronged and oppressed Welsh were so tempting that many were led away to support his cause, unfortunately for themselves and their connections.

Throughout the Principality there was only one family of which the Duke was deeply apprehensive, and that was the house of Tudor. That house included Dafydd, whom he had just cause to fear. His personal hatred towards him was by no means diminished because he bore in recollection the recent mortification he experienced at the reception Ap Jevan had given him upon the Mona coast. Owen Tudor, too, was at Harlech; now therefore was the time to show his animosity, and wreak his vengeance upon the race he detested. To imprison Dafydd in his own castle had been long the secret wish of his heart, and he exulted in the probable attainment of his darling object. He determined that his campaign should commence with the siege of Harlech; the obdurate men of Merioneth, once deprived of their daring leader, would soon be brought to acknowledge allegiance to the house of York.

Dafydd was not ignorant of the Duke's intentions, for he had friends in a quarter little suspected, who gave him timely warning of the approaching danger. Not a moment was wasted in vain regrets, no idle lamentations were heard, not an expression of either hope or fear escaped their lips; all felt the urgency of the case, and commenced at once the preparations for defence. Dafydd and his sons were present everywhere, indefatigable in their efforts, working night and day until their preparations were completed. The castle was filled with as many stout hearts as were requisite for its defence, and that its circuit could accommodate. Private injunctions were issued for the men in Merioneth to hold themselves in readiness to take up arms at a moment's warning; while every suggestion of importance was carried out calculated to secure the fortress during a long siege.

The bustle and confusion of the preparations over, Ap Jevan could not divest himself of anxiety; not so much on his own account, as on that of his noble kinsman Owen Tudor, who from the time of his dismissal from court had been a sojourner at Harlech. He recalled the many unfortunate circumstances which had befallen him. The Duke of York had never ceased to persecute him. He had been the sole instigator of his discharge from the royal household, as well as of all the less important disasters which had befallen him since the death of his consort, the dowager Queen Catherine.

'I have been thinking that our arch enemy the Duke has got wind of your present position,' observed Dafydd, on joining Owen Tudor in the long gallery of the castle. 'It is as much on your account as mine that we are indebted to him for the honour of this visitation.'

'Och! Dafydd, I should be sorry if I thought that was true,' said Owen, with much seriousness. 'May the foul winds take him! He is never happy but when he is hunting after the blood of a Tudor. This is not the first time by many that he has driven me to cover. Och! Dafydd, if this is the case, we must brace ourselves to the uttermost, and let courage and self-devotion be our watchword. Let us keep this savage fiend at bay till he has had enough of us.'

'We have many to contend with, and too many are our own countrymen,' observed Dafydd, lowering his voice.

'I know it,' was the laconic reply.

After a short pause, Owen continued:—

'For my own part, Dafydd, I have no fear. I would back you and your handful of men against York and his legions. You are no child at arms. I am surprised at the Duke's audacity in attempting to storm a castle, when Dafydd ap Jevan, the Hero of Montargis, is the commander.'

They were interrupted by the entrance of a youth from one of the watch towers of the castle, who communicated intelligence that the army of the Yorkists was in sight.

The confidence of Owen Tudor in the courage and experience of Ap Jevan was fully justifiable. This confidence was seconded by the well-known strength of the castle. No place of defence could be better adapted for observation as well as resistance. No enemy could approach the walls unobserved—this magnificent stronghold of Ap Jevan was as remarkable for its commanding position as for its beauty and grandeur. It was a noted site from the earliest ages. The conquerors of the world had a fortress here, upon the wreck of which another was built by the Briton Maelgwyn Gwynedd. Upon this, the present building was founded by Edward I. The sea face arose from the brink of a rock, ascending perpendicularly from the shore that opened far and wide under the haughty towers which darkened over it. The face of the rock, steep as the walls which crowned it, and almost indistinguishable from the dark grey masonry, united with them, presenting an aspect of one uniform gigantic front, defying hostile approach. The fortress was square. The angles were defended by circular towers, and these had on their summits small watch-towers like the eagle tower at Caernarvon. The walls of immense thickness, on the side accessible from the land, were protected by a broad ditch of considerable depth, excavated in the solid rock. The entrance, with its guard room, was admirably flanked, and defended first by a barbican, next by the moveable bridge across the ditch, and then by a second portcullis in the inner work, besides that in the barbican. The principal and state apartments were on the inner side of that court, which was pierced for the portal or entrance. These apartments rose to the height of three stories.

The grand banqueting hall was situated on the opposite side

of the court, looking outwards upon a wide extent of sea, from a height which made the boldest head dizzy to look down upon the vast level before it. On the right of the entrance was the chapel, in which half a century before, Owen Glyndwr had worshipped, when in arms against Henry IV., and now the family of Einion paid their daily devotions there. From the summit of the watchtowers, in the direction of the land, rock and mountain, cliff and wood, vale and stream, varied the prospect; crags and hills rose one beyond another in noble perspective. Nor was the castle itself destitute of romantic history. On the contrary it bore charmed traditions like—

> The story of Cambuscan bold,
> Of Camball and of Algarcife,
> And who had Canace to wife
> That own'd the virtuous ring and glass.

Traditions, not well-vouched history, told that Bronwen, the fair necked sister of Bran ap Lyr, Duke of Cornwall, inhabited a castle where the present stood, and yet stands, called 'Twr-y-Bronwen'. She married one of the fabulous kings with which Irish history delights to swell its barbarous annals. Under the government of ap Jevan at this time, the loftiest tower of his proud abode bore the name of this fair Bronwen, who once kept her court at Harlech, ages before Edward I erected his strong castle there. In proof of the fact, what means Harlech but 'the fair rock'?

To return;—standing upon such a lofty site as the Bronwen tower, no enemy could approach unobserved. It was a brilliant day, just such a day as often follows a tempestuous night; when everything in nature looks fresh and cheerful again. The tide was fast receding upon the seashore. Thousands of sea-gulls had collected, arranging themselves in companies along the sandy beach, where they appeared to be enjoying the mid-day sun, and glutting themselves with a banquet, which on the previous night had been thrown on shore by the angry elements.

Dafydd and his companion, with all the weight of care upon their minds at that moment, were struck with the loveliness of the scene. A beam of pleasure flashed across their features, so pensive just before. But they soon returned to their former more thoughtful expression, as they watched the progress of the advancing enemy.

'Our foes are pouring down upon the sands,' said Kynfin, who had joined them, 'and soft enough, methinks, they will find them, after the storm last night.'

'It will serve them for a plaster for their feet,' replied his brother, laughing. 'You may rest assured that after their rough march, every man is more or less foot-sore.'

'Anyhow, I should not like to stand in their boots,' observed another of the party.

'O'r anwyl! nor I neither, you may be certain they will have the worst of it,' repeated several voices.

Many similar remarks helped to beguile the hours, till night once more dropped her curtain, and Dafydd and his companions became aware that their inexorable foe had encamped with his troops below the proud fortress. Within a few weeks, it was even possible within a few days, their towers would be mutilated, their property destroyed, and death and desolation spread around their hearths. Dafydd did not allow himself to dwell upon this melancholy prospect. On the contrary, he was in excellent spirits. He felt confidence in his men; in Owen Tudor as an able adviser, and in the walls of his castle. The rest he left to Providence.

The whole of the following day nothing of importance occurred, save that some slight disturbance was observed amongst the soldiers in the enemy's camp. The Duke was frequently seen mounted on a white charger, addressing his men. Towards dusk several individuals were bold enough to reconnoitre quite close to the defences of the castle, which it was the object of their ambition to subdue. It was now raising its grey turrets to the sky, amid awful stillness, in haughty defiance of its foes. No signal of animosity—no sounds of preparation for the coming fight were seen or heard. All was so calm and placid that the tall towers looked like funeral monuments over the dead of departed years, rather than a part of a fortress on the eve of being besieged.

As hours passed, Dafydd became more impatient. He scarcely ever quitted the battlements, where he could mark unobserved every movement of the enemy. The moon had risen and gone down. Again the greater luminary appeared from behind the distant hills, tinging with roseate hue the mountain, the sea, and the plain, when long columns of smoke arose from the camp below, and Dafydd thought he could perceive a movement among the enemy's troops.

'The sun sets not before those caitiffs have felt the force of our arrows and missiles to their cost,' said Dafydd, soliloquizing, with throbbing pulse and flashing eye, as the vivid picture of the scene about to ensue crossed his imagination.

He was right in his conjecture; for scarcely had an hour elapsed, when the Duke of York, at the head of two hundred chosen men, was scaling the precipitous crag on which the castle stood.

With what eagerness of feeling did Ap Jevan and his trusty adherents watch the movements and await the time for action in death-like stillness! Nearer and nearer the enemy approached to the walls; but not an arrow, not a missile, impeded his advance.

'Do the men of Merioneth intend to make no resistance?' said the Duke of York, casting hurried glances at the high towers above him, as with his followers he stood for an instant to recover breath after their rapid ascent of the steep.

It was at that moment the Warden, whose eye had followed the Duke's movements, gave the word. In an instant a deadly flight of arrows poured from the towers and loop-holes of the castle, spreading consternation amongst the besiegers, many of them struck, fell headlong over the cliffs. The Duke, a little in advance, seeing the imminent danger of his position, rushed forward, shouting to his men to follow him like brave Englishmen. They obeyed, and rushing precipitately onward, gained the precincts of the moat, when the Yorkists' trumpets, and the stentorian war cry, vibrated along the walls of old Harlech, proclaiming a temporary triumph, soon to be followed by an unexpected reverse.

Dafydd, with his usual prudent ingenuity, had contrived several pit-traps, the use of which he had learned in France, where they were called *trou de loups*. It was these yawning graves which checked the zeal of the besiegers, who at the sight of so many of their comrades disappearing into them before their eyes, became panic-stricken. At this critical moment the Duke was pierced by an arrow in the breast, and staggering forward fell to the ground. Immediately afterwards his body-guard, alarmed for his safety, bore him away insensible from the scene of action.

The siege continued, but the Duke was confined to his tent, and could take no active part in the operations. The chagrin and mortification which he hourly experienced at his ill success retarded his recovery. He felt the error he had committed in thus early besieging so strong a fortress. He weakened his forces, losing instead of gaining ground in the great work he had undertaken, 'should he resign the hope of overcoming the brave men of Merioneth, and making them serve under his banner?' It was a mortifying reflection for an ambitious spirit. Yet deprived of his presence before the castle walls, success was uncertain. Nevil next in command, had done all in his power to achieve success, but he himself, he imagined, would have done better. One trusty officer named Brook was taken prisoner, with several other able soldiers. 'Could he afford to lose them—to lose others equally of importance to his future campaign?' With these reflections the Duke called a council of war.

'To continue the siege will be no easy task,' observed the Earl of Salisbury, one of the council present, as the Duke repeated the foregoing query. 'You are not aware of the difficulties with which we have to cope. The Cambrian chief is a warlike leader of great experience. Even if we could bring him to open combat, we should not be sure of success, much less behind defences so strong as those of Harlech.'

'Not so, by St George!' answered the Duke, passionately. 'Were it not that time is precious, I would never abandon the siege until I had placed his bleeding head on the battlements of his impregnable fortress. There was a time when a dungeon for his home would have contented me; now blood, blood alone will appease my anger with this contumacious rebel.'

'Your highness must wait an indefinite period, I fear, for

that gratification,' replied Nevil; 'you observe truly that time is precious; letters have just arrived from the Duke of Devonshire; your highness will see that affairs of greater importance are demanding your presence elsewhere. Queen Margaret's influence is hourly increasing, and her partisans are mustering from all quarters. Can it be well to protract the siege of this remote fortress, while our enemies all over the realm ripen their designs unmolested?'

CHAPTER III

The Siege—Margaret of Anjou— Bloreheath

LEAVING the Duke occupied with his council and serious reflections on his position in the camp before Harlech, balancing the probability of final success with the dangers which might occur to his cause in other parts of the kingdom, the more attractive scenes within the castle became possessed of redoubled interest. Still arose unscathed those proud towers, like giants keeping watch at night over the beleaguered country beneath.

Dafydd had no sooner assured himself that the enemy had retired to their quarters for the night, and that each fresh sentinel was placed at his post, than he hastened to communicate in person to the ladies of his household the joyful intelligence of that day's success, and of their own safety. The attack had been unusually fierce. Twice had the enemy approached so near as to endeavour, but unsuccessfully, to fire the castle. They had been repulsed with great loss in both attempts. Mistress Tudor had passed the hours of combat in the deepest anxiety for the welfare of her lord and sons. It was now amidst convulsive sobs that she embraced her lord, offering a prayer of thanks to heaven for his preservation, and that of his offspring, who were also spared to her.

The garrison of the keep had gathered around their chief lord in their congratulations. Every eye watched him with a respectful and grateful glance as he moved from one place to another. Now he spoke cheering words to the wounded, giving prompt orders that every attention should be paid to them. Few lives had been sacrificed. The only member of the family on whom injury had been inflicted was Kynfin. He came into the presence of his mother, whom he alarmed, with a cut across his forehead, which he assured her was merely a scratch, adding with a hearty laugh, his fears that there would be no scar left to become a memorial of that day's achievement.

'Let me tell you, my dear mother,' said Kynfin with his wonted merriment, 'the scoundrel who gave me this memorandum in my forehead—mind, it is no Cain brand— that scoundrel is one of the Duke's favourites; he is now my prisoner.'

The moment mutual congratulations had been exchanged, and the wounded had received professional aid, the warden assembled his family in the chapel to offer up a prayer of thankfulness and gratitude to Him who had so signally favoured them during that eventful day. This duty completed, they repaired to the hall, where a substantial supper smoked upon the long massy tables; and, according to the custom of the olden time, the members of the family and officers took their respective places at the tables on the dais, the space below being crowded with the extra numerous garrison and the domestics of the establishment.

At the head of the hall sat Ap Jevan; surrounded by his affectionate family and friends. The warlike and determined expression which had marked the countenance of this brave soldier in the morning in action, had entirely vanished, and cheered by his success, was beaming with kindness and dignity. It was a scene not easily effaced from the memory of those, who, sharing in the hospitality of that day, proclaimed him their chief, their deliverer, and their friend. He himself addressed all present in the most spirited manner, but more particularly his noble kinsman Owen Tudor. At times he made racy and piquant remarks upon the Duke of York's discipline, and military character. Then he spoke kind words of approbation to his sons in relation to the gallant conduct of some of the garrison during the contest, which had come under his own observation. To his amiable consort who sat at his right hand, he spoke in soothing accents, and with great tenderness, words calculated to allay any fears she might entertain of the termination of the siege to their disadvantage.

During the evening Dafydd questioned his sons respecting the number and rank of the prisoners taken during the different sallies they had made in the morning. It appeared that there were ten knights and esquires, and more than triple that number of the common soldiers. The wolf traps had proved of greater importance than they had imagined.

Midnight appeared, and most of the family retired to rest. Dafydd and Owen remained discussing the affairs of the day, and forming plans for the future, should the siege continue.

'Another such a day will damp the zeal of our opponents,' said Owen, rising to place another faggot upon the hearth. 'I should not marvel if the Duke embrace some opportunity of seeking a reconciliation.'

'Time only will reveal that,' said Dafydd, 'meanwhile I shall keep my fortress in readiness to resist any sudden attack. Our antagonist shall see that it is no child's work to capture the key of the north.'

'Are you aware,' observed Owen turning the conversation, 'that among the prisoners of whom we were speaking a short time since, there is one with whom you are not altogether unacquainted, too whom I have some reason to remember?'

'Indeed!' answered Dafydd; 'to whom are you alluding?'

'To that braggart the English baron Brook. For years that has been my secret foe.'

'Have you seen him?' inquired Ap Jevan.

'I have not: he is in the dungeon prison. What say you to paying the caitiff a visit? I would fain meet him face to face. He shall then know my opinion of him, base-born upstart as he is.'

'He is but a tool in the hands of York,' remarked Dafydd, 'unworthy of our notice; we must recollect too that he is our prisoner. To upbraid a poor devil in irons, would be ungenerous.'

'Perhaps you are right,' replied Owen with a thoughtful expression; 'still, Dafydd, I feel I should be happier if I knew I had planted a thorn in that man's heart. He and York are the only two on earth whom I regard with mortal hatred; revenge on them would be sweet to me.'

'Och! Owen, you are mistaken, gratified revenge imparts no real comfort to the breast. The evil on both sides falls back upon us. It is best we leave the repayment of injuries to a higher power.'

'I would I possessed a disposition half as magnanimous as thine,' replied Owen, with unusual earnestness. Shortly afterwards the friends separated for the night.

Dafydd's excitement would not allow him to take repose. The night was passed upon the battlements. His watchfulness was fortunate. Scarcely had the day-break faintly appeared when the well-known cry arose of 'The Saxons under the walls.' Unexpected as those sounds arose the warden was ready from without. Shout answered shout, both on the part of the assailants and the garrison, and blow answered to blow, too, as the Duke's men, with great daring, attempted to force the gate, and scale the outer works. Again they were repelled. The dim morning preventing the pit-falls from being perceived, many more of the Yorkists were precipitated into them. Richard Nevil, the Earl of Salisbury, was slightly wounded, and again the enemy withdrew from before the castle, under the exulting shouts of its gallant defenders from the battlements.

The Duke of York, still unable to lead his troops in person, waxed angry at being a second time baffled; and in the heat of the moment reproached his officers with want of perseverance, and even of courage.

The Earl of Salisbury and others were displeased at such language from their prince. Had the latter not made an apology to them for his heat, the difference might have ended disastrously for the Yorkist's cause. Tranquillity was at length restored. Shortly after this incident the Duke, in close conference with a council of war, came to the determination to relinquish the siege, provided Dafydd would restore his prisoners.

'We must relinquish the siege in any case,' Nevil insisted. 'Remember Queen Margaret is raising England. As to this Welsh chieftain, we may try a treaty with him, although I have doubts of our success.'

'Confound him; confound all the Welsh race,' exclaimed the Duke of York, giving vent to half-suppressed anger. 'He must be induced to consent to my stipulations, whatever it cost

us. I have said it, Richard Nevil; you have now only to see
that my will is fulfilled.'

Salisbury quitted the Duke's presence without losing a
moment, and lost no time in making known to Dafydd the
Duke's inclinations.

After much controversy, Dafydd consented to deliver up
the prisoners, with the exception of four of the knights, whom
he proposed to keep as hostages. The treaty was thus ratified.

On the following day, to the delight of the inhabitants of
Harlech, they beheld the army of the white rose break up camp,
and saw its departure from their vicinity. Then there arose in all
bosoms a feeling of pride; every heart experienced a joy for a
long time before unfelt. The Saxons had quailed before their
arrows and missiles. The rebel York had been baffled in his
attempts, while the banner of the red rose floated still over
Harlech's proud battlements, and their chief was safe.

In less than a month after this event, worthy of the
exultation evinced on the occasion, the departure of Owen
Tudor, and the two sons of their much-loved chief, caused a
fresh sensation in Harlech. Owen Tudor had been summoned
by Margaret of Anjou, through his son, Jasper Tudor. Jasper
was a great favourite with the king; so much so that he always
kept him near his person. Owen was to raise what troops he
was able, and to join the Queen at Coventry.

Tudor and Kynfin, hearing of the Queen's commands,
entreated their father to allow them to accompany their noble
relation. Dafydd, after some consideration, ultimately
consented to their wishes. He himself felt some desire to join
in the cause, but he had important duties to perform nearer
home. There was no foreseeing when the Yorkists might pay
them another visit. Their party was daily becoming more

powerful, and the struggle for Lancaster promised to be fiercer than ever.

On the arrival of Owen Tudor at court, the Queen received him most graciously, expressing at the same time her regrets at the misunderstanding which had subsisted between them. The sole author of that misunderstanding was the selfish and ambitious Duke of York. She now declared she would make atonement for the past, and, if successful, the house of Tudor should be crowned with such honours as its services and noble lineage deserved.

The condescending and pleasing manners of Margaret had rendered her an object of the greatest interest in the midland counties, more particularly at Coventry. But, notwithstanding all this loyalty of feeling, she was painfully aware of the terrible contest in which she was about to be engaged. With warm solicitude for her consort, whose health would neither admit of bodily nor mental exertion, Margaret took the whole of the state affairs upon herself, acting as the king's delegate. Thus having duly considered the best policy to be adopted, the council decided upon trifling no longer with the Duke of York's presumptuous claims. They determined to meet the rebel, and by a decisive blow, crush those fearful disturbances, which were preying upon the vitals of the country.

Previous to this bold step, Margaret commanded the young Prince Edward to present the leaders in her army with a silver swan. This was a representation of his own badge and that of his great ancestor, Edward the Third. While the hope of Lancaster distributed these insignia with his infant hand, he expressed a wish, with all a child's eagerness, 'that they would wear them for his sake, and fight bravely for the good cause of Lancaster.'

The engaging innocence of the young Prince gained their hearts; while the cries of 'God bless his soul!' 'God bless the noble boy!' 'Long live our Prince Edward!' 'Long live the house of Lancaster!' rung on all sides.

Tudor and Kynfin were not forgotten upon this occasion. The heir of Lancaster exhibited a great partiality towards them both, after their instalment in the Queen's household. The child's first impulse, upon the silver swans being given into his possession, was to run and present one to each of his Welsh friends; and further, to the no small surprise of those present, he laid another upon his little palm, and holding it out, said—

'Here, Tudor ap Dafydd, you must send this to your brave father, who kept the Yorkists from his castle. Tell him Prince Edward asks in exchange the bow which sent the arrow into the rebel York.'

The Queen now learned for the first time that Salisbury, at the head of a potent army, was approaching. Her anxiety for the King's security increased, as he was too ill to leave his chamber. No alternative remained but to urge Audley to lose no time in meeting the white-rose party, lest her liege lord should be in danger. With these feelings she left the King, accompanied by the Prince, and hastened in person to communicate her wishes to her general, already strengthened by a reinforcement of ten thousand men. A long conference took place. The following were the Queen's valedictory words:—

'Good speed!—the Virgin help thee, Audley!—remember Salisbury! Salisbury! Dead or alive!'

Margaret had never been present at a battle. She determined upon witnessing that which was about to take place on Bloreheath. Did she repent her intention?—Who can tell? It was a fearful sight for her, yet she looked on a long time, until, eagerly clasping her child in her arms, she shrieked with a bursting heart—

'They fly! They fly! Our valiant army flies before the banner of the white rose! Audley! Somerset! This is a reverse I did not indeed count upon!'

'Your Highness is in danger!' said a kind and sympathizing voice, close at hand; and Tudor ap Dafydd, with his two companions, stood before her, ready to assist her flight. Every moment was of importance. Her conductors hurried forward with breathless anxiety. The little Prince clung to his Welsh friend. In a half whisper the child inquired if Kynfin was safe, and why he was not with him? The questions were answered in a few monosyllables, and clasping the child closer to his breast, Tudor strode on rapidly. At a turn in the road Kynfin, with horses and a small escort, suddenly appeared; and before the curfew had tolled that evening, the fugitives were beyond the reach of their pursuers.

Notwithstanding Margaret's poignant grief at the sight of the slaughter and defeat of her trusty adherents, the bright sun of the morning infused fresh energy into her soul. All the warlike spirit of her noble race kindled in her veins. She resolved in future to take the field herself, and by her personal encouragement lead on an army to contend for the right of her husband and child, determined not to rest till every possible struggle had been made to crown her endeavours with success.

'The battle of Bloreheath can never be effaced from my memory,' said the Queen some time after that unfortunate defeat. 'Our hearts are touched at the melancholy sacrifice of our subjects; but never will we be discouraged at York's temporary triumph. Rather shall it be an incentive to spur us on to conquer the rebellion or perish at the sword's point. The scourge of our land must be overcome before tranquillity can be restored—he must die. In this emergency, my faithful and zealous adherents, I look still to you for support. Let us continue to fight manfully for our anointed sovereign and lawful prince.'

CHAPTER IV

The Maid of Honour—The Royal Flight

Soon after the battle of Bloreheath the Queen, with her royal
Consort, repaired to Ludlow, to meet the insurgents upon the
borders of Wales. The King was in better health than he had
been for some time before. Margaret persuaded him to issue
a proclamation to the purport that all nobles, esquires, and
subordinates, who would return to their lawful sovereign
should receive a free pardon. This proved a fortunate measure.
No sooner had the proclamation been published than hundreds
deserted from the rebel party. Seemingly too glad of an
opportunity of quitting their unprincipled leader, they
exchanged the pale for the dark rose.

At this unforeseen change of affairs the Duke of York
became alarmed, and leaving the Duchess and his family at
the castle of Ludlow, fled with a few faithful followers to
Ireland. His bold allies, Salisbury and Warwick, sought refuge
in France. Under these auspicious events England for a short
time enjoyed tranquillity.

Notwithstanding the excitement throughout the late
campaign, the sons of the Welsh chieftain, who had been
introduced at Court under the distinguished patronage of
their noble kinsman, Owen Tudor, had not been unrewarded
by the royal pair. After their courageous and heroic
behaviour at the battle of Bloreheath, and subsequently, in
aiding the Queen's flight from that terrible scene, the

brothers had been promoted to distinguished offices in the royal household.

The Court at this time was held at Windsor. It was during, the winter festivities there that Aliano, one of the maids of honour to the Queen, became an object of deep interest to Tudor, who found, during his sojourn there, frequent opportunities of enjoying her society. The time passed in uninterrupted happiness. At length vows were proffered and the troth given. Tudor felt, what he had never before experienced, that he had reached the height of happiness. Aliano was all the world to him. Her presence dispersed every shadow that darkened across his path. He imagined that he had become another being. Too soon the spell was broken, for Aliano became suddenly changed: her cheeks grew pale, her steps slow and sad. She was missing; and where she had disappeared was unknown to the Queen and her companions. It was said she had fled the Court to incarcerate her fair form within the walls of a distant convent. She left behind no trace of her road—no clue by which to discover her retreat.

The sudden and mysterious disappearance of the 'Lily', as she was frequently called, occasioned excitement amongst the gay assemblages at Court. She was much regretted, and her grandfather, her only surviving relative, was inconsolable.

It was whispered that the handsome Cambrian youth Tudor ap Dafydd had trifled with her affections, and that in a state of despair she had taken some precipitous step. Tudor, who was not less changed in his appearance than Aliano, shortly after requested leave of absence, and it was granted.

He immediately started for his native hills. With a light step he bounded over crag and morass, through wood and glen, and thought that the land of his forefathers never appeared so lovely. Nature, in her wild, uncultivated state, seemed to be dressed in smiles to welcome the wanderer, cheering him at every step, till he reached his uncle Grono's hospitable dwelling. He there felt once more happy, compared to the later period of his residence at Windsor.

During these mysterious incidents which had caused so much gossiping at court, Kynfin was in France, having been sent thither by the Queen with a special message to the Duke of Somerset, who was then absent from the realm. Thus it happened that the brothers had been separated.

Queen Margaret, with her natural discernment, had discriminated the characters of the youthful Tudors. Independently of being connected by a collateral branch with the house of Tudor herself, she felt from their personal merits, a real interest in their welfare. At the same time she considered herself fortunate in having two individuals so useful among her retinue. Tudor, with his strikingly handsome lineaments, noble bearing, and generous disposition, was an ornament to her court. He had proved himself a good soldier and a faithful subject. Kynfin, less favoured in personal appearance, she found an apt and suitable envoy, ever ready to fly upon her missions abroad or at home, and executing them with a promptitude and judgment which would have done honour to the most accomplished diplomatist. Margaret remarked that for a long time she had not met with one so attentive, so energetic, and yet so steady in principle as the beardless boy, the son of the valorous Welsh chieftain.

A few months after these incidents Tudor and Kynfin once more met together in the royal household. Much had occurred, to interrupt tranquillity at court. A fatality appeared to darken over England. It was once more threatened with civil war. The

Duke of York was in arms again, and on his march to the capital.

This startling intelligence raised fearful forebodings. Margaret with surprising readiness convoked her adherents, and set out at the head of a powerful army to give battle to her implacable foe. They met near Northampton. There the dauntless Queen drew up her forces in battle array. A terrible encounter took place. During the greater part of the action, the red-rose party had a decided advantage; and would have gained the victory, had not that contemptible traitor to his friends Grey de Ruthyn gone over to the White Roses and betrayed the cause of Lancaster, by introducing the enemy into the very tent of his royal master, when the King was immediately taken prisoner.

By this ignoble and base act, a panic spread through the Queen's army. Margaret with all her endeavours to rally her men had no control in the confusion. The Red Roses were again obliged to fly before the banners of the white.

The first thought of the Queen was to gain possession of her offspring: and so agonized were her feelings that she would have plunged into the enemy's camp, sooner than have fled without her child. The sons of the Welsh chieftain were with the royal mistress in the trying hour. Kynfin participating in, and sympathizing with her distress, knowing the locality of the young Prince, hurriedly disappeared, and quickly returned, rejoining the illustrious lady with the infant Prince Edward in his arms.

As they fled before the exulting enemy, the shouts of victory, still sounding in their ears, made the unhappy Queen too painfully aware of the danger of her position. She hastened her flight with redoubled energy till the Bishopric of Durham was gained, where she remained but a few days. At the expiration of that time, through the entreaty of the Tudors, seconded by the Duke of Somerset, Margaret consented to seek a safe retreat within the mountain barriers of North Wales.

The Yorkists were hourly gaining ground. Too well the Queen knew that it was unsafe to tarry longer in the North, even for an hour.

Under these distressing circumstances, the hapless fugitive set out on her weary route. She was previously assured by her kind and faithful followers that they would adopt every expedient in their power to ameliorate the fatigue of the journey, and secure her safety on the way.

Her escort was so limited that Margaret dreaded an encounter with any of the detached parties of the Yorkists. At every step her anxiety increased, from the perils by which it was too evident she was surrounded.

'If we could once reach our mountains,' said Kynfin, addressing the Duke of Somerset, who had just been communicating the Queen's fears, 'I have no hesitation in answering for our safety. Among our wilds there beats many a stout heart for Lancaster, within whose dwellings we can not only obtain shelter during the night, but ensure protection and hospitality to cheer us on our way.'

On the following day the marshes were reached. At the sight of the blue mountains every heart rejoiced. Margaret stood and gazed intently upon the lovely prospect which thus suddenly appeared before her.

'Oh, land of nature's beauty!' exclaimed the delighted Margaret, placing her hand to her brow as if to compass the whole of the lovely landscape; 'an unhappy fugitive is come to seek shelter under the shadow of those towering heights. But, woe is me! there remains still too many a weary mile to traverse before that comforting period will have arrived.'

Towards the close of evening, as the little band slowly proceeded, their horses jaded, and themselves overcome by fatigue, they were alarmed by the tramp of horses; and the next moment surrounded by a band of ruffians, who, regardless of the Queen's presence, and her melancholy situation, rushed forward, rapier in hand, declaring they would spare no one, not even the child, if resistance were made. One of them approached the Queen, seized upon the bridle of her palfrey, and demanded her jewels.

'Audacious wretches!' cried Tudor, who was near the Queen's person, indignant at the insult offered to his royal mistress, as he fell upon the robber with great precipitation. A furious struggle ensued, when Kynfin, seeing the danger of the royal lady, caught the reins of her horse, and dashed off into the thickest part of an adjoining wood.

'We are safe here, I think,' said Margaret, with a look of bewilderment. 'Kynfin ap Dafydd, lose no time for the Virgin's sake! Go back to the assistance of your brother and the rest of my faithful attendants. My anxiety on their account is great. Heaven protect them!'

It was well Kynfin returned to his friends, since the contest had become desperate. The boldness and self-possession of the twin brothers proved the safety of the fugitive party. Their encouraging voices, their active and dauntless conduct, were an incitement as well as an example to their companions, who fought gallantly by their side, till at length the marauders retreated. A party of them, however, seizing some of the Queen's luggage, had fled, followed by the rest of the band, leaving their wounded comrades to the mercy of their opponents.

By this catastrophe two or three were killed and several wounded. Delay was dangerous—the wounded were left behind with some of the party to administer to their wants.

The hour grew late. They pursued their way over many a weary mile before they halted. This took place only to relieve the animals of the escort that could proceed no further from fatigue. It was a warm moonlight night in July, and the Queen was herself thankful to rest until the morning. A shelter of rock, and beds of heath, rich in beauty and perfume, offered on their purple blossoms the only rest for the exhausted travellers.

The little Prince was already asleep. Kynfin, who had the special charge of the royal child, laid him down with all the gentleness of a practised nurse, on mantles spread for the accommodation of both Margaret and the precious infant. He then retired to a respectful distance from the royal sleepers, and kept guard with several of the party, who alternately watched and slept.

The sun was high in the heavens before Margaret awoke from her slumber; the first she had enjoyed since they commenced their journey. The morning was beautiful, a gentle wind blowing from the tops of the mountains—the earth teeming with freshness, and wild flowers exhaling their delicious sweetness; the bleating of the sheep was heard afar, and the gurgling of the numerous mountain-streamlets fell in gentle cadence upon the ear. There was a tranquil charm around, to which even Margaret was not insensible in her painful situation; for, as she advanced towards her attendants, there was a mingled expression of pleasure and sadness visible in her countenance.

After a hasty repast from their vagrant provisions, they set out again upon their pilgrimage. As at each step they drew nearer to scenery more wild, and beautiful, expressions of admiration escaped even Margaret's lips; and, for a time, she seemed to forget her perilous situation in admiring the impressive scenery around. It was but transitory. As the beauty of the morning changed, so the illustrious lady relapsed into her former depression. This increased as gaping chasms, barren moors, and turbid torrents, ever and anon impeded their progress.

Contemplating the deplorable state to which Margaret was reduced, it is marvellous her depression was not greater. Her escort, since the brutal attack of the marauders, was reduced to eight. Her wardrobe had been wholly carried off, and still there were many miles between the party and their place of destination.

In the midst of her troubles, Margaret felt thankful that she had the protection of the Tudors. Her whole trust was centred in them. They alone of the party knew the country, and understood the language. She was contented in continuing to Kynfin the entire charge of the hope of Lancaster, and he was unremitting in his attentions. Tudor quitted not the side of his royal mistress, but walked the greater part of the way to lead her palfrey over the rough and uncertain ground, which marked the character of the wild and unbeaten track they had entered upon.

Travelling on in this manner for some time, the party suddenly came upon table-land overlooking a picturesque valley beneath. Night was rapidly approaching. A thick mist was hovering over the tops of the mountains, awaiting the sunset to drop down with its usual impetuosity upon the lower cliffs. Tudor at this moment turned to address the royal lady, with a look of care and sadness, and in a few sentences made known their definite position,—

'Please, your highness, my uncle's house lies in that direction,' said he, drawing the Queen's attention to a certain part of the valley; 'just a mile and a half distant in a straight line. This path, down the crags, would lead us directly thither. Supposing we take the bridle road, it will be several miles round, independent of our being obliged to pass through a nest of Yorkists. If we would gain my uncle's before midnight, and avoid this dangerous and weary march, there remains the alternative; and that, please your highness, is to descend these crags on foot.'

It was now that Margaret, with a look of despair, exclaimed in touching accents—

'The Virgin help me! Will danger never cease? Shall we never reach the strong towers of Harlech?'

Tudor assured her in cheering and respectful tones that there was no real cause for alarm, if she would place herself under his protection. He would pledge himself to conduct her in safety to the vale below.

Margaret uttered a few words of thanks, and dismounted without raising another objection. Immediately after, placing her hand upon the arm of her fearless guide, she commenced descending the dangerous path, while many of her party stood hesitating upon the brink.

Kynfin took the lead, and with the hope of Lancaster upon his shoulders, bounded from crag to crag with the agility of a chamois hunter, to the alarm and astonishment of his Saxon companions, who were treading the ground with so much circumspection. Margaret, too, at first was alarmed for the safety of her child, but her confidence in the chieftain's son overcame her fears, and she stood for a few moments an admiring spectator.

'I envy you mountaineers,' said the Queen, turning to address her companion; 'your courage and activity are marvellous. I would I were as fleet of foot. In such adversity as mine, methinks, Tudor, I need it.'

She sighed, and a melancholy smile for an instant lit up her countenance.

After some slight delay, the whole party reached the foot of the precipitous crags in safety.

The horses and ponies were taking a more circuitous path, further down, followed by shepherd boys; who shortly afterwards drove them up to the spot where the anxious travellers awaited them.

Once more the noble lady vaulted into her saddle, and ap Dafydd, grasping the reins of her horse, began urging it on by various coaxing tones in the vernacular tongue.

A drizzling rain had already set in, and night was overtaking them. Each drew his cloak closer around him, proceeding silently, as the rain beat in his face.

There was something dreary to all in that prospect, conjoined with the silence of human voices coming on so suddenly. The clattering of the horses' hoofs echoing and re-echoing among the rocks and eminences, which skirted the road on either side, the roaring of the distant torrents, the far-off cry of the solitary otter, the barking of the sheep dogs, the notes of the wild birds disturbed from their nests, to which must be added the gloom of the approaching night,—all combined to render the scene sombre as well as wild.

'There, there it is, at length,' cried ap Dafydd, suddenly

breaking the silence, as the weary party rounded a large mass of rock; 'there is a roof which shelters as stout a heart for Lancaster as any in the British dominion, and let me assure your highness that he, veteran as he is, would serve your Majesty's house to the last drop of his heart's blood.'

Having said this, he placed a bugle horn to his lips, and gave one long thrilling blast. It was returned by many a wild echo among the hills. Another blast was given, and another, when immediately afterwards figures were seen standing on an overhanging terrace, bearing blazing torches.

At this cheering sight, the exhausted travellers hurried forward, and with rejoicing hearts prepared to ascend the winding stone steps which fed directly to the entrance of the curiously constructed abode of Grono ap Meredyth ap Tudor, who advanced in haste to welcome the royal fugitives.

CHAPTER V

Welcome to Harlech—The Spy

IF the light torches gleaming in the distance had proved so
cheering to the benighted travellers, how great must have been
their joy, when the venerable Grono conducted them into the
spacious hall of his renowned forefathers! There, the blazing
hearth, the well supplied board, the smiling faces of the
attendants, proclaimed a welcome that might well gladden the
souls of fugitives so elevated yet unfortunate.

Exhausted and dispirited after her fatigues, Margaret was
overcome with thankfulness at finding herself suddenly
transported to a scene so cheering. She found it some
consolation to reflect that she was no more exposed to the
vengeance of her implacable foe, no more unsheltered from
the elements.

The evening's festivities, for there was joy in the household
of ap Grono to be so honoured, were checked early on account
of the Queen's fatigue. Tudor had disappeared upon the first
arrival of the party at the hall; the Queen remarked the
circumstance, but none volunteered an explanation. He
reappeared as usual on the morning of the next day. In this
hospitable asylum Margaret consented to remain a short time;
Grono rejoicing that he was thus able to contribute to the
comfort and safety of his royal mistress. When the time
arrived for her departure, he endeavoured to prevail upon his
royal mistress to prolong her visit, assuring her that it would

re-establish her health, and she would then be better able to encounter the remainder of her perilous journey.

'Detain me not, my venerable friend,' replied the Queen; 'in these critical times it does not become us either to consult our inclinations or comforts. You are already aware that the Yorkists infest the adjoining district; they will hear of my presence with you. The more haste I make in quitting the spot, the better for us both. Let me assure you, my faithful subject, I feel deeply grateful for the protection you have afforded me. In remembrance of your hospitality you will accept this token—would it were worthier.' The Queen then unclasped a golden cross, richly inlaid with jewels, and placed it in Grono's hand. Immediately after which she descended the winding steps from the terrace, and joined her escort that was already in waiting.

The sun at that moment had risen over the grey hills, tinging with rosy hue the clouds which rolled in strange forms above their summits, and then disappeared among the numerous fissures and chasms of that rough and rocky district.

At the Queen's desire, Tudor took his accustomed place by the side of her palfrey, and Kynfin once more received the royal child under his especial charge. In this manner the travellers continued on their way, sometimes fording rivers, scaling heights, and eluding straggling parties of Yorkists that caused the fugitives moments of intense alarm for the safety of the Queen and Prince.

The chieftain of Harlech awaited their arrival at the castle with great anxiety. Preparations had been made for the reception of the fugitives some time before; but the strictest precautions had been taken to prevent the country from hearing of the royal lady's expected arrival. When a messenger brought word that the illustrious party was within a few miles of Harlech, Dafydd neither sent an escort, nor went himself to meet the Queen, lest it might excite suspicion. But with what unfeigned pleasure, with what genuine sympathy, did the noble and kind-hearted chieftain welcome his liege lady, the moment she set foot upon the threshold of the castle!

Margaret of Anjou had never before seen the brave defender of her house. She had been familiarised with his name in connection with many anecdotes of the French war. This had created a desire on the part of the Queen to become personally acquainted with him. With what pleasure, then, did she behold his open countenance and unsophisticated manners, his well-proportioned, yet almost gigantic figure, as he hastened forward to throw himself at her feet and swear to her fealty!

The hour was late when the fugitives reached Harlech, where the minister of the crown, the Duke of Somerset, had already arrived. Margaret, completely exhausted by mental as well as bodily exertions, retired immediately to the apartments appointed for her use; where the lady of the castle, the Mistress Tudor,[1] with her natural kindness, proffered her services. Everything that could be done to ensure the comfort and happiness of her distinguished guest she had anticipated.

With feelings of deep commiseration did the good Mistress Tudor gaze upon the sorrowful Queen on her arrival. Her long, dishevelled hair flowed over her shoulders, her once costly and elegant garments were hanging about her person soiled and neglected.

---

[1] The maiden name in those times was retained after marriage, and is to this day among the humbler classes.

'Was royalty ever before brought to such extremities?' thought the good lady of the castle, while casting furtive glances at her beautiful companion—beautiful notwithstanding her forlorn condition in regard to dress.

Margaret for some minutes hung over the sleeping child, the tears struggling in her eyelids, and then falling silently down her pallid cheeks.

'O Arglwyddes *bach* anwyl! [2] I am sorry in my heart for you,' exclaimed Mistress Tudor, no longer able to control her feelings. She then threw herself upon her knees before the object of her pity, and continued:—

'Would that it were in my power, noble lady, to comfort you in your distress. These are sad times, but the God of heaven will not forsake you.'

Margaret was affected by this artless language, and confessed the value she set upon her sympathy.

The child moving and appearing uneasy, Mistress Tudor took the little prince in her arms, undressed him and put him in bed, imprinting a warm kiss upon his cheek, and repeating with native pathos—

'O bach anwyl fy machgen bach anwyl (my darling little boy), you shall sleep here in peace, and none shall touch you as long as my good lord can unsheathe a sword for the house of Lancaster.'

The manners and customs of the Welsh were entirely unknown to the fair descendant of Anjou, but she soon learned

---

[2] Dear, dear lady. The literal translation of bach is 'little', and takes vach in the feminine, but this word is more frequently used as a term of endearment, in the same manner 'chen' is by the Germans, and in that sense does not change in the feminine.

to appreciate their warm, disinterested character; and in the noble partner of ap Jevan the Queen found a faithful friend and valuable companion to cheer her exile.

Mistress Tudor's first consideration and care was to replenish the illustrious lady's wardrobe. Margaret was even amused amid her sadness at the various articles of clothing which were brought for her inspection. She was pleased to select those made in the country, adding that while she was in Wales she would dress as the native ladies did, and patronize their artisans.

One day after the arrival of the royal party, Dafydd early in the morning repaired to the battlements; with his arms folded across his manly chest, he paced to and fro, glancing his vision from side to side with a restlessness not habitual. He had risen from his bed after a sleepless night, and was now endeavouring to shake off the unpleasant forebodings which had entered his mind.

'Why should I apprehend danger? Why look for evils which may never visit us?' argued Dafydd. 'York may come again with increased numbers. He may be more persevering, but Harlech is strong, and the men of Merioneth are brave. We can still hold our ground. Protector of King Henry's consort, I will not forfeit that high post, while the confidence with which the Queen honours me shall not be found misplaced.' Here Dafydd suddenly stood still, and clasping his hands in the attitude of prayer, exclaimed:—

'Margaret, Queen of England, my sovereign, anxiety for your welfare, and that of your royal child, preys upon my heart. The responsibility I incur is great. God answer my orisons in your behalf, and give me strength to prevent any disgrace of this weighty trust on my part.'

Scarcely had he uttered this ejaculation, when his quick eye detected an individual skulking along near the entrenchment without the castle. Dafydd, for a few minutes riveted to the spot, eagerly watched the movements of the stranger.

'He is a Saxon, by my sword, he is!' Then turning to one of the sentinels, he continued—

'Here, Howel, I want your eyesight to confirm my own— what figure is that?'

No sooner had the words been spoken, than the sturdy sentinel sprang forward, his eye searching in the direction to which ap Jevan pointed.

For a few minutes he was silent, and then, unusually excited, he cried,—

'I see him, the Saxon thief! Look yonder, master, to the left, there is another skulking villain.'

'They are spies,' said Dafydd, thoughtfully; 'Howel, there is no time to be lost; these fellows must not escape us.'

The Warden reached the hall with a quick step, and ordered Howel, whose duties as sentinel had just then expired, to fetch a woman's petticoat and upper garment, and to join him at the postern.

Howel quickly fulfilled his errand, and soon found his master metamorphosed into a countryman—with a sack of loose litter upon his back.

'Now Howel, make a woman of yourself. Hasten; take this peat basket.—There, that will do, come along with me.' Both quitted by the sally port together, and both carried rapiers under their garments.

A storm at this moment came sweeping up from the sea most opportunely, and for a while they were both hidden from the sight. Dafydd and his companion continued their way, well knowing in what locality they were proceeding.

'We are on the right track,' whispered Howel.

'Aye! Aye!' replied the Warden, in a still lower key; 'the Saxons are both under the rock. We have only to go on in the same direction, and they are ours.'

Howel obediently followed in the footsteps of his master. Suddenly they came up to the unsuspecting foe. Not a word was uttered. The attack was not anticipated. The Harlech chieftain disarmed and took them both prisoners. In his powerful grasp, it was vain to make resistance. The prisoners did not afterwards attempt it, but allowed themselves to be led passively forward, obstinately refusing to answer any questions which were put to them.

They were now approaching the castle. The Warden, provoked at their dogged silence, hurried them into the courtyard, and throwing off his disguise, at once resumed his accustomed authority as lord of the fortress.

'By my sword, we shall soon teach you to change your bearing,' said he, casting a withering glance at his prisoners; 'we may put you to the question.'

Several of the garrison had come into the court, and some of the household. Dafydd, with a commanding look and wave of the hand, kept them at a distance, while he continued:—

'Listen, Yorkist spies, hatched in the nest of traitors—your confession? If you lie—by St David and all the saints, I will splinter you before the sun goes down. Did the arch-rebel York send you hither, or came you with a horde conducted by another of his party?—answer me.—What, no reply?—are your intellects fled after your speech, mewn gwironedd?—do not think to deceive me in this manner.'

He then gave one of them a violent shake, as if to recall him to his senses, being impatient to discover their design.

Roused by this sudden insult, they both sprang with the fury of tigers upon Ap Jevan. But they soon found the Harlech chief was more than a match for them. A blow from his powerful arm laid one of them at his feet; seizing the other by the collar, he lifted him on high, and, drawing his sword, he placed the naked blade at the Saxon's breast, exclaiming:—

'Confess, traitor, or prepare for the question and another world.'

Still no syllable came from his terrified victim.

'You will not confess?' resumed the Warden, his anger increasing as he waved his glittering weapon over the youth. 'Learn then, your doom is sealed.'

'Hold—the holy saints preserve me,' gasped the Saxon, death with its appalling horrors flashing across his mind. 'Give me a short time to consider.'

'No,' retorted Dafydd, 'I have given you time, traitor, to answer my question; speak, I am in earnest.'

The firmness with which this was uttered, and the resolute expression of the speaker, told the culprit that hesitation would be immediate death.

With large drops of perspiration falling from his brow, and reduced to the extremity of death or obedience, the Saxon muttered between his clenched teeth:—

'The Earl of Warwick—yes, the Earl sent us to ascertain whether Queen Margaret had taken up her quarters here.'

'Wfft,' muttered Ap Jevan; 'and have you gained the information you sought?'

'No,' replied the youth, recoiling from the searching glance of his interrogator.

'You have some better idea of what brought you into Wales,

than such an idle story as that. Beware how you trifle with me further.'

'I speak the truth,' said the Saxon; 'we followed Queen Margaret in her flight from Northampton, and kept the fugitives at a little distance before us, the greater part of the way. One evening, when in the heart of the mountains, the weather misty and wet, we lost our way. Since then, we have not been able to discover her track. Some of our party went in one direction, and some in another, but to no purpose.'

'Go on,' said Ap Jevan, as the prisoner stammered and was about to curtail the particulars. 'What brought you into this neighbourhood, of all places—did you dream to find the royal fugitives here?'

'We had been informed by a shepherd boy that soldiers, baggage, and horses, had been seen passing through the glen a few days before. Our intention was to remain in this vicinity till our suspicions were removed or confirmed.'

'What would have been your next step?'

'To return to the Earl of Warwick and acquaint him with our discovery.'

'Enough,' said the Warden. 'I shall only ask two more questions; where are the remainder of your band—and what is their number?'

'They were twelve in all. We did not deem that a sufficient number to attack the Red Roses; particularly when we had just heard of the blunder of which John Cleger, the avaricious serf of my Lord Stanley, had been guilty.'

'But your companions, where are they now?'

'Among the mountains somewhere; we parted with them a week back.'

Dafydd then commanded the prisoners to be placed in close

confinement, to await his further pleasure. He then communicated the event to the Duke of Somerset, who received the intelligence with some alarm.

'Conceal the incident from the Queen. It would be best not to cast a shadow over her fancied security. She places implicit faith in you, Ap Jevan.' Such was the minister's thoughtful reply.

Dafydd now felt his anxiety for the Queen's safety increased. He determined to be continually at his post, and set a secret watch among the mountains. He felt that every precaution must be taken to prevent an unforeseen attack from the enemy.

Meanwhile, Margaret, by her affable and condescending manners, had gained the hearts of the good people of Harlech. The hall of the castle daily became more crowded with guests. Dafydd, from interested motives, sent secret invitations to all those whom he knew to be staunch friends of the house of Lancaster that they might pay due homage to their Queen and youthful Prince.

This conduct was gratifying to the royal exile. Notwithstanding her solicitude for her consort, and her anxiety as to public affairs, she had thus a few scanty moments of real enjoyment. She felt no apprehension amongst the simple-hearted Welsh. Their homely and independent life had a charm for one whose years were passed in cares and trouble, so that she almost envied them. Accompanied by a small escort, she rode about the country, and sometimes a tiny skiff was observed gliding sweetly over the waters in Cardigan's lovely bay, bearing the daughter of Anjou's proud race.

As the royal party was returning from one of these pleasant excursions, it was overtaken by a storm. The Queen was forced to seek shelter in a cottage by the roadside, the dwelling of a poor shoemaker.

Struck with the poverty and wretchedness of the abode, Margaret made inquiries about the family. The cottager had recently lost his wife, and he was left to be the sole support of a numerous progeny; but, notwithstanding his industrious habits and good character, he was unable to satisfy their many wants by his labour.

The Queen was deeply touched at the tale, and ordered him to make shoes for her retinue. Then pointing to an intelligent, open-countenanced youth she added:—

'Send this son of yours to the castle; he shall return with me to England, care shall be taken of him.'

The shoemaker did not understand the Queen's kindness. His knowledge of Saxon was very indifferent, not indeed beyond a few phrases. But upon Kynfin repeating Margaret's words in the Welsh tongue, informing him at the same time that the Lady was King Henry's consort, he started up and flinging aside the implements of his trade, prostrated himself before his benefactress, tears of gratitude glittering on his sunken cheeks. 'He was incapable,' he said, 'of making shoes of a quality fit for great people. He could only make plain shoes for his countrymen. If there was anything else he could do to show his duty and gratitude for her highness's kindness to his son, let the labour be ever so great he would not shrink from its performance.'

'I shall not forget your proffered services,' said Margaret with much dignity and suavity of manner, and, placing a piece of gold upon the table, quitted the cottage.

CHAPTER VI

Royal Sorrows—Ambition thwarted— The Adieu to the Castle

'MADAM,' said the Duke of Somerset, entering the Queen's apartments with a look of great bewilderment and uneasiness, 'Richard, Duke of York, has been proclaimed by the King and people heir-apparent to the crown of England and protector of the realm. I have received the act passed by the parliament;—I tremble indeed for the house of Lancaster.'

The little hope of the red rose banner was sitting at his mother's feet with his full blue eyes fixed upon her maternal face, as if asking an explanation of the minister's hurried intelligence.

'My child, my sweet child,' said Margaret in mental perturbation, clasping him to her bosom. 'Oh! cruel fate, what ill has it not in store for thee! Can it be possible, Henry thy father, my liege lord!—what phantom of the brain, what evil influence, what weakness has induced you to wrong this your son, your only son, this our darling child? No, it cannot be. A royal father to disinherit his offspring! and that offspring the only hope of Lancaster.'

As the words fell from her lips, an unusual lustre shot from her beautiful eyes. It was the concentration of a grief too deep for tears, of too much magnitude to raise even a sigh, all was reflected back upon a heart nearly breaking. For some moments she sat heedless in appearance of the simple questions reiterated by her infant son. She mechanically pressed him nearer to her heart, and remained the speechless image of silent woe.

The minister stood awaiting her commands for some time unheeded. At length, she roused herself, and rallying her energies with surprising composure, considering her previous state, she thus addressed him:—

'My lord, you will perhaps imagine this to be a weakness of mine not suitable to the moment; I hardly feel that it is suitable, but it is past. I am now ready to hear all you think needful to communicate; after that we can concert active measures. I well know, my lord Beaufort, that, despair is not policy, and that despondency is a weak substitute for the restoration of hope. Let me hear how you came so quickly in possession of these writings; it is not possible that Morgan the shoemaker, who was the messenger sent to procure them, has gone and returned in so short a time.'

'Your highness must know that I obtained them through his activity. The poor shoemaker has achieved what few others could accomplish, and at present awaits my further orders.'

'Providence has timely given me a useful though humble friend; would I could bestow on the poor man adequate reward.'—While the Queen slowly articulated the last sentence, she was unfolding the papers and letters, and soon, as she read them carefully over, became wholly abstracted.

It appeared that Henry had unexpectedly arrived in London, surrounded by the lords of his court, who, since the battle of Northampton, treated him with marked respect. Continually vacillating, they now appeared almost as warm for the Red Rose, as they had formerly been for the White. A parliament was summoned; the Duke of York, who was then in Ireland, was desired to be present. He was prevented from crossing the channel by the weather, and did not reach London until after the opening of Parliament, while the affair between the White and Red Roses was warmly debating.

Without waiting to refresh himself after the journey, the Duke rode down to Westminster, entered the House of Lords, and approaching the canopy, placed his hand upon the throne, in the vain hope that the House would clamorously demand that he should seat himself there. An ominous pause followed; the sensation his sudden appearance had caused, too clearly indicated that this act of daring presumption was not universally approved.

This unexpected hesitation of the nobles confused the Duke: his face, which on his entrance looked pale and haggard, became deeply flushed. His confusion increased, when the Archbishop of Canterbury approaching him, coolly asked, 'if he would not go and pay his respects to the King?'

'I know no one to whom I owe the honour of such an acknowledgment,' replied the Duke with increased mortification, as bridling himself up to his full height, he glanced with a contemptuous air on the assembled peers, and immediately, with rapid strides, left the House.

So much had he relied upon having the crown offered to him on that occasion that he remained for some hours afterwards in a state which scarcely permitted him to recall clearly what had passed. Before he retired to rest, however, he had recovered himself, and adopted a determination to let the world know his sentiments. Accordingly, the very next day he addressed himself by letter to the Parliament, stating the reasons upon which his pretensions to the crown of England were founded. Great excitement and heavy anxiety were felt throughout the kingdom during the debate that ensued and continued for some days: it was ultimately resolved that Henry should retain the crown until his demise: it was further provided that the Duke of York should be his successor. If Henry in any way disregarded this resolution, the crown would at once pass to the Duke of York and his heirs.

Queen Margaret was no sooner acquainted with these facts, than she ordered letters to be written to her agents in the capital. The necessity of her departure from Harlech was urgent, but resources in money were required for that purpose. Letters were therefore once more placed in the hands of the trustworthy Morgan, who left the castle the same night mounted on a sturdy pony, and with great cheerfulness he commenced his unsuspected errand over his native mountains.

Margaret consulted Ap Jevan upon the most secure mode of leaving his hospitable castle. She spoke so touchingly to him that many, who were much less sympathising than Dafydd, would have felt unmanned. She entered minutely into the distressing particulars of her position, and lastly, declared her intention of going from thence to Scotland, at the court of which country she hoped to gain efficient support, and contend once more for the rights of her consort and child.

Dafydd listened to all that the Queen had to communicate, with deference and attention. Having well weighed all the circumstances, he suggested that she should go by water, rather than again subject herself to the hardships and difficulties of an overland journey. He proposed that with his sons he should carry her to the Menai in one of their own boats, in which operation there would be little hazard incurred; she could then proceed to Scotland at her own pleasure.

All this appeared so feasible to Margaret that she awaited Morgan's return with impatience, in order to proceed as Dafydd had suggested.

After the family had retired, Dafydd and his two sons, sitting before the hall hearth, talked over the contemplated departure of their royal guest.

'Someone should go into Carnarvonshire, and see that a vessel is ready to be under weigh at a moment's warning,' remarked Kynfin.

'You are right, my son, I have taken that into consideration,' replied the Warden; 'our cousin at Penmynnydd, I have been thinking, will be the best person to receive the Queen, before she embarks. Weather, or some unforeseen event, may prevent her setting sail immediately upon her arrival in the Straits; preparations, such as you propose, are necessary. The sooner it is done the better; our energetic messenger, Morgan the shoemaker, may be back sooner than we count upon.'

'Well, father, you have only to command,' said Tudor, 'and I will start at once. The moon is now high in the heavens; my little skiff will skim like a swallow over the sea; you had better let me go. We all feel that the duty of today should not be deferred till tomorrow.'

Dafydd consented; Tudor waited not another command, but hastened from the hall to the seaside, and was soon, with his only companion, a pilot, gliding over the waters on his secret mission.

The Warden and Kynfin stood upon one of the towers, watching the speck that glittered in the moonbeams, as it bore away the favourite youth, who had but a few minutes before stood in their presence with an eager look and dauntless mien. Their hearts glowed within them, and both felt proud of

Tudor; little thinking that he whom they loved so dearly, was leaving his home to return no more.

A week elapsed after Tudor ap Dafydd and the grateful Morgan had each set out different ways on their adventurous errands. Margaret still remained under the shadow of the old walls of Harlech. Tidings had arrived from Tudor that their cousin, Llewelyn ap Dorwyn, had succeeded in procuring a vessel with a crew of volunteers and that he was now only awaiting the arrival of the Queen.

Margaret was sitting at an open window overlooking the bay, fanned by the fresh breezes as they swept along, and contemplating the crossing of the waters below, when the Duke of Somerset's voice attracted her attention. Looking suddenly round, she was startled by the strange expression of his countenance.

'What news—anything the matter, my lord,' eagerly inquired Margaret; 'the messenger has returned I see by those letters,' and she held out her hand to receive them.

'They are the expected letters containing the money, so far all is well; but your highness will be distressed to hear that our royal master has been compelled to issue a mandate for the immediate return of your highness and the Prince to London: should you refuse to obey, it will be denominated high treason. A party of Yorkists are on their way to deliver this strange injunction. Before sunrise, it is feared, they will be at these gates, thundering for admittance.'

'Enough, my lord,' said the Queen, imperatively. 'Go, tell my brave protector, Ap Jevan, that it is my pleasure to set off as soon as the boats can be got ready.'

The castle was thrown into great confusion in arranging for the Queen's hasty decision. In a few hours all was prepared for embarkation. Notwithstanding the hour was late, the good people of Harlech crowded on all sides, to take leave of their beloved Queen. She was dressed in the simplest attire, and accompanied by the Duke of Somerset, the Warden, Kynfin, and several esquires, she descended the rugged and slippery path which led to the seashore. Many ran before her, bearing torches. At the same moment the bards, who had composed a song for the occasion, struck up the mournful notes—

'Ffarwel iti Peggy ban.'

The Warden and his lady took their last leave of their illustrious guest. In the first instance it had been Dafydd's intention to escort the royal lady himself as far as Mona isle, but upon the intelligence being received that the Yorkists were already on their way to demand the person of the Queen, he was obliged to forego the honour.

The boat was scarcely ready to put off, when the moon rose from behind a dark, low cloud, casting her soft, silvery beams upon the picturesque group, as if to cheer them over the white glistening foam that broke gently on the castle-beach.

Margaret, with deep emotion, waved her white handkerchief as she left the land.

'Adieu, adieu, all my generous Welsh friends, the happy days passed among you shall never be forgotten by your Queen.'

The anchor being lifted with an off-shore breeze, fearlessly did the little bark glide onward with her canvas spread to the breeze. The proud castle of Harlech was soon left far behind.

Notwithstanding the wind was in Margaret's favour, the passage was tedious; and all felt thankful when they reached the hospitable roof of another of the clan of Tudor. Margaret was more than usually fatigued, and retired to her chamber. Sleep, however, did not visit her eyes.

The greater part of her time was passed in forming plans for her future proceedings against the unsuspecting Yorkists. She had much confidence in the nobles of the northern counties, and by the aid of Scotland, great efforts might yet be made in her behalf.

'Yes, I will check-mate York—check-mate him, before he is aware I have left the impregnable fortress in Wales.'

Unrefreshed and fevered from thought, she rose at an early hour the morning after her arrival, having herself completed her toilet, before her retinue were moving.

Nothing could exceed the restlessness and impatience exhibited by Margaret upon this occasion. Minutes appeared hours in her anxiety; nor did these feelings abate till she was on board the vessel, rapidly leaving the rocky headlands of the Welsh coast.

Tudor and Kynfin, at the Queen's desire, retained their places in her suite. They had been her companions in misfortune, and she now hoped they would be the same in her triumph. They were so much favourites of the Queen that she never hesitated giving the young Prince entirely into their charge.

CHAPTER VII

A Regal Victress—A Secret developed—The Deathbed of Youth

MARGARET was graciously received by the King of Scotland; and the assistance she sought willingly granted. Her adherents were, therefore, greatly encouraged; and the heroic Queen soon set out at the head of a formidable army; crossed the Scottish borders, and joined the chivalry of the northern counties, with every expectation of success. She flew onwards with an eagle's swoop, amid exulting cries of confidence and loyalty, until she reached the gates of York, defying the leaders of the White Rose to their astonishment and dismay.

No sooner had the Duke of York been informed of the decided and daring proceedings of the intrepid Queen, than he left London with the Earl of Salisbury, and hastened, with all the forces he could muster, to check the rapid advance of the incensed Lady, whom he was wont to designate as the 'Lancastrian tigress'.

Upon reaching Sandal Castle, the Duke resolved to remain there till the arrival of his son, the handsome young Earl of March, who was expected with reinforcements from the borders. These were hours of suspense and anxiety to the Duke. Every moment he grew more exasperated as he beheld the tide of fortune flowing in another channel, and the author of the calamity a feeble woman.

Margaret entered Wakefield, and stood with her brave soldiers under the walls of his castle. Elated by her good fortune, and impatient to dispute her cause with the sword-point, the Queen sent repeated messages to the Duke, inquiring why he kept himself like a frightened bird in a cage? Was he too much alarmed to take a view of his enemy from the towers of his castle? Was he afraid to meet a woman? He who called himself the heir-apparent to the crown of England?

'Go tell him, Queen Margaret, his opponent, says—he is no more than a dissembling coward, a disgrace to his nation.'

Roused to the highest pitch of anger, the Duke swore he would wait no longer for the assistance of his son, disdaining the counsel of all—even that of his friend, old Sir Davy Hall; who, with tears in his eyes, implored him to delay his rash intention. Nothing could divert him from his purpose. Angrily turning from the old man's sound advice, he quitted his stronghold, and advanced in the name of God and St George. Rushing upon the vanguard of the Queen, he vainly hoped that by daring intrepidity, his female opponent would be scared from the field.

He was mistaken. Anjou's proud spirit was not to be thus daunted. With admirable calculation and forethought, she drew up her army in three divisions. The centre she led herself, issuing her commands through the Earl of Somerset, who rode beside her spirited charger. The wings were under the command of the Earl of Wiltshire and Lord Clifford. In this order she well knew her own security, and without a shadow of alarm, pressed onward with her more numerous forces. The wings, perceiving the ill-judged situation of the enemy, at once closed in upon and enveloped both flanks of the enemy. The slaughter that ensued was terrible, and in less than half an hour, three thousand of the Yorkists were lifeless upon the field. The remainder, alarmed for their own safety, fled before the victors.

Clifford, a man of little feeling or humanity, excited by success, pursuing the fugitives, seized upon the young Earl of Rutland, who was made prisoner, murdering him in cold blood. He returned to the camp, bearing on his lance the sanguinary head, severed from the body of the Duke, who had fallen.

Loud and deafening were the shouts of rejoicing, intermingled with jeers, that rent the air when Clifford appeared among them, exhibiting the bleeding head crowned with paper.

'Madam, your work is done—here is your King's ransom,' said he, presenting it to Margaret, who at that moment rode up to the spot.

Margaret was unprepared for such a spectacle. At first her feminine nature recoiled, and she turned away, but soon recovered herself. Her distaste was supplanted by revengeful pleasure. She turned and looked again upon the pale and bleeding head—it was that of the great enemy of her house. My consort, my child, our enemy is no more! A wild laugh escaped her as she galloped away from the sanguinary scene.

Cruel as Margaret thus appeared, she possessed many amiable qualities and kindly feelings. Upon hearing that her faithful adherents, Tudor ap Dafydd and his brother, were severely wounded, she expressed the greatest concern. No sooner had she given orders for marching to the capital on the following morning that she might set her captive lord free, than she went to visit the brothers in their tent.

'This misfortune I did not look for,' said the Queen, bending over the wounded youths. 'I had hoped that you would have accompanied me in my triumph to the Metropolis. God grant that you may soon be restored. I have arranged that you be taken to a kinsman of one of my nobles, who resides not far from hence. Care will be taken of you.'

Many cheering expressions dropped from her lips. Again assuring them of her solicitude, she quitted the tent.

Thus, in the midst of her triumph, Margaret remembered the sons of her valiant protector. It was after midnight before she returned to her own quarters. The turmoil of the camp was hushed, and the memorable day terminated.

The sons of the Welsh chief had been removed to the abode of the English Baron. Kynfin, who had been slightly wounded, was soon able to leave his couch. Fortune had not been so lenient to Tudor, who hourly grew worse. Fever quickly reduced his fine athletic frame to a shadow. Kynfin, in deep despair, beheld the change which had taken place.

Mistress Elinor, a lady who presided over the Baron's establishment, his own favourite sister, endeavoured to do all in her power to relieve the sufferings of the invalid. She assured Kynfin that, in time, Tudor would recover from his wounds.

'Come, come!' said she, in gentle accents, 'you must brighten up, and not look so dispirited.'

'Kindness itself!' muttered Kynfin, as the door closed upon the good-hearted lady. 'Little will it avail my poor brother. Oh anwyl! anwyl! would we had both died upon the battlefield. There would have been glory in that! My mother, how shall I ever return to you without your first-born, your favourite son; the life, the joy of our fireside; the sunny ray which dispersed every cloud that appeared on the horizon of our domestic felicity? None can be aware of the extent of our loss. Cambria will be deprived of a brave soldier, and I shall lose my companion, the friend of my bosom.'

His head sunk low upon his breast, and a groan escaped him when he thought of losing his brother.

Tudor's fever increased, and he became more and more restless. When alone, he called Kynfin, and affectionately pressing his hand, begged he would keep near him, for he had much to say. His whole frame trembled. There was an unnatural wildness, too, in his eyes, as he continued—

'Kynfin, my end is near; I fain would have lived, or died upon the battle-field. God's will be done. I dare not repine. I am punished for the deception which I have practised upon my family. Start not, my brother, listen! I have important matter to communicate.'

He paused to recover himself, and then proceded—

'Kynfin, since we have been in the Queen's household, we have been frequently separated. It was while you were in France, I formed an attachment to one of the maids of honour— Lady Aliano Stanop. She was a Saxon maiden, and you know, Kynfin, how strong an objection my father has for any of his house to form an alliance with that race. Disregardful of his wish, disobedient to his commands, I sought the maiden's affections, and won them; we were happy in the bright prospect that we imagined lay before us. I must be brief; life is ebbing. Aliano, in a paroxysm of grief, one day revealed to me that her grandfather's intention was to marry her to a man of great wealth, distinction, and advanced age. This intelligence was a fearful blow to us both. It almost drove me to madness. I was tempted to propose to my mistress to solemnise our nuptials in private. Aliano at first objected, but on our being driven to the last extremity, she consented; and we were united in the dead of night by a monk, not far from Windsor, in the presence of Bridget of Windsor, the mother of Aliano's foster mother. A parting letter was written to her grandfather. In that letter, I made Aliano state that she had renounced the world, and would take the veil in a distant convent; the rigid rules of which would prevent her having any communication with her family. She gave up all for me—fortune, friends and country.'

Tudor paused; his agitation seeming to stifle farther utterance.

'Raise me up, dear brother, I feel that I am going; yet I have much to say.'

Then looking steadfastly in Kynfin's face, he proceeded—

'Chide me, yes, chide me! you who have been the companion of my childhood; you who have ever been open with me, and ever loved me with a devotion uncommon even between brothers. I have deceived your confidence, I have been ungrateful and unworthy of your love in this matter.'

'Reproach not yourself, Tudor,' said Kynfin, tenderly supporting him, while a look of anguish passed over the sufferer's face. 'I forgive you—we all forgive you.'

Thus encouraged, Tudor went on with his narration:—

'I was alarmed lest my absence from the palace should occasion suspicion. Thus the immediate parting from my bride was unavoidable. I privately sent for some of our countrymen. I placed Aliano and her maid, disguised as a nobleman and his page, under their escort. I knew she would be safely conducted to the house of our good uncle Grono ap Meredyth, where she has ever since resided. I avoided trusting my secret to any. I said that Aliano was a young nobleman in great difficulties, a friend of mine, in whose welfare I was particularly interested.'

'She was at Grono's, then, the night we arrived with the Queen, and your repeated disappearance during our stay is accounted for?' said Kynfin, mournfully.

'Truly so; but that was not the first time of our meeting after our marriage. I obtained leave of absence. I was at my uncle Grono's a month before you returned from France. The last time I beheld my beloved wife was when I left home on a pretended visit to our cousins, a short time after the Queen arrived at Harlech. Thus you perceive, Kynfin, my duplicity has been kept up to the last. With deep remorse I am about to leave you without any atonement! My father! oh! my father! I would ask his forgiveness and die happy!'

The accents lingered upon his lips, as he sank back exhausted.

After attempting two or three times to speak, and when he had somewhat recovered, he asked Kynfin to lift him up higher. Looking round the room, he fixed his eyes upon a small packet on a table, carefully tied up and sealed.

'Take that,' said he, 'take it, Kynfin, and give it to Aliano, my cherished wife. Would to God she were here to receive my last embrace! Would that my father were here that I might receive his forgiveness! Kynfin, ask him to be kind to her, to comfort her, and protect her for my sake. She cannot go back to her country. She has sacrificed all for me. My mother, my father, centre the love you bear your son in his relict, his gentle Aliano! Atonement—pardon—my mother—father—Aliano!—Aliano!'

These were the last hurried words which fell from the lips of young Tudor. Before sunrise he was no more.

CHAPTER VIII

The Young Widow—Scene at the Castle—Singular Revelations

THE funeral rites celebrated in due respect over the remains of the brave, the handsome, and lamented Tudor—Kynfin, broken-spirited and dejected, bade a hasty farewell to his kind and sympathising hostess. He departed to convey to his friends in Wales the melancholy intelligence of the irreparable loss they had sustained. He had also to communicate the strange confession disclosed upon his brother's death-bed. These things so absorbed his thoughts that, as he travelled, he became lost to all around him. Night or day, storm or sunshine, came unheeded to the unhappy traveller. Over rock and across moor, through valleys or along plains, he pursued the same unbroken silence, until he reached the solitary habitation of his uncle, which without ceremony or notice he immediately entered.

The surprise and amazement of the venerable Grono at this sudden appearance of his kinsman, it is not easy to describe. There was no warm welcome given. Looks only were proffered on either side; and a delicate young female, who was his uncle's only companion, changed colour repeatedly, as she cast inquiring glances at the stranger.

'Kynfin,' at length articulated Ap Meredyth, in a tone of doubt and apprehension, 'what brings you here? Is it your spirit or yourself? Speak, boy!—speak!'

'I am the bearer of ill tidings,' replied Kynfin, in a sepulchral voice, as he sank down upon a seat which stood near.

'He comes from the battlefield! Yes! He comes from the side of Tudor!' cried Aliano, distractedly, the instant she heard the name. Springing to the side of the stranger, she continued, in a supplicating tone,—

'Kynfin, have pity on me! Tell me how you left my own Tudor—my kindest, best of husbands! Keep me not in suspense! Is he wounded?—sick!—dead! Oh! merciful God! he is dead!'

A wild shriek burst from her agonized heart, and she threw herself unconsciously into the arms of the venerable Grono.

Kynfin's looks had betrayed that to which his speech refused to give utterance.

Aliano was conveyed at once to her chamber, where unremitting attention was paid to her by her faithful maidens.

When the first shock was over, and Grono found himself alone with Kynfin, he learned the particulars of the last moments of his young kinsman. Recent circumstances had drawn uncle and nephew so much together that the old man, more than ever attached to Tudor, was now not able longer to suppress his feelings, and wept bitterly.

How very still his solitary abode remained during that night! If the angel of death had been there, his influence could not have imparted a graver aspect to everything around. Noiselessly the domestics moved from room to room. The only sounds which fell upon the ear were stifled sobs, and occasionally hollow, broken sentences from mourners in different parts of the house.

Many days elapsed before Aliano could in any way rouse

herself from the depression into which her sorrow had plunged her.

Grono entered her room, endeavouring to soothe her with more than paternal solicitude. His efforts availed little. Genuine grief is not to be comforted: it must run its course to its exhaustion.

The old man, from sorrow and anxiety, had a severe attack of illness. This fortunately diverted Aliano in some degree, by the cares it involved, from the suffering her own bereavement inflicted.

Kind and affectionate towards her friend and protector, she rose at once from the couch of sorrow, and came to attend upon Grono. She refused to leave his bedside to others until he was able once more to take his accustomed seat in the hall.

Aliano had seen Kynfin but once after the announcement of the melancholy event. And that was but for a few minutes in Grono's darkened chamber. She was anxious to talk with him alone: she had many questions to ask about her lamented Tudor, and grew still more impatient for an interview. Yet still she delayed, and it was long before she summoned up resolution to send for him. He came, in obedience to her request, to her apartment; and as he silently approached her, he was struck by her delicate beauty. She immediately extended her hand, and in gentle accents requested he would seat himself.

The interview was extremely painful, yet the fortitude shown by Aliano was surprising. At her request many sentences uttered by her departed Tudor were repeated over and over again, while the varying colour on her cheek betrayed the deep emotion of a desolate heart.

Before they separated, she gave several letters into Kynfin's hands, and begged him to peruse them with attention. 'They will reveal much to dear Tudor's advantage,' she added, keeping her eyes to the last upon the precious packet.

Tudor's scruples for keeping his marriage secret, even from his own family, were more fully explained in those letters, and much was to be said in his defence. In other letters sentences were addressed to his parents, imploring their forgiveness. Then again he spoke much on the behalf of his widow, who had left her home, her relations, and friends, to join her destiny with his own. If he knew that they would take her, and cherish her for his sake, and be a father and mother to her, as they had been to him, it would smooth his deathbed.

Many similar expressions showed how much disturbed in mind he must have been for some time before his decease.

Kynfin ever afterwards took an interest in his brother's widow. A link seemed to have connected them. Without reserve, Aliano learned to speak to him of her sorrow, and they felt their sympathy reciprocal.

Kynfin was now anxious to reach Harlech. Aliano would have accompanied him, but Grono felt unwilling to part with his fair companion; thus their departure was from day to day delayed. One of ap Meredyth's domestics had already been sent to Harlech with the particulars of Tudor's last moments. He now returned with an answer from the Warden.

The letter was urgent and peremptory:— 'Return my son; the heart of thy mother is withering, come and comfort her. Come not without the relict of our dear child, our much-lamented Tudor.'

Kynfin gave this letter to Grono, and after reading it carefully, much to their surprise he said,

'Infirm as I am, I will go with you, and introduce my sweet

charge to her unknown relations and new home. I have taken a prominent part in all belonging to your affairs, my child. Should a reconciliation between you and my good kinsfolk be necessary, I am the party to come forward and effect it. We will start tomorrow morning. I shall be ready at any hour you please to indicate.'

Aliano consented to this arrangement, and thanked Grono repeatedly for his consideration and kindness.

The party started an hour before sunrise for Harlech. The meeting between Kynfin and his parents was touching. After the first paroxysm of grief was passed, they turned to welcome the sorrowing young widow, lifting up their voices and blessing her as she entered.

'This, my child, is to be thy future home,' said Ap Jevan. 'You are welcomed with a parent's welcome.'

These words sank deep into Aliano's heart; she felt a strong filial affection towards him who uttered them.

Under the mournful circumstances existent, the sombre appearance of the great hall, indeed of the whole castle, was oppressive to the spirits, and particularly to Kynfin. He saw something to remind him of his departed brother everywhere. His strongbow remained suspended in the hall. Others of his weapons were scattered about in different places, or hung in other apartments. He reflected that his brother's voice, once heard there so joyous and happy, was now forever silent. He continually repeated, 'Would that death had not torn you from my side, my brother, my friend, my companion!'

It was sometime after the arrival of Aliano, before cheerfulness gradually brightened again within the walls of Harlech. The voice of an infant innocent, too, was heard. Dafydd ap Jevan, with a happy look, held upon his knee the offspring of his first-born, tracing in her delicate features a resemblance to her lamented father. Dame Tudor, who had been scarcely known to smile after the death of her son, now gazed with delight upon the blooming child. She called it endearing names, and became its second mother. That mother alone was not more happy than Dame Tudor, as she clasped her infant in her arms, and felt that it had come like a gentle zephyr on a warm summer's eve to refresh her drooping spirits.

After Kynfin's return he became much changed in his personal character. His careless and merry countenance now bore traces of melancholy, even of dejection. His low spirits were at first attributed to the loss he had sustained in his brother's death; but time wore on, and with it appeared no alteration; at last he became a subject of anxiety to his parents. His restless spirit never seemed at peace. He continually absented himself, roving from place to place, seeking danger wherever it offered, and acting apparently without reflection. In stormy nights, he was in the bay buffeting the angry elements, as if they could alone soothe his spirit. His manner towards his family became strange and unaccountable. Occasionally a burst of affection would escape him, and his manly cheek appear bedewed with tears. Invariably upon these occasions it was observed that he hastily left his home, as if he were ashamed, or annoyed, at betraying his real feelings.

Aliano, well aware how Kynfin's singular conduct distressed his parents, at length determined to make him give some explanation of a course of conduct so foreign to his pristine habits. Kynfin had been from home several days. Aliano awaited his return with more than usual impatience.

The family had retired; she was alone in the great hall, watching the fragments of a smouldering log upon the hearth, and doubting whether her brother-in-law would come home for the night.

'Kynfin, Kynfin!' she ejaculated aloud, 'why do you act so cruelly towards those who love you? Why throw a shadow across their path, which has already been darkened by so much sorrow?'

'You may well ask why, Aliano,' said a voice close to her ear; and Kynfin himself stood before her. 'I am miserable, unutterably miserable. In pity spare me, my sister.'

'I will spare you—I will make every allowance for you, only tell me what it is that makes you unutterably miserable?'

Kynfin's face grew paler and paler, while he ran his slender fingers through his hair, and fixed his wild eyes upon his companion.

'Were I to tell you, Aliano, you would say I was wrong, very wrong; you would scorn me—you would hate me. Yet Heaven destined that we should see each other. Heaven has given you a voice which probes the inmost recesses of my soul, and has thrown me out of myself. Aliano, I love you with a passion I cannot control.'

His voice was agitated, and his whole frame trembled, as he continued—

'Yes, Aliano, it is this uncontrollable passion which has made me miserable, made me wander from my home; made me neglect my parents when they wanted comfort, and received pain. It is this that is destroying my brain and draining my existence. Now I have told you all. Despise me, hate me!' Then covering his face with his hands, he sank upon his knees before her.

Surprise and distress unutterable, were depicted upon the beautiful countenance of the young widow; with all the natural gentleness and kindness of her heart, she was shocked and grieved. For some minutes she was unable to articulate a word. Kynfin still bent his head, kneeling before her. At length she said, with a firm but gentle voice:

'Kynfin, my brother, arise! If you love me as you profess to do, have a regard for my feelings, and your own duty. I am your brother's widow. I cannot so easily forget the memory of one, whom I cherished with an affection, such as you described. Kynfin you must pray to heaven for strength of mind. You must strive to conquer the passion you have avowed. For my sake, for that of your family, for your own peace of mind, endeavour it, I will then be grateful and regard you with a sister's love. Cease to distress me. Cease to make me the cause of darkening your paternal home, and of bringing down the grey hairs of our parents with sorrow to the grave.'

Thus saying, she arose from her seat and retired to her apartment, where she gave way to the bitter grief which the unexpected address of Kynfin had caused, but which in his presence it became her to restrain from a sense of her own self-respect, leaving him half unconscious of her departure.

CHAPTER IX

Siege of Harlech—Magnanimous Conduct of Sir Richard Herbert

THE sun was setting superbly, tinging Cardigan's deep blue waters with the colours of the radiant bow. Flickering clouds of gold and purple took new shapes, emitting a thousand hues of the richest character, then breaking and dispersing in rivalry of glory. They vanished at last, as if into another wide and distant sea, our own concealing that brilliant orb, the departure of which they had so gorgeously adorned with colours dipped in heaven—that orb, which had, as it were, but a moment before seemed reluctant to part from a scene so fair.

'Gone! gone!' said Aliano to her little girl, as she stood by Ap Jevan's side, watching, from one of the towers, the lovely sunset. 'It is after all a gloomy parting,' she observed. Then she held up her little one to kiss its grandfather and bid him a good night.

'Why hurry away?' said the chieftain; 'the child is not sleepy. Stay, my spirits are low, very low.'

'You suffer the affairs of the nation to interest you too deeply,' replied Aliano, in a tone of gentle reprimand. 'The impending dangers may be great, yet, my dear father, we should not forget that the same mighty hand which has just concealed the sun from our eyes dictates and governs all, not only in heaven but also on the earth.'

'I know it, my child. I pray fervently that the misfortunes, both public and private, which I feel must come sooner or later, may be received in a spirit of resignation and fortitude.'

Several years passed, and great changes happened, after Margaret of Anjou set out on her triumphant march to London. Three battles had been fought, and to the queen's sorrow, she had found in the young Earl of Marche a more powerful antagonist than his father. The king was still a prisoner. After the defeat of the Red Roses at Towton, Margaret with the Prince of Wales fled to France, leaving the Earl of Marche at the zenith of his ambition, and King of England.

During this period he had sent repeated threats to the stubborn enemy of his house, Dafydd ap Jevan, to deliver up the key of the north, or that he should suffer on Tower Hill. The Warden kept everything quiet, yet still some uneasiness was felt in the little town of Harlech. Ill omens were rumoured as being observed, and the country's superstition was excited.

About an hour after the sun had set, and Aliano had left the battlements with her infant charge, Dafydd was suddenly roused from his reverie by loud shouts from the town below. He immediately hastened to the spot. A body of armed men had entered Harlech, and proceeding to the habitation of Morgan, had seized and bound him hand and foot, to the astonishment of the unhappy captive.

'What have I done?' cried the poor shoemaker, 'to deserve this brutal treatment? In truth good Saxons, you must have mistaken your man.'

'Mistaken our man, indeed! I trow we know our business better than that, you Lancastrian dog. It is only such fools as you, blind buzzard, who get mixed up with politics, and by way of a reward are finished with a knock on the head.'

The ruffians laughed in chorus, and gave Morgan a kick to keep him from struggling.

'By St George, you had better keep quiet or you will have the worst of it,' vociferated one of them with an angry expression. 'I would as soon deal with a brute or an idiot as with one of these Welsh boors! There now, hold your crying, baby,' continued the speaker savagely striking a little child, who was affectionately clinging about his father's knees, and sobbing piteously. The blow was of so severe a nature that the luckless child fell down senseless. A crowd assembled. Loud shrieks from the women rent the air, and anger was roused in the hearts of the brave men of Harlech. They took up arms and ran to the spot.

In the midst of this uproar, the chieftain appeared, who, without a moment's hesitation (calling upon his men to keep close to his side), fell upon the disturbers of the town, and released Morgan from their clutches.

At this sudden change of affairs, the English soldiers were crest-fallen and confounded. They were all led in chains to the castle.

In this way commenced Ap Jevan's misfortunes. No sooner had Edward of York received tidings of the affair, than he became violently excited. Recalling his father's injunctions, he swore a terrible oath that this daring outlaw, the Captain of Harlech, should pay the penalty of his animosity to the house of York.

'I will trifle no longer with this Lancastrian,' continued Edward. 'Let my own sword taste my blood if I do. Not a shadow of mercy shall be shown to him, or his family. You,' he added turning to William Herbert, Earl of Pembroke, 'we expect to execute our commands without delay.'

With infinite difficulty the English general led his army through the Alpine regions of Wales, and in less than a fortnight, greatly worn by fatigue and deprivation, they reached their destination, not much to the delight of the soldiers. They stood gazing upon the strong grey turrets, jutting out and frowning in bold relief. It was evidently a fortress not easy to be subdued. From the dark expanse of sea, whence came the wild notes of the sea birds, in numbers more than they had ever before seen, the murmur of the waves floated on the breeze, and the whole presented a novel arena for military warfare.

After the siege had been carried on for little more than a week, the Earl of Pembroke assigned the conduct of the operations to his brother Sir Richard, a valiant hero of his day, nearly as renowned for his feats of bravery, as the intrepid and invincible Dafydd himself. One of the first things he did was to dispatch a peremptory summons in the name of the king for the immediate surrender of Harlech. Dafydd received the message with scorn, and fixing his steady gaze upon the envoy, gave the following ready reply:—

'Go tell your general I held a tower in France till the old women in Wales heard of it; and now I will let the old women in France hear how I defend my fortress in Wales.'

The Saxon knight was not so much surprised as pleased with the Welsh chieftain's bold reply, and exclaimed with much animation;—

'Bravo! bravo! a Welshman to boot! I should like to make the chieftain's acquaintance. His heart is in the right place. On my soul, I admire his spirit! Aye, and, I trow, it is a great shame, a sad reflection on us not to leave this renowned hero of the French wars alone. He has served his country well; and now he is declining in life, these proceedings ought not to occur.'

With noble feelings towards Dafydd and his family, Sir Richard went to pay his respects to the Warden and was courteously received. He was evidently struck with something about the beautiful, young widow, and without disguise took a lively interest in the whole family; nor did he retire from their presence before he had formed a resolution to intercede with the King in their behalf.

Dispatches were immediately sent off to his royal master with the true state of affairs, acquainting the monarch with the nobleness of Ap Jevan's conduct, and the harmlessness of his nature, when left undisturbed; and, finally, hoping the King would consider the difficulties attending such a siege, particularly with regard to the invincible strength of this fortress. The siege expense would be enormous.

On receiving this statement, the King only became more angry, and passionately exclaimed:—

'Go tell that blind fool of a knight I will not be hampered with these useless dispatches. I will be obeyed. My commands are unalterable. The siege shall be carried on, if it drain my coffers, and cost in time all my life to take the place.'

The siege was conducted, in consequence, with vigour and skill. Yet for some time the besiegers had the mortification to see that their efforts were of no avail.

Dafydd had well stocked the fortress with provisions and, by the aid of a secret passage underground, managed from time to time to get fresh supplies unknown to the enemy.

This state of things long continued. The besiegers were puzzled to discover how the garrison subsisted. No egress from the castle was left unguarded. At last the Saxons began to suspect there was some subterranean communication, which with incessant activity they endeavoured to discover.

It was the faithful Howel who, pale and breathless, brought the intelligence that the enemy had been seen near the mouth of the cave in which was the entrance to the passage. They had also captured a boat laden with provisions. This was a death-blow to the defence, and Dafydd felt the danger, there was only the alternative to block up the entrance of the passage and starve. Before the night after the discovery had elapsed, the passage was blocked up, and Dafydd sat in his hall, surrounded by his family, suffering under the most painful reflections. Those he loved so dearly he must see die before his eyes, or give them up to an insulting enemy, to be ill-used and, perhaps, led to the block.

His little grandchild was standing with her hand upon his knee. He pushed her away, as if he could not trust himself, and strode rapidly up and down the apartment. Mistress Tudor, with a deep melancholy settled on her features, in a high-backed chair, mechanically running out her thread at her spinning-wheel, and glancing thoughtfully first at one, and then at another. Aliano was sitting with her hands clasped together, following the chieftain with her anxious gaze, as he moved to and fro. Kynfin was watching her with that strange countenance which had lately identified him. Not a lip moved: suppressed sighs alone mingled with the monotonous buzzing of the wheel. It was a scene of woe.

Little Gladys—for that was the name of Tudor's infant daughter—little Gladys had been standing for some time with her face turned away, offended at the harsh and unusual treatment of her grandfather. She did not cry, though tears were wetting her tiny fingers. At length a succession of sobs burst forth from her little heart, drawing the general attention.

Ap Jevan immediately approached, and taking her in his arms, fondly caressed her.

'Fy mheth bach,' (my own little darling) 'bach anwyl,' murmured he, deeply affected, 'I am not content being myself miserable, but I must embitter thy tender years. Come, little one, cheer up—stroke your grandfather's cheek. You shall be happy. We will all live to make you happy,' he concluded, in a wild and unnatural exclamation.

At that moment a knocking at the outer gates interrupted the touching scene.

'Command that he be shown in,' said Ap Jevan, upon Kynfin informing him that Sir Richard the Saxon stood before the gates. Then putting down his grandchild, he stood erect, to receive his generous opponent.

The terrified infant clung to her grandsire's knees, lisping impassionately, 'A Saxon! a Saxon! cruel Saxons! I hate the Saxons!'

Sir Richard, who had come with the hope of sparing life, advanced towards the ladies, and bowed with his usual gallantry. Then, turning to accost the Warden, he offered him his hand, and said—

'I do not see, my noble captain, why, privately and individually, we should not be on terms of friendship. It is my misfortune to be publicly your foe. Let me pray you to consider it only in that point of view. Whenever it is in my power to befriend you, I will do so. I have now come on a mission to work a reconciliation between you and my royal master. It is with sorrow I look upon these massive walls, so gloriously defended by your ancestors and yourself, and think how soon they must be polluted by the vulgar soldiers, ravening for plunder. The siege must terminate in the way I have described. You, a great chieftain, and, perhaps, all your family, as well as your brave followers, if not previously starved to death, will most probably, without trial or further ceremony, be executed upon Tower Hill. All that I have said you must see is correct. Rapid foresight and discernment belong to so great a soldier as yourself. I seek to avoid this direful calamity. For the sake of your family, then, chief of a noble line, I call upon you to deliver up these walls without further resistance. It is painful and trying; but think of your position. King Edward has taken a solemn oath that, if he should drain his coffers to the last shilling, he will go on with the siege till Harlech is in his keeping. Think well, then, of your present position, and choose the least of two evils. I swear by all that is holy I will intercede for you and your family. I will make excuses to his highness. By giving me up the castle, you will place me in a position to plead your cause; and I will plead it, if I lose my own life. Hero of far-famed renown, I have said it.'

'Enough! enough! Saxon knight,' repeated the distracted chief. 'Recall not Ap Jevan's days of glory. They are gone; and what has been will soon be forgotten. Ochan! ochan! national and private grief has worn and broken a spirit that was once bold and fearless. Do with me what you please. Death would terminate my sorrow! Death would hide from the world a disgraced and neglected old man! Take me on honourable conditions that may spare my wife and children. I may stipulate that they do not suffer for my faithfulness to another royal house—for the virtue of constancy. Good Sir Knight, I stipulate that my family shall not be cast out vagrants upon the earth, or linger out their existence in a dungeon. On these conditions alone—it is a matter of honour between us—

I will deliver up to you alone the home to which my soul clings.'

Ap Jevan could utter no more. He sank into a chair and groaned as he had never been heard to do; for when before had a groan escaped his breast?

Aliano, who had breathlessly listened to every word he spoke, kneeling down by his side, addressed him a few words cheering and comforting. Little Gladys clung closer and closer to her distracted grandsire. She laid her cheek upon his hand, and, looking tenderly into his face, inquired why they did not send the cruel Saxon away. 'Taid anwyl[3] had never been unhappy till the cruel Saxons came under their walls.'

---

[3] Dear grandfather.

CHAPTER X

Imprisonment of Ap Jevan— He and his Family pardoned

ON the arrival of the Welsh chieftain in the capital, with fifty of his brave adherents, all gentlemen of good descent, a deep sensation was evinced amongst those who favoured the house of Lancaster. They deplored in secret the fate of these brave and zealous adherents from Wales, who were at once placed under close confinement in the Tower.

At this reverse of fortune, Dafydd ap Jevan had much with which to struggle. Since he had last been in England's metropolis, the contrast was too great, not to force comparisons. Vividly did the whole scene come before him. Once he had been borne along in triumph, the excited and fickle populace had flocked to gaze upon the Cambrian warrior, the hero of the French wars, filling the air with loud acclamations, now like a felon, he was dragged through the streets. Contempt and ill-feeling were upon the lips of the same populace, from which loud, vulgar, and insulting merriment confused the ears and harassed the spirits of the weary prisoners. They were even thankful to gain the quiet of the Tower dungeon. Such was the change in minds destitute of honour and principle— such the evanescence of popular applause.

Sir Richard, to whom the prisoners had surrendered, sought an interview with the King. The monarch was at supper, seated with his amiable queen, on his right hand; his mother, the Duchess of York, on his left, while Lord Rivers, Lord Scales, and several members of the royal family besides, were partaking of the banquet.

'So ho! trusty Knight!' exclaimed Edward courteously, motioning him to be seated. 'You are the bearer of glorious news, I hear, arrived *apropos* with yourself, to enliven our evening's entertainment. All will join with me in drinking a toast—our hearty thanks to brave Sir Richard Herbert for ridding the nation of the contumacious Lancastrian, who, I can scarcely believe it, is at last safely deposited in the Tower. By St George, we must lose no time in striking off the head of that traitor, lest he escape us. More of this in private, good Sir Richard, blood at banqueting with ladies does not assimilate. Come, amuse us with an account of your exploit. I was alarmed by your last despatch, lest you should take years to become master of the keep.'

'True, your Highness; the Welsh chief would at this moment have been still the possessor of Harlech's impregnable fort, had I not made overtures to him by promising that I would intercede on behalf of his family and himself. Upon this mission I have arrived here, and feel assured when your Highness has heard the particulars of the affair, you will not refuse the request, it being a matter of honour. The select assemblage which I have the honour of addressing is perhaps not aware that the chief of Harlech is the same brave soldier who, long before the unhappy contention between the pale and the dark Roses, fought for England's glory and distinguished himself in the French wars. He is now declining in years. His family have implored me to be a mediator between my royal master and their beloved parent. Restore him to his family, and gratitude alone will keep him from raising his hand against your noble house. Besides this, your Highness will not dishonour me by breaking the terms of the capitulation.'

As Sir Richard concluded this sentence, every eye was turned upon him, all being interested by the various questions which were asked by the company. It was not thus with the King. The royal countenance had fallen. Instead of the animated and smiling expression which it had before borne, it was now one of severity and suppressed anger.

'What! sir Knight? your language amazes me; keep capitulations with traitors? Demand pardon for an enemy of our house that it has cost so many years to subdue. Can I forget that my father was disgraced through his means, and that the fiery little Queen, through him, escaped our hands. No, by the powers of heaven! no interceding shall avail. He shall die the death of a traitor on Tower Hill tomorrow. His family shall suffer with him.'

The Queen who, in the lifetime of her first husband Sir John Grey, had been a staunch friend to the house of Lancaster, felt a secret interest in the fate of the unfortunate Welshman, whose person and character were not altogether unknown to her. Dafydd had in early years rendered her deceased lord great services. Tears filled her eyes, and placing her trembling hand upon the arm of her consort, and looking imploringly in her face, she said in gentle accents—

'Be not angry with me, my Lord, at interfering. Let it please your Highness that the Welsh chief be brought forthwith into our presence. We can then hear what he has to say in his defence. Will my liege lord grant me this favour?'

So soft did these words fall upon the King's ear, and so

sweet was the expression of the eyes which were turned upon him that, like the charm of an Orphean lyre upon the beasts of the forest, it made the savage breast of the monarch relent. He immediately turned to Sir Richard, and ordered him to see that the Queen's wish was fulfilled.

The hour was late when Dafydd appeared before the King. There was something imposing in the bearing of the captured chief, as he stood with his noble figure and open countenance, not unmarked nor unworn with cares and sorrows.

'Have you anything to communicate?' inquired the Queen, looking steadily into Dafydd's face, as if she wished to ascertain if he recognized her.

'Have you ought to say in your defence?' rejoined the King with an angry gesture; at the same time inwardly gratified at the sight of his intended victim. The question had to be repeated before Dafydd vouchsafed a reply.

'I understand what your Highness has spoken—Ap Jevan has nothing to say in his defence. You state yourself to be the rightful heir to the crown, I have not yet acknowledged your Highness as such, consequently I am a traitor in the eyes of your court, and therefore must die. But,' he continued, turning mournfully towards the Queen, 'I would say much on behalf of my family. It is hard they should suffer. It is for them, gentle lady, I would implore mercy.'

His voice faltered, and throwing himself upon his knees, before the consort of his revengeful foe, he caught hold of her robe, and looking wildly into her face, repeated vehemently:—

'Heaven touch your heart, my liege lady, to exert your influence on behalf of my wife and children. They surrendered with their home on conditions of honour.'

Edward began to be alarmed lest Dafydd should work upon

the feelings of the fair sex present. Turning to some of his attendants, he said,

'This act of presumption is too much. Take the dissembling old man out of my presence. Let him be removed back to the Tower; where he will not long await his execution.'

It was now that Sir Richard Herbert's heart burned within him. Stepping forward, he said in a firm and determined tone—

'Let not your Highness be hasty in your decision. The life of this noble Welshman lies on my honour—you, Sire, will not destroy that?'

'My words are unalterable,' replied the King coolly: 'he shall die the death of a traitor.'

'That shall not be, Sire,' retorted the valiant and daring Knight. 'You may, if you please, take my life in lieu of that of the Welsh captain, but I will not be disgraced—I will not be dishonoured. I am a soldier, a zealous subject, to whom death is less a calamity than disgrace. I will place Dafydd again in his castle, and your Highness may send whom you please to take him out.'

No sooner had Sir Richard Herbert concluded these words, than he strode out of the apartment, followed by Ap Jevan.

Disappointed and incensed at his request being refused, and his honour stained, Sir Richard was preparing to put his threat into execution, when a messenger arrived from the King with a summons for his immediate attendance. Sir Richard obeyed, and as he passed along one of the corridors, on his way to the royal apartments, a page touched him on the shoulder, and whispered—

'All's well, Sir Knight, the Queen has succeeded; the Welsh chief is pardoned.'

The Queen, with her extraordinary influence, had spoken

long and earnestly to her royal consort. She pointed out to him the impolicy of offending Sir Richard by a violation of his honour. She observed he was a man who possessed so much talent, and was so useful, that the crown would lose a staunch friend and warm adherent, all for an old man, who could now effect little for any party. On the other hand, would it not be greatly to the royal advantage to indulge Sir Richard in his request? Was not the royal honour implicated in that of his servant, Sir Richard? Depriving the chief and his family of their castle and their lands, was surely a sufficient punishment.

Thus the Queen had argued, and when Sir Richard was ushered into the King's apartment, he was surprised to find the monarch in a better humour. The Knight immediately inquired if he had altered his mind about the captive.

'Sir Knight, I was hasty yesterday. The Welsh rebel and his family are pardoned; but the pardon is conditional. Should a second offence be given to my crown, he shall be considered an outlaw, and all his family. Sir Knight, do you not think we could bring the Welsh captain over to our side? What think you of sending a thief to catch a thief? We might make him useful to us. In that case, I would permit this favourite of yours to remain in his castle, and perhaps make a peer of him at last, if he did us the right kind of service.'

Here the monarch laughed. Sir Richard, with a serious air, replied—

'No, Sire, that is impossible. Dafydd would rather die a hundred deaths than change from a great principle which he thinks just.'

'Confound his soul,' retorted the King pettishly; 'I think he might make a bargain for his life.'

'He did that in the capitulation, please your Highness.'

'Expel him and his family with all their household goods, friends or foes; and remember that they take themselves clean out of Harlech, and leave no trace of their footsteps behind them,' vociferated the King.

The same apartment in the Castle of Harlech, which had in former years been occupied by the illustrious Margaret of Anjou, now contained the unhappy family of Dafydd, prisoners in their own abode.

The arrangement had been made by Sir Richard Herbert, who consulted their comforts in all he did. He gave orders that they should be deprived of nothing save their liberty, during the absence of himself and Ap Jevan, until the King's pleasure was made known.

During their captivity, therefore, Kynfin and Aliano were much together. Since the secret had been revealed, there appeared to be an understanding between them. Kynfin would often speak to Aliano, and her influence over him was gradually working a change in his behaviour.

One evening, as they were sitting over the wood-fire, which cast, by flashes, a brilliant light over the spacious and gloomy apartment, all speaking in suppressed tones—Gladys, who was sitting on her mother's knee, covered her face with her little hands, repeating that she could not bear to be always sitting in that room.

'Why were the Saxon soldiers in the hall? Why did her anwyl Daid go away with the unkind Saxon. Anwyl Daid had said he would never let the wicked Saxons come into the hall. Why, why,' she continued, bursting into tears, 'will you not tell me all about it, my dear mother? I am so unhappy.'

Aliano sighed, and endeavoured to explain the reason of their painful position. The child was not satisfied.

Kynfin, who had been sitting at a little distance motionless, supporting his pale, lank features upon his hands, his dark penetrating eyes fixed upon the mother and child, now rose, and approaching, took the child off its mother's lap.

'Come,' said he, 'fy mheth bach,' while he stroked the dark locks from off her sweet innocent face. 'I will tell you a tale.'

And he repeated something which sounded so mysterious that the child's attention was immediately diverted. She looked quite happy.

'But why, uncle Kynfin,' cried Gladys, at length interrupting him with a wild gesticulation, 'why shall I not hate the Saxons? I do hate them. They are horrid wicked people.'

Aliano's cheek, which, but a few minutes before, had been of so pale a hue, was now suffused with red. She felt an inward pang. 'Kynfin will not betray me. Poor little innocent, thou shalt never know that thy mother is one of the hated Saxons.'

The silence which followed, was broken by confused noises in the court. Footsteps sounded in the gallery, and stopped at the door, which was instantly thrown open, and Dafydd and Sir Richard stood before them. Loud exclamations of joy resounded through the apartments. How warm a welcome was given to the chief by those he held most dear on earth!

'Fy nghalon bach anwyl,' cried Dafydd in the most endearing tones, while he clasped the child who ran with open arms to meet him. 'Your old grandsire has indeed returned, but brings sad, sad news!'

The child had thrown her arms round his neck, and began sobbing upon his venerable bosom.

'O fy mheth bach anwyl! Cheer up little one; what ails thee, child?' continued the chief, looking tenderly in her face.

'I am sick at heart! I thought the Saxons would kill you, or put you in a dungeon, and I should never see you more,' whimpered Gladys, smiling through her tears, and stroking his cheek with her hand.

'The Saxons are not all bad, fy nghalon bach,' said Dafydd. 'If it had not been for this good Knight, you never would have seen me more. How shall we ever repay this debt of gratitude?' continued he, addressing his wife. 'If Edward of York had followed his own inclination, he would ere this have hoisted my bleeding head upon the battlements of London Bridge gates. You, my beloved family, would have been all placed in confinement. But the Almighty has so willed it that through the interposition of the Queen and our kind friend Sir Richard, the King has softened his edict. Our lives are spared, but we must leave these walls for ever. Harlech, the home of my ancestors, is no longer our home.'

How bitter were these words, and though in bitterness they were spoken, Dafydd uttered them without faltering in his accents. He could have greeted death with joy, but for the sake of those he loved he hailed life, and was thankful.

Before Sir Richard withdrew, he spoke to the widow of Ap Dafydd. His words were repeated in an undertone, but so urgent in manner that Kynfin's attention was attracted by them. He only overheard the last sentence—'That he would return in a few hours.'

No sooner had the Saxon Knight closed the door, than Aliano turned in her gentle and affectionate manner to comfort Dame Tudor, who had sunk into a species of stupor.

'Dear mother, he is spared to us,' said she; 'never mind about leaving the castle, wherever we go we shall be together, and live to make one another happy. Oh, yes! we may still be happy! Do not fret about it.'

Mistress Tudor clasped the hand of her beloved husband, who stood close by her side, and looked up into Aliano's face with an expression which could not be misunderstood.

The hour of midnight arrived—the revelry of the soldiers in the great hall was hushed, and, according to promise, Sir Richard made his appearance. Once more he was observed to speak to Aliano, who looked startled and uneasy; he then approached Dafydd, and said—

'My brave and noble friend, during the last few hours, according to the King's commands, I have been making arrangements for your departure. I have taken preventive measures to conceal from the soldiers the King's edict, in order that you may make your journey to the mountains unknown, both to friends and foes. This I consider of importance, for your present and future safety. The great point is to keep your retreat from the King's knowledge. I have no dependence upon him. Kings have long arms and short memories. King Edward has secret agents, who would not hesitate to commit any foul deed, if they but pleased their master, and could finger gold in payment. I grieve deeply for you all, to be thus obliged to drive you from under the roof which sheltered you from your earliest years. Would that it were in my power to spare you this trial, but such are the miseries of civil war. I have only to add, noble chieftain, since necessity urges your flight, be ready at this hour to-morrow night. You shall have a few faithful followers to conduct you to that wild spot in the mountains, which you named to me this morning. Tell me what you desire to retain of your household goods. You might take all, only it will be necessary to send them after you by secret means. Those things you would take with you, name them to-night, and they shall be packed tomorrow. Perhaps you will permit your daughter to accompany me, and point out the objects most needful to travel with you, as well as those you wish to follow in your steps?'

'Yes, dear father, I will go with Sir Richard,' said Aliano, interpreting the Saxon's looks. 'No harm can befall me. I know where everything is, and I think I know what you would select, and what you would leave behind?'

Sir Richard took his lamp, and Aliano, with light steps, followed her companion from room to room, selecting those articles of which they were in search. Scarcely a word passed between them till they reached that apartment which Sir Richard had taken for his own private use, where none of the servants were likely to intrude.

It was then the Knight closed the door, and setting down the light, turned to greet his fair companion in the following familiar words—

'Aliano, my sweet little cousin! How strange, surpassing strange, to find you in this remote land! And these are the grey old walls, and not a convent, which hid from the world one so much beloved and admired—one so deeply regretted by all? Aliano, how came it to pass that you, so young and amiable, could have played a part so deep as to elude discovery?'

Aliano shaded her eyes with her hands, and trembled violently.

'I stand condemned before you, cousin Richard. In mercy do not betray me!'

'Put away all fear, my Aliano,' said Sir Richard, kindly. 'I would not for worlds cause you a moment's pain.'

Aliano returned the pressure of his hand and inquired if her grandfather was alive.

'No: he has been in his grave the last two years. He never forgave himself for his cruelty to you.'

Aliano sighed.

'Will you be surprised,' continued the knight, 'the old man had a presentiment that you would someday return to the world, and left his property to you in the event of your reappearance? This is good news for you, my sweet cousin. From the day I recognised you, I have longed for this moment. I seem to have been sent by Providence to render you assistance in the hour of need. Your present situation is indeed lamentable. The hardships which await this unfortunate family you can never support. Aliano, time is urgent, and what I have to say must be said in a few words. Let me take you and your child to your friends and your fortune.'

'Treason to my feelings, good kinsman!' cried Aliano, with energy. 'I cannot desert the family of my lamented husband. I cannot be so ungrateful to forget, under the peculiar circumstances, the welcome I received upon my first arrival at Harlech, the love and devotion which have ever since been lavished upon me and my beloved child. No, Richard; you have a kind heart: do not urge me to take so heartless a step. I have lived with them in affluence and power. Can I leave them in adversity?—bowed down with sorrow? Oh! no, playfellow and companion of my early years, my career is marked out for me. I am contented and happy to follow those who are so dear to me, wherever fate decrees, until the grave receives both them and myself.'

CHAPTER XI

Dafydd and his Family expelled from Harlech

'THE son of Harlech[4] is missing,' cried Howel, with a look of despair, as he hurried into the courtyard where the family had assembled to take their departure.

'Ochan! Ochan! The lad has not been himself since the death of my first-born,' murmured Ap Jevan, struggling to retain that fortitude which every slight and unexpected grievance seemed ready to disorder.

The hour, the painful hour had arrived. They could wait no longer for him. Dafydd bowed his head—his frame trembled—he stood for the last time upon the threshold of his fathers. His heart beat violently; but he slowly moved on, giving orders mechanically to Howel that every care should be taken of Tudor's widow.

'Lead the way—lead the way,' said he, hurriedly, as soon as his daughter was seated in her saddle. 'I will see to the mistress and the little one.'

A tall figure was standing outside the gate, wrapped in a dark mantle, as Howel and Aliano made their appearance. It was Sir Richard Herbert. In an instant he drew up close, and

---

[4] The "son of such a place" is a term generally used in Wales.

whispered a hurried and feeling address to his cousin. After wringing her hand in silence, and bidding her a last farewell, he turned to witness the bearing of the fallen chieftain, as the heavy gate grated on its hinges, excluding him for ever from the home of his forefathers.

In the midst of all this bitterness of soul, Dafydd did not forget to express grateful thanks to his friend, who turned away painfully overcome, as the party hurried forward, and left him the solitary spectator of the pathetic scene far behind.

The night was gloomy, the wind whistled mournfully, howling through the fissures of the jutting rooks, which overhung both sides of the path that led to the secluded dwelling of Howel's father, in the heart of the mountains.

In former years often had Ap Jevan and his sons traversed that glen during the chase, and often from Carreg-y-Saeth, the 'rock of the arrow', had they struck a deer to the earth, and performed feats of skill of which anecdotes were still related.

This hollow was called by the natives 'Cwm Bychan'. It seemed formed by nature as a place of refuge for the hapless children of the soil. Ap Jevan felt grateful for so secure an asylum. Though their deprivations were great, not a murmur escaped them.

The moment Ap Meredyth heard of the fate of his relatives, he sent repeated messages to request his kinsman and family would come and live with him. But Ap Jevan refused. He felt it would be hostile to his feelings of independence. But he could see no reason why Aliano and her child should not avail themselves of the offer. There they would not be deprived of the luxuries and comforts to which they had been accustomed. They would not be so exposed to the inclemency of the weather, and be safer from the common foe than with him.

Thus Ap Jevan argued, despite his secret anguish at the thoughts of parting from connections that had entwined themselves so closely around his heart as to seem necessary to his existence. Still, with his noble, unselfish nature, he was urgent they should agree to Grono's proposal.

Dafydd was spared this trial of their absence. Aliano would not consent to leave him.

'No, no, dear father, never mention the subject more,' she replied, with an affectionate eagerness, which was peculiar to her, and never failed to win the hearts of those with whom she lived. 'I am quite happy, and fully contented to live in poverty with you. To share your joys and trials is to me a high privilege.'

How cheering, how warming these few words came home to Harlech's fallen chief. In haste he arose to embrace his daughter. Then a solemn prayer was repeated, and a fervent blessing implored upon her head.

Soon after these points had been decided, Dafydd, with his usual mental activity, formed a plan for building a strong and commodious habitation among the surrounding rocks, by that means to ameliorate their sufferings and discomforts. The spot which he fixed upon was farther up the valley than the place of their present sojourn. It was a site so remote that it was entirely concealed from any intruders who might merely enter the cwm. Howel was a good mason; and by the assistance of some of the mountaineers, Dafydd found his work advance rapidly towards completion. Some of the rooms were partly excavated in the rock. The building, though extensive, was so arranged that few could have distinguished, from a little distance, any human habitation on the spot. The place appeared from a distance nothing more than a pile of fallen and broken rocks, heaped promiscuously together.

During the construction of this refuge Kynfin suddenly arrived among them, to the great joy of his family, that welcomed him with more than its usual affection.

Little Gladys hung upon his neck, caressing him, until the eccentric son of Harlech was overcome, and in vain endeavoured to conceal his tears. Kynfin was passionately fond of children. He gave no explanation of his disappearance from Harlech; and none but Aliano ventured to ask it, but it was out of the hearing of others.

The building of the new home was not only an amusement to Ap Jevan, but also to Kynfin. They daily superintended the workmen. Kynfin at times energetically applied his hands to the labour, while the same gloom continued to rest on his brow, with his thoughts absorbed on the image of the gentle Aliano. To make her comfortable and to smooth her sufferings seemed to be now his sole anxiety.

The winter was unfortunately severe. Aliano, like a tender plant uprooted, and carried away from England's warm and cultivated land, and transplanted into this wild, desolate region, shrank from the bleak mountain blast, and appeared to be fading in health. Paler and paler became her cheek, her step and voice grew weaker; but she never complained, and her spirits knew no change.

Early in the spring, 'Cader y Cil',[5] for thus Kynfin had denominated the new structure, was finished.

A quantity of household furniture which Sir Richard Herbert had contrived to secure them, was arranged in the new dwelling. Several articles which the chieftain and his son had amused themselves by carving during the winter, contributed both to the comfort and ornament of their wild and singular abode.

---

[5] A stronghold in a retreat.

The life they led, was like that of colonists. Kynfin continually followed his field sports, and always well supplied the larder. The chieftain often participated in the amusement, but yet more frequently shared in Howel's agricultural undertakings. These proved fortunately, very successful, for the family exiled from their ancient comforts. They enabled them to partake of luxuries, which in their most sanguine moments, they had never anticipated to find in so rude a spot.

Summer was approaching, during which, several of the Harlech inhabitants, after many a fruitless search discovered the retreat of their beloved chief. They were overwhelmed with joy, many quitting their houses by stealth, came and settled in the glen that they might be near their friend the champion of their youth. They sympathized with him in adversity, and more firmly than ever vowed fealty to him.

Ap Jevan was greatly affected at this mark of their attachment. More and more, he became united in heart and soul to those good people. He now appeared like a parent watching over his numerous offspring, rather than the renowned chieftain over the men of his clan.

To Ap Jevan a new interest thus arose to cheer and reconcile him to adversity. With what pleasure did he gaze upon the well-known faces assembled around him, as of old. His path was planted with thorns, but they did not wither every flower which struggled to rise into blossom among them.

As the family were about retiring to rest one night at a late hour, they were alarmed by the furious barking of the dogs, and an uninterrupted knocking at the gate. Their fears were soon dispersed; the stranger demanding admittance being no other than their Saxon friend, Sir Richard Herbert, who had been sent on some government duty into Wales. He could not resist a visit to the family in whose interest and welfare he had taken such a conspicuous part.

Ap Jevan had been, since his arrival among the mountains, so great a recluse that of the political events of the day he was profoundly ignorant; of Edward's increasing tyranny, and of the still hopeless state of the house of Lancaster.

Sir Richard informed them of the melancholy end of Morgan the shoe-maker. The wretched man had been put to the question on the rack by the judges, in order to extort from him the names of the parties concerned in Queen Margaret's correspondence during her sojourn at Harlech. The excruciating agony which his slight frame underwent was of no avail; not a single name nor any of the circumstances could they get him to divulge.

King Edward heard of the unfortunate Welshman's unflinching endurance, and swore in a paroxysm of rage, he should be made to feel, commanding he should be pinched to death with the red-hot implements of his trade, adding, with the vindictive feelings of a royal Nero, that he half felt inclined to witness this frightful and barbarous spectacle himself.

The good people in the cwm lamented the loss of Morgan. His children were immediately taken by his late neighbours, who divided them among different families, and brought them up to manhood.

Sir Richard expressed great anxiety on Ap Jevan's account. Some of Queen Margaret's letters written from Harlech had got into the king's hands.

'Your name,' said Sir Richard, addressing the chief, 'was frequently mentioned in them, your virtues, your bravery, and your zeal for the Red Rose party were all stated. I lament that it has roused Edward's anger. His agents are at work to discover your locality. I warn you, as a secret friend, to be upon your guard. Let your friends be upon the watch to give you the alarm, should any of these blood-hounds get upon the right scent.'

'Anwyl! Anwyl!' ejaculated Dame Tudor, sorrowfully, 'if they should discover us here, we shall indeed be undone. Ow, ow! (woe's me!) Dafydd, would that you had never anything to do with either the Red or the White Roses. They will never rest satisfied till they have laid your head upon the block.'

'Good Mistress Tudor, do not take it to heart so much,' said the knight soothingly, 'with a little caution it would take a life-time to discover such a retreat as you have here. It is rumoured that you have sought shelter under Grono ap Meredyth's roof. Your friends, myself, among the number, encourage that idea.'

Sir Richard was distressed, at the change which had taken place in his cousin's health since they parted at the gates of Harlech. He was struck with Kynfin's peculiar manner towards her, and longed for a little private conversation. On the following day he spent several hours alone with her. Kynfin, who watched every movement of Aliano, was disturbed at observing this interview. His wild and restless eyes were continually fixed upon the Saxon, as if demanding an explanation of such a familiar intercourse. Aliano had not told him that Sir Richard was her cousin, her early friend and play-fellow. Burning with jealousy and uncontrollable passion, he sought Aliano that night, after the rest of the family had retired.

'What is the matter with you, Kynfin?' she said, in one of her gentlest tones, as soon as the door of the room was closed behind them, and they stood face to face.

'Language cannot interpret my feelings,' replied Kynfin, placing his hand before his expanded eyes, as if he thought they would frighten his companion.

'Kynfin, this is like what you were at Harlech, not what you have been of late. I began to persuade myself that you had some control over your feelings that you were changing for the better.'

'Changing! No Aliano, never, never, how can you speak thus calmly? Cruel, heartless Aliano, why have you deceived me? Why did you not tell me before that this Saxon had gained that heart, which I have strived in vain to obtain?' He waited not a reply, but continued with frightful rapidity:—

'I see through it all, my suspicions at Harlech were not unfounded, the look you returned the Saxon, the words that Saxon whispered, all reveal the dreaded truth, shatter my hopes, and destroy the peace of my soul for ever! Aliano, I will become a vagrant upon the face of the earth. I will never more return to my home. It will be your hand which will have done it. Aliano, listen. Let my last request touch your heart— pray that death may soon terminate my miserable existence.'

Aliano's gentle nature, weakened by ill-health was terrified at Kynfin's frenzied manner. Several times she attempted an explanation, but the words died upon her lips, and she fainted.

The blood instantly rushed to Kynfin's head, then back to his heart, leaving his face as pale as that of his insensible companion whom he supported in his arms. His passion was now gone; with a strange calmness he looked upon her beautiful face, and repeated in a voice foreign to his own:—

'Aliano, my own Aliano, I have loved you with unalterable, undying love—love that has stood on the brink of madness. You told me that it was sin to love a brother's widow; you said that it was unlawful in the eyes of God; if it is so, God forgive me. Oh Aliano! this is not the barrier which rises between us now—another—a Saxon! My brain! My brain!' He laid her gently down, looked long and earnestly upon her sweet features, impressed an impassioned kiss upon her brow, and fled with the swiftness of an arrow from a home which contained all that was dear to him on earth.

The noises of the doors opening and shutting, roused Sir Richard Herbert, who had retired to a room contiguous to that which Kynfin so lately quitted. In a few minutes he was at Aliano's side, bathing her temples, and wondering what strange circumstance had left her in this distressing state. It was long before she came to herself, and then she was too weak to answer her kinsman's anxious inquiries. Sir Richard was obliged to leave her that morning, to his deep regret, and never learned the truth of the event of that night.

Aliano was never the same again that she had been; she frequently asked if there were any tidings of Kynfin, and upon the reply in the negative relapsed into silence and dejection. The cold blasts of winter had already set in, and she became alarmingly worse. The seeds of a fatal malady had long been sown, it was now making frightful inroads upon her constitution. Her anxious parents watched over their child with tender and untiring solicitude; hoping against hope that she might yet be spared to them. But the fiat of death had been issued, that awful fiat which no power on earth can recall.

A few days before her decease she spoke to Ap Jevan regarding Kynfin. She related how she had been the destroyer of his peace, that she had driven him from his home, and made them all unhappy. Anguish was depicted in her face, she spoke long and earnestly, yet left half the tale untold.

'Oh Kynfin, would you were here, to listen to my last confession!' frequently fell from her lips, and one night, with more than usual excitement, she exclaimed—

'Tell him, my dear father, if ever he returns to you that the Saxon was the child of my mother's favourite sister. It was natural that he should take an interest in me. Through him a portion of my property has been sent to me, and those last few hours I spent in his society; we were arranging about my affairs, to make you all more comfortable. Tell him, dear father, that no one has possessed the whole of my heart, but Tudor, my ever-lamented Tudor. Yet, dear Kynfin, comfort him, for he had a large share of my affection and sympathy.'

CHAPTER XII

AP JEVAN's head became bent upon his bosom, and his locks white as the snow upon the hill summit, his gait marked in every step the aged man. That sweet spirit, which in the hour of adversity had poured into the hearts of his family comfort and resignation, had passed away from earth in prayer, and left her child to cheer and watch alone the declining years of her afflicted grand-parents.

With what manly fortitude had the chieftain triumphed over his past trials. He had seen his first-born son taken from him, he had watched the unnatural and painful change in the conduct of his remaining offspring,—he had borne up against the misfortunes of the house of Lancaster—he had witnessed the cherished home of his forefathers torn from his possession, and himself left in poverty, an exile, and almost an outlaw. Yet, not until now, did both his moral and physical courage seem to give way. The honoured chief, the defender of Harlech, at last appeared utterly disconsolate.

Often would he repair to the little chapel and take his accustomed seat near the tomb, which had been hewn out of the rock for Aliano's last dwelling place. There he would pour out his soul in sorrow. For a time not even the innocent voice of his 'wyres bach'[6] could call one ray of joy into his melancholy face. In vain she attempted to lead him out upon the hills, or told him of some deer browsing near the

---

[6] Dear little grand-child.

homestead, or endeavoured in a thousand ways to comfort him. He was inconsolable.

With her grandmother, Gladys found it not so difficult a task, for she could not listen to the childish voice, and look upon the pleading face of her 'wyres bach' without being touched. Great as was her affliction in the loss of her daughter, and the deep uncertainty as to the fate of her son—her only son; she clung close to the child of her firstborn, her 'little comfort' as she called her, and bore up against the trials with surprising energy.

Some months after their bereavement, when the snow had melted from the mountain tops, and the rich bloom of the heath was already tinging the adjacent hills with its beautiful purple, one of the men from the hamlet, suddenly appeared at the door, and reported that there were two Saxons, who wished to see the chief on urgent business. They added that they were of the Red Rose party, or they would not have brought the message.

'Let them be conducted here immediately,' replied Ap Jevan; 'I will see them.'

Soon afterwards the brother of the late Duke of Somerset, with the Earl of Oxford, introduced themselves to Ap Jevan. He received them with a warm welcome. It had been raining heavily, so that the travellers were not sorry to disencumber themselves of their wet garments, and close in round a turf fire, which looked cheerful, even at that time of the year.

A substantial meal was soon served upon the boards, and highly appreciated by the hungry visitors, who declared they had not partaken of such good fare for many a long day.

'Since the battle of Barnet, we have had rough work,' observed the Earl of Somerset.

'Aye,' replied Oxford; 'and there is much more in store for us before all is settled. This defeat has been a ruinous affair to our cause, Ap Jevan. It will take a long time before we can recover it, unless we make a desperate struggle.'

'Misfortune is ever ready to cast a shadow over the house of Lancaster,' rejoined Dafydd; 'I have not heard more of the battle than that I hear the great Warwick is dead.'

'Yes, and his brother the Marquis of Montague. They fought valiantly to the last. It is a blow, indeed, to the Red Roses. Aye, it has shaken our very foundation. An individual like Warwick is not to be often met with. He was a man of surpassing power and talent; well qualified to lead in our cause. Search history through, you will seldom find another, like him the populace call a great "maker and unmaker of kings". You say you have heard but little of the bloody contest. The moment Warwick was among the slain, the whole field became a scene of confusion and slaughter. The Yorkists had gained the day, but Edward was not contented with his success. Cruel and revengeful as he is by nature, he issued an order that no quarter should be given. My heart sickens at the recollection of the scene of carnage that ensued, and drove the Earl of Somerset and myself from the field; we know not the full extent of the havoc. We have now come to seek shelter for a time among the mountain barriers, where we know there breathes many a stout heart for Lancaster. Our attendant is a son of the unfortunate Morgan, of Harlech town—you remember the lad? He has been in my service since Queen Margaret went to France; he revealed your retreat and conducted us to this glen. I have long wished to see you, Dafydd ap Jevan. I earnestly desire you should no longer bury yourself in these mountains, but come to the seat of war. It is possible the great chief of Harlech, may be willing to plunge once more into the roar of battle, and join us in making another effort to regain the crown, and rid England of a hated tyrant.'

A pause followed, and then a few casual remarks passed between Somerset and the Earl of Oxford. Little Gladys whispered to her grandmother. The large dogs moved impatiently from one side to the other of the apartment, as if expecting to share a meal. There was a look of excitement, mingled with sadness, in Dafydd's countenance. Mistress Tudor glanced anxiously at one individual and then at the other, without venturing a remark; she was in terror, lest her beloved partner should accede to the Earl of Oxford's wishes. She listened with earnest ears to the discourse between Somerset and the chief.

'Well, Ap Jevan, you will think of what the Earl of Oxford says. Perhaps you do not know the state of public affairs sufficiently to enter into our feelings. Within the last few years, Edward has become so tyrannical, so odious to the nation, that if we only play our game well, I feel sure Lancaster will win the day. You cannot dream of the licentiousness that is daily indulged in at court. I aver with truth that those who were lately Edward's best friends, are now becoming his enemies—if not openly, yet secretly. Would it not be a national service to rid England of the monster, and place our anointed sovereign once more upon his throne. Let us fight for the good cause of Lancaster, my noble-hearted friend. We have once more taken up arms, let us not lay them down till victory shall crown our efforts. Margaret, our queen, and the young prince, are in England. Let us still defend their cause, and with hands of iron and hearts of sympathy, prove that our proud land will have no king to rule over it who disgraces his court, and stains his hands with deeds too hellish for the light of day to visit. A glorious hope yet survives. Come, therefore and share it, come and wield your battle-axe for your anointed king, your prince, and your unhappy queen.—You will not refuse?'

Dafydd rose from his chair, walked several times across the apartment, looked earnestly into his wife's face, and then sat down, and taking Gladys upon his knee, kissed her. This was all the act of a moment. He started up again from his seat, and with the warm blood of a soldier kindling along his veins, he grasped the hilt of his sword and exclaimed:—

'The old man will no longer sit by his hearth mourning; no, my good friend, though my locks are grey and my strength diminishing, I will not refuse to go with you to fight, and spill the last drop of my blood for the cause of Lancaster.'

'Bravely spoken, Ap Jevan,' Somerset and the Earl of Oxford ejaculated at the same breath. 'It is a pleasure to see that the vicissitudes and misfortunes which have so long overshadowed your house, have not destroyed the spirit of a patriot, any more than the valour of a soldier.'

'Ochain, ochain, Dafydd bach, surely you will not leave us?' interrupted Dame Tudor, in a pleading tone. 'Remember Edward of York's cruel and heartless threat. Dafydd bach anwyl, you will not leave us? Recollect his agents are now seeking to destroy you. Think of me, Dafydd, your wretched wife. You know how deeply we have all drank of the cup of bitterness. Will you now leave me alone to drain it to the dregs? Dafydd bach, don't leave us!'

'Fy ngwraig anwyl,'[7] murmured the chieftain fondly, and looking intently toward Mistress Tudor; 'add not to my sorrow by repeating these words; my country calls me. A sanguinary tyrant governs our land; I appeal to your judgment. Would you have me neglect so sacred a call? If you value my love, say no more. Let me go and end my career, if it is the will of God. This is better than to die here, an inactive, miserable, and broken-hearted old man.'

A profound silence reigned as Ap Jevan concluded these words, so decided as to his intentions. Gladys's full eyes were riveted on the chieftain's countenance. Howel, who had stopped to listen, stood pale and trembling behind his master, muttering at intervals:—

'O'r Tad! o'r Tad!' Even the dogs seemed to know that something unusual was the matter. They got up from the hearth, and came rubbing themselves backwards and forwards against their master's legs, and licking his hands. Old Katherine, Howel's spouse, at this moment entered the room to summon the child to bed. Gladys immediately threw herself into her grandfather's arms.

'Fy nhaid bach anwyl anwyl, (my dear, dear grandfather),' cried the child, in an agony of distress; 'do not go away, the sun will never more shine upon us. We shall sit in the gloomy chapel and die. Fy nhaid anwyl! Stay, stay with us.' She was taken from the apartment sobbing.

The Duke and the Earl of Oxford remained for a short time at Cader y Cil. They sent off Ivor (Morgan's son) to Jasper of Hatfield, Earl of Pembroke, who was levying troops in South Wales, to apprize him of their arrival in that locality, and their

---

[7]   My beloved wife.

intention of being at a certain village on a fixed day, when they hoped he would join them.

It was scarcely daylight when Dafydd and his noble companions commenced their journey one morning over the mountains, to join the Earl of Pembroke. The roughness and unevenness of the road they travelled was fatiguing, particularly to the Englishmen, though they appeared highly pleased at the end of the first day's march, to stretch their weary limbs upon straw under a half-covered shed. For amusement they talked over the good fare of which they had partaken under Dafydd's hospitable roof, the venison steaks, the dried salt geese, and fish with 'cwrw da' (the good ale), and the sweet flavoured mead. This retrospection did not tend to appease their hunger. They looked out in vain for a habitation, and were obliged at last to content themselves by going to sleep. The drowsy god soon came to their aid. They slept, and dreamed, and slept, and dreamed again, of battle fields, of banqueting halls—just then so much needed—and of warlike glory. Then the scene changed to precipices, disgrace and danger, all huddled unconnectedly together in wild confusion.

It was not so with Dafydd; after reposing for an hour or two, he rose and left his slumbering companions. He was too ill at ease to dose his eyes. He was heart-sick as he stood in a leaning attitude against a projecting rock, whence he surveyed a wide stretch of country, softly lit up by the midnight luminary of the heavens;—rocks, hills, woods, lakes, and glens, were aft visible, one below another, to the margin of the distant sea; the last was so faintly seen that it required a keen eye to distinguish it from the clouds.

'My country, my beloved country, fare thee well!' said the

veteran warrior, in mournful accents; 'it is my last farewell. I feel that I have soon a longer journey to take than the present. May the great and mighty being who created this fair scene before me, receive me, unworthy as I am, into His glorious kingdom; may He bless you, my best of wives, and you, my wyres bach (most beloved of children); you will lose one protector, but there is another you cannot lose, who never slumbers nor sleeps: I leave you with Him. My unfortunate son, God protect him also, and restore him to his home.'

The eastern horizon warned Dafydd it was time to retrace his steps to the shed. He roused his companions, and they were soon again upon their journey.

At a late hour at night they gained the appointed village. The first person who greeted them was Ivor; he had arrived with the Earl of Pembroke but a few hours before; and immediately conducted them to a small inn, where Jasper of Hatfield and his party had already taken up their quarters.

In a rude, dirty, small apartment, these three distinguished noblemen talked over Barnet's bloody field. The conduct of the battle was canvassed with much seriousness on the part of Jasper Tudor. Their future plans were next discussed: and all agreed that no time should be lost in proceeding with the utmost expedition to the aid of the heroic queen and her noble son, whose youth and inexperience greatly needed their counsel.

CHAPTER XIII

Battle of the 'Bloody Meadow'—
Death of Ap Jevan

AFTER many days of weary marching, the little company of partisans for the cause of Lancaster arrived before the gates of Beaulieu Abbey in Hampshire. Margaret of Anjou and the Prince with his bride had there taken refuge. On their route they were joined by the Earl of Devonshire, Lord Wenlock, and John Beauforte, brother of the Duke of Somerset. All were equally anxious to behold their illustrious queen and to assure her of their continued fidelity to her cause.

Margaret had received so great a blow by the death of Warwick, and the defeat at Barnet, that she could not rouse herself from her despondency. For some days she had kept her room, and was pale and haggard in appearance, when Somerset, with the rest of her friends, were ushered into her presence.

They were struck with the change which had taken place in the unhappy queen. She seemed to have lost all the natural energy of her character. For a long time she would listen to no proposals for meeting the Yorkists again in the field herself, nor would she consent to her son being placed at the head of an army against the White Rose.

Somerset, and the other Lords, said much to revive her hopes. The Prince argued long and earnestly with his mother, entreating her to listen to her friends. She remained inflexible.

There was a momentary pause, and Margaret turning her eyes towards Ap Jevan's tall figure, the colour immediately mounted to her cheeks.

'Somerset,' said she, 'surely that is a face I know; I cannot be mistaken?'

'It is your Highness's brave protector at Harlech, Dafydd ap Jevan ap Einion, who has come from his native mountains to spend his remaining strength and energy in the cause he has so long warmly embraced.'

'Enough, Somerset,' said the Queen, impatiently, 'tell the brave Dafydd I would speak with him.'

The Welsh chieftain immediately approached and Margaret courteously extended her hand to him. A smile, touched with sad remembrances, for a moment irradiated her grief-worn features.

'Verily, this is an unlooked-for kindness, noble Ap Jevan,' said she. 'The meeting with an old friend is cheering. It affords me an opportunity I have long wished for, to sympathize with you in your misfortunes. The years which have rolled away since I took my departure from your hospitable roof, comprised for both of us a painful period of hope and apprehension, grief and disappointment. In the midst of my own trials, Dafydd, I did not forget yours. In thought I have often travelled back to the days I sojourned at Harlech, recalling the genuine kindness of yourself and family. Dafydd, there are few in the world who possess so noble a heart as yours. I have seen much of human character since we parted; I have learned it too by bitter experience.'

'I am not worthy of all that your Highness has been pleased to say in my favour,' replied Dafydd, bowing low.

'I would I could have shown my feelings towards you in

action, rather than word. Had misfortune not been so liberal with her gifts; had I been victorious, you should not only have been installed into your former position, but have received those honours your matchless conduct so well deserves. But alas! where is now our kingdom? A prospect of desolation, misery, and death alone remains. My nobles will not agree with me, Ap Jevan, that it would be madness to attempt to take the field again. My own wish is to abandon the cause, and seek an asylum once more in France, where we should, at least, live in peace. Speak, I would hear your opinions upon this important subject.'

'Your gracious Highness will excuse my giving an opinion,' replied Dafydd, 'taken as I am by surprise. Of late years I have been buried in the mountains. I am totally inexperienced upon these points.'

'I have no occasion to follow your advice, good Dafydd. I only desire to have it,' said the Queen.

'Then, please your Highness, though you have received a fearful shock, and been disheartened, you have still many stout hearts burning with indignation against Edward of York. I can vouch for my own countrymen. Gather them together from all quarters. Muster an army superior to any that has yet been marshalled under the banner of the Red Rose. Let every effort possible be strained. If not, let the contest rest where it is.'

'Dafydd's remarks are to the point,' observed the Prince. 'Be guided by them, honoured mother.'

Importuned on all sides, Margaret at length consented; and almost immediately afterwards her friends dispersed themselves in different parts of the country, levying troops. Jasper Tudor returned to Wales; but Dafydd remained with the Duke of Somerset.

Previous to Jasper of Hatfield's departure, he had a long interview with the Queen and young Somerset. Before he quitted the Abbey, he impressed upon their minds the necessity of remaining in seclusion till he arrived with the Welsh troops he should levy.

He seemed to feel a presentiment that something would go wrong; for he turned again, and repeated the request:—

'Remember my parting words—'Go not to the field till you see me at the head of my Welsh legions.'

The whole country was again plunged into excitement; and as the new levies passed from village to village, mothers and grandmothers, maidens and children, felt forebodings that fresh evil was coming upon them, and wept in silence for their absent relations in the ranks of war.

Margaret at length left Beaulieu and proceeded to Bath, where she was surrounded by an army that was every hour increasing. Jasper of Hatfield was shortly expected on the borders. It was intended to concentrate there. The Queen and her valiant son set out at the head of their troops, and marched with surprising rapidity towards Bristol, and from thence to Gloucester.

'My anxiety is great,' said the Queen, 'lest our implacable antagonist should come upon us before we cross the Severn and join Jasper Tudor's army. Somerset,' she added, with a tremulous voice, 'let us not forget Pembroke's last injunction.'

Repeated messages were brought of Edward's rapid march towards the Severn, and of the increase of his followers. She and her friends saw, perhaps too late, what the great Warwick's death had done, and that with him really rested the fortune of the Red Roses. A still darker shade overspread the once brilliant brow of Anjou's fair descendant. She turned to look upon the youthful face of her son, glowing with excitement, and said with a long, heavy sigh—'Something within tells me, my child, that you will never wear England's disputed crown!'

She was roused from these gloomy reflections by the near approach of her troops to Gloucester. There they discovered, to their unutterable confusion, that the men of the city had fortified the bridge, and obstinately refused to permit the Queen and her friends to pass over. Threats and entreaties were of no avail: the citizens kept the post in dogged silence.

Provoked to the extreme, Margaret commanded an interview of those individuals with whom she was acquainted in the town. She offered them large bribes, if they would only use their influence in her favour. It was to no purpose.

'It is the Duke's special command!' shouted the men of Gloucester on every side. 'To permit your Highness to pass over would be to sign our death warrant.'

'To Tewksbury! To Tewksbury!' cried the Queen, in a bewilderment. 'There remains no alternative.'

She rode forward in front of her troops, and waving her hand, continued:—

'On!—on!—for God's sake! Speed, my brave, my zealous followers! It is of no use wrangling with these graceless clowns. Let us gain but the Welsh borders—let us cross the Severn at Tewksbury, and all will be well.'

She then turned her charger round, and dashed off in the direction of Tewksbury, followed by her devoted army. Margaret was now herself once more. The dauntless spirit of their leader re-animated every heart; and pushing forward rapidly, they gained the town in so short a time that all, save the impatient Margaret, marvelled at the progress they had made.

But their hopes and efforts were cast down for ever. Scarcely had they arrived at Tewksbury, when intelligence was brought that King Edward was but a few miles distant, having pushed on by rapid marches. He would be up in battle array before they could pass the Severn, or even place the Avon between them and their foe.

'Insupportable misery!' ejaculated the Queen, turning deadly pale. 'Heaven and the saints are against us. Edward will be on our rear. My son! my son! we are ruined!'

Scarcely had the words fallen from her lips before she regretted their utterance. Seized with a dauntless determination not to be dispirited, she turned immediately to the Prior of St John, who was standing near her, and said in an imperative tone:—

'Let not this alarming circumstance interrupt our march. Let us make more speed to pass over, and gain the Welsh borders. Where is Somerset, that imprudent youth? Seek him—send him to me.'

'After so long a march, we thought your Highness would need repose. Consequently orders have been issued to that effect.'

'Repose! fatigue!' repeated Margaret, with a mingled look of scorn and vexation. 'Methinks you are mighty solicitous for my comfort! In a time like the present, Master Prior, the enemy well-nigh up with us, short of our Welsh friends, to let fatigue and repose intrude upon duty, we sacrifice moments which are life and death to us. Send me Somerset and Wenlock. Let me not have to repeat my words.'

She bit her lips in anger.

The non-appearance of either of the generals caused Margaret great uneasiness at such a moment. She at length went in search of them herself, when, to her unutterable dismay, she found entrenchments actively throwing up, and the Severn in the rear.

'What!' cried the Queen, bewildered, 'entrenchments? The saints protect us!'

She placed her hands in agony to her temples, and called aloud for Somerset.

'Why do you not come?—This audacious neglect is not to be borne.'

The Duke at last made his appearance, and the queen irritated, addressed him:—

'How is it my commands are disregarded, my Lord? You have incurred my great displeasure. Withdraw these orders instantaneously, Edward Beaufort; we must continue our march, this night, this instant. The river on our left flank, the enemy approaching our right and rear, we are undone!'

'That is impossible, I cannot withdraw the orders, please your Highness,' said the Duke with provoking calmness; 'I thought the Park here so advantageous, we could not do better than give battle here. To make alterations now, would be injurious; it is too late. Where could we find a place more suitable for entrenchments?'

'With our rear on the brink of a river! There is generalship! Jasper of Hatfield too, is not here,' replied Margaret, with a despairing look.

'No, but before the sun rises, I expect he will be here,' replied the Duke.

'But if not,' interrupted Margaret, laying a stress on the negative.

'We must fight with redoubled energy, we must take our chance,' answered the Duke, suddenly becoming aware of the responsibility that had devolved upon himself. He now became greatly annoyed at having acted without consulting his royal patron.

'Insolent pertinacity!' ejaculated the Queen, the moment the Duke had quitted her presence. 'It is well he is a Beaufort; heaven knows that to no other fiery spirit would I have submitted to such ill-judged conduct. Somerset, Somerset! The blood of those who have served me so well, will by this act of folly be wasted to our ruin.'

With a heavy heart, the Queen returned to her tent. There upon her knees she poured out the anguish of her heart, not in words, but in thoughts. One slight female form knelt by her side, joining in her supplications. It was a young and interesting bride, her daughter-in-law, the great Warwick's child. Soft, gentle in manner, she was ever ready to comfort the distressed, and soothe the wounded in spirit. Her words were few, but they sank deep into the soul of the sorrowing Margaret, who cherished her from feeling her superior virtues.

The beautiful light at the dawn of a lovely spring morning roused the unhappy Margaret from her slumbers, on the day, as she had anticipated, that was to end the many conflicts between the Red and the White Roses. Hope and despair alternately governed her thoughts. She dressed in haste, to meet her generals in consultation, before the attack Edward was on the eve of making upon her.

Margaret desired that Somerset and his brother should lead the wings, but that the van should be conducted by the Prince of Wales, under the superintendence of Lord Wenlock, the Prior of St John's, and by her special request, the faithful Dafydd ap Jevan, who was to take his station at the side of his royal master; marshalled in that mead, which was to be handed down to posterity as the 'bloody meadow', and by which name it is still known.

The Queen and the Prince then rode about the field encouraging the troops.

'Give me this victory, my faithful followers,' cried Margaret, with the blood of her warrior forefathers kindling in every vein, 'and promotion and happiness shall be your reward—unlimited promotion—uninterrupted happiness!'

These words were articulated with a clear and powerful voice; her cheeks were flushed, and that peculiar lustre visited her eyes which when seen, could never be forgotten.

Deafening cries that Edward of York was rushing upon them, soon after resounded in the ranks. Where was Jasper of Hatfield? What had been his last prophetic words? The recollection of them fell upon Margaret's ears like a death-knell.

'Victory or death!' cried the Queen, as she rode towards the thickest of the fight; her dear voice heard rallying the troops.

Somerset at this moment dashed up on his reeking charger, fiery and ungovernable as himself, and inquired with passionate gesture,—

'Where is that fool, Wenlock?—The tardy scoundrel—he is not at his post! By the saints, we shall lose the day!'

Wenlock was not at his post. The distracted Duke, boiling with indignation, galloped off in another direction.

'Where is Wenlock?' he again vociferated.

Wenlock he at length discovered, talking unconcernedly, with some of his men, in the marketplace, as if the crisis of their cause was not at hand. This unpardonable conduct was beyond endurance.

'Is this your post?' thundered the young general in a frenzy of excitement. 'Thou foul traitor to the Queen! Thou shalt no more betray friends or foes,' he raised his battle-axe, and deft the skull of Wenlock on the spot.

This frightful spectacle had an unfortunate effect upon the men under Wenlock's banner. They stood for a few minutes, appalled at the death of their chief, and then took to flight, causing so much confusion that Margaret saw in terror, the day was against them.

'Let me but die, let me die! I cannot live through this day,' shrieked the distracted Queen. She sprang from her horse, and would have rushed headlong into the hottest of the fight, had not Dafydd, her old and faithful friend, seen her intention.

'Stay, royal lady, Queen-consort of my revered master!' cried Ap Jevan, throwing himself before her to intercept her progress.

'Your life is precious to us, to the King, and to the Prince!'

'What? you—you, Dafydd?—will you wring my heart, by reminding me at such an hour, of that most dear to me? Leave me to die—leave me to die; I declared it should be victory or death!—victory or death!'

Overcome, at length, with fatigue and agitation, and half insensible, the venerable chieftain conveyed her to a dwelling in the Park, and seeing that she was safe, returned to the scene of action, where the first objects he encountered were Prince Edward in a desperate hand-in-hand combat with Gloucester, the ferocious hunchback duke of that name.

Ap Jevan saw the imminent danger of the stripling, and rushed forward to his assistance. His former strength seemed to reanimate his declining frame. He stood between them, and by one of his sturdy blows, the King's brother was repelled some distance from his prey. The ill-shapen Duke, however, was not to be thwarted. He arose from the ground on which he had staggered and fallen, and rushed furiously upon the hoary chief of Harlech.

'I know you,' shouted he, in a hoarse voice, 'I know you,— enemy of our house. If you breathe, after I have done with you, let the vixen Margaret wash her hands, to her heart's content, in Richard of Gloucester's blood!'

Sir Richard Crofts and other Yorkists collected round the spot. Dafydd found himself attacked on all sides, but boldly stood his ground, till a battle-axe blow aimed at him from behind by the cowardly hand of Sir Richard Crofts, felled the veteran to the earth.

A malicious smile passed over the ill-features of the Duke, who started forward and cleft the already bleeding head of Harlech's bold and valiant defender. His courageous spirit fled;—hushed for ever now, were the cares and sorrows of his long-troubled heart.

When the youthful Edward beheld his champion cut down, and saw him expire under the blows of Gloucester; he was struck with horror. The Duke had quitted the spot in haste, summoned by the king, to share the pleasure of entering the enemy's camp. The Queen's troops were put to flight, without further resistance.

Edward of Lancaster stood alone, closed in on all sides by the enemy. Not a friend or adviser was near to aid or counsel him. The Earl of Devonshire, and Sir John Beaufort, the brother of the Duke of Somerset, were both slain. Somerset, exasperated at the turn the battle had taken, acted like a madman, and became incapable of issuing further orders.

Such was the unfortunate position of the ill-fated Plantagenet and her son.

'It shall not be said the heir of Lancaster fled before the enemy,' said the Prince, placing himself against the trunk of a sturdy oak. In that situation he kept his opponents at bay, till Sir Richard Crofts appeared once more, bearing in triumph, as his prisoner, the Prior of St John's, who, upon approaching Edward, entreated him to lay down his arms, and surrender, as he himself had done, to Sir Richard, who spontaneously promised to plead on their behalf.

Exhausted from the fight, and persuaded that destruction was inevitable, the Prince at length yielded to the monk's solicitations; but not before he had turned to gaze once more on the melancholy remains of his devoted friend, Dafydd ap Jevan. For his cause, Ap Jevan had left his home, and for that, had perished, far away from his friends and much-loved mountain land.

CHAPTER XIV

*Murder of Edward of Lancaster—
And of King Henry*

TEMPTED by Edward's offer of a large bribe, the mercenary Sir Richard Croft had sought to obtain possession of the person of the young Plantagenet. Elated by his good fortune, and utterly disregarding his promises to the Prince, he hastened to conduct him into the royal presence.

Edward on the impulse of the moment, with his accustomed unfeeling levity, whispered;—

'By St George! Richard, he is a noble youngster, he has robbed many a maiden of her heart!'

The young Prince continued standing in a dauntless attitude before the scrutinizing gaze of the unappeasable tyrant.

'Rash, presumptuous youth, what brought you into my kingdom with banners displayed against me?'

This he demanded in an insulting tone, suddenly changing to an angry lowering cast his countenance, before so expressive of pleasure at his success.

'To recover my father's crown, and my own inheritance,' replied Edward haughtily.

'Beware how you express yourself thus,' retorted the king, with an angry gesture, striking him a violent blow in the face with his gauntlet. At the same time, Edward exchanged a look with Gloucester; this was the royal signal to murder the scion of the house of Lancaster.

The Duke sprang forward, followed by his brother Clarence, and the Earls of Dorset and Hastings. They fell upon the unarmed stripling with the ferocity of unrelenting savages, and terminated in this brutal manner the existence of one, who had gained the favour of all by whom he had been served.

This savage deed cast terror upon friends and foes, not a voice was raised in its favour. Every face exhibited signs of dissatisfaction. Gloucester handed his gauntlet and sleeve to an attendant. They were reeking with the blood of his victim. He withdrew the first from the scene of his own sanguinary baseness. As he passed through the crowd, his withered arm was convulsively grasped, and an unearthly voice, which he recognized, whispered in his ear;—

'Richard of Gloucester, there will be retribution. This crime of blood *shall* be appeased.'

Trembling violently the Duke staggered back, and when he had recovered himself, a spare, dark figure passed before him and vanished.

'The Devil take her,' he muttered to himself, his conscience smiting him at the words he had heard: he quickened his footsteps.

On the following morning, as King Edward was on his way to Worcester, Sir William Stanley came up, and requested him to halt.

'We have discovered,' said Stanley, 'the place of the Queen's concealment.'

His royal master asking a full explanation, he at once gave it.

'By St George, that is good. Methinks fortune smiles upon me,' rejoined Edward. 'I have vanquished the enemy at last.

Although it cost me so many sanguinary fights, it was worth the blood spilt. It was a Caesar's triumph. Stay, Stanley, I am a fool to bray here, before Margaret is secured. Where did you say the tigress lurked in cover?'

'In the Nunnery near Tewkesbury,' replied Sir William. 'Anne of Warwick, the Countess of Devonshire, and Lady Vaux, are also there.'

'Go then, Sir Knight, place a strong guard around the house; guard well the saints within; they are the holy leaven of the Yorkists' batch. There await my further commands.'

Sir William Stanley owed Margaret a personal grudge. He insisted upon being shown into the Queen's apartments; for he was very desirous to witness the misery which the intelligence of her son's death would inflict on the unfortunate Queen.

Margaret raised her head as he entered and delivered the intelligence of the murder of the Prince. She fixed her eyes upon the speaker, then raised her arms towards heaven, speechless from magnitude of grief. Her lips became pale as her care-worn cheeks. She remained motionless as a statue.

A loud piercing shriek burst from the agonized breast of Edward's young bride, but it roused not the grief-stricken mother. The scene well-nigh affected the hard-hearted Stanley, a family name as renowned for inconstancy as want of principle. He never forgot that moment, if it raised no pity in a bosom insensible to ought save its own interests.

Sir William received orders soon afterwards, for conveying Margaret to Coventry; Edward was then there. Shortly after, the selfish conqueror entered the metropolis, bearing along in his triumph the broken-spirited Margaret, and the widowed consort of her son, whom he had murdered.

In the same chariot, clasped in one another's arms, the illustrious prisoners were conveyed through the streets of London, to the Tower. On reaching the gloomy precincts they were instantly separated. The Queen was left alone to deplore her fate in a dark and loathsome dungeon. Unhappy Margaret! The desolation of her sorrowing heart may be imagined, not described, as she sat brooding over her misfortunes. Her beloved consort, whom she had not seen for years, she well knew to be within a few doors of her own cell. Her spirit yearned to mingle her tears with his, and sympathize in the irreparable loss of their idolized offspring. But even this consolation was denied her amid her magnitude of woe.

On the same night as the Queen reached the Tower, Gloucester contemplated the committal of the long-premeditated murder of King Henry, her husband. Scarcely had the glass run out the midnight hour, when he repaired to the chamber of the unsuspecting monarch. Henry had but a few hours before been made acquainted with the death of his son, and the total overthrow of his royal house. In deep meditation upon these distressing events, these heart-rending calamities, the pious, feeble-minded Henry was sitting at a rude, worm-eaten table; a pet bird was upon his shoulder. He was turning over the leaves of a religious book, when he caught the sound of approaching footsteps. The gaoler had long before brought him his evening meal; and he had no thought of being again disturbed for that night. He listened, confused voices fell upon his ear, and that of Gloucester's was distinctly heard. The monarch shuddered as if he anticipated some dreadful evil to himself. Naturally of a nervous temperament, he started upon his feet, at the same time looking towards the door; Richard of Gloucester and three ill-looking banditti, like himself, all armed, entered the gloomy cell.

'St Henry,' cried Gloucester, sarcastically, 'how have you borne your affliction? Has the spirit of your son visited you? Spirits contemn dungeon doors. My dagger was steeped hilt deep in his blood. Sanctified, you may express it, ex-King of England. I may do service to more of your family, paper-crowned monarch!'

These words uttered, Gloucester threw himself upon his unhappy victim, not willing to miss the merit of a crime. He grasped Henry violently by the garment, and dashed him on the floor. The King had scarcely time to clasp his hands together in the attitude of prayer. The Duke and his assassin colleagues then plunged their daggers into the body of the unfortunate monarch.

'There lies the imbecile! It is done at last,' muttered Gloucester, with a fiendish laugh. Hastily quitting the murdered body, the Duke passed down the gloomy passage with hurried steps, as if he feared the spirit of the murdered monarch was tracking his footsteps.

A voice was heard as if issuing from the vault, the counterpart of that which addressed him at Tewksbury.

'The blood of the Lord's anointed shall be avenged on thee, Richard of Gloucester.'

Gloucester trembled till he reached the King's apartment, where he made a strong effort to shake off the terror of those accents, while he was assuring his royal brother that his throne was secure.

Edward looked at him with an inquiring expression of countenance.

'Do you doubt me?' said Gloucester, hastily. 'The deed is done; the throne is ours.'

'So far it is well,' articulated the King; 'on my soul, Richard, you have done bravely, what I could not have dared to do.'

'What!' said the Duke, with a self-satisfied air. 'What, I should like to know, would not Richard of Gloucester dare to do?' He then laughed outright, and reminded Edward that Queen Margaret was still in their power.

'Aye, Richard, but she is deprived of her weapons and her claims—She is now harmless. We need not extend our vengeance further.'

'What do you mean?' said the Duke; 'have you forgotten her taunts—her persecutions? By heaven, Edward, she was the worst of the three.'

'That may be,' said the King in a firm tone, 'but our vengeance must end here. No Plantagenet has ever stained his hands with the blood of a female. We have already performed much to requite her for the evil she has done to our house. Deprived her of her consort; bereaved her of her son; taken her from the zenith of power, and plunged her into abject misery. On my soul, Richard, what would you have more?'

'If anything could be done to add a few more drops of bitterness to her cup, I would do it,' said Gloucester, with a sardonic smile.

CHAPTER XV

Kynfin Finds the Body of His Father— The Awenydhion

THE roar of battle, the shrieks and groans of the wounded, and the shouts of the victors had scarcely been hushed, when Jasper of Hatfield with his strong and numerous army of Welsh partisans reached the vicinity of Tewksbury. With bitter disappointment he heard of the total defeat of the Lancastrian army. The queen's generals had not listened to his parting words, and had become the victims of their own ignorance of warfare, and glaring indiscretion.

Pembroke, deeply distressed upon hearing of the brutal murder of young Prince Edward, saw every expectation of vengeance and success, which he had till now cherished, vanished into thin air.

The hope of Lancaster was utterly gone; the ground both he and his forces occupied was a post of imminent danger. Hastily disbanding his levies, the jealous Welsh returned to their mountains to grieve in silence over the obliteration of the Red Rose standard.

One tall slender figure followed not in the footsteps of his countrymen. Hastily bidding them farewell, he pursued his lonely way to the fatal battle-field. The clouds were chasing each other hurriedly athwart the heavens, which seemed to have changed with the fortunes of the day. The moon in fitful glances looked down upon the solitary wanderer over the scene of death, Hundreds of the slain lay heaped together, preparatory to interment on the field. The contortions of the features of the dead, marked here in rigid character the stern determination of hostile anger, and there the placid sleep of passion had been quenched under the unexpected blow.

The stranger passed on among heaps of dead, from pile to pile, in a hurried search of some particular body. Eagerly his dark wild eyes traversed in one direction and then in its opposite, until they were suddenly riveted on a noble form dabbled in blood, but too well known to be mistaken for any other.

'My father! my father!' cried the son of Harlech in anguish; 'dear to me as life, aye, once dearer to me than existence, though my affection was so ill exhibited—to thee an unnatural, an unfeeling son, despite my filial regard; worthless descendant that I am of a noble line.' Here Kynfin paused amid his grief, for he became aware of footsteps approaching. Turning round, he saw only a solitary individual, who was busy among the bodies in search of plunder; so busy as scarcely to notice him.

In silent self-condemnation, Kynfin passed his hands against his temples, and kneeling on the earth, trampled and gory as it was, remained some time in a half-insensible state.

The day-dawn, dispersing the mist that had covered the horizon, recalled his own position to his distracted mind. To remain and become a prisoner of the Yorkists, drunk with insolence and victory, could be of no benefit to the fallen cause, to his noble father's remains, or to himself. He observed the sword still in the cold hand of Harlech's chieftain. He reflected it was a valued relic of his ancestors. He took it, pressed it passionately to his lips, gave a wild, farewell glance at the mangled remains of his brave sire, and withdrew from the scene of the tragedy, with a pace as rapid as he thought was consistent with avoiding the notice of the Yorkists, who might be returning from the pursuit of the Lancastrians. He saw none, even the joy of victory was silenced in the fatigues they had undergone; all being wrapped in slumber.

Kynfin reflected upon the demands of duty towards his sole remaining parent, his mother, and directed his steps to his late father's home. He proceeded unobserved. At the close of the second day from leaving the blood-stained field of Tewkesbury, he felt greatly fatigued. This induced him to seek a night's lodging at all hazards, in a small inn near the road-side. He approached the door, and a loud laugh of revelry caught his ear. He knocked, and was at once conducted into a low roomy kitchen, where several persons were seated round a table, covered with homely provisions, and in the midst of them a bowl of warm ale.

The night was boisterous and rainy, and as the drops pattered against the casement, and the wind whistled without, the cheerfulness within was appreciated, even by Kynfin, oppressed as he was with thoughts of his own condition.

On the entrance of the stranger, the men seated at the table cast upon Kynfin a suspicious look.

'A soaking wet night, young man,' said one of them—a tall, dark, ill-looking Englishman. 'Not sorry to get under shelter; excellent provender, we can strongly recommend it,' and he struck his hand upon the well-supplied board. His words were lost upon Kynfin, who had thrown himself into a chair on the opposite side of the apartment, and only answered these remarks by wildly staring at the party.

The company, somewhat surprised, exchanged glances with one another, then whispered and laughed alternately.

'Come, come, gentlemen,' said one of them, named Jervis ap Griffith; 'I am a Welshman; if I am not mistaken, this stranger is a countryman.' Then lowering his voice, he continued: 'I think I am right, he is neither a madman nor an idiot, but what we call in our good Welsh, an Awenydhion.'[8]

'By the beads of St Jerom, that is a long jabbering word, what does it mean?' inquired Sir Roger, the name by which they addressed the dark Englishman. All the rest laughed in chorus.

Ap Griffith looked annoyed; but upon again being asked to give an explanation of what an Awenydhion meant, replied:

'An Awenydhion means, gentlemen, a person visited with a poetic genius, or, if you will have it so, possessed by an invisible spirit, who puts a written scroll into his mouth, that gives him supernatural power. Such persons are sometimes silent, and sometimes seized with a fit of frantic enthusiasm. But to cut the story short, these people can be made useful, for example, in a case like ours, Sir Roger.' Thus concluded Jervis, laying a stress upon the last sentence, and giving his companion a knowing wink.

'Indeed!' said Sir Roger, rubbing his hands with incredulous look.

'If you have these strange animals in your country, on my life I should not like to live among you,' observed one of the company. Many similar remarks were made, and the subject brought to a close by drinking to the health of the Awenydhion. The cries for more ale continued, vulgar jokes,

---

8   See Warrington's *History of Wales*.

and songs of little harmony, fell confusedly upon the ear. At length they drank so deeply that the presence of the stranger and the tale of the Awenydhion completely escaped their memory. Ap Griffith and his dark companion talked aside from the rest; but as the bowl was replenished, the speakers began to be more unguarded in their conversation.

'You have not struck the bargain yet, Sir Roger,' said Ap Griffith, pertinaciously; 'say, clear and smooth, what is the reward for the Earl of Pembroke and his nephew, dead or alive? I know the sanctified hypocrite well. I have a grudge against him; I lived once under his castle walls, and slaughtered scores of his deer, for which he threatened to hang me. Mewn gwirionedd! if I don't strangle him first, the Lancastrian dog, yn enw goodness! I wonder how he feels after such a scattering of the Red Rose leaves.' After these comments, Ap Griffith rose and staggered forward, shouting with extreme eagerness:—

'Edward of York for ever! Down with the Lancastrians, down with their blood for ever.'

'Bravo, Ap Griffith, you are the fellow for me, y-e-s, y-e-s, you are the fellow for me,' repeated Sir Roger, scarcely able to articulate. 'Bring me that rebel, Pembroke, dead or alive, you shall be made a gentleman of, as sure as King Edward sits upon the throne of England. Y-es, you shall be made a gentleman of. By the beads of St Jerom, you shall.'

'Do you think he will make a knight of me, Sir Roger? Why, that is the height of my ambition. Ha, ha! that would be grand. Well, if you will keep the bargain, I will undertake to trap the Earl in the neighbourhood of his own castle. I'll let him know, too, that his friend the deer-stalker did it.'

Sir Roger fell asleep, and soon afterwards the bacchanalian

party broke up for the night, leaving Kynfin alone in the kitchen. Embers were still gleaming upon the hearth, and all around was silent, save the chirping of the crickets. The intention which had just been divulged, was so agitating to the feelings of the son of Harlech that, weary and feverish from fatigue as he was, he could not sleep. The moment he was alone, he rose, opened the window, and felt refreshed by the external air, though damp. The rain was still falling, white misty clouds were resting on, and breaking over the adjacent hills.

'I have been taken for an Awenydhion, indeed! Drunken fools!' ejaculated Kynfin to himself; 'they shall not be undeceived. Jasper of Hatfield, you shall not perish by one of Edward's villainous agents, without my making every endeavour to rescue you from such an end. They think that I am possessed. I will bear with them till my point is gained! They shall find to their cost that the stranger was no Awenydhion, nor an idiot; mad! well I may be mad, misfortune may make me so. My home, my desolate home, how can I ever return to thee? I even now see it—my shadow will make it darker. Can my mother—my devoted mother—be cheered by the presence of him who has been the author of this desolation?' Absorbed by bitter reflections, the son of Harlech remained before the window till the sun rose.

At an early hour, preparations for departure were in busy progress, on the part of the inmates of the house. Horses and ponies stood ready saddled in the yard, surrounded by men and boys jabbering half English, half Welsh.

The son of Harlech hired a strong pony, and was the first to sit down to the morning repast. While he was at the table, Sir Roger and Ap Griffith made their appearance.

'By the beads of St Jerom! If the poetic genius is not down before us,' cried the knight, facetiously. 'Whither are you bound, friend? Do you travel west?'

'To the mountains, twenty miles this side of Pembroke,' said Kynfin, abstractedly.

Ap Griffith took a seat near him, and immediately entered into conversation in his own language. Kynfin soon knew the character of the man, and how to play his part. He managed with this understanding to work deeply on Ap Griffith's weak and superstitious mind.

'"What is the greatest folly in a man?" was Caturg's[9] inquiry of the seven learned men,' observed Kynfin, looking steadily into his companion's face. 'Ystyffan, the Bard of Teilo, gave this reply:—"The wish to injure another without having the power to effect it." That power, man, thou lackest.'

'Under your guidance I shall have that power, I entreat you to go with us,' said Ap Griffith, respectfully.

'Twenty miles this side of Pembroke I travel. If you would have my company follow me. I follow no mortal.' His wild eyes were upon them all; starting upon his feet, he repeated various incoherent sentences, and the next moment was in the yard.

'He is a wizard, or a madman, I'll stake my life! Why, nothing can be done with such a fellow as that,' exclaimed Sir Roger.

'Indeed, truth, Sir Roger. I no like not to go with him, he can be of great use to us,' said Ap Griffith, cramming his

---

[9]   Caturg was an Abbot of Llancarfan, in Glamorgan. He was surnamed
       the Wise, and is numbered among the saints of the sixth century.
       Taliesin, the chief of the Bards, completed his education under this
       celebrated sage, whose Truisms and Aphorisms are still extant.

mouthful and preparing to leave the table. 'We have a bevy
of Lancastrians to pass through, remember that, Sir Roger.
You do not know the nature of these Awenydhions, come, let
us go with him; indeed, truth, the aid we require he will
bestow upon us,—we shall get out of him what we want.'

'The devil only knows what you do want,' retorted Sir
Roger, annoyed at being disturbed at his breakfast. 'You
Welshmen are, without exception, the most superstitious dogs
I ever came across,'

Ap Griffith looked angry, and Sir Roger, dependent upon
him, thought it prudent to yield.

'I suppose you must have it all your own way,' said he; 'all
I can say is, I would sacrifice much if I could only be certain
of getting Pembroke and young Richmond into my power.
Aye, by the beads of St Jerom! I would go a great length to
stain my fingers with their blood, to finish the Lancastrians,
the last of the Lancastrians.'

When they appeared in the yard, the first person they beheld
was the son of Harlech, leaning over the back of his pony,
gazing intently upon the hills before him. Suddenly he sprang
upon his nag, and trotted out of the stable yard, leaving the
Englishman and his companion to follow at their leisure. They
had hardly gone a mile, and had reached a bare extensive
moor, where all halted but Kynfin, who simulated to exhibit
a strange power over his steed. After violently snorting in the
air, and striking his fore feet upon the turf, the nag dashed over
the dangerous and uneven ground, and left all the rest of the
party far behind.

'Stop, stop! For mercy's sake stop!' cried Sir Roger, quite
out of breath. 'I can't stand this horrid work. Let our guide,
who can be no other than a devil, go to the devil.'

They drew up, and some of the party seemed highly amused at the swiftness with which the poetic genius rode over the marsh. Many remarks were made, jokes intervening, and the whole of the company at length was restored to good humour, before rejoining their strange companion.

Several other adventures, and some singular manoeuvres on the part of the Awenydhion, as they deemed him, occurred before they reached the town. There he had previously told them he should take his leave. During the ride, Ap Griffith found many opportunities of holding conversation with the genius, and had given him his confidence and received a satisfactory reply. There was a good understanding built up between them. Ap Griffith appeared in high glee. He assured Sir Roger he might consider the Earl and his nephew already secured.

Kynfin hastened forward to gain the castle of Pembroke before the morning, if possible. He left his companions at a public house to regale themselves in the same way as they had done the previous night.

On his admittance to the castle, Kynfin was shown into the presence of Jasper Tudor and his nephew.

'What! Kynfin, the son of Harlech? This is an unexpected pleasure,' exclaimed the Earl, warmly shaking him by the hand. 'You have soon followed on our steps. What tidings do you bring of our shattered house? Not cheering, I fear. Edward is not likely to show us mercy.'

'Your words are too true, Jasper of Hatfield,' replied Kynfin, sorrowfully. 'I have come on an errand of the utmost importance. The disclosure will cause you great anxiety. Edward is seeking, by foul means, to destroy the last of the Lancastrians.'

'How,' cried Pembroke, looking alarmed, 'how came you by this information?'

'By a strange coincidence.'

The son of Harlech then related the particulars of his meeting with Sir Roger and his accomplices—how he had worked upon the deer-stalker's weak mind, and had learned from him the most minute particulars of their scheme.

'My spirit, I have told Ap Griffith, shall wander over Coed Gwyll, the spot they have fixed upon to accomplish the bloody sacrifice.'

A faint smile passed over Kynfin's face, and he continued:—

'Sir Roger is to write a letter to you, signed with the names of several leading Lancastrians in the neighbourhood, in which he will request the favour of your company, on a particular night, at a secret meeting, to be held at the Monastery of Pendergast, an hour before midnight. This is a ruse to entrap you on your road, waylay, and murder you. Their perfidious intentions do not end here. The moment they have succeeded with you, they are to repair immediately to the castle, with a fictitious message from yourself, commanding the Earl of Richmond, your nephew, to join them without a moment's hesitation. Relying upon their success here, their determination is to dispatch him on the spot where your assassination will have been perpetrated, and then to bury you both in the same grave, afterwards bearing the welcome news to the King.'

'Most treacherous!' ejaculated the Earl of Pembroke. 'A fearful escape for us! We are greatly indebted to you, my worthy kinsman, for our preservation. We must now see how we can best make this premeditated villainy re-act upon its authors.'

CHAPTER XVI

Treachery Frustrated—A Stratagem— Justifiable Doubts

THE Earl of Pembroke and his nephew impatiently awaited the arrival of the letter from Sir Roger. Kynfin, at their request, took up his temporary quarters at the Castle.

In a few days the expected letter arrived. It was couched in language agreeing well with what Kynfin had already stated in substance. The bearer of this treacherous epistle, a lad, was instructed to wait for a reply. The Earl asked the messenger some simple questions. He then wrote that he would be punctual at the Monastery.

'They will think they have me, Kynfin,' said Jasper Tudor, suddenly appearing in the hall with the letter in his hand. 'Here is the invitation. Unthinking knaves! dearly indeed will we make them pay for their conspiracy. Let us settle upon our arrangements immediately. We have no time to lose. Suppose Sir Roger should have more men in ambush than we calculate. It is advisable that we should be prepared for them.'

'We cannot be too cautious,' answered Kynfin. 'I would recommend you to send a score of men, disguised as freebooters, to conceal themselves in Coed Gwyll, to remain quiet till they hear a call from your bugle.'

'It shall be done,' said Pembroke.

'Put mail under your jerkin, and take all the arms you can conceal,' added Kynfin.

'Am I to understand the son of Harlech will risk his life with mine?' rejoined Pembroke.

'Assuredly, my lord; yet I can take no active part in the contest. Blood! Blood! I have enough on my conscience.'

A cloud passed over his face, and his words died upon his pale lips. The soft eyes of Aliano, and the mangled remains of his father, appeared to his imagination, and he became absent and silent.

Pembroke and the son of Harlech mounted their horses at the appointed time, and left the castle to pursue their hazardous ride to 'Coed Gwyll.'

'We have a good six miles,' observed Kynfin. 'The night favours us.'

'Aye, methinks, if the monks of St Martin knew of this atrocious design, they would in right earnest offer up their prayers on our behalf.'

The moment they reached the beaten track which leads to the Priory of Pendergast, they travelled briskly, setting their horses on the trot. They now and then exchanged a few words—no more. An hour had elapsed. The clump of dark trees, standing a little to the right, warned them of approaching the place of danger. Pembroke felt for his bugle, and remarked, with some little nervousness, that the moon was rising, and would opportunely come to their aid.

To this Kynfin made no reply. On entering the wood, he remarked, in a whisper, that the watchword must not be forgotten, and that it would be necessary to be careful of their own men. They proceeded in silence for a short distance further, when Kynfin again whispered,—

'Pembroke, I see them—be wary!'

The words hardly passed Ap Dafydd's lip, before Jervis darted forward and seized the reins of his horse. In an instant they were surrounded by Sir Roger and his accomplices.

A blast from the Earl's bugle gave the alarm. At the same moment, Kynfin, in an expert manner, threw a loose hood over Ap Griffith's head, and sprang from his horse. This was the work of a moment. Pembroke's men made their appearance, and Sir Roger, in attempting to drag the Earl from his saddle, received a dagger in his breast, and expired.

Ap Griffith, who had discovered the Awenydhion, was giving him the most abusive language, when his brains were dashed out by the Earl's men; and thus closed his career of villainy.

Young Henry of Richmond received his uncle with breathless eagerness, and learned the details of the murderous affair with deep emotion.

'You may thank Kynfin for this success,' said the Earl of Pembroke. 'He has not only acted the part of a kinsman and a friend, but of a daring and experienced soldier. He accomplished his purpose unarmed, in a manner worthy of his name.'

'Speak not so of me,' interrupted Kynfin, 'you will drive me from you. I hate commendation, of which I am undeserving; my private history is not known to you, Jasper of Hatfield.'

Notwithstanding this eccentricity, the Earl of Pembroke and the whole household became daily more attached to Kynfin.

Young Henry, with a very natural curiosity, endeavoured, but in vain, to discover a clue to his peculiar character. That some secret affair dwelt upon his mind, everyone was aware; he was pitied in consequence, though no one knew the cause.

A day or two after the foregoing defeat of the conspirators, the Countess Dowager of Pembroke, Lady Herbert, who for several years had been a second mother to young Henry of Richmond, came on a visit to the Castle. The first wish she expressed was to see Kynfin Tudor,[10] their preserver.

The son of Harlech was embarrassed in the society of the Countess and her daughters. They brought up bitter recollections, increased the wildness of his eyes, and made him more restless than ordinary. After a few days' usage to their society, he became more reconciled; Lady Herbert's gentle kindness evidently won upon him.

Jasper of Hatfield would not hear of Kynfin leaving the Castle. He had frequently urged it, for he felt, though at times he would shrink from the thought, that he had duties to perform elsewhere. This was fortunate, because hostilities were again impending over the persecuted noblemen.

One day, after the family had partaken of the evening meal, Kynfin, touching Jasper of Hatfield on the shoulder, requested some private conversation.

'Let the Countess and her children leave the Castle tonight, my lord,' were Kynfin's startling expressions.

'Are you in earnest?' inquired the Earl of Pembroke, looking bewildered.

'In right earnest,' repeated Kynfin; 'Morgan Thomas, brother-in-law to Sir Roger Vaughan, has hostile intentions. He has been bribed by King Edward, and is now raising troops to lay siege to this stronghold. Leave the care of the Countess to me; I will escort her to her residence this night, while you begin your preparations for defence.'

---

[10] The second son always takes the mother's maiden name in Wales.

An hour or two later, the Countess and her family left the fortress well mounted; and before day-break reached their destination in safety. The Countess took leave of the son of Harlech with regret, giving him a valuable ring in remembrance of his services.

Ap Dafydd returned to the Castle, and found the inmates in great confusion, being under no small alarm.

'This is a serious affair,' remarked Pembroke; 'but only what I expected. I fear, Kynfin, with our handful of men, we shall find it a difficult undertaking to resist Morgan's army.'

Kynfin was silent, he replied only by a movement of the head, in way of an answer.

The besiegers were before the castle. Every hour Kynfin's manner became more and more reserved. Some of the garrison declared they had seen him at night, going over to the enemy's border. This was correct. He had let himself out at the portal; had stood under the castle-walls, contemplating the enemy's camp, the gleaming bivouac fires, and the discordant voices, not yet hushed. It was equally true he had stealthily passed on to the moat, crossed it and entered the neglectful enemy's camp. There he ventured to inquire for Dafydd Thomas, assuring the sentinel who challenged him, that Thomas was a great friend, and he had business with him which would admit of no delay. Happily, the sentinel whom he accosted, was under Dafydd Thomas's orders, and the man, without hesitation, conducted him to his master's tent. There a cordial greeting took place between the friends.

Dafydd Thomas and Kynfin in early life had been on terms of intimate friendship. During Margaret's sojourn at Harlech, Dafydd Thomas had accompanied his uncle thither to pay her homage. From that time, a friendship had commenced between Kynfin and himself. They had followed and fought together under the banner of the Red Rose, and had joined their voices in the cry of victory at the battle of Wakefield.

They talked over the perils and adventures of those days. Kynfin found Dafydd the same generous, kind-hearted friend as ever. Dafydd lamented the changed appearance of Kynfin, and sympathized with him in his misfortune. In speaking of his own affairs, he regretted deeply the savage disposition of his brother.

'Well, Dafydd,' said Kynfin, at length, wishing to introduce the subject which had brought on his visit; 'I am about to ask you a great favour. When I heard that you were here, I could scarcely credit that you could raise your hand against the house of Lancaster, whose cause you once so warmly embraced. To me it is incomprehensible. I find it is too true you are running with the current, instead of standing out to the last in supporting the few individuals remaining of that noble-hearted line. Now, Dafydd, I must tell you that the Earl of Pembroke and his nephew, are my friends and relations. I come on their account to plead that you will not deliver them to the tyrant Edward; but save them from persecution and death. I know the castle cannot stand a long siege, that it must fall into the hands of your brother, sooner or later. I know that no mercy will be shown them, unless you, Dafydd—you aid them to escape.'

Dafydd appeared not a little embarrassed. Drawing nearer to his friend, he said:

'I own I am under the banner of the White Rose. Circumstances have brought me to this. Let me undeceive you my heart remains warm in the cause of the Red Rose. In their adversity, no one sympathizes with them more than myself. I have formed plans to place them far beyond the reach of their persecutors. A vessel is now at Tenby, in which I intend they shall sail for France. This cannot be accomplished till the castle is in our hands, and they are our prisoners. Thus, Dafydd Thomas is the same Dafydd Thomas as ever, in heart and soul, if forced to appear otherwise.'

Kynfin shook his hand warmly. The friends talked over their plans to deceive Morgan, and assist the escape of the Earl of Pembroke and his nephew.

It was agreed that Kynfin should return to the castle, and deliver up the fortress to his brother Dafydd Thomas; then Dafydd should persuade his brother to give Kynfin a high office in the castle, out of gratitude. In that manner he would be able to communicate with the prisoners, when the arrangements for them to be secretly conveyed to Tenby could be carried into effect.

Kynfin at first hesitated at these arrangements; but seeing there were no other that could be adopted, he consented.

The friends then separated, each to play his part in deceiving Morgan Thomas. Upon retracing his steps, the first person Kynfin met in the castle was young Henry, who immediately exclaimed:

'Well, Ap Dafydd; may I ask what has kept you so long from your post? My uncle thinks your conduct strange.'

Kynfin instantly coloured, and inquired where he was.

'In the hall,' replied Henry of Richmond; 'and in bad spirits.'

The spacious apartment looked more than usually gloomy. As he entered, Jasper Tudor, who had his back towards him, started at Kynfin's footsteps; but, upon seeing his kinsman, smiled at his own fears while he inquired,

'What news?'

Ap Dafydd wore his usual sorrowful expression, as he said:

'He was afraid there was no chance of escaping the enemy; and the castle must be sacrificed. But, Jasper of Hatfield,' continued he, 'be not alarmed, the savage Morgan Thomas shall not deliver you over into Edward's hands.'

Although these words were delivered with much warmth of manner, both the Earl of Pembroke and his nephew felt ill at ease.

When Kynfin had withdrawn, Henry of Richmond expressed his fears that Kynfin's assurances were of little worth. He was so eccentric in his conduct, so changeable in character, that it was impossible to place entire confidence in him. 'If the castle is sacrificed,' said he, 'we are sacrificed.'

'Henry, you wrong him,' said Pembroke; 'I have more confidence in Kynfin than in any one living besides.'

Early on the following morning a furious attack was made. Everyone was at his post, and acted with great bravery. Kynfin of a sudden was missed. The next instant young Henry rushed into the presence of the Earl of Pembroke, exclaiming:—

'My uncle, Kynfin Tudor has betrayed us. The castle is taken.'

'Impossible,' cried Pembroke; but before he could utter a second sentence the apartment was filled with armed men, and they were instantly made prisoners. Kynfin was amongst the number, and assisted in binding them.

'Did I not tell you, uncle, that I could place no trust in the eccentric son of Harlech?' said Henry of Richmond, as they dragged them along together.

Jasper of Hatfield was petrified with astonishment; he endeavoured to catch Kynfin Tudor's eye, but its glance was averted.

CHAPTER XVII

The Agreeable Surprise—An Ocean Refuge—Foreign Courtiers— The Unexpected Captivity

AN entire night and the whole of the following day the captives were left to themselves in the cheerless dungeons of their own castle. Young Henry's reproaches were bitter against Ap Dafydd; the Earl of Pembroke pointedly avoided the subject, and never mentioned his name.

Both had thrown themselves upon their straw beds; the young Earl had just fallen into a broken slumber, when the sound of approaching footsteps caught Pembroke's ear. He started up, the heavy bars of the dungeon were quickly drawn back, and Kynfin Tudor, with his friend stood before him.

'Jasper of Hatfield, haste!—Dress in these clothes,' cried Kynfin, placing a bundle of raiment before him; 'young Henry of Richmond will do the same.'

'Kynfin, Kynfin!' ejaculated Pembroke in a tone of suppressed joy, 'you have not forsaken us, I knew you would not.'

The son of Harlech again urged them to lose no time.

'Step lightly—follow us,' pursued Kynfin; 'we hope soon to place you beyond the reach of your persecutors.'

They passed hastily through dark rooms and winding galleries, and reached the outer gates in safety. But their perils

159

did not end there. They had to follow their conductors through the heart of the camp, where they were liable to be continually intercepted by sentinels. Dafydd had foreseen and prepared for their challenges. He evaded all questions, gave the watch-word of the night, and passed on. In this manner the fugitives gained a farm-house, where they mounted horses ready in waiting, without causing suspicion.

Arriving in safety at Tenby, they embarked on board the merchant vessel procured for their use. Fortunately the wind and tide being in their favour, they were soon under weigh.

Their deliverer had accompanied Pembroke and young Richmond to the beach; and as they were about to step into the skiff, to reach the ship, moored a little distance off, Kynfin took Pembroke's hand, and said:—

'Jasper of Hatfield, permit me to go with you to France. My home here is overshadowed. I cannot return to it. My country rises before my sight like a barren wilderness;—my heart is blighted;—let me then go with you, I shall be happier in a foreign land.'

'Welcome, welcome,' replied the Earl, 'I shall enjoy the society of one to whom I owe so much, whom I sincerely regard—share my exile! Kynfin, draw my affection still closer round you. It will contribute to our mutual happiness.'

The skiff pushed from the shore, Kynfin was at the helm, he sat with his eyes riveted on the land, the expression of his countenance changed. Greater sadness gathered upon his brow, and then a momentary gleam of pleasure came over his careworn features.

He was abandoning his home, perhaps, for ever, and how keenly did that word 'home' pierce his heart! His mother, he knew, was happier without his presence. He loved her with a deep earnest love; but she would not see his careworn face, watch his restless and peculiar habits, and not be deeply pained.

All this by his absence would be spared, she would be far happier without her miserable son.

He turned and looked into the reflecting waters, and seemed as if he expected them to respond, 'Yes, far happier—far—far happier.'

'Luff, luff; come alongside, lads!' repeated the rough voice of the skipper from the deck. In an instant, Kynfin roused from his melancholy reflections, steered the boat as he was directed. They were soon on board, and were received by the crew with marked respect.

During the passage, Pembroke had opportunities of studying Kynfin's character. The more he penetrated into his motives, the more he saw reason to admire him. There was thus exhibited a benevolence and refinement which a superficial observer would not discover, reserve was a prominent trait in his character. He was never known to utter a bitter word against anyone but himself. He shrank from the presence of strangers, avoiding society; yet there was something so prepossessing about him that he always attracted attention, and imperceptibly drew every heart towards him.

One evening while they were on deck, they were struck by the appearance of the atmosphere.

'We shall have a storm,' observed Kynfin, 'our boat is not one to weather a tempest.'

'You think there is danger then?' said Pembroke.

'We shall require all hands on deck!' continued the son of Harlech, and went in search of the captain, who said:—

'We are not far off the French coast; to be candid, I do not half like the squall that lowers in the distance. If my Lord

Pembroke had not expressed a wish to be landed farther up the Channel, we should do better in running further down; with such a wind as this in our teeth, we shall not easily work up against it.'

With the darkness of the night, the storm increased. 'All hands on deck,' was the skipper's first order. Kynfin's services were most valuable. The greater the danger, the more calm he appeared, to the surprise of all; nautical activity and skill were shown on his part very prominently on that fearful occasion.

As it was, they were driven on the coast of Brittany, where they were compelled to land. The vessel had received considerable damage, and was not in a condition to proceed further towards her original destination. Pembroke disappointed at this delay, resolved not to wait for the vessel, but go on at once to Paris. They remained at a small fishing village to recover themselves from their fatigues.

Jasper of Hatfield proposed that since they had arrived in the dominions of Francis, Duke of Brittany, they could hardly be so devoid of politeness as not to pay him their respects.

Kynfin was averse to such a visit. He urged that no time should be lost in proceeding to Paris.

Henry of Richmond, on the contrary, set his heart upon going to the Duke, and begged his uncle to disregard Kynfin's scruples. It was therefore arranged that they should start the following morning to pay court to the voluptuous Francis of Brittany.

Kynfin disappeared for a time the same night, and just as they were on the point of passing out of the stable court, came up to Jasper of Hatfield, breathless, and taking hold of his horse's head, exclaimed:—

'Jasper of Hatfield, turn to the west; you will repent of the step you are taking!'

The young Earl of Richmond again interposed. The good Earl of Pembroke and his nephew then proceeded upon their route to the court.

'Kynfin is not in his senses, I am sure of that,' remarked the young Earl, laughingly.

'He is a peculiar man,' was Pembroke's laconic reply.

'You always take his side,' answered his nephew, evidently a little piqued.

'If I do,' replied Pembroke, in a hasty manner, 'I have good cause for doing so.'

After a tedious ride, the Duke's summer residence came in sight of the visitors, who were struck at the magnificence of the structure. They soon after gained admittance, and were conducted into the presence of the Duke, who received them with coldness. One person of his court only remained in his presence during the interview. That person was Landois, who proved afterwards the greatest enemy of the accomplished strangers; he was the Duke's prime minister.

'To quit your realm without first waiting upon your Highness,' said Pembroke, much embarrassed at the reception which had been given him, 'would have been discourteous; we are on our way to Paris. This will be a sufficient excuse for our brief visit.'

The moment these words had escaped him, he felt he had betrayed himself.

Scornful exultation faintly portrayed itself upon the visage of Landois at that moment, while an expression of the Duke's seconded his suspicion. A rapid dialogue passed between them in the Italian tongue. The grand favourite then made his exit, and did not return for some time. During that interval, the Duke became more affable, conversed upon the topics of the day, and, save England, all foreign powers were touched upon. He led his guests into a noble saloon, where refreshments were served up to them in great state, and the time was passed until Landois's re-appearance, in company with another of the Duke's favourites, Lescun, whose presence was as forbidding as that of the minister Landois himself, but who had not, like the latter, touched a bribe from the King of England.

Ill at ease, the Lancastrian nobles rose to take their departure. The Duke bowed with great courtesy, and said in good English,—

'Gentlemen, at the gates my mandate awaits you.'

Lost in conjecture, Pembroke and his nephew strode hastily down the long corridor, at the termination of which, they were surrounded by the Duke's serfs; these immediately presented them with a scroll of paper, having the Duke's signature and seal attached. To Pembroke's surprise, it contained an order that they were not to cross the borders of the dukedom; but to remain at Vannes, where they would enjoy the comforts and luxuries of an establishment suited to their rank and station. Should they attempt to evade that mandate, they were threatened with imprisonment.

Thus they were kept in a kind of honourable custody. Pembroke thought of returning at once to the Duke, and upbraiding him with his inhospitable conduct. Upon mature consideration, he forbore, and permitted himself to be attended by the Duke's guards as far as the village, where they proposed remaining for the night.

'Had I but listened to Kynfin Tudor,' said Pembroke, bitterly; 'see, Henry, how we have been requited!—Edward of York is the author of this insult.'

As he alighted from his saddle, and was about to enter the

inn, Kynfin ap Dafydd appeared in the doorway. He had been uneasy about them, had followed their footsteps from the fishing village, and had only now to learn the latest misfortune, which had befallen the last of the Lancastrians.

CHAPTER XVIII

A Foreign Home—The Conspiracy— The Plotters Defeated—A Leave-taking

BUT a few days passed before the Duke of Brittany sent an escort to conduct the exiles to Vannes. A residence had been prepared for their reception. Kynfin accompanied them. In the most painful state of reflection on the future, they travelled in profound silence.

On approaching Vannes, they were received by the inhabitants with cordiality, a gratifying circumstance to the Earl of Pembroke and his nephew, as it removed from their minds much reasonable apprehension. 'Happiness, or at least tranquillity, may be yet in store for us,' flashed across Jasper Tudor's mind, as he resolved that he would reconcile himself to his fate.

Several months passed after they had settled in their foreign home. Kynfin was considered of the household. His singularity rather increased than diminished. He spent whole days upon the ocean, greatly to the Earl of Pembroke's anxiety, who felt occasionally something like disappointment in the son of Harlech. He had watched an opportunity to speak to him in private, but was unsuccessful, until one evening he found him upon the beach alone, when he addressed him:

'Well, worthy kinsman, ever solitary and disconsolate, of late you have avoided me.—What has wrought this change?'

'I have much upon my mind, Jasper of Hatfield. Think not, for a moment, that I am changed towards you, my kind and generous friend.' This was uttered with deep pathos.

'If you were less reserved, and more confiding in your friends, you would be happier, Kynfin,' replied the Earl, in a kind tone of voice. 'I own that of late there have been many circumstances which have created suspicion in others, and caused me anxiety.'

Kynfin sighed—Pembroke continued:

'I have watched you going more than once to yonder vessel, at her moorings. It is a privateer, I imagine?'

'It is,' replied the son of Harlech, rashly. 'I have on board her, some good friends.'

'Friends!' repeated the Earl, with a look of astonishment; 'I should have deemed you the last individual with whom I am acquainted, who would have held communication with such lawless people?'

'It is so,' replied Kynfin Tudor, colouring. He then drew the Earl's arm within his own, directing their footsteps towards the rocks, where they would be screened from observation. He was well aware they were watched.

'Kynfin,' said the Earl, looking earnestly at him; 'mystery tinctures all your actions. It would require supernatural power to unravel the intricacies of such a mind. Tell me what you apprehend—who is watching us? You are fanciful.'

'I would it were so, and that I could say there was no danger.'

'Danger,' repeated the Earl; 'what mean you, Kynfin?'

'Imminent danger,' replied Kynfin; 'I have long had suspicion, but not till lately have I been able to discover that there is a conspiracy against your life, and that of your nephew. Edward of York, your old enemy, is again at his intrigues.'

'Is Francis of Brittany in league with him?' demanded the Earl, with increasing anxiety.

'No! We must do the Duke justice, of acquitting him of any share in so base a plot. Edward is too sensible of this disgrace; any scheme against your life would reflect upon him in the sight of the Duke. He does not deem his ground secure there. He is afraid of the Duke turning against him, and he is cautious, though thirsting still for the blood of the Lancastrians. But he does not the less labour to gratify his vengeance, violating sound policy. I am not suspected, good Earl of Pembroke, therefore it is easier for me to acquire information of what is plotting.'

'An enviable position is ours,' remarked the Earl; 'tell me the particulars of this conspiracy, and how you made the discovery?'

'You have heard me speak of *la petite* Jacqueline, Jasper of Hatfield, and you have seen the child once.'

'Yes, I remember, methinks *la petite enfant* has a strange hold upon your affection. This is not the first time you have mentioned her name to me.'

'I am fond of children,' said Kynfin, with a smile passing over his features, not unmingled with sadness. 'It is true, I own, it may appear strange that the little innocent possesses such an influence over my feelings; in confidence I impart it, she is the only one to whom I speak of my sorrow. Her sympathy is sweet, she is an angel monitor. Her innocent ways repel demon thoughts, at least for a time. Tell me not of gloomy monks, of repenting saints, of cunning priests; they have never conferred upon me half the benefit that this innocent child has worked for me. I will tell you how she is connected with my unravelling the existence of a plot, which concerns us all so deeply. One Jean de Groits, a confederate of the minister Landois, is to be a chief actor in the project with the child's uncle. *La petite* happening to hear him and the others talking over their plan, which included ourselves, she, though only half comprehending what she heard, became alarmed on my account, and in the most artless manner related it to me. She mentioned that they were only waiting an opportunity to murder you, and talked of throwing your bodies into the sea. She said she was afraid her father had some connection with the conspiracy, which made her unhappy. He was her only parent, and she was sure if he were concerned, it was to oblige her wicked uncle, her dislike of whom, for his malicious character, she always declared. When she lost her mother, he told her she might soon get another as good. "How cruel," said the poor child, "I hated him from that day." To relate the many incidents which happened in tracing out the design of our enemies, would occupy too much time. After meeting several of the conspirators at Louis Agustine's house, I repeatedly followed, the ruffians unseen, to the rendezvous in the outskirts of the town, and overheard their unguarded remarks. Repeatedly heard them dispute, and regret they had taken Louis Agustine into their confidence. Landois's name was frequently mentioned in connection with their plans. More than once, Jasper of Hatfield, that man himself, in disguise, I have seen among the conspirators. The main point with them, was to keep the secret of their intermeddling in the murder from Duke Francis. You may ask why I did not earlier acquaint you with these circumstances. I reply that as long as there remained an uncertainty with regard to securing and defeating their villainy, it was impolitic. The tables are now about to be turned. At a certain hour tonight, they hope to accomplish their atrocious deed, therefore keep at home. Go not to the banquet in the city, where you are expected. Snares are laid for the assassins; they will be foiled. The vessel, as I said, contains friends, countrymen of my own. The captain and his officers are gentlemen of good family, who before the time of the late troubles, possessed lands and property to a large amount. Since then, they have been deprived of their estates by the Yorkists, and expatriated. They have found a home upon the seas. They have taken to roam the ocean in order to live, and stand at bay with virtue to evade want. Habit has somewhat degenerated them, I own, but they still support the cause of Lancaster, whenever opportunity occurs. They are no shuffling renegades from a noble cause. I know their leader; I knew him in better times, opulent and honest. He has invited me to join them on the condition of rendering me assistance to defeat the emissaries of Edward. Jasper of Hatfield, your look distresses me. I cannot recall my words— the promise was given; the conditions are signed. I depart before the recession of another tide; and with me two of the conspirators of Edward shall be carried off, bound hand and foot. In the hold of that bark, the *Eryr*, they shall repent in irons of their foul design. In her course, a wanderer over the waste of waters, I shall be borne from those whose memory will be dear to me, with the consolation that I have not ineffectually served them.'

'You will not leave us, Kynfin?' said the Earl of Pembroke, greatly agitated. 'There can be no necessity for your joining the pirates on our account. I have treasure; I will ransom you. Remain with your friend Jasper, for his sake remain, if from no other motive.'

Kynfin refused to listen to the entreaties of his friend.

The Earl proposed that the villain should be at once seized. It was clear the Duke Francis had no concern in the atrocious affair. He would order condign punishment upon its authors. His favourite Landois should be exposed.

'That man carries dangerous weapons, Jasper of Hatfield; whoever crosses his designs, though unawares, will have to suffer bitterly all that unsparing vengeance can inflict. I have made a promise to *la petite* not to expose her father. Louis Agustine would, in the event of my discovering the plot, be brought to shame, and to public execution. I should never forgive myself. Therefore, let me keep my peace of mind, I pray you. I have bound you to secrecy; you will honourably keep it, I know. What I have arranged must not be undone. I have not time to enter into all the windings and turnings of this intricate affair—it would now be a valueless narration. Let me assure you I have acted with pure devotion to our common cause. We may meet again, my good friend, under happier auspices. The step I have taken will not condemn me in your eyes at least. Bear in mind that I seek not a pirate's life from choice, but an overwhelming necessity.'

Kynfin was seen afterwards scaling the rocks, having left his companion to pursue his way back across the sands alone. He then repaired to pay his hurried farewell to his little friend.

A gentle knock at Louis Agustine's spacious saloon entrance, caused the agile Jacqueline to spring forward to the door, to receive the well-known visitor.

'Oh, Monsieur Kynfin, I am so happy you are come! What made you so late?' exclaimed the child, taking him by the hand, and leading him up to her father, who was seated at a small table, with some wine, bread, and fruit before him.

Looking up into Kynfin's sorrowful countenance, she

assayed a guess at what was passing in his mind, but it was a vain conjecture.

'I am come to take leave of my little friend, and of Monsieur Agustine,' said Kynfin, seating himself, and placing the child upon his knee.

'What! Monsieur,' cried Louis, 'are you going away from Vannes? Wherefore?' he eagerly inquired, and his face grew at once pale and anxious.

'Urgent circumstances call me, or, rather, send me away,' replied Kynfin, fixing his gaze steadily upon that of Agustine, who cast down his eyes and looked every moment more confused.

'Go into the garden, Jacqueline, *ma petite*,' whispered Kynfin. 'I will seek you there presently. I must talk to your father in private.'

Scarcely had the door closed, when the son of Harlech turned to address his companion:—

'Louis Agustine, you can half imagine my reason for quitting Vannes thus hastily, after what I mentioned to you yesterday. You can half guess that I know you to be a confederate in this conspiracy against the lives of the two English Earls, who took refuge in your country, relying upon an hospitality which you intend to violate. You know all the vile concoctors of this base plot—you have aided and abetted them. You know as well that you have been acting contrary to the honour of the Duke, your ruler and governor. You are aware that Duke Francis issued an edict to the effect that, should anyone in his Dukedom injure either of the noble English refugees, he should be punished according to the strict laws of Brittany. You know, Monsieur Agustine, you and your brother have been in correspondence with Edward of England;

and Landois, the Duke's minister, is at the bottom of all. Tempted by bribes to enter into a conspiracy, and finally become a foul assassin, you would sacrifice my friends and companions in exile, and you would destroy your own soul for a little paltry gold. Attempt no justification of what admits not of extenuation. I am in possession of letters which have passed between you and the degraded agents of Edward of York. I have discovered the secret of your plot. Tremble, flagitious man! you may well tremble! My whisper would at this moment place the axe of the executioner over your neck, and send you, with your accomplices, to share the reward of the first murderer!'

Louis Agustine felt a chill come upon his heart; for a moment he became paralyzed; then he fell upon his knees, and in abject terror implored mercy.

Kynfin's excitement cooled, when Jacqueline's innocent voice sounded from the garden. The man before him was that child's only parent. His contempt and indignation were in an instant exchanged for pity.

'I did not come here,' Kynfin continued, 'for the sole purpose of upbraiding you. I came to hear a confession of penitence, and then to part friends.'

Kynfin here took two or three turns up and down the room, as if to restore his self-possession, and proceeded:—

'Though it is in my power to bring you to condign punishment, I shall not do so. I feel that you are not bad by nature, but too apt to err at the solicitation of others, rather than from your own impulses. Remain here unsuspected, and regarded as before by the citizens. Let my words prove a salutary warning. None shall know of your guilt. In return, Monsieur, I demand that you enter into no more degrading negotiations for the committal of foul offences, nor into more conspiracies against unfortunate exiled nobles, and, if not an earnest friend to my noble kinsmen, that you prove in their behalf a man of uprightness and virtue—that you will warn them against any danger which you may know is impending over their heads—and I shall be recompensed for my forbearance towards you.'

The Frenchman, spare of person, and not of an ill disposition by nature, felt for a moment unable to rise from his kneeling posture, so much was he agitated. He felt his guilt. He acknowledged Kynfin's forbearance, and, sincerely repenting, would have blessed the son of Harlech, could he have uttered assurances of which his quivering tongue refused to articulate a syllable.

'I have parted good friends with your father, Jacqueline, *ma petite*, now I have come to look at you and speak to you for the last time,' said Kynfin, as he entered the garden.

'These are cruel words, Monsieur Kynfin,' said the child, as she presented him with a garland of flowers for a keepsake. 'If you had not told me that you were going away to do some good, I should never again be happy. What shall I do when you are gone, dear, kind Monsieur Kynfin? No one will speak to me of England, your beautiful country, of which I do love to hear; and do you know why, Monsieur?'

'Because, Jacqueline, you lived there when you were a very little girl.'

'It was my mother's native land. All that belonged to her remains dear to me. But, Kynfin Tudor, you are going away from me, and I have so many things to say I can remember none. Tell me when you will come back to Vannes? The days will be weary when you are gone. Do not say that you will never more come to cheer me. I shall wander about the garden alone, and often repeat your name there—yes, a thousand times. I shall whisper to my flowers how unhappy I am. Why do you leave us? Why make me so unhappy?'

She then threw her arms around his neck, and placed her lips to his. Her little heart beat convulsively, and tears started into her eyes.

'You must not weep in this way, my Jacqueline bach. You make our parting still more sad.'

Kynfin pressed the child affectionately to his breast, and then whispered in her ear:—

'You know, Jacqueline, *ma petite*, that it is to save your father, I leave this sunny land. I promised his safety should be secured. Go and comfort him. He is unhappy. Teach him, as you have taught me, to know from what source comfort may be had.'

Once more the son of Harlech kissed the child, telling her that the hour was approaching, and he dared not remain longer.

Farewells were repeated again and again. Kynfin then turned hurriedly from the flower-garden, bounded down a flight of steps which led directly to the seashore, and looked across the bay to discover if anyone was yet moving on board the '*Eryr* bach'. The jolly-boat at that moment was in the act of being lowered. Shortly after, she pushed off, manned by some of the *Eryr*'s fearless crew. The son of Harlech gave a shrill whistle, which brought them to the spot where he stood.

'Good luck to tricking the Frenchmen!—good luck!' repeated each voice, as they stepped upon the shore. Two of the crew remained in the boat, while the rest accompanied Kynfin Tudor through the outskirts of the town, till they gained the spot where the assassins were to pass on their murderous errand.

Night was over the streets that had become wholly deserted. The pirates watched for their prey with increasing anxiety. At length the unsuspicious wretches made their appearance, and were at once easily overpowered by the strong hands of the sea-rovers, who gagged and bound them almost before they could recover from their amazement. Thus were the men secured, dragged into the boat, and without the smallest disturbance in either the town or neighbourhood, embarked in the freebooters' vessel, to be conveyed to a far-distant land, from whence return was hopeless.

The white sails of the *Eryr* were loosened, and she flew along like a swallow on the wings of the wind. The French coast soon faded in the horizon, and the home of Ap Dafydd was now the pirate's bark.

END OF VOL. I

VOL. II

CHAPTER I

A Youthful Captive—Juvenile Patriotism—Family Fears Alleviated

CLOUDS were gathering thick upon the hills, a drizzling rain was falling, which at times driven along by the gale through the narrow passes, abounding in the vicinity of Cwm Bychan, almost blinded Sir Gilbert Stacey and his companions, as they were returning from the chase to Harlech Castle, Edward of York having some time before appointed that Knight the keeper of the fortress, not long after its ancient chieftain and his family had been driven from the walls.

The rain soon became doubly disagreeable to sportsmen weary with fatigue. Slipping at every step, the fog becoming every moment more dense, and fearing to be bewildered, they were ready to abandon the idea of reaching their destination that night, could they but discover any kind of shelter.

'Marry! I would give a king's ransom if we could find a cottage, or even a shed,' cried Sir Gilbert. 'I fear we shall lose ourselves in this accursed fog; and it won't be the first time either, since I came into this uncivilized land. Spear me, if it were not for a fine buck now and then, I would see these outlandish, heathenish places at the devil, before I would set my foot in them again. Curse the stones! I shall break my neck,' exclaimed Sir Gilbert, loudly and pettishly, while he halted for the fiftieth time to recover a false step.

His companions, who were a little in advance, simply responded by a loud laugh, and throwing themselves down amongst the heath on the side of the path, awaited his arrival patiently.

The moment Sir Gilbert joined them, he declared he would go no further, and immediately sent off some of the younger of the party in search of a shelter.

Scarcely had they taken their departure, when a light footstep coming down some rude stone steps, a little distance from Cader y Cil, attracted their attention. The figure of a little maiden, with flowing locks of raven hue, appeared bounding along with deer-like agility, until she suddenly halted at a mass of rock, just opposite where the Saxons had seated themselves.

Surprised at the sight of the strangers, she cast at them a hasty and searching glance from her brilliant eyes, and then bounded up the steps again, without uttering a word.

Sir Gilbert called to the child, and entreated her to stop; but the fairy-like form had vanished. Two esquires, at the Knight's request, set off in her pursuit. Even the exhausted keeper rose, and put himself on the look-out, muttering:

'We are near a habitation, no doubt; we have only to secure the frightened child, and we shall be housed for the night.'

At length, after searching in every direction, they were returning to Sir Gilbert, when the little creature was discovered behind a shelving rock. She had concealed herself there, in hopes her pursuers would pass without observing her.

The noisy exclamation which proceeded from the Saxon strangers on the discovery, thrilled through the child's frame. Scarcely knowing what she did, she placed herself in a defensive attitude, ridiculously enough. In the interim, Sir

Gilbert and his party came up, and though they pressed round her, she kept the same bold front.

'Out upon you! Little saucy wench; what makes you show so formidable? We have no wish to hurt you,' said one of the party, approaching to take her by the hand.

'You shall not touch me,' cried the child, clinging close to the cliff, and holding up a knotted stick, which she shook in a menacing manner; while she repeated in good English:

'You Saxons shall not touch me; you have no right to come here and disturb my happy glen; you have no right to shoot my red deer. Away with you—you shall not touch one, you Saxons!'

'Marry! Who told you, my saucy little lass—who told you, my little minx, that we had no right to follow the chase here? I should like to know that,' observed Sir Gilbert, arriving just in time to hear the last two sentences.

'I tell you!' replied the child, looking extremely indignant; 'you are cruel-hearted Saxons. I won't tell you anything.'

'There is fire; there is spirit for you!' said one of the esquires, moving a few steps from the child, and joining the rest of his companions in a hearty laugh.

Sir Gilbert alone declared it was no laughing matter, standing in the wind and rain, and night coming on rapidly.

'Seize that child!' he cried. 'Depend upon it she belongs to the freebooters who have made such havoc among my black cattle. None but a freebooter's brat would act in this way. Secure her!'

'That is if we can catch the wild cat, Sir Knight,' said several voices present, laughing immoderately, and approaching the child.

'Come, no more of this nonsense,' resumed the Keeper, with increasing impatience. 'I tell you what, little minx—

conduct us to a dwelling where we can find accommodation for the night, or we will take you a prisoner to Harlech.'

'I won't conduct you anywhere,' replied the child, with a look of scorn, rather than fear. 'There are no dwellings here for Saxon Yorkists; no, no, none for them; I know of none.'

'Beshrew me! You obstinate minx, you shall suffer for this. Bring her along,' cried Sir Gilbert, in an ill humour; and he began his return homeward.

The child could make no further resistance. They kept her prisoner, and with a strong girdle attached round her waist, she was led along by Henry Stourton, Sir Gilbert's nephew. They proceeded till they were joined by young Stacey and his party, who had been seeking in vain for a shelter in which to pass the night.

'Confound the fog! I have lost my black terrier,' exclaimed Stacey, the moment he reached his companions. 'I have been whistling and hooting for the last hour, and all to no purpose. What are all you jabbering about?—what a nice little lass!— Where did you pick her up?'

'You have lost a little fun in her capture,' said one of the party, who gave Stacey the particulars.

'What are you going to do with her?' he demanded.

'Take the little wench to the castle. She is one of the freebooters' children. You know they have done us more harm than good,' rejoined Sir Gilbert.

At every step the wind and rain increased. It was with difficulty they kept the right path, and long after midnight when they reached Harlech.

During their journey over the bleak hills, little Gladys, who was in reality the captive child, was silent and dejected about her grandmother. She thought how she would be distracted at her absence, and how poor Howel and Katherine would be wandering over the rocks in search of her, and return in despair. She thought of trying to escape, and how joyful would be the meeting with her grandmother. While she was thus occupied in thought, the party and their prisoner stood before the portal of Harlech.

'My honoured Sir Gilbert, what has been the matter; what has detained you?' cried Lady Stacey, hastening to meet them as they entered the hall.

'Nothing serious, mother,' replied young Stacey; 'we strayed rather further than usual, and were overtaken by the mist. We have brought something for you, mother—something from the mountains.'

Here he pushed little Gladys forward.

In mute astonishment the poor child glanced around her. The doors were closed, a large, blazing fire illuminated the hall of her ancestors. The same old tapestry, as before, hung upon the walls: even some of the rude carved furniture was familiar to her. But then where was Ap Jevan? Where was her mother, her grandmother, her uncle, Kynfin? They were all once there. Now she was there alone, among Saxon Yorkists. Strange voices were in her ears; strange faces around her. She saw and heard it all, and stood in the midst of her enemies, as if unconscious of their scrutinizing gaze.

'Who are your parents?' inquired Maud Stacey, with some curiosity.

Gladys made no reply. Again she was importuned by questions.

'Y Saison! Y Saison!' repeated she, with strong emphasis; then springing across the apartment, she hid herself in one of the recesses in the wall.

'What a strange little creature,' remarked Maud; 'are you

sure, father, that you have not got hold of some mountain idiot? What do you think we can do with such a nonentity? Why did you bring her here?'

'Don't weary me with questions; I want my supper,' answered Sir Gilbert. 'Leave the child alone. We will have at her presently, and she shall be made to confess who stole Sir Gilbert Stacey's black cattle.'

'What! Does she belong to some of those barbarous people?'

'Aye, I believe you, or she would not have been here now,' said the Knight, as he raised a goblet of ale to his parched lips; and then taking his seat at the board, helped himself bountifully to the smoking dish of venison before him.

'I never felt so hungry, weary, and thirsty, in my life, mother,' said young Stacey, securing a place by her side; 'you have no idea how wretched and comfortless we have been all day.'

'Yes, I have,' said Lady Stacey, smiling, 'for it has been wretched enough here. That poor child, what is to be done with her? She must be as hungry as you are.'

Stacey immediately rose, and after some reluctance on the part of the child, she was placed at the table.

Everyone, as they sat round the good cheer, appeared happy and contented, save the hapless mountain girl, whose food remained untouched before her, while her dark blue eyes wandered from one strange face to another, with an expression not to be misunderstood.

Maud began examining the child's dress, and observed to her mother that it was of no common texture.

'See here, father, if she has not got the Lancastrian badge,' pointing to a silver swan, which fastened the kerchief round her neck. 'How came a freebooter's child by this?'

'Best known to herself,' remarked Sir Gilbert: 'if not by

fair, by foul means.' He then turned toward Gladys, who had become the object of general attraction.

'What a commanding and singular expression she has,' observed Henry Stourton to his companion; 'there is much incipient intellect concealed under those long lashes, and that spacious forehead; she is a little beauty too!'

'There is no disputing that, but she bears signs of becoming a very haughty one,' replied his companion.

'We ought to make some allowances for her position,' rejoined the charitable Henry Stourton.

When the sportsmen had made a hasty repast, they withdrew to their respective chambers, having unanimously agreed that the examination of the captive child should be deferred until the morrow.

When Gladys found herself alone in her chamber, she fell upon her knees, buried her face in her hands, and wept. She thought of those in the Cwm, what a night they would pass, and all from her own folly. Had she but spoken more guardedly and less feelingly, she might still have been by the side of her dear grandmother. These thoughts tended to increase her palpitation, and make her still more pained to be absent from Cader y Cil. She at length fell asleep from exhaustion, and did not awake till summoned before Sir Gilbert, at a late hour, on the following morning.

'I hope the fire of yesterday has been damped, young minx. I shall have, I trust, a more reasonable child to deal with today,' said the keeper.

'Let me impress upon you, little one, that upon your answers to my questions your fate depends. If you are not the child of a freebooter, you know who stole my black cattle—you cannot deny it.'

'I cannot tell you,' said Gladys in a calm tone, 'I cannot utter a word to injure my own people. If the Saxons encroach upon our land, they must expect such things.'

'You had better take care, young one, and not speak thus boldly,' said her interrogator, evidently surprised at the mountain girl's good address. 'Is your father a Lancastrian?'

'Our private history is our own secret,' replied Gladys, mournfully.

'Well, well, we won't hamper about that; all I want to know is about these confounded freebooters, who have been persecuting me ever since I came into the country. If you will only tell me, my little wench, the honest truth, you shall return to your home laden with presents from Mistress Stacey, and all the rest of the family here.'

'No,' replied Gladys, 'I would not accept a present from a Saxon and a Yorkist.'

'How dare you use these insinuations against the Saxons? I ask once more, who was the leader of those who stole my black cattle? At your peril, refuse to answer me,' cried Sir Gilbert, with an angry gesture.

A haughty expression passed over Gladys's face, and yet her answer was in a soft and gentle tone:—

'No, Saxon knight, you may use threats if you please, but I will not betray my people. I am not afraid of anyone, as long as I know I am doing right.'

'Singe a Jew! if this is to be borne,' cried the keeper, in a frenzy of passion; 'and from one so young, too. I have not done with you yet, you pert minx. You shall be stretched upon the rack, and made to tell. If civil words won't do—on the rack, yes, on the rack, you obstinacious little fool!' and he started up, and dragged the child across the hall.

'No, no, Sir Gilbert, this must not be!' cried Lady Stacey, flying to the child's rescue with her maternal feeling in her heart. 'What, my honoured sir! put so tender a frame in irons, in torture—no, I will not permit such barbarity. It would disgrace us for life.'

'Very well, madam,' replied Sir Gilbert, white with rage; 'if the rack is done away with, why, then, do away with our holy religion! Dreadful innovations on time-honoured customs. Well, if it shall not be the rack, it shall be the dungeon. Interfere in that, at your peril. I am determined I will know who stole my black cattle.'

Lady Stacey, with her usual tact, said no more. He had been so repeatedly annoyed by the mountain horde that it was always a sore point to touch. He was now more than usually nettled. Lady Stacey pressed Gladys's hand tenderly; and as the gaoler disappeared with the little captive, she could not refrain from tears.

The mountain child was conducted to a comfortless apartment, where scarce a loop-hole let in a ray of light. Never till now did she feel the hopelessness of her situation. The outer gate grated on its hinges; she heard it close and shut her out from all that was dear to her upon earth. The national hatred against her Saxon neighbours was increased. She lifted up her voice in piteous wailing; it was unheard save by an echo from the neighbouring cell. She shrieked, and with the weariness of her grief sank to sleep at last, in her cheerless abode, a prisoner within the walls which justice called her own. Here Gladys, poor girl, passed many weary nights.

The evening when Gladys disappeared from the Cwm was never to be forgotten there. From the setting sun to the rising day, faithful Howel and his wife were upon the hills seeking for her.

Ap Jevan's widow paced from room to room in agony of mind, calling upon the name of her 'wyres bach'. The words vibrated along the lone walls of Cader y Cil, and left her more disconsolate than before. Katherine returned in the morning with no intelligence of her mistress bach. Howel collected some of his neighbours, and went once more up the glen, in another direction, on the same enquiry.

'Someone has been here,' said Howel, examining the ground. 'Listen! I thought I heard a sound.'

A piteous moaning of some animal in distress immediately drew their attention to the spot, where a little black terrier was discovered wedged in between the rocks. The creature had fallen from the height above, and one of its legs was broken.

'Dyn anwyl! Why, this belongs to the Saxon knight,' said one of the men. 'Depend upon it, they were here last night, and have carried away our mistress bach.'

'I will find that out,' said Howel. Taking the animal under his arm, he set out at once, buoyed up by the hope of discovering the child. Howel was a man not to be daunted. By much manoeuvring, he got admitted into the castle, and gained the desired information, with which he returned to Cader y Cil.

Distressed as all were there, it was a satisfaction to know that the child was safe. She had neither been drowned in the lake, fallen over a precipice, nor been gored to death by a stag. These reflections were consolatory. For a time they lessened their grief by planning a thousand stratagems for the restoration of the wyres bach. One was no sooner formed, than it was rejected for another, and that in its turn gave place to one which shared a like fate. It is fortunate for humanity that shadowy consolations will so often lighten substantial misery.

CHAPTER II

A Contrabandist—The Weird Lady— The Incantation—Superstitious Dupes

'DYN anwyl! Shonyn! there is a vessel in the bay. I can't say any how I like the cut of her gib, I believe she comes from the French coast, but she is not our sort, that's as clear as a herring.'

Thus spoke the hoarse voice of a short, square-built sailor, as he entered a smuggler's cottage upon the beach, and taking off his wet jacket, threw it over a barrel before the fire to dry.

'Well now, did not I tell you, Morgan, that we were a set of fools to let our men be off before our kegs were safe stowed away among the hills,' said his companion sullenly; 'mewn gwirionedd! if you ever catch me talked over again. She is a revenue shark, I'll be bound, and a nice glory hole we are in.'

'Yn enw'r Brenhin! I am vexing in my heart about it,' responded Morgan, sorrowfully. 'I only wish the kegs were two hundred miles from this spot, and then I would say Shonyn Goch. I would not care a cockle for any one of them sharp-toothed gentry—but what is to be done? We shall be nabbed.'

'Mewn gwirionedd! if I'll be nabbed,' said Shonyn, starting up with a grim smile; then moving to the entrance, he placed a strong bar across the door. On returning to his seat, he eyed his comrade for a few minutes in silence, and turning to a young female who was busily engaged at the further end of the room, he exclaimed with sharpness:—

'Peggy, girl, don't be shifting about there, but serve up our supper. We want to be off.'

'Yn enw Tad! What's in the wind now?' exclaimed Morgan. 'Shonyn, you are not going to cut and run, and leave the kegs?'

'Twt, nonsense! Do you think the smuggler of Madoc, bold Shonyn Goch, would do that?—not he. I'll tell you what I am about to do—I am going to pay the Dewines[11] of Gêst a visit. She will set our heads above water, if we only promise the old lady a keg of the best spirits.'

'Dyn anwyl,' ejaculated his companion, 'you had better not count upon that. Should she be in one of her dark humours, she will not have the civility even to admit you.'

'Twt, twt, nonsense! I know better than that. Whenever I propose anything, Morgan, you are sure to douse the glim, and make it all pitch colour; you'd better send us clean overboard at once.'

'Well, well! Shonyn, my lad, don't lose temper, I don't want to quarrel,' replied his companion, soothingly. 'Let us drink to our success, and you, Peggy bach, will too, won't you, girl?' added he, holding the cup to the young woman's lips.

'No, no, Morgan! It would not come from my heart if I did,' said Peggy, hastily pushing the mug from her. 'No good will come from getting the Dewines to hoist up her curse upon the strange vessel.'

'O'r beth wirion! Why, what is the matter with the girl?' cried the sailor, much surprised.

'She is a fool, gone mad, and if she repeats that again, I will

---

11   The witch or prophetess.

cut her tongue out of her head,' retorted the smuggler, with much irritation.

Morgan smiled, the girl remained perfectly still, as if she had been too long accustomed to abusive language, to take any notice of the insult. Shortly afterwards, Shonyn and his companion quitted the cottage for the house of Gêst.

Shonyn was out of humour. They walked on in silence till they reached the knoll which brought them in full view of the picturesque creek of Borth, where the strong and commodious mansion in which the Dewines resided was situated.

'Why, the old lady is illuminated,' cried Morgan, stopping to take breath, and fixing his eyes upon the stream of light which shone from several windows, again reflected in the fast advancing tide. 'I guess she has company.'

'Come on, come on,' said Shonyn, impatiently; 'if she has, it is of no consequence. I will see her, anyhow.'

'You have never seen her, lad,' inquired his companion, 'have you?' placing his hand familiarly on his friend's shoulder.

'No,' replied his comrade, moodily. Again they pursued their way, both relapsing into silence, till they reached the steps leading to the entrance of the ominous habitation, when Shonyn suddenly addressed his companion:—

'I have been thinking, Morgan, you had better remain here. She is a ticklish creature to manage. One of us will be enough for her at a time. You may rest assured, I'll lay on the tallow, and do the uttermost to make all run smooth.'

Morgan was more pleased than otherwise at this arrangement, and accordingly waited outside while Shonyn hastened up the steps, and knocked for admittance. Several times he knocked before the door was flung rudely open, and then closed immediately on the smuggler of Madoc.

After some awkward explanation with regard to the purport of his visit, the far-famed Dewines of Gêst thus harangued her unwelcome visitor:—

'What! You blind beetle, you think, do you, like all the rest of your scrubby, cowardly tribe, that by fat rewards and wheedling, you can turn the Lady of Gêst round your finger, as you would an eel, ha! ha! Let me tell you that you are mistaken, you shall not fling a custard in my face. What care I for your kegs of extra fine spirits. Aha! You may well turn pale, master smuggler, the Lady of Gêst has enough already to sail your sloop in, and drown yourself. She will do this if you give her more of your flattering words, you trembling caitiff. Whist! whist! have a care, I say, lest, before you look me in the face, I send you headlong into the devil's dominions.'

Shonyn hastily rose, and, putting his cap over his death-like features, began mechanically to move towards the door, hoping to make a stealthy exit.

The witch saw his object, and immediately exclaimed, 'So, ho! blind beetle, you would escape like a terrified fly from a spider. The web has caught you; try the latch, master Madoc.' As she concluded these words, she started from off her stool with a wild gesture, and laughed louder than before: 'So, ho! here is a wedding, it seems, between an ass's mouth and a bundle of thistles.' Then, stretching herself upwards to her full height, which was nearly five feet eleven, she pushed her cap from her forehead, and throwing down two sticks crosswise upon the floor, began dancing with the agility of a girl in her teens, cutting capers in the air and screaming with strange delight at her own wonderful achievements.

Never had Shonyn Goch been so awe-stricken in his life.

The peculiarly wild expression of her large, yet acute features, were now rendered perfectly hideous by long straggling grey hairs, which had broken loose and were waving and shaking in all directions over her gaunt boney shoulders. The green fire of her widely expanded eyes, gleamed through her locks, her nostrils dilated, her parchment skin wrinkled and grew more sallow as her excitement increased. Her thin long frame terminated in spindle legs, ornamented with yellow clocks upon red hose, exposed as far as the knee, added still more to the singularity of her appearance.

Poor Madoc! Minutes were hours as he stood with his eyes riveted upon the supernatural female dancing before him, and declaiming in words of which he could not guess the import. Every muscle in his face seemed to quiver to each step she took, and a thousand resolutions were internally forming at the same time that should the ogress permit him to leave her dwelling, he would never again cross her threshold, or knowingly come within two hundred cable-lengths of her house. Still the Lady of Gêst danced on and on. The poor wretched man standing in the same petrified position, endeavouring to prevent his teeth from chattering in vain, and his knees from knocking together. He called to his recollection the number of bloody fights and cruel scenes to which he had been privy from his youth; but none, frightful and appalling as they might have been, had caused him the terror that this witch of Gêst inspired. She must, he thought, be a genuine daughter of hell. He shuddered, turned giddy, became chill and sick, and then sank into a chair, no longer able to preserve his self-control.

'You infant, you trembling coward,' cried the Lady of Gêst, suddenly desisting from her amusement, and striding up to the spot where the smuggler sat: 'We have had enough of each other,' she screamed, and immediately seizing him by the arms under the magic of terror, which she had inspired, pinioned them to his side. She then pushed him along the passage, shouting in his ears:—

'Go fool! else shall the mandrake's shriek
Startle thy brain so soft and weak!
I'll kill an infant, hearest thou that!
And rub thy brow with the innocent's fat—
Thou shalt drink from the hollow charnel-house skull,
Where the black cat lapped till her stomach was full.
Of the mad dog's foam, and the owlet's brain,
And drops from the gibbeted murderer's chain.
Mixed with herb-juice that grows on the tomb
Of the wretch self-slain, when his hour had come!—
Away! Or else by my magic I swear
I will bring to torment thee the demon of air,
That shall rend thee, as hell-dogs rend their brood
When tempted to virtue by spirits good:
Dost thou think to cozen one like me?
Avaunt, I will nothing achieve for thee!'

With these concluding words the Dewines hurled him over the steps, slamming the door violently upon its hinges, and the smuggler of Madoc fell prostrate beyond the threshold.

The night had by this time become palpably dark. A low murmuring breeze whistled through the stunted oaks which surrounded the building, and the continued dashing of the waves against the rocks made the spot still more cheerless.

There for some time the smuggler lay, stupefied by his fall, if not by fear. When he at length attempted to rise, he felt like a child. His iron sinews became flaccid, his limbs were palsied. He heard his companion calling to him from the sands, but had no power to reply.

Morgan, guessing something wrong had occurred, hastened to the spot. He was alarmed at finding his companion seated upon the ground, to which posture only he had as yet been able to raise himself. He was almost speechless.

'O Duw anwyl, Shonyn, what has the Dewines done to you?' exclaimed he, stooping down and endeavouring to lift him up.

'Och! take me away, take me away, Morgan gwâs,' muttered the smuggler; 'I would rather be hung than die at this woman's door.'

After some difficulty, Morgan succeeded in moving him from the dreaded precincts.

Scarcely half an hour had passed away, when a boat under full sail rounded the point, and was making for the creek. The crew landed just below the house of Gêst. Six rough-looking fellows leaped out of her, and immediately ran up the steps of the mansion as if they had been long accustomed to do so.

'Mother, good mother,' repeated the foremost of the figures, drawing his fingers across the window, 'recall what you last said, I am sorry for what has passed. You would not have Dhu ap Rhys and his brave men perish. We have stretched a long arm to gain the house of Gêst tonight. Let us in, pray let us in, good mother?'

'What, is it you, Dhu, my own brave boy himself?' eagerly responded the witch, drawing back the huge bolts and throwing the door open.

'However you have requited me, Ap Rhys, however much

you have pained me, it shall never be said the Lady of Gêst refused to admit the bold Dhu, who made the Yorkists feel his stout hand, who spilled their blood upon the plain, who took the rebels in their own nets, and still lives to annoy them. Welcome, thrice welcome, rover of the seas.' She then held out her sinewy hands to the handsome young man, and conducted him to a seat, while a strange gleam of pleasure flashed across her features as she gazed intently upon his face.

The rest of the party now entered the apartment, and quickly arranged themselves on a long settle, as they were directed.

'Serve the men,' shrieked the hostess. Immediately a dwarfish child, with broad high shoulders and a huge head, made his appearance, and after going backwards and forwards from the kitchen to the apartment where the table stood, several times, laden with dishes, an excellent and plentiful meal was served up.

The men talked among themselves, while Dhu, his mate, and their hostess, scarcely volunteered a remark.

'Mother,' at length exclaimed Dhu, 'have you heard anything of the strange vessel? She is making for this part of the coast, and we expect will be down with the tide in the morning. We are in great trouble about it, mother. Our cargo, as you know, is not yet run in land. What would you recommend us to do? These revenue fellows are not pleasant to deal with.' Dhu hesitated; he perceived the Dewines change colour, as the wildness in her eyes became more remarkable.

'What are you after, boy?' said she, in a stern commanding tone. 'Why do you not speak out plain, instead of beating about the bush? this is unlike you, Dhu.'

'Well, mother, to be honest, I did not know how you would

take it—you remember how I incurred your displeasure last time—but here goes! Mother, you can help us—the knot, the fatal double knot!'

The same thing had been requested by the smuggler of Madoc. She had refused him in the manner which has already been seen. But what could she say now, when Dhu ap Rhys, the commander of the *Eryr* bach, was the supplicator?

'Rovers of the sea, your hearts are of iron, but your heads of self,' muttered the Dewines, as slowly taking the ominous handkerchief from her bosom, she held it up before them.

'Dhu Ap Rhys, I will do what you wish; yet you will be sorry for it.'

In repeating the last sentence, she placed her hand across her brow, and stared full into the face of the melancholy-looking man, who was sitting opposite. His eyes met hers, and an involuntary shudder passed over his frame.

Ap Rhys, struck by the Dewines's strange manner towards his mate, took no notice, but merely asked the Lady of Gêst why she spoke so ominously.

'I shall not satisfy you,' responded the witch, gloomily.

Moving away from him, she sat down upon a low stool, arranging her dishevelled hair. Some minutes afterwards, she again held up the handkerchief, and then exclaimed with a wild gesture:—

'See, Dhu ap Rhys! The deed has not yet been done. Shall it be done?'

'Yes, good mother,' replied the pirate, impatiently.

The handkerchief fell instantly upon her lap; and looking up at them all, she tied the fatal double knot. Then she began humming a low dirge, and continued it at intervals the rest of the evening, much to Dhu's annoyance. He tried in various ways to divert her attention. She would give no heed to him, and at length, rising suddenly, retired to her own apartment.

The men now ranged themselves round the fire for the night, counting upon some hours' rest, when they were suddenly roused by loud blasts of wind, which shook the foundation of the building with its terrible gusts. The feathers and shells, which hung in festoons upon the walls, flapped and rattled. Some old pieces of tapestry swung to and fro, with ceaseless motion; the very chairs appeared to be restless; while there was a mingling of sounds altogether confusing; the moment seemed marked by something unearthly.

Dhu felt strangely uneasy. Starting upon his feet, he endeavoured to compose himself. Then walking up and down the apartment, he discovered that his mate was missing. Astonished at the circumstance, he hastily interrogated his sleeping comrades, who seemed equally as much astounded as their captain.

'He and that confounded woman are in league against me. I know something passed between them. I saw it. Zookers! the fellow could not have got out without her being privy to it. Such bolts! Such locks! Aha! I don't like the look of affairs: bad—decidedly bad! On my soul! Ap Dafydd, I thought you were an honourable man!'

Suspicion was a failing in the rover's character. It was now roused, and not easily quelled. He once more threw himself upon his sheep's-skin pallet, but it was not till break of day that sleep visited his eyes.

While it was yet early, the witch of Gêst strode into the large room. Stooping over the yet slumbering men, she inquired in a sepulchral tone if they had not been disturbed by the wailings of the drowning crew.

'No, good mother, no,' hastily replied Ap Rhys. 'On my soul! it has been a terrific night, enough to awake the dead.'

'What! boy, has no female form appeared to you, nor piteous wailings rung in your ears? I have seen her. I have heard them. The blood of the innocent be upon you!' cried the witch; and a fierce flash from her large eyes made even the daring pirate feel awed.

'The deed was done for you, rover of the seas—done for you,' continued she. 'It will be a blot upon my conscience. It was done for you, Ap Rhys. I would never have wrecked that vessel for another mortal. For you I could die.'

No sooner had she uttered these words than she began shaking the men violently by the shoulders, and screaming at the top of her voice:—

'Whist! Whist! The sun is high. This is no longer a place for you. Rise, sluggards!—begone!'

'But, good lady of Gêst, listen to me,' interposed Dhu ap Rhys.

'No, Dhu, I listened to your voice last night, when to all others I was deaf. Go, ask the smuggler of Madoc of the reception he received at my hands. You could not have treated a Jew or a dog worse than I did that man; and that, too, was done for you. I knew he had injured the commander of the *Eryr*, and was jealous of him—fool as he was—but wits make nooses for themselves, Dhu, ha!'

A flash of deep red mounted into Dhu's face for a moment. He reproached himself for the ill will he had felt towards her, while he exclaimed:—

'Your actions are so mysterious that I do not understand you, mother. What has become of my mate? You assisted him to escape last night.'

'Whist! Whist! Out upon you! Ap Rhys. You doubt my sincerity, ungrateful boy: you take friends for enemies, and enemies for friends. You make much ado about nothing, hot-brained younker! Begone! I say begone! and never come again upon such a mission as you did last night. May your heart be lighter when we next meet. Bear not down on the coast to-day, keep in land, and go stow your lumbering kegs in the hills. Whist! Whist! Think of turns and tides like a man, and be ready for all. Not another word! Commander of the *Eryr*, begone!'

The pirate, followed by his men, with the voice of the Dewines still sounding in their ears, reached the spot where they had on the previous night so securely moored their boat.

'She is gone!' repeated every voice, and each looked at the other in mute astonishment.

Dhu, whose indignation and rage knew no bounds, was the first to break the silence by invoking the hottest vengeance upon the Lady of Gêst. So loud and excited was his voice that it must have reached her ears; and no doubt she laughed long and loud at the rover's superstition and folly.

'Zookers! I have been duped long enough by this accursed woman. I will bear it no longer. I have as good a mind as ever I had in my life to go back and strangle her. Confusion! The devil take her and my mate too! I said they were in league against me—and all under the mask of friendship!'

'Aros, aros, be calm, captain,' said Gam, who was a good-hearted fellow, worthy of a more honest employment than that of a smuggler and a pirate; placing his hand upon his fiery commander's arm, Gam repeated eagerly:—

'Curse not that woman, we shall vex on it. Take patience, take patience, and think on it a little longer; let us go up to the valley, and look after the nags that we may lose no time in running our cargo. The tide will serve in a couple of hours, and we can then bring them up in the sprat boat; see here I have the key the Dewines gave me as I passed out, and she tell me very good, all would go well. "Ie yn wir", ap Rhys, all will go well, I am quite certain; she no go to play the old devil with us, as you talk, no indeed, truth, she, she care too much for you, captain, quite certain, quite certain.'

'Hold, you jabbering idiot,' shouted Dhu, shaking off the hand which retained him. 'Get out of my way, all of you, leave me to myself.'

'To the foot of the rocks, captain,' persisted Gam, with a good-tempered smile. 'If you see on it good, we will go.'

'Aye, go to the devil, if you like, you provoking rascal,' retorted the rover; 'but zookers! mind, carry that hag, witch, Dewines, or whatever you choose to call her, along with you.'

CHAPTER III

A Disaster at Sea—The Rescue— Parental Anxiety Relieved

'LUFF, man, square her yards to the wind, in with the main-sail, double reef the top-sail, set the storm-jib, get her under snug canvas,' roared the hoarse voice of the captain on board the strange vessel, which had caused the smugglers so much alarm.

'Holy St Katherine, how gloomily the miserable land looms in the distance,' muttered a spare sickly-looking Frenchman, addressing the commander; 'is there any chance of our reaching Harlech before morning?'

'Not a hope, we shall have enough to do to keep off the land, with such a sea, and such a coast for a lee-shore,' replied the captain. 'It is a shame that those lubberly Welshmen did not tell me before that the coast was dangerous, and there was a difficulty in procuring a pilot. I would not have run her down here, not I. Deuce take the rascals! There is one satisfaction, they will share our fate, come what may.'

'Holy St Katherine, save us,' murmured the Frenchman, and shrugging up his shoulders, half buried himself in his cloak.

'Santa Maria will help us,' whispered a soft voice in the Frenchman's ear; 'only let us pray, dear father, let us hope we shall yet gain the fortress before the tide turns in the morning.'

'Holy St Katherine! May your words come true, my child,'

cried Louis Agustine, pressing his daughter to his heart; 'but see,' he would have said, as he anxiously looked around, 'those dark black clouds, the shrieking birds, these forerunners, do not look like it?'

Jacqueline saw what was passing in his mind, and remained silently gazing in the direction of the castle, which, with the moon, had suddenly disappeared from their sight. She continued occasionally lifting up her thoughts in prayer, and hoping for the best.

Though the hour was late, and the moon remained invisible from the thickness of the atmosphere, the Frenchman and his daughter stayed upon deck. Nothing would induce them to go below. In mute despair they sat clinging to each other. A kind-hearted sailor lashed them to the rail, to prevent them from being washed overboard, if the sea rose higher.

'Santa Maria! Holy St Katherine! The Holy Saints of Jerusalem have mercy on us!' were words which continually fell from the Frenchman's lips, as the darkness and the roaring of the wind among the rigging, the shouting, the voice of the captain, and the dashing of the angry waves smote his ear in loud and continual repetition, sure harbingers of danger.

In the midst of all these confusing sounds Jacqueline started; she thought she heard wailing sounds. The next moment, Gito, the cabin-boy, seized her garments, and repeated in a trembling voice:—

'Wele, wele! (see, see!) Meistres bach! There goes the spirit of the seas, the Dewines! The Dewines! Her double-knotted handkerchief flaps in the wind. We are lost! We are lost!'

The captain at that moment came up, and exclaimed in an angry voice:—

'See there, Monsieur Agustine, see those cowardly

scoundrels! There is not a man that will raise his hand to save my ship. Those beggarly, superstitious Welshmen have turned the heads of the rest of my crew; they have seen the spirit of the seas—fools! the terrible woman of Gêst, forsooth. They say no power on earth can save our vessel, and so they will not try.'

'Wele, wele, the Dewines! the Dewines! Her double-knotted handkerchief flaps in the wind. We are lost! We are lost!' again rung in their ears.

Scarcely had the exclamation died away, when the foam-crested waves ran higher, for the gale still freshened. The ship heaved and plunged, the seas broke clean over the decks; utter darkness prevailed, for a red lantern light on the tops, which before gleamed across the deck, swung loose from its lashings, and fell into the sea.

The steersman was not at the helm; no sailors at the sheets; no look-out forward. Left to chance, the unfortunate vessel, unmanageable, scudded before the wind with frightful rapidity. All on board felt destruction inevitable.

'*Mon Dieu*! *Mon Dieu*! Save the ship, save my child!' shrieked Louis Agustine, in agony. 'Santa Maria! Holy St Katherine, save her, save my child!'

Jacqueline was on her knees, and with uplifted hands gazed into the dark firmament, occasionally illumined by vivid flashes of lightning. She prayed with a fervency her spirit had never felt before.

Still the vessel drove onward in her destructive course. The land loomed near, the rocks, the dangerous rocks on which the surge broke, and the foam flashed and leaped with frantic energy, surrounded them on all sides. They were embayed. At length with one simultaneous cry from the affrighted crew, the vessel struck and bilged at the same moment.

That part of the ship occupied by the Frenchman and his daughter at the moment, happened to get so firmly wedged in a cleft of rock where she had struck that they were apparently in safety; save from the angry foam which flew over them and drenched them to the skin. The ship had parted, and they were left almost alone on the part of the wreck to which they were fixed. They heard the cries of the crew engulfed in the raging waters. They heard, but could not see them, still less render them assistance. Very soon those cries were hushed in death, amid the raging of the angry waters.

After some time the father and child, who had remained almost in an unconscious state upon the part of the wreck on which they were preserved, wet, cold, and exhausted, saw the darkness which had for so many hours veiled the land, begin to disperse, and daylight appear. Jacqueline, rousing herself, soon became aware that they were close under the land.

'Oh father,' said she, 'we are safe, we are close to the shore.'

'Impossible,' ejaculated the Frenchman unclosing his eyes, and fixing them a moment upon the deep waters which surrounded them. Then he again relapsed into a state of stupor.

'Santa Maria! What shall I do?' cried Jacqueline, looking anxiously into his face. 'He is so cold and wet, he will die for want of warmth.' She endeavoured to unfasten the rope by which they had been secured to the timber by the sailor who had perished. The tide had fallen, the portion of the deck on which they rested, was now left high and dry. She looked about for aid.

Her father's first word was to bless his child, and thank the saints for having preserved their lives. He began to look wildly about him; his back was to the land.

'Give me your hand, *ma petite*,' said he, attempting to rise and disentangle the rope. 'I think I can stand now. Where is the shore?'

'Stay an instant,' cried the maiden, disentangling the rope from herself, when a moment before so happy and joyous, but too hasty in her efforts, she lost her balance and fell over the wreck into the waves beneath.

The agony of the father was wrought up to madness. He raved, shrieked aloud, called upon the angry waters to deliver up his child, and struggled in vain to set himself free from the rope which still attached him to the ship's rail, but the more he tried the less was his success.

'Let me die with her, only let me go to her. Ye saints in heaven, ye saints on earth, are you all deaf to the distracted entreaties of a parent? Give me back my child—give me back my child.'

He soon became exhausted. Strange noises sounded in his ears, and he sank down insensible.

A light-built boat, with snow-white sails, appeared at this moment making for the wreck. One person alone was in the stern sheets. He had heard the cry of the afflicted parent, and was about to render him assistance, when the light garment of Jacqueline floating on the waves drew his attention. She was safely lifted into his boat.

'The Dewines was right, her prophetic words have come true,' muttered Kynfin Tudor, as he stroked back the long flowing hair, and looked into the pale face of the maiden, who, though no longer a child, still retained sufficient traces of her former person to be recognized.

'Jacqueline! *ma petite* Jacqueline! Have I come too late to save thee?' He clasped her affectionately in his arms, and tried if her heart still beat. 'She breathes,' said he, hastily wrapping her in his boat cloak. He then gave her a little wine from a bottle in the locker. The next instant he boarded the remnant of the wreck on which her father lay prostrate and half insensible. No sooner had he reached the Frenchman than he cut away the cords. He carefully placed him at the side of his daughter, and steered towards Cricceath, the nearest haven, resolving to seek assistance from the castle at that place. It was not long before he reached the shore, and driving his boat up among the large stones of the beach, he hallooed for assistance. An answer was instantly given from the rocks above, and shortly after a noble-looking youth made his appearance upon the shore.

'There was a wreck last night, I know,' exclaimed he, addressing the stranger. 'I am glad to see you have saved some of the unfortunate people, you have only to bring them up to the castle. We will take care of them. What, a lady? I hope she is not dead?'

'I hope not,' repeated the mate of the *Eryr*, for such Kynfin had become, taking her in his arms, and without another remark scaling the rocks with surprising rapidity, never stopping till he had given Jacqueline into the hands of the good mistress of the castle.

'Restore her, restore her,' he cried with energy. 'Something must be done immediately, or she will die. For the love of heaven do all you can for the maiden, good lady.'

The next moment Kynfin Tudor retraced his steps to the beach, and delivered up Louis Agustine to the care of young Conyers. This all executed in a very short time, he became again sole tenant of his boat, beating about amongst the breakers. It soon bore away and looked a speck upon the horizon.

When Monsieur Agustine was in some degree recovered from the shock he had experienced, and the stupor which the sudden disappearance of his child had caused, Mistress Conyers assured him that his daughter was recovering rapidly, and conducted him to her room that he might be convinced her pleasing announcement was correct.

The bewildered man looked long upon her face, and pressed her hand to his lips.

'How can this be?' said he. 'Jacqueline, my child, I saw you die with my own eyes. I heard your cry. I saw you immersed in the boiling waves. Did I dream it? It must have been a dream surely? My child is spared to me—she is spared to me;' and the Frenchman wept for joy.'

For some days they remained at Cricceath, Mistress Conyers loading them with attentions.

One afternoon Louis Agustine inquired the particulars of their escape from the wreck, and to whom they were indebted.

'Why,' replied Ethelred Conyers, 'I can hardly tell you. He was a singular-looking man, gentleman-like in manner, but half pirate in look, with such a strange, wild pair of eyes.'

'Were his eyes dark, and was he tall and slender?' inquired the maiden.

'Yes, and his hair was thrown very much back from his ample forehead,' was the reply.

'It is he! It is he, no doubt!' cried Jacqueline, 'it is my old friend.'

CHAPTER IV

The Wreck Visited—Local Superstition—A Pilots Caution against Weird Women—Explanation

'THE vessel is wrecked, and every soul on board lost,' cried young Stacey, suddenly entering the apartment at Harlech, where the family were assembled at breakfast.

'Wrecked! Lost!' responded every voice round the table, with a mingled look of horror and surprise.

'I fear there can be no mistake about that,' replied the youth; 'they say one end of her can be seen upon the rocks—that her masts are gone, and several of her timbers have already been picked up on the coast.'

'Woe is me! This is sad indeed, my little niece, my poor sister's only child,' ejaculated Lady Stacey, in deep distress. Mistress Maud turned pale, and immediately followed her mother out of the room.

'On my sword! This is an unfortunate affair,' muttered Sir Gilbert, suddenly becoming serious. Walking across the apartment he stood for some time looking out of the window.

'I have been thinking, Edward,' said he, hastily turning round, 'that this is a mere rumour. Some of the people on board may have been saved. Go over to the other side and ascertain the particulars. Go too, if you can go, to the wreck.'

Young Stacey hastened down the cliffs in company with his

kinsman, Henry Stourton. They leaped into a boat and steered their course to the Carnarvonshire shore.

After beating about some time in the bay with a head wind, the tide too, dead against them, they were divided in opinion as to what course they should take. The creek of Madoc was before them, and the boatman informed them that some of the bodies had been washed up there. This only increased their anxiety to reach the spot. The tide was still ebbing, and there were doubts whether there would be sufficient water to take them down the channel.

'Come, Edward, I will settle the matter,' cried Henry Stourton; 'suppose we go to the wreck first, and to Madoc on our way back. We will just look at the hull, or what is left of it. It is not likely it will stand another tide.'

'With all my heart,' responded young Stacey; 'mind the sheet, we had better not carry so much canvas. It will be squally round that point—Eh, pilot?'

'Ie yn wir (yes, indeed); my jacket, Master Edward. We shall catch it presently,' answered the sailor, scanning the horizon, and putting on rather a serious face.

'Pshaw, master pilot, there is no occasion to look so serious. We are not boys to grow faint-hearted. Let her come round a little—there; that will do. Now for a wet beard. We are in for it. How the surf flies about our ears,' vociferated young Stacey, as it dashed in white foam over the bows. The little boat bounded over the billows with surprising sea-worthiness notwithstanding.

They were within a cable's length or two of the wreck, when the pirate's boat, with its white sails, came driving before the wind, dipping its bow into the water as it darted close along-side them.

'That's a proud little thing as ever I saw,' exclaimed young Stacey.

'Ie yn wir, Master Edward; she is one to do her work,' replied Griffith, shutting one eye, and fixing the other, which sparkled through its shaggy eyebrow upon the object in question. 'I don't believe there's a boat on the coast that can beat her.'

'By St George she is a clean-built thing,' rejoined Edward, admiringly; 'can't you tell us, old fellow, to whom she belongs?'

'Why, people say on it, about here, that Dhu ap Rhys owns her, as well as the vessel you see yonder, moored under the rocks,' answered the pilot, with some little hesitation.

'And who is this Dhu ap Rhys, I don't recollect having heard his name?'

'The fishes! Master Edward. What, you never heard of Dhu, the great pirate, and most daring smuggler on this coast? There never was such a daring sea-bird. He beats the government chaps like nothing at all. As to Shonyn Goch, he is a new-born infant to him. I suppose you have heard of that man?'

'Yes, the smuggler of Madoc, you mean. We all know that fellow, and you too, Griff—you know more of him than you will own. You are deep fellows in these parts. Take care you are not hauled up some of these days.'

'Indeed, truth, Master Edward, I fear you grow very harsh upon us, Shonyn Goch is no friend of mine.'

'Well, Griff, you have some good points about you, but you must not blow the gaff upon us—soho! here is the wreck.'

'Master Henry is right, these timbers won't hold another tide. Haul down the jib—steady. You want to go aboard, I suppose, young gentleman?' said the pilot.

'To be sure we do,' was the reply, and they were quickly scrambling upon the wreck. They discovered some property belonging to the Frenchman yet safe, and stowed it away in their boat. Having satisfied their curiosity, they pushed off, up sail, and away in the direction of Madoc.

The tide was coming in fast. There was much flood in the river, and they got up the channel without difficulty, running ashore just below Shonyn's cottage.

'Suppose we go and inquire of the people here; I should like to know if any of the poor souls escaped,' said Edward.

'I should like to see a smuggler's cottage. Let us go in,' rejoined Henry.

'What sort of looking fellow is this rascal, Shonyn Goch?' asked Edward. 'Not very handsome, I have heard.'

'No! Something of the carrot about him,' replied Griff, drily, 'with eyes like that little creature you Saxons call a ferret.'

'Ie yn wir, Master Edward, something like on it, that way.'

'What a description,' said Edward. His companion laughed heartily, and they took their way to the hut. To their annoyance the smuggler's cottage was locked, and even the windows barricaded.

'Yn enw Tâd! there is something the matter here,' said Griff, investigating the premises minutely. 'The old shark is either hiding himself, or has cut clean away.'

'Well, this is provoking,' said Edward, with a look of much disappointment. 'We are losing time, too, had we not better go to those people on the beach? They may be able to give us a more accurate account of the wreck. We want to see the poor fellows thrown ashore. Aha, who knows, the poor Frenchman may be one of them.'

On reaching the spot they found several women standing over the bodies of two of the sailors, washed up on a piece of the wreck. The pilot asked them some questions in his own language.

'What are all these gesticulations? What do these women mean with grave faces, pointing all in the same direction?' inquired young Stacey, with impatience, and no little curiosity.

'They say,' said Griff, 'that the Dewines of Gêst was on the waters last night. She was the cause of the vessel being lost.'

The pilot purposely avoided entering into particulars the moment Edward Stacey began to question him. He hurried them away, on the plea that if they did not go out with the tide, they would not return to Harlech that night.

After they had pushed off from the shore, young Stacey, in a determined tone, again asked the pilot to tell them all about this wonderful woman, this Dewines of Gêst, and what she could have to do with drowning a set of honest fellows.

Griff grinned, was silent, and shook his head, with an indication of dislike to enter upon the subject.

'Come, come, old fellow, this won't do, you shall satisfy us upon this point. You know all about her,' interrupted young Stacey.

'I believe the man is afraid of her,' said Henry, laughing.

'To be sure he is,' replied his companion. 'He thinks she could upset our boat and drown us in a calm, strangle us without a cord, and send us puff into the lower regions with her breath.'

'Don't talk on it that light way, Master Edward; no, don't; if you knew all I do about the Dewines, you would be more careful what you say.'

'Well, old fellow, perhaps we should, if you would but tell

us.'

'I never comes upon the waters, Master Edward, never,' said Griff, with great emphasis on the negative, 'without I says to myself, St Cyric[12] keep me from coming across the spirit of the seas, save me from her curse. Young Saxons may laugh, but the day may come that they will be sorry for it. I am not the only one that can tell you that she has been seen scores of times, floating with her knotted handkerchief over the waves of this bay. She was here last night, and you know what she has done.'

'Now do you really believe it?' said young Stacey, with a smile. 'On my honour, master pilot, when one looks at your broad shoulders and muscular frame, one wonders such whimsies can make you fear. But to the point, I should like to see this extraordinary woman, who frightens so many stout hearts. Some of these days I will go and pay the old Dewines a visit.'

'O, Duw anwyl! Master Edward, you had better not, you would never come back with your head safe upon your shoulders—she hates a Yorkist as we do the devil.'

'So—ho, she condescends then to take a part in the affairs of the nation,' retorted young Stacey.

'Why, yes, Master Edward, I hear-ed say she has good reason. The White Rose party has been no friend to her.'

'How?' inquired Stacey, deeply interested; 'come, you, Griff, know the secrets of her history—let us have them.'

'The fishes! not I, Master Edward; why, if you were to promise me a ship load of the best spirits, I could not tell you—the devil only knows them.'

---

[12] The patron saint of the Welsh mariners.

'Perhaps you can inform us how long she has been in this part of the country?'

'About ten years; but she comes and goes continually, no one knows whither.'

'You don't know then, from whence she comes?'

'No, I heard someone say that she had been seen at the battle of Tewkesbury.'

'Indeed, have you ever seen her, Griff?'

'Yes, master Edward, I have seen her once, only once,' repeated the seaman, in a tremulous voice, while his weather-beaten cheeks became livid.

'Do you know of anyone besides, who has seen this witch spirit; what sort of looking animal is she?'

'Ie yn wir; I know a few who have, and she nearly frightened their souls out of their bodies. As to her looks, she is tall, has large saucer eyes, and very long grey hair.'

The pilot shuddered as he finished the sentence, and taking up some of the tackle of the boat, moved forward, evidently anxious that they should run into the land.

'There goes the smuggler's bark,' exclaimed young Stacey, turning round; 'there is no mistaking her, with her light build and white sails. By St George, if she is not making for the creek of Borth. It does not look as if he were much afraid of the she-wolf. How is that, Griff?'

'Why, people say on it here, master Edward, that Ap Rhys himself has a bit of the devil about him, and he and the Dewines go hand in hand together. All I know is that she has vaults which lie deep under the water, and there she always lets him store away his goods. The fishes! Master Edward, if it were not for her, he could not defy man and the devil in the way he does. The whole country is afraid of them.'

'Ho, ho, master pilot, she aids the smugglers, does she?' cried young Stacey, with a look of triumph. 'The truth is out at last. This is the way the rascals carry on their trade. Why, Griff, what an old fool you are. You and your countrymen allow yourselves to be duped in this barefaced way? Henry, I say,' added he, turning to his cousin, 'this affair must be probed.'

'O'r Tad! Master Edward, if you hold your own life dear, listen to me,' cried Griff, with a look of terror; 'have nothing to do with this woman—have nothing to do with her; none ever meddled with her without repenting. Indeed, truth, master Edward, don't have anything to do with her. Anwyl! Anwyl! I wish I had never opened my lips about her. I would have cut my tongue out of my head if I had thought, master Edward, you would have taken it in this way. St Cyric save us!'

'You provoking old fellow; I never saw your equal in superstition. Mark me, Griff, if you don't disclose all you know about the proceedings of this woman; if you equivocate, as sure as the clouds are over our heads, I will make you all suffer for it; spear me if I don't.'

Griff became more alarmed than before, and stammered with an equivocal and deploring look:

'Indeed, indeed, truth, master Edward, you will be sorry in your heart. Have nothing to do with the Dewines, she is a hard one to show game.'

'That is not answering my question; you are a fool, Griff, if you think to intimidate me by your superstitious nonsense. Tell me at once all you know about this woman smuggler, this female pirate; or, by St George! I will have you up before the justice,' said Stacey, much irritated.

'The fishes! Master Edward, I no think you would take it

in that way. I am no smuggler, and I know nothing more about the Dewines than what I have told you.'

The pilot shook the wet from off his jacket, and endeavoured to look more easy. He remained silent, running his tar-stained fingers across his hairy face, and eyeing his companions with gloomy forebodings.

Young Stacey and his cousin passed severe censures upon Wales, and all the superstitions of Welshmen.

The boat had now run up through the surf, and they landed upon the sands. On parting with the pilot, he turned and called after them:

'Sleep on it, young gentleman, ie yn wir; have no dealings with the Dewines. The work she did last night ought to frighten every Jack of us. Take care she does not make a wreck of you as well as of the vessel.'

'I defy her,' cried young Stacey, with a loud laugh; the young men then hurried on towards the castle of Harlech.

'You defy her, young gentlemen,' muttered Griff, when they were out of hearing; 'it would be a lean fly challenging an elephant.'

'Well, mother, we have been unsuccessful,' said young Stacey, on entering the apartment which Lady Stacey occupied; 'no female has yet been washed up on the coast. What has happened? You greet me with smiles.'

'They are saved!' replied his mother, with a joyous expression of feature. She then told him that someone had rescued the Frenchman and his daughter from the wreck, and had taken them to Cricceath, where they were now under the hospitable roof of good Mistress Conyers; and that as soon as they were sufficiently recovered, the young masters of the castle had promised to bring them over. This intelligence had restored them all to good spirits.

'Where is my father?' inquired the young man, throwing himself into a chair and beckoning a lad to take off his boots. 'We have had a terrible wild day of it. I am dead beat: however, I am pleased to hear of the rescue. If you had seen the wreck, mother, you would say that a miracle had been wrought.'

Upon hearing that Sir Gilbert was in the next room, waiting with great impatience for supper, the young men immediately adjourned thither, and were not sorry to sit down to an inviting repast.

'Well, Henry, after all the pilot's words the witch of Gêst has not robbed me of my cousin. I wonder what he would say now?' said young Stacey, leaning forward behind his sister's chair, and laughing heartily.

'I have no doubt he would make up some outlandish tale, and say the Dewines, by her supernatural hand, had saved them. Who knows but she and her emissaries, the smugglers, might really have had something to do with the rescue?'

'Well done, Henry,' cried Stacey, throwing himself back. 'I believe you have a secret faith in the witch after all. By St George! How Griff would show every tooth in his head, did he but know that he had made a disciple of you.'

'I think it is to be regretted he does not know it,' said Henry, laughing; 'the old fellow will not be overburdened with sleep to-night.'

'I don't think he relished my threats,' replied young Stacey; 'he deeply repents having mentioned a word about the witch.'

'What witch—what do you mean?' inquired Sir Gilbert, tossing off a goblet of wine, and smacking his lips; 'you appear to have met with some adventure this morning.'

'We have indeed—we have passed a very strange day, and

came back wiser than we went; neither you nor I, nor any of us knew before, that this bay swarms with smugglers. The house of Gêst is their rendezvous; the woman who lives there is called the Dewines, or the witch, and is their great ally. By what I can make out, she is their agent. What is more, the hatred she bears to the White Rose is unlimited.'

'That is easily accounted for,' remarked Sir Gilbert, pushing his plate from him, and looking stern. 'If all you say is true, we must look into the affair. Smugglers are dangerous fellows to deal with, hard-headed, tough dogs at tossing a pike, or handling a cutlass. I would nip them in the bud—nip them in the bud, I say, and give them no quarter. They are rebels too, travelling under two masks. For instance, we have seen it in the bastard of Fauconbridge, that ungrateful rascal, who gave his Highness so much trouble and annoyance. That fellow turned pirate; you were too young to recollect the circumstances. It caused a great sensation in those days.'

'His name seems familiar to me,' replied young Stacey; 'I should like much to hear all about the affair.'

'It is soon told,' rejoined Sir Gilbert; 'that young dare-devil, in the first place was spoiled by his patron, the Earl of Warwick. Through the Earl's interest, when quite a youth, he was made vice-admiral of the channel. There was a fine opening for him, if he had conducted himself with propriety. But what was the conduct of the rascal; only a few years afterwards, when the Yorkists came into power, he turned pirate; plundered a number of Portuguese vessels, and set everyone at defiance. On the death of Warwick he appeared in arms upon the coast of Kent, and while Edward was on his route to Tewksbury, landed and proceeded on his way to London at the head of seventeen thousand men, who called themselves Lancastrians in place of vile rebels. He soon became master of Southward and had it not been for the dauntless conduct of the good citizens of London, the metropolis would have suffered great injury under his hands. As it was, he was repelled, and forced to retire to Sandwich, where he strongly fortified himself. The King repaired thither immediately after the battle of Tewksbury. The traitor ought then to have been seized and executed, of this there is no doubt. I was with the king at the time, and as others did, tried to persuade him to do justice.

'The King assented in the first instance. He even went so far as to sign Nevil's death-warrant. Suddenly he changed his royal mind, yielded to the terms young Fauconbridge offered, pardoned the rascal, and even knighted him. The pirate rebel once more became vice-admiral of the channel. We were mortified as well as astonished that the King should thus act contrary to his own interest and the wishes of his nobles. There was a report that some evil spirit appeared from behind the arras, seized the warrant out of Sir William Stanley's hand, and committed it to the flames. This idle tale was soon afterwards contradicted. We never knew the King's real motive for acting in this affair in the manner he did. He was sorry for it afterwards, and wished he had listened to our counsel in the first instance. That unmitigated scoundrel, violent as ever for the Red Rose cause, had not been long restored to office, when I discovered he was in communication with some of the Lancastrians, and at his old habit again of plundering upon the high seas. I immediately reported him to the King, who became very angry. You should have seen Thomas Nevil's rage, when his old enemy went to visit him in his prison. I did not conceal from him that I should move heaven and earth to rid the nation of his presence. So sure as I had the blood of a Stacey flowing in my veins, so certainly I declared King Edward should not again pardon him.'

'How an old enemy? What do you mean by that, father?' inquired young Stacey, with not a little curiosity.

'Aha! yes—you don't know I owed him a private grudge,' replied Sir Gilbert, turning first red and then white. 'He made mischief between me and Warwick. We were never friends afterwards. But we won't speak of that matter,' continued the Keeper, with still greater confusion, and he immediately changed the conversation once more to the smugglers in the bay.

'I believe there are many such as Fauconbridge, if the truth were known,' remarked young Stacey. 'I am afraid the present disturbed state of the country creates its own enemies to a frightful extent.'

'There is much truth in your remark,' replied the Keeper. 'When we consider that fret, we ought to seek out the aggressors and make an example of them. Marry! if I don't investigate the whole matter, and acquaint our royal master with their proceedings. We will see if we can't catch the caitiffs, and make a reformation in this heathenish land.'

'I entreat you to have no concern in any such matter,' cried Lady Stacey, with a very anxious expression of countenance. 'We are Saxons and strangers here. You will only bring us into trouble, and be hated still more by the people. Listen to me, my honoured Lord. I am sure it would be very unwise, even dangerous, to meddle with so lawless a set.'

'Madam, when I have a duty to perform, it is not usual for me to neglect it. You timid women don't understand these affairs. Leave them to us,' said the Keeper authoritatively.

Henry Stourton and Edward now began amusing Mistress Maud with the adventures of the morning. Although she appeared highly entertained at the narration, her cheeks continually changed colour, and she expressed much fear at the ominous old woman of the bay, declaring heartily that she hoped they would take the pilot's advice and never go near her dwelling.

During this recital, Sir Gilbert had thrown himself back in his chair, and gone off to sleep. Two fine staghounds lay panting before the burning faggots; and Lady Stacey, with a thoughtful countenance, occupied as usual with her spinning wheel, completed the group.

CHAPTER V

The Handsome Stranger—A Feudal Treaty—An Unexpected Friend— A Dip into Politics

'MY curiosity is excited to know who that interesting girl is, wandering so sorrowfully about the castle. No one seems to take any notice of her,' said Jacqueline to his cousin, the morning after her arrival at Harlech. 'She reminds me of someone for whom I have a deep regard. Those lovely eyes—that beautiful face quite infatuates me. Maud, tell me who she is?'

'You amuse me, Jacqueline,' said her companion, smiling sarcastically. 'I cannot enter into your enthusiasm with regard to that girl. I think her beauty entirely spoiled by her being so haughty and revengeful. To tell you candidly, I have long ceased to take any interest in her.'

'Well, I should not have thought her revengeful; haughty she may be,' said Jacqueline, thoughtfully. 'Yet still, Maud, you have not told me who she is, and from whence she comes.'

'It is a long tale,' replied Maud, carelessly; 'she has been a prisoner in the fortress for four years. I hate the name of the girl, she has caused us so much trouble and annoyance. I declare, for the first year, we never knew what it was to have a moment's peace. There was always some difference arising between my father and mother about the child, destroying the comfort and happiness of our family circle. For the first six months, too, I was nearly frightened to death by continual attacks of her savage people, who were outrageous at our retaining the child.'

'She is of Welsh extraction, then,' said Jacqueline, with a gesture of surprise. 'I am still more puzzled to know why, under those circumstances, you kept her a prisoner. Why did you not let her return to her family, and the benefit would have been reciprocal?'

'It would be impossible to enter minutely into the particulars of this affair. We are in a manner compelled to keep Gladys as an hostage for our personal safety. When we first came to Harlech, we were grossly persecuted by a mountain horde of freebooters, who were constantly in the habit of paying us nocturnal visits, carrying off our black cattle, and destroying our property. In a word, doing everything to annoy their Saxon neighbours, who they openly acknowledge they deeply hate. It happened one day that my father, with a party of friends, was shooting among the hills, and came across the girl in question. Upon discovering that she was by a collateral source connected with our hostile neighbours the freebooters, she was taken captive and brought to the castle. My father was in hopes that by threats she would reveal to him the locality, and the names of some of the lawless horde. He was mistaken. She remained inflexible, and provoked my father to such a degree that he placed her in strict confinement for six months. Then it was the marauders became ten times more violent. They murdered several of our serfs, shot and poisoned our bloodhounds, and attempted to set fire to the castle. In fact, it had arisen to such an extent that we found it necessary to come to some understanding with them. Stipulations were agreed to that if they would promise to desist from their hostile persecutions, Gladys should be permitted to have the full range of the castle, to be treated kindly, and placed upon a footing with the family. On the other hand, upon their disapproving of these terms, my father declared positively that the child should be sent to the king of England, who knowing her to be the daughter of a Lancastrian of some standing, would show her no mercy.

'This threat alarmed them. They immediately consented, and we have never since been annoyed by them. So you see, my dear cousin, that retaining the Welsh girl as an hostage, is a necessary evil.'

'So it appears,' rejoined Jacqueline, with a sigh. 'Tell me, Maud, was Gladys's father of gentle blood? If so, how is it she is in any way connected with a set of lawless freebooters? It sounds shocking.'

'Father Nutze says that these freebooters, as we call them, are of the fallen race of Lancastrians. They persecute us, he says, not from a love of plunder, but of revenge against their Saxon neighbours, and consider it a point of duty—poor savages! We think that by many little incidents that have occurred, Gladys is the daughter of the chief of their clan, who in all probability perished in one of the battles of the Roses. She can speak English fluently, and has some little knowledge of history—and—'

'Yes, plays the harp with a scientific hand,' said Jacqueline, finishing the sentence. 'Well, I think, poor girl, she is to be pitied. You must not be angry with me, Maud, if I take an interest in her.'

'She will never permit you to take an interest in her,'

answered Maud, evidently annoyed. 'She only opens her lips to Father Nutze, and occasionally to my mother, and my cousin Henry, who has lowered himself extremely in my eyes, by persisting in paying her attention, when she receives it with such indifference. Perhaps, Jacqueline, in my cousin you will find as enthusiastic an admirer of the Welsh beauty as yourself.'

These words were repeated so sarcastically that Jacqueline, with her exceeding gentleness, looked at her companion in amazement, as she hastily quitted the apartment, wondering if she were in earnest.

For several days Jacqueline watched the captive maiden in silent admiration. She generally sat opposite at her at meals, but had never found an opportunity of exchanging a word with her. One evening, after she and her cousin had returned from an excursion among the mountains, she found Gladys alone in the hall, stringing her harp.

'Gladys,' said Jacqueline, approaching the Welsh maiden, 'your history has been related to me. You do not know how deep an interest I take in you. Do not avoid me; let us be friends.'

Gladys looked up in surprise, the gentleness of the tones and the accents were both foreign to her.

'My history,' she repeated, in a mournful voice, 'none here know my history.'

Jacqueline said with one of her sweet smiles, 'I know that your home was among the mountains. We have been roving over them today, Gladys, and shall I tell you that the captive maiden whom we had left behind, was in my thoughts the whole day. I wished that you had been by my side that your native breezes might have fanned your cheeks, and the sweet perfume of the wild flowers greeted you—Gladys, I grieve for you.'

At that moment, voices were heard in the long gallery, and Jacqueline hastened away to take off her things and prepare for supper.

Louis Agustine looked tenderly towards his child as she entered the room.

'You don't know how thankful I feel, *ma petite* Jacqueline, that we are safely lodged under the roof of our dear relatives,' said he, drawing her to him, and imprinting a warm kiss upon her glowing cheek. 'Does *ma petite* think she will like this country? *Je le trouve bien froid.*'

'I have had a most charming day. I have been in raptures with everything. I love the wild scenery here,' said Jacqueline, with almost child-like glee. She then turned to look at Gladys, and exchanged a smile.

During the meal, the conversation turned upon the Welsh, and many unfeeling remarks were made upon them, particularly by Sir Gilbert, who finished by invoking a hearty curse upon one of the menials, who happened to be a son of the soil, and had neglected to execute a command, which had been delivered to him in the morning.

These little incidents made Jacqueline feel more sympathy for Gladys, who evidently was pained by what she heard.

Changing the conversation, Sir Gilbert asked Monsieur Agustine if he knew what had become of the Earls of Pembroke and Richmond. It was not a wise thing on the part of Edward, to let them escape from the country.

'They are in the power of the Duke of Brittany, are they not?'

'*Parbleu!* sir knight, I believe you,' cried the Frenchman, shrugging his shoulders, 'there is not a word nor action expressed that is not repeated at the palace. A severe punishment awaits them if they attempt to cross the borders of his dukedom. The king of England wanted our duke to deliver them up to him; but no, thank you, the old fox is too knowing, he has his own interest in view.'

'Was it true that their lives were attempted a few years back?' inquired Sir Gilbert.

'There was some talk about it, but that was soon hushed up,' replied Louis Agustine, who, in spite of all his endeavours, turned pale, and Jacqueline felt the blood mount to her cheeks. With not a little skill, he immediately diverted the attention of Sir Gilbert, by asking him if he had taken any interest in Louis the Eleventh's hostile proceedings against the Dukes of Burgundy and Brittany, assuring him that it had of late caused general excitement upon the continent, and that Louis's base and unprincipled conduct was greatly censured by the European powers. England was likely to go to war with France.

'Yes, I have watched those movements with a great share of interest,' replied Sir Gilbert, becoming more than usually animated. 'What is your opinion, I should like to know, of that knave, the constable of St Pol; a pretty part he has played in the eyes of the world. Ha! ha! a nice trio for working up scenes of intrigue, I trow—Louis, King of France, Charles, Duke of Burgundy, and their arch accomplice, the constable.'

'Parbleu! Mon ami, although you live in those wild mountains and in this outlandish spot, you have not lost your old taste for politics, you keep pace with the rest of the world. Was not that a terrible affair the death of Guyenne, the poisoned peach to the widow d'Amboise, given by the churchman? One

should have thought him a cardinal whose vices are the seven deadly sins; he was only a monk that poisoned for the king of France, one as fond of dainty cheer as if he were of the conclave. It was a ruthless thing, methinks, because Louis was afraid of a reunion between the Duke of Guyenne and the beautiful heiress of Burgundy, thus to take life. It was a severe blow to the noble Duke. It had been the cherished wish of his heart that their nuptials should have taken place. It is very difficult to define what the chequered movements of these potentates are aiming at. Ambition is their food; inquisition and intrigue, their playthings; don't you think so, *Monsieur*?'

'These are dangerous times. Holy St Katherine, keep us from being mixed up with the dark deeds of our period. It is better policy, far better policy, to steer clear of them. Ha! ha! *mon ami*, I see you are fond of a dip into politics.'

'I am,' replied Sir Gilbert. 'I always say it was a mistake, a grievous misfortune to England, that I was not in the cabinet. Yes, I am fond of politics, I understand them well. Beshrew me! but you and I shall get on uncommonly well together. You have just come from the centre, where all these intrigues have been carried on, and will be competent to enlighten me upon some points, that I have never thoroughly been able to understand, in this remote place. You say the king of France destroyed his own brother, the Duke de Berri—bah! I mean Guyenne; he dropped that title of late. Well, and what was the next movement?'

'Why, Charles, Duke of Burgundy, in a fury came down with his army upon Picardy, and by way of revenge, slaughtered the ill-fated population. He then proceeded on his route to Beauvais, and would no doubt have committed fearful devastation there, had he not been opposed by the brave

Jeanne Hachette, whose valour upon this occasion will long be remembered by the inhabitants.'

'Marry! I don't recollect hearing of this second Joan of Arc. There appears to have been some fearful massacres in several parts of France.'

'True, true! Our country, I regret to say, is in a disturbed state and given up to anarchy. I am glad to be out of it.'

'Now, if the Dukes of Brittany and Burgundy take a part with our king Edward, and go to war with the French monarch, he will be in a critical position—at all events, not in an enviable one.'

'So much the better,' answered the Frenchman. 'I have a deep hatred of that royal personage. By the bye, Sir Gilbert, now I think of it, what has become of Margaret of Anjou, is she still in the Tower?'

Gladys, who had been sitting behind Jacqueline, started as she heard the familiar name of their beloved queen, and so earnestly were her eyes riveted upon the Frenchman's face that everyone present noticed it.

'Oh, no! she has been some time removed from those dreary precincts,' replied Sir Gilbert, 'she is now in Wallingford castle. You are aware that King Edward has something allowed him by King René for her subsistence. She is permitted to have the full range of the castle.'

Again Gladys looked up, and though she cast a haughty look upon all, tears glistened in her eyes at the recollection of what had been early impressed upon her mind.

'Poor Margaret of Anjou!' ejaculated Lady Stacey; 'how gloriously she commenced her career, and how sadly is it closing.'

'It is only what she deserves,' said Sir Gilbert, severely;

'she had no business to interfere in our politics. Why, madam, if it had not been for her, some of England's best blood would have been spared, and the horrors of a civil war would not now be darkening England with its sad effects. We may look upon that woman, madam, as the sole instigator of our misfortunes. She has been a curse to our land; and for my part, I should be glad when her foot no longer treads its soil.'

The name of Anjou put the keeper out of temper. Gladys had retired from the scene, and was pouring out her sorrow in sweet melodies upon her harp in a distant apartment. Henry Stourton guessed her intention as she made her exit, and looked wistfully after her; and Jacqueline would have given worlds to have followed in her steps.

Some days after this quiet evening, Jacqueline, who had been out with her cousin upon the beach, sought Gladys, to show her some seaweeds and shells she had gathered upon the sands. Not finding her in the hall nor in the sitting-room, she ascended one of the towers, which she knew to be a favourite retreat of the captive. There she found her, with a loose mantle thrown around her elegant figure, leaning over the battlements, watching, with an eager eye, a bark with its white sails, gliding over the blue waters beneath. Her harp and book lay by her side untouched; and she did not turn round at the sound of footsteps.

'Do not say I am an intruder,' said Jacqueline, approaching and placing her hand gently upon her shoulder. 'I have so long wished for this moment to be alone with you, dear Gladys.'

The daughter of Harlech rested her lovely eyes upon her companion, and answered only by a pressure of the hand and a smile; but that smile was so melancholy, Jacqueline could not forbear exclaiming:—

'Dear Gladys, I wish you were not so sad—so unhappy. I wish a thousand times you could be joyous like our maidens of the South. Sometimes I cannot sleep, when I think of you. It is so strange—so very strange that youth and beauty should be thus overshadowed. Why is it you are so fond of being alone, and treat everyone and everything with such marked indifference?'

'I would not intentionally treat the kind, the gentle Jacqueline with indifference,' said Gladys, drawing her companion nearer to her, and looking steadfastly in her face. 'And do I then interest you? The reserved, the gloomy, the forbidden alien in this house, is it on her account your rest is sometimes disturbed? Jacqueline, we are comparatively strangers, and yet I feel that I can love you, and that if I were to tell you all the sorrows of my heart, you would sympathize with me, and understand me. You ask me why I look so sad; why I am so fond of being alone. I am a stranger and a captive among my enemies, the enemies of my people. Were it not even so; Mistress Maud, I feel instinctively, is not one to soothe or listen to the outburstings of an unhappy heart. Her severity of manner rather drives me away—it quite repels me. Lady Stacey, though very kind to me, and I am grateful, is the wife of a man whom my soul loathes. You wish, Jacqueline, that I was joyous, like your maidens in the South. That can never be while I am a captive. When I think of my home and my loved grandmother, without a soul to comfort her declining years, my heart yearns in bitterness. In me, her grandchild, the last of our noble house, she had centered all her love, her care and her thoughts. In vain she now listens to hear my voice; in vain she tries to catch a view of my face. She sits in the chimney-corner inconsolable, and prays for my return. Oh, Jacqueline, ask me not again, why I am so melancholy; you know it now. That is not all: these grey old walls, these proud battlements, which keep me from my beloved parent, are by right my own. Within these walls, I first saw the light of heaven; within these walls, I was taught to lisp names, both sacred and dear. Jacqueline, I breathe to you a tale which none here know: I am the grandchild of the mighty chieftain, the once bold defender of this fortress, Dafydd ap Jevan ap Einion. Keep my secret.'

The daughter of Harlech and the French maiden sat long upon the battlements that day, and mingled their tears together.

CHAPTER VI

A Maternal Reception—The Legacy— Painful Reflections—A Stratagem

'KYNFIN! Kynfin! My son—my beloved son, have you come at last to comfort your afflicted parent, bereaved of all, even of her wyres bach?' cried the widow of Ap Jevan, as she threw herself into the arms of her son, and burst into a flood of tears.

The long-lost son had indeed returned. Clasped in one another's arms, neither mother nor son could speak; sobs alone were heard throughout the chamber. So touching and unexpected was the meeting that the faithful Howel stood motionless, with eyes wide open and arms extended. Katherine, his wife, trembling violently, had averted her face to conceal her emotion.

Kynfin, in broken accents, inquired what his mother meant about the child.

'Am I to understand the child is gone?—Gladys, the joy, the hope, the sole remaining hope of our fallen house—that she is no more? Why has Heaven judged us so hardly? My mother, in my bitterest moments I never looked for this!'

As he repeated these hurried words, his manner grew more singular and wild, and his lank, worn face became of a pallid hue. The disappointment was gall to his soul.

'No, Kynfin; let me undeceive you,' cried his mother, with a tremulous voice. 'The child is not dead. She has been stolen from her home by our enemies, the merciless Yorkists. For nearly four years, she has pined away her youthful days among them. She is a prisoner in those walls which once we called our own.'

Kynfin Tudor indignantly exclaimed:—

'What, mother! Were there none—none of my people that had courage enough to rescue her from their hands? None who had the heart to save their chieftain's grandchild from the polluted presence of the Yorkists! Not one, mother—not one? Would that I had returned before that luckless day!'

'Would that you had, my son,' repeated the widow of Ap Jevan, sorrowfully. 'Since they have torn from my bosom the last remaining joy of my heart, my life's blood has lessened within me. I should soon have passed into the grave for which my soul yearned, had I not seen your face and pressed you once more to my bosom, my long-lost son. Year after year I have watched and mourned for you; at times thinking that you too had passed from this weary world, to another and a better. I never thought I should again run my dim sight across your much-loved features. Ow, ow, I have suffered much, Kynfin, my beloved child; you know not how pure, how unadulterated, how unalterable and undying is a parent's love!'

'Forgive me!—forgive your undutiful, wretched son,' cried the conscience-stricken Kynfin, bending before her upon his knees, and looking imploringly in her countenance, now embrowned by time, like the autumnal leaf. 'Mother, mother, I acknowledge that I have been what I ought not. I stand before you a criminal, a wretched man, blighted by ungovernable passions; yet forgive me, forgive me, I pray!'

'O fy, anwyl, Kynfin bach, you have my forgiveness, my

free forgiveness, from my heart, and may my blessing,' continued Mistress Tudor, placing both her hands upon her son's head—'yes, a mother's blessing overshadow your offences. Let them pass into oblivion as if they had never been!'

Time lapsed, and the son of Harlech still sat by the side of his mother. She poured into his eager and attentive ear many a painful tale of bygone days. She told him how Aliano had passed away from earth to heaven. How deeply she had loved him, with a pure, sisterly love. That the Saxon, her kinsman, had no peculiar share in her affection, beyond kindly relationship. How she had yearned to see him, and to bid him a last farewell. How frequently and fervently had been her prayers that he might be comforted: and thus, even to her dying hour she had evinced deep sympathy and regard for him.

These tidings sunk deep into Kynfin's heart. He mechanically held out his hand for a roll of paper which his mother offered, telling him that it was what Aliano had intrusted to her charge, with the special injunction that it should be given to him upon his return. The son of Harlech eyed the packet for an instant, then concealed it within the folds of his vest. An hour afterwards, he was sitting among the shadowy rocks of his mountain land. One of the papers was lying open before him, as he devoured with eager and bewildered vision the following lines:

'To you, Kynfin, I bequeath my child, for the sake of those who were dear to you, but are now no more. Be a father to my darling, Gladys. Keep her steps from harm. To be a father to the orphan is a sacred charge; yet shrink not, Kynfin, from that charge. It is the dying request of your loving sister, Aliano.'

The son of Harlech repeated the words over and over again—'Be a father to my darling Gladys. Keep her steps from harm. Be a father to the orphan. It is a sacred charge, yet shrink not from it.'

Kynfin remained pouring out his soul in prayer, and straining his eyes over the precious lines, till night obliterated them from his vision. Devotion is ever the refuge of the mountain lover in affliction. He then hastily arose, and retraced his steps to Cader y Cil; soliloquizing, he went on his solitary way:—

'How dear to me is thy memory, my Aliano. Eight long years have passed since those beloved characters were written. How have I fulfilled the post allotted me? Sacred as the charge is, it is not I that have shrunk from it. Had I received the request before, I would not have neglected it, unworthy as I feel of so responsible, so holy a charge. I would not have turned from it, but have embraced the duty which devolves upon a parent. Aliano, could I have foreseen your bequest, and that your child would have been taken from her mountain home, her tender years been clouded by misfortune—her noble, yet youthful mind, poisoned by the seducing influence of our enemies, the Yorkists—I would never have sought a foreign land, but have hastened to watch over my sacred charge. I should then have been happy, even blessed in the consideration that I was fulfilling your last bequest. Destiny wrenched the power from my hand. To benefit others, not myself, I have fallen into snares from which I have been unable to escape. Had I known, Nevil, you were a headstrong perpetrator of all that is exciting, daring, and vicious, I would never have stepped upon the deck of the *Eryr*—I would never have bound myself to you by a promise of secrecy. Why was this my destiny? I love not crime, yet I have been an accomplice in crime. I love not blood, yet I have been a participant in pouring it out. What is worse, my chains cannot be snapped asunder. I must go on a miserable bondman, trammelled and enslaved, upon the gory decks of the *Eryr* for another year!'

Kynfin was so disturbed by these reflections that for some minutes he walked up and down before the gates of Cader y Cil, to calm himself before he ventured again to appear in the presence of his mother. When he was about to seek admittance, Howel suddenly appeared from behind a large stone.

'What has brought you here?' demanded Kynfin in a stern voice. 'I did not know I was to be subjected to intrusion. Do you want me?'

'Please you, my good master, I was unhappy because you were so. I thought, may be, I could speak to the son of Harlech a few words of comfort. I have loved his father and I love his son; and Howel, the old sentinel, is sore cut up about the "wyres bach".'

The manner and the tones in which this was spoken touched the heart of Kynfin, who immediately said—

'Well, well, Howel, that is kind and sympathizing. I have never doubted your sincerity: soon I shall have to put it to the test. The wyres bach must be brought to her rocky nest. You must first tell me all you know about the child. Have you seen her since she has been carried to the castle?'

'No, my good master.'

'You do know if she still cares for her people. They may have prejudiced her, she was so young when taken a captive. They may have influenced her tender heart, and weaned her affections from us.'

'No, no, son of Harlech, that would be impossible. You don't know my meistres-bach, if you speak in that way.'

'My soul yearns to see her,' said Kynfin, in a thick voice.

A long pause followed. Both were looking up at the pale face of the moon rising slowly from some dark clouds rolling that moment along the heights, and leaving the rugged outline standing in bold relief. The shepherd dogs were barking. Two large stag-hounds, ancient in look, were rubbing themselves affectionately against the legs of their long-absent master, and seemed, at intervals, to evince their joy at his return.

Kynfin and the faithful domestic now entered the house. They found the good old lady had retired to rest, having been so overcome by that day's excitement, that to pour out her gratitude to the author of her late happiness and to retire to her bed seemed as much as her feeble frame could perform.

Howel heaped turf upon the fire. The master and the worthy domestic resumed the theme of their conversation. The old servant explained how many fruitless attempts had been made to recapture the daughter of Harlech; and how Sir Gilbert had threatened to punish the child, and to send her to the cruel King Edward.

'It was then our hearts sank within us. Sir Gilbert said he knew she was of gentle blood; and we trembled lest he should discover that she was the granddaughter of our lamented chieftain. He would then reveal the secret to the tyrant King of England, and she would have no mercy. Placing these fears aside, we thought it better she should remain under the roof of the Yorkists in our own country, than that her sweet face should be looked upon by the bad people in the royal court. This alone made us rest quiet and obedient to our sorrow.'

'And, perhaps, it was as well you were so,' replied the son of Harlech, with a sigh.

Stroking the shaggy sides of his dogs, he remained silent and thoughtful, while Howel rose to place more turf upon the hearth.

'Howel,' said his master, after a short silence, 'the child must be seen; a message must be given to her; she must speak herself. We must know what are her feelings before we can take our ground and act. Let Katherine go to the castle when Sir Gilbert is out. She may feign to be wild in her head, and linger about the courtyard till she catches sight of the daughter of Harlech. Katherine is no fool: she can play her part well. Wrong in the head, and pretending to sleight of hand, she may convey a letter to her meistres bach.'

CHAPTER VII

A Rustic Ramble—The Fair Musician— The Stratagem Successful

AFTER the shipwreck in the bay, the families of the Staceys and Conyers became intimate. Sir Gilbert and his lady accepted an invitation from Mistress Conyers to pass some days at Cricceath. The good dame had returned with her guests for a short time, accompanied by her three sons, Ethelred, Stephen, and little Tyrrel, who from that time had been constantly skimming in their boat across the bay, either to or from the rival castles, which stood facing each other on the opposite shores.

This intimacy was highly appreciated by the young people, particularly by the inmates of Harlech, who, had it not been for the attention of the noble youths of Cricceath, would, in all probability, have found it dull during the absence of Edward Stacey and M. Agustine, who had been summoned to France a short time after the arrival of the latter in Wales. Jacqueline was left behind, under the care of her aunt.

The winter was over. The bright days of spring which succeeded, frequently induced the young people to seek adventures among the hills, taking refreshments with them. Many hours were thus happily passed either on the borders of a limpid stream, or in exploring the picturesque glens in the neighbourhood of Harlech.

Upon one of these excursions, when the little party was descending a deep defile, Ethelred and Jacqueline were lingering behind. After a break in the conversation for a short time, the youth turned round, and looking at his companion, laughed and said:—

'Well, Mistress Jacqueline, me thinks we are dull companions. Half an hour since, you were the merriest of the party. I wonder how it is we are both so silent now?'

'I was thinking of the poor captive whom we have left unhappy and solitary behind us,' replied his companion. 'I wonder what you were thinking of?' looking up into Ethelred's countenance, as he helped her over a fence.

The colour mounted to his face in an instant.

'Our silence is accounted for,' said Jacqueline, smiling. 'Poor dear Gladys! Don't you feel for her? Would you not like to place her here in this romantic glen, and then watch the expression of her beautiful features? She is so enthusiastic about her country, so fond of her mountain land, that she feels her captivity bitterly.'

'Why is she kept a prisoner?' Ethelred, endeavouring to appear calm at the appeal. 'Surely if you were to ask your uncle he would let her come with us occasionally?'

'No, my uncle has refused me that request several times. Let him take anything into his head, and he is as immovable as the rocks we stand upon. I suppose it is treason to say so, but I think Sir Gilbert is heartless and cruel. I wish my aunt, my good kind aunt, had never married him.'

'I should like to set the captive maiden free,' cried Ethelred, 'but this too is treason.'

'In me you would find a willing coadjutor,' replied the French maiden, with a lively gesture, 'treason or no treason.'

At the same instant they both started, Jacqueline suppressing a faint scream. Little Tyrrel having suddenly leaped over an intervening rock, was standing before them.

'You are a pretty fellow, Master Ethelred,' said he, 'running off with a damsel in this fashion, frightening us all out of our senses about you. We began to fear you had taken a love leap over a precipice, and expired in one another's arms. What a romantic tale I should have had to relate to the good people in Carnarvonshire. Are you aware that it is getting late? Remember we have a long sail to reach Cricceath. We shall not arrive home before the moon sets. My mother will be anxious.'

'My sword, Tyrrel, you little odd fish, nobody can understand half you say,' replied his brother, moving away from the spot, and carefully leading his fair companion over the large stones that lay in their path. 'Be off, you little rascal. Go tell Mistress Maud that we are in the rear, and not inclined to commit self-destruction.'

The moment the party entered the gates of the castle, they were attracted by the soft melancholy strains of the harp, issuing from one of the towers.

'A sad welcome! Poor Gladys!' said Jacqueline.

'I am sure you need not make yourself unhappy about her,' said Maud, 'it is only done to excite sympathy. Take care you are not duped by her, my good cousin. I have lived with her longer than you have.'

When they had reached the hall, Ethelred Conyers was missing.

'Where is your brother?' enquired Lady Stacey, addressing Stephen. 'You must not think of going home tonight, it is late, and besides Sir Gilbert wishes you to accompany him to the chase in the morning.'

At an early hour the next day the sportsmen hurried over their breakfast, in order to reach the hills in good time. The confusion, the running to and fro of the boys, the baying of the dogs, the loud whistling of the retainers, the deafening blast of Ethelred Conyers's bugle, combined to give an animated appearance to the castle court.

Several hours had elapsed after the noisy party had quitted the precincts of the old fortress, when a low growl and an occasional bark from a fierce mastiff in the court, drew Lady Stacey's attention.

'Shall I go and see what is the matter?' said Jacqueline, darting across the room in her usual good spirits. Immediately afterwards she disappeared in company with Gladys.

'O meistres bach! meistres bach,' cried a female voice, in a high sharp tone. 'No let that dog bite. That dog will kill me. Wele! Wele!' she continued, pointing her finger towards the porter. 'He will kill me, and the dog will kill me.' Immediately running up to them, she crouched down close to the ground, once more repeating:—'Wele, wele! The man is going to kill me.'

'Aye, aye, my good woman, have a care how you behave yourself, or the dog eat me if I don't make mincemeat of you,' said Black Donald, the spirit-drinking Scot, with a savage grin.

'Cease, my good man,' said Jacqueline in an interceding tone. 'The poor creature can do no harm. You are frightening her out of her senses. What have you there? What have you in your basket?'

'Cockles, meistres bach, very good cockles. I very hungry. I no nothing to eat for one, two days.' She then held out her two fingers in order that she might make them thoroughly understand her.

Mistress Maud now made her appearance, and the strange
woman upon inquiring who she was, instantly took up a
handful of the shell-fish, and with a low curtsey and a smile,
approached her, exclaiming in a high tone:—

'Take present—take present! Cockles very good.'

'Why, the woman must be mad to suppose I would touch
those nasty things with my fingers,' said Mistress Maud,
motioning the offering from her.

In an instant, with a blank look of despair, the woman let
the cockles fall from her hand upon the ground. The next
moment, as if a sudden thought struck her, she fell upon her
knees, and scrambling them up into her apron, presented them
to Jacqueline and Gladys, repeating the same words:—

'Take present! Take present! Cockles very good!'

'Poor woman,' exclaimed Jacqueline, 'she means well, and
this time her feelings shall not be hurt I will go and fetch
something to put them in. Tell her so, Gladys, and take care
that neither the dog nor the man hurt her.'

'I will,' replied Gladys. At that instant Katherine seized the
opportunity of slipping the letter into her hand, followed by a
rapid dialogue.

'O Katherine, bach anwyl Katherine,' cried Gladys, in a
whisper. It was with the greatest difficulty she could refrain from
throwing herself into the arms of her nurse, but she recollected
that Maud's eye was upon her, and immediately stooped over the
basket to conceal her face. Taking up a piece of seaweed which
lay among the cockles, she appeared to be carefully examining
it, while she conversed the whole time in an undertone.

'I wonder how you can stoop over those filthy smelling
cockles,' said Maud, 'and you,' continued she, addressing
Jacqueline, who at that instant returned. 'I am still more

surprised at your indulging the woman by accepting those miserable shellfish; such a low idea.'

'Well, never mind, Maud,' said the light-hearted French girl, laughing, 'I am not quite as fastidious as you are, cousin. Who knows but Gladys and I may enjoy our supper off them.'

'Really, Jacqueline, I am astonished at you,' retorted Maud with a toss of the head. 'Let the woman go. What is she jabbering about?'

'Pray let her stay a little longer,' said Jacqueline, in a pleading tone. 'I am sure it must give pleasure to Gladys to converse in her own tongue. It sounds so strange. I like to hear them.'

'Nonsense, cousin, your solicitation for Gladys is carried to too great an extreme,' said Mistress Maud, no longer able to conceal her annoyance. 'Black Donald,' cried she, turning to the porter, 'show that woman out of the gates.'

At the approach of the man the poor woman screamed. Lady Stacey ran out in alarm to see what was the matter.

'Poor thing! I should think she is not quite right in her head,' remarked the kind matron, after having heard the particulars from Maud.

Then approaching the woman, and placing a trifle in her hand, she said kindly:—

'My poor woman, you had better go; we are not fond of cockles at the castle.'

'No, mistress, you no like cockles, no,' then suddenly changing her voice, she added:—'I like mistress very good. I see on it, very good. You no like cockles. Well, well. Mistress I bring you present; no cockles. Mistress very good. I bring you present.' Then turning a beseeching look at the lady, she cried:— 'O mistress! I no like go that way; I fear in my heart the dog will kill me.'

'Gladys, go with her, and assure her the dog will not hurt her,' said Lady Stacey, compassionately.

With what a secret pleasure did the captive approach her nurse, and accompany her to the gate.

So well had Katherine played her part that not an individual in the castle suspected what had taken place.

'How pale you look, Gladys,' said the French maiden, who had waited for her return. 'Let us go upon the battlements—do you feel ill?'

'Yes,' whispered the captive, in broken accents. Scarcely had they reached the desired spot, before Gladys fainted. Jacqueline was alarmed, but by a simple remedy she soon recovered.

'I hope no one in the castle knows that I have been ill,' said Gladys, the moment she could speak. Upon being assured to the contrary, she appeared satisfied, and sat looking upon the sea for some minutes, her face still so pale, that her companion felt anxious, and loaded her with friendly attentions.

'Kind Jacqueline,' cried she, and throwing her arms around her friend, she burst into a flood of tears.

'Ah, Jacqueline! Did you suspect that anything had passed between myself and the woman?' resumed Gladys, recovering from her grief, 'That woman, that dear old woman, was my nurse. She told me all about my home. She has given me many messages from my own dear grandmother, and has also brought me a letter from my uncle. Oh, Jacqueline! You must not tell,' said she, lowering her voice; 'my uncle says he will not rest till I am restored to my mountain home. Is not this kind? Is not this good of him? And I shall be restored—I am certain I shall be restored, for uncle Kynfin never says what he does not mean.'

'Kynfin! Kynfin!' repeated Jacqueline, 'Kynfin Tudor! Can he be your uncle?'

'Yes, he is my uncle,' answered Gladys; 'why do you ask, why do you look surprised?'

'He told me never to breathe his name. Oh, Gladys! It was he who was so kind, so good to me at Vannes; it was he of whom I have so frequently spoken. I owe all to him. He saved my father from the scaffold. It was he, I feel convinced it could not have been any other, who preserved me and father from a watery grave. Kynfin Tudor! Can it be possible; the man I loved next to my father, the most in the world in those days of my childhood, was your uncle, my dear Gladys.'

Jacqueline shed tears of joy.

'Did not I feel there was a link between us?' said the captive maiden, returning Jacqueline's warm embrace. Once more the daughter of Harlech and the French maiden mingled their tears together.

As usual, the sportsmen did not return till dusk. When Sir Gilbert had refreshed himself by exchanging his attire, he repaired to the banqueting hall, and sinking into a chair, exclaimed, with not a little raillery, 'So, ho! Mistress Stacey, there has been a scuffle among you womankind, since we left this morning.'

'No black eyes, I hope,' cried little Tyrrel, staring into Jacqueline's face, and chuckling as if amused.

'No, not quite come to that; I am happy to see,' resumed Sir Gilbert, falling back into his chair and laughing immoderately.

'I don't half understand all this joking,' said Lady Stacey; 'what is it, Maud?' I should be glad of an explanation.'

'Ha! Ha! Good Mistress Stacey, you were all at drawn swords in the court yard, to-day.'

'Well, to be sure,' replied Lady Stacey, laughing in her turn, 'who could have told you?—Black Donald, I suppose. After all, what was it; a slight dispute about a poor crazy woman, who was frightened at the dog.'

'It was not Black Donald who gave me the account, graphic as life,' once more resumed the keeper, enjoying the puzzled look of Lady Stacey and the peculiarly uneasy expression of Mistress Maud. Little Tyrrel then became an amusement to him, as he sat eyeing the party with his waggish expression of countenance.

During the discussion, Ethelred was standing at the lower end of the apartment, in the recess of one of the windows, close to Gladys. She was winding thread for Lady Stacey. After watching her a few minutes, he addressed her in a deep tone:—

'Although the sun had scarcely risen this morning, I saw you upon the battlements, Mistress Gladys. Dare I venture to tell you that the further I left the grey old turrets behind, the more frequently did my heart wander back to you?'

Gladys made no reply, but her thin taper fingers ran more nimbly over her work. The youth continued:—

'I am afraid you are angry with me for what I said yesterday. Why will you not accept of sympathy? Why not let me brighten your captivity? Mistress Gladys, you do not know how deep an interest I take in you, and that one cold look, one cold word from you, gives me pain.' As Ethelred finished this sentence, he leant forward, and looked earnestly in her face. Gladys involuntarily raised her dark blue eyes. The moment they met his, a deep blush mantled her cheeks.

She gradually recovered herself, and answered firmly and decisively:—

'I am not angry, though your words pain me, Ethelred Conyers. How often shall I have to request of you not to speak thus. I cannot accept your sympathy. Don't ask me why—I cannot.' The colour mounted again into her face.

'Mistress Gladys, I must know why,' said Ethelred, drawing nearer to her and looking still more in earnest; 'there can be no valid reason why not. I implore you not to be so unkind— Tell me why not?'

Gladys dropped the thread from her fingers and with much hesitation, continued:—

'Oh! Ethelred Conyers, why do you ask me? I would keep it from you, but you will not let me. I cannot accept of any sympathy, or be under any obligation to a Saxon, one of that race who are the persecutors of our land, our common foes. Alas! Even my having any intercourse with you (did my people know it), would lower me in their eyes. Never speak thus again.'

'And because I am of that unfortunate lineage, publicly, not privately, the enemies of this wild land, I must be hated and despised by one in whom the whole of my happiness is centred,' said Ethelred, in a broken, disappointed tone. 'Oh, Gladys! These are bitter words.' His face turned deadly pale, as he at the same time crushed a rejected sprig of heather between his clenched fingers.

Gladys saw the deadly hue upon his cheek, as her eyes once more met his earnest gaze, but neither of them spoke. A moment after, she felt a thrill pass through her veins; for he was gone.

'Well, master Ethelred! Do you intend to go without your

supper?' cried little Tyrrel, looking towards the window which the youth had only that moment quitted. Taking his place before the smoking viands, he continued:—

'Master Ethelred is always fond of speaking to the ladies without a third person being present; is he not, mistress Jacqueline?' looking very archly at the French girl.

'Well, he is not singular,' replied Jacqueline, laughing, 'a third person often makes me feel stiff and formal.'

'Perhaps so,' replied little Tyrrel, highly amused, and he whispered to his companion:—

'There are two who are fond of talking to each other, mistress Maud and Henry Stourton. They say they are betrothed; I don't believe it. I don't think he is very devoted, he admires the captive maiden.'

'Hush!' said Jacqueline. Tyrrel immediately turned his eye upon Gladys, who had just taken a seat opposite to them, and was silent.

'Where is Ethelred?' now became the general inquiry. No one could answer the question, till half an hour afterwards one of the attendants informed them that the master of Cricceath had gone across the bay. The boatmen had left word to that effect.

They looked at each other with surprise, and Gladys waited with impatience an opportunity of escaping. To her, it had been an eventful day.

The following morning, Stephen and little Tyrrel took their departure from Harlech, and were accompanied as far as the boat by mistress Maud, Jacqueline, and Henry Stourton. The morning being fine, they extended their walk upon the sands, when they suddenly came in contact with Griff, the pilot.

'Well, master Henry,' said the Pilot, in a very familiar tone, 'I hear-ed master Edward is gone to fight the French, and good luck to him, says I, and far better says I, than breaking loose into a smuggler's den. Ha! Ha! master Henry, I thought you would think on it, and not cut your own throats.'

'By my troth! old Griff, you are very free,' cried Henry, laughing and shaking the pilot's hand off his shoulder, 'Let me undeceive you, old Griff, if you suppose that it is fear which prevents us from taking immediate measures against those lawless fellows. Not a bit of it, we shall have them yet, some of these days, when they least expect it.'

'The Dewines, master Henry; you have not forgotten what I told you about her?'

'Come away, Henry,' said mistress Maud, looking half disgusted, half frightened at the speaker. 'I wish you would not listen to him. What a horrid old man.'

'And you are not afraid of the fierce Ap Rhys, neither, master Henry?' persisted the Pilot; 'that man who has the courage of a lion the savageness of a wolf, and the cunning of a fox. You had better take my advice, master Henry. Have no dealings with him; cross not his path.'

The old pilot became so energetic in his entreaty that he once more placed his rough hand upon Henry.

'Do come away, Henry,' once more exclaimed mistress Maud. 'He frightens me.'

'The fishes! the fishes! Mistress Stacey. I think it is a pity on it that you don't know who your friend is. But I am an old foul, an old fool, to trouble my head about any of you. I'll never speak to you any more, none of you, kith or kin. So farewell, master Henry; this is my last warning. Put not your finger in the fire, for it will burn; nor your hand into the hive, the bees will sting. Remember this when the evil day comes; and that those were the words of old Griff, the pilot.'

CHAPTER VIII

The Successful Emissary— Mountaineers Aroused— Pirate Superstition—The Prophecy Repeated—An Unexpected Departure

'I HAVE seen her!—I have seen her!' cried the breathless and exhausted Katherine, as she hurried into the presence of Kynfin Tudor and his mother. 'I have seen the daughter of Harlech. I am proud in my heart of her. She looks the picture of what she is, the grandchild of our dead chief, my dear old master! Oh, how like she is to her father!'

'And did you speak to her, and did you hear her voice?' inquired Ap Dafydd, hurriedly.

'Yes, son of Harlech; she said her days were spent in yearning for her people,' replied Katherine.

'And what more did my wyres bach say?' asked the widow of Ap Jevan, with extreme eagerness.

'Her first words were to inquire after you, good mistress; and to tell me, by night and by day, she longed to be by your side. Her thoughts were ever in the Cwm.'

'O, fy mheth bach anwyl! My own wyres bach!' cried the old lady, clasping her hands together, while the tears rolled down her cheeks.

'Did you ask, Katherine, if they were kind to her?' inquired the son of Harlech, greatly moved.

'Yes, she told me that mistress Stacey was good to her; but mistress Maud was harsh, and watches her with the eye of a falcon.'

'And did she say anything of Sir Gilbert?'

'That he had been very severe and cruel to her, but that now he took little notice of her save that he was always causing her pain by using bitter words against our people and our country.'

'Fy mheth bach anwyl! Would that she were here once more,' murmured the grandmother. 'How could anyone find it in their hearts to be cruel to my wyres bach?'

'Did she not speak of the French maiden, no kind words for her?' again inquired Kynfin.

'Yes, son of Harlech, much; she had never known a happy day till mistress Jacqueline came to the castle. She is good and kind. So different from mistress Maud. Had it not been for her, our words would have been few. She spoke gently, and seemed to be fond of meistres bach.'

Kynfin Tudor bent his head upon his band and remained for some time silent.

'Katherine,' at length he exclaimed, 'what did the child say about our restoring her to her home?'

'It made her heart bound within her; but she told me to tell you, son of Harlech, that Sir Gilbert was a hard man, and a favourite of Edward of York. For the future safety of the Cwm, you were to be careful how you acted. She would be grieved that her freedom should be at the cost of the good people there.'

'The child is right,' murmured Ap Dafydd: 'she has the forethought of her grandsire, and the kind, unselfish heart of her mother. I know the part we have to play is a desperate one;

yet it must be played. St David help us! The child shall no longer be under the roof of that Saxon tyrant. It must not be!— Men of Harlech! Men of Merioneth! I will appeal to you! Sir Gilbert must be overcome. You will not refuse to aid me when you know who is concerned in it!'

Ap Dafydd wandered forth into the open air, to calm his excited feelings and mature his plans. Howel crossed his path, laden with provisions for the homestead.

'Howel, you are the very man I want!' he exclaimed, suddenly arresting his attention. 'Go tonight to the honest people in the Cwm, and tell them that the son of Harlech desires to speak with them at dusk, tomorrow evening. Let them gather themselves together, secretly, both young men and old.'

On the following evening, though wet and gloomy, Kynfin Tudor, accompanied by the hale old man, Howel, tracked their way through the wild and cheerless glen, until they reached the rudely constructed building, used sometimes for a chapel, and sometimes for clandestine meetings similar to the present.

The son of Harlech had no sooner appeared among the mountaineers, than a rush was made to reach and wring the hand of their late chieftain's son; and to express one by one their heartfelt joy at his return.

Kynfin was moved by their touching conduct. He acknowledged their devotion in a manner worthy of a descendant of the great Ap Jevan. The old men heaped blessings upon his head, the young spontaneously swore to support him and his house.

At length he waved his hand as a signal that he was about to harangue them. They stood before him with their heads uncovered, and an expression of earnest desire to catch his words.

'Since last I stood among you, my noble, faithful countrymen, melancholy changes have taken place, changes which we could neither foresee nor control. Alas! my friends, I have returned to my home to find it desolate, to my beloved mother to find her sitting by her hearth solitary and broken in spirit, bereaved of her last comfort. The child, the only hope of our noble house, the grand-daughter of your lamented chieftain, torn from her. By what means she was stolen from her grandmother's side you are already well aware.

'I hear that you have mourned over her fate, and are mourning still—that you have endeavoured to the uttermost of your power to restore her to the lone walls of Cader y Cil, but have failed in your endeavours. I feel grateful for your solicitude. I am at the same time keenly alive to the child's position. Bitterness touches my soul; my heart is overshadowed. At night my dreams are haunted by the spirit of her parents, who are ever crying to me, to fly to the rescue of their child. Their cries shall be heard. Let me tell you, brave men of Merioneth—brave men of the Cwm, that I have gathered you together tonight to ask you to lend me your aid in a scheme for the recapture of our beloved child. The daughter of Harlech has expressed a wish that her freedom should not be purchased at the sacrifice of any of her beloved people. Let us hope that it may be so. To gain possession of the person of Sir Gilbert, the merciless persecutor of our child and country, is necessary for our present and future safety in the Cwm. I do not wish for his blood, but to bind him hand and foot, and place him where he can never more see the day. The next time we meet I will explain the whole plan, meanwhile I request you to be ready at a moment's notice, to enter with me into a daring undertaking, perhaps to fight manfully in the cause of the restoration of the daughter of Harlech.'

Clamorous and enthusiastic were the voices which resounded on all sides. 'We will risk everything, home, children, life, for the daughter of Harlech, the grandchild of our lamented chief. Yes, son of Harlech, we shall be proud and happy to hazard all for her restoration, should it be necessary.'

'Enough, enough,' replied Kynfin, 'you are what I thought you to be, the faithful and devoted. When I come here again in a day or two hence, or it may be in a week, be ready.'

Shortly after, in company with his old retainer, he disappeared among the crowd, and retraced his steps to Cader y Cil.

'Is that you, Kynfin Tudor?' said a youthful voice, just as the son of Harlech and the old sentinel were about to descend a steep defile, not above two hundred paces from the house of meeting.

'Is it Roderike ap Maelgwyn who asks that question?' inquired Kynfin in a tone of surprise. 'What are you doing here?'

'In search of the mate of the *Eryr*. I did not look for the good fortune of finding you so soon,' replied the young man. 'I am the bearer of a message of great importance. The Dewines calls for you. There has been a terrible affair since you were absent. I expect a desperate struggle will take place before they have done with us. King Edward is acquainted with our handiwork in the neighbourhood, through that pic-fingering Sir Gilbert Stacey and his son, he who went a few months back to join the King's troops in France. The old knave will pay dearly; you know what sort of a man Ap Rhys is when roused—savage as a tiger. But come, Ap Dafydd, we must not be wasting time here, when our immediate presence is required elsewhere. Did you hear the message? The Dewines calls for you.'

'Then I must go,' murmured Kynfin, and turning to his trusty servant, he said:—

'Howel, my good man, return to Cader y Cil, and when my mother inquires for me, tell her that her son has been called away upon urgent business, but will return shortly.'

The amazement with which the old man overheard the dialogue between his master and the stranger, can scarcely be imagined. He turned away with a heavy heart, and pursued his route in silence, forming a thousand conjectures as to what his master could be about. What could he have to do with that terrible woman on the opposite shore? He must belong to some lawless band, that was as clear as noonday. 'O'r Tad! O'r Tad!' muttered the old man mournfully, 'what will it all come to? Ow, ow, all goes very differently to what it was in my early days! St David preserve my young master from any fresh trouble.'

Ap Dafydd with his young companion now hurried over the hills in the contrary direction. 'Now, Roderike, let me hear the particulars of these government proceedings. How came you by this information?'

'It was Griff, the pilot, who first put us upon the scent; you know when we once get upon it what dogs we are to track out the game. I fear the old keeper has not the slightest chance of his life. Our captain has sworn as sure as there is sand upon the sea-shore, he will not quit the coast till he has laid him low. Perhaps, Ap Dafydd, you are not aware that he is an old enemy of Thomas Nevil, the bastard of Fauconbridge. Terrible work there would be if he wore to get into the hands of the man who they think has long ago perished by the executioner's axe. Imagine King Edward's amazement, his wrath, upon discovering Fauconbridge is living—the man he so dreaded;—but this is dangerous language, even in these wild parts.'

'What does the Dewines say to it all? She was the chief mover in the artifice,' said Kynfin, scarcely noticing Ap Maelgwyn's last words.

'She is boiling and bubbling up at a fearful rate. She curses King Edward, whom she still calls Earl of Marche, and sends every member of his family to the bottomless pit. "That vain old Duchess," said she, meaning the King's mother, "I should like to see her stripped of her gay feathers, tied in a sack, and thrown into the Thames, for the mud eels to fatten upon." I should like to know the secrets of the Dewines's history, coloured as I imagine they are by intrigue, tragedy, and deception.'

'There is a strange link between the Dewines and Dhu, I cannot make out what it is,' remarked the son of Harlech.

'I have often thought so,' rejoined Ap Maelgwyn. Both walked on in silence for some distance. At length they reached the beach opposite to the creek of Borth, and Ap Maelgwyn conducted his companion to the boat a little way down.

'The wind is with us, we shall be over in little time,' said the youth, hauling up the sails and putting the boat in trim.

'It was old Griff who warned you of the impending danger,' said Kynfin Tudor, taking his seat in the boat. 'You have not explained the nature of it, you merely say that King Edward has been made acquainted with our locality.'

'Did I not?' answered his companion, 'why then I must

inform you that an armed force has arrived in our vicinity, with a royal mandate to give no quarter to the smugglers, or in other words, to secure them dead or alive. The knights and esquires in the neighbourhood have promised to render every assistance in their power. Two of the revenue crafts are hovering about the coast. You may be certain they already count upon having secured their game. Aye, aye, those revenue rascals—but it is well they think so. They are much mistaken. Who, I should like to know, ever beat Ap Rhys, when he was supported by the Dewines? We are going to be beforehand with them, Kynfin Tudor. It is on that account the good mother literally pushed me out of her doors, and told me to make as much speed as if the devil was at my heels. I was not to return without the mate of the *Eryr*. She declared she would not stir a finger in the matter till you made your appearance. She also spoke of two individuals in the castle who interested not only you, but herself. Dhu was out of temper with her.'

'What are their plans?' demanded the son of Harlech, with greater eagerness.

'I cannot enlighten you in that particular,' replied Roderike. 'I left them arguing the point. Dhu was for one thing, and the good lady for another, as usual. All I know is that an attack will be made upon Harlech at night. You are to take a prominent part on account of the interest you have in the affair, and the knowledge of the fortress.'

Ap Dafydd remained silent.

'Can't you give me a cast to the other side?' cried a voice from the sands; and the next instant Griff, the pilot, after wading knee-deep in the water, leaped into the boat.

'The fishes! young man,' cried he, 'what are you doing

here, playing upon the waters, when the devil is about to play the very fishes with you? Yn enw, goodness! you should have taken my warning, as the smuggler of Madoc did, buried his kegs half a mile in the sands, and was then off by the first tide in the morning.'

'Aye, aye, Griff, that may appear very judicious in your eyes,' replied Roderike, 'but we are of a different mould to Shonyn Goch. We have our game to play, he has his; time will show who displayed most skill upon the occasion. Shonyn has to get clear of the bar and the revenue boats, as well as we.'

'I know that of old,' replied the pilot. 'I know you to be sharp fellows, of very different mould to the smuggler of Madoc. I think it is as well to tell you that the old keeper has scudded over to-day to have a talk with the government chaps. They will be upon you before you are aware of it, sharp as you are, good masters. Keep a good look out.'

'But Sir Gilbert returns every night to Harlech?' resumed Roderike, inquiringly.

'Always, either over the Traeth Bychan or over the Traeth Mawr,' replied the pilot.

'I don't care a dead shark's tooth about the case,' said Roderike, running the boat in among the rocks, and setting the pilot ashore. 'Thank you for your warning, Griff, time will show if we shall pay attention to it.' He waved his hand as the boat ran for the creek of Borth. In a few minutes they arrived before the house of Gêst.

'Welcome, son of Harlech, mate of the *Eryr*,' said the Lady of Gêst, giving him a nod of recognition, and motioning him to be seated. 'Thou hast done well, aye wisely, not to tarry when I called for you.'

'Good Lady of Gêst, I would know what it is you expect of

me. Let it not be your request that Ap Dafydd shall take the life of any!'

'Ha! Ha! Ha!' laughed the Dewines. 'See how alarmed he is! Dhu, you said it would be so. Ha! Ha! Have you never yet spilled blood, you innocent?'

Kynfin moved across the apartment, struck his breast, and muttered several incoherent sentences.

'Whist! Whist!' continued the Dewines, once more addressing the son of Harlech. 'Blind beetle that you are, to make so much ado about nothing! There's no occasion for you to dabble your fingers in blood. Dhu ap Rhys will spare you that trouble. You need not be in sight, or even within reach of the gore that is about to be spilled. So now drive away your fears and give me all your attention. So the son of Harlech took upon himself to act without consulting the Lady of Gêst? Her eyes have been upon you. It so happens that all is well. The followers of the Red Rose, the brave men in the Cwm, whom you harangued in the meeting-house, will be in great request tomorrow night. Son of Harlech, I have an important post for you to fill, and much has to be done, anticipating the appointed hour. Before sunrise you must be skimming again across the bay. You must obtain an interview with Rowland, and give him this packet,' presenting it to Kynfin, consisting of a small parcel of paper folded carefully. 'Tell him that it is the Dewines who sends it him. Bid him heed her words that it may be well with him. To disobey will bring down a curse upon his head, aye, bring his grey locks to the grave. Impress upon him that the two maidens must be ready to deliver themselves up to you at the moment of the onset. He must admit you into the fortress. He must give the garrison that powder which is in the packet in their drink at supper. It will intoxicate them. Those pills are for the porter and his dog, deadly enough in their effect. They are to be sacrificed, and Sir Gilbert must be sacrificed. We will leave that to Dhu.'

Kynfin Tudor shuddered, and averted his gaze, while he said solemnly:— 'St David preserve us! Good mother, do you not fear the judgment?'

'Whist! Whist! Out on you! You have the heart of a chicken.'

'Good Lady of Gêst,' cried Ap Dafydd, looking wildly round, 'Blood! Blood!'

'Zookers!' interposed Dhu, 'surely, Ap Dafydd, you don't suppose I would suffer that sordid villain to escape my vengeance, when an opportunity offers!—that double smooth-faced scoundrel! the base, meddling hypocrite!—the greatest enemy I ever had! No—on my soul! I will not spare him. How many times has he tried to take my life? He has persecuted me from my cradle, that demon!'

'Whist! Whist! Dhu, speak not in that way,' said the witch, putting her hand upon his shoulder. 'Lose not your temper, hot-brained rover, nor again interrupt me, till I have delivered my injunctions.

'That the Lady Stacey may not witness the bloody deed— she has been kind to the captive maiden,' continued the Dewines; 'Rowland must be told to give Sir Gilbert the alarm that the freebooters are coming down upon his cattle. This will be a sure means of enticing him from his chamber. He will fall into Ap Rhys's embrace.'

'Oh! cannot this be avoided, good mother?' hastily responded Kynfin, with an imploring look. 'We can take him prisoner, but not slay him.'

'Zookers! the furies take you, Kynfin Tudor!' cried Dhu, in

an angry voice, 'would you have us all sacrificed for the sake of that base, pampered fool of a Keeper, who would deprive himself of his beef and bowl, which he thinks more of than anything else, that we might be hanged. I should have thought you, Ap Dafydd, would have been as glad to have got rid of the vile persecutor of your land, as I shall be of my old enemy. The base villain! I shall give him what he deserves. Don't preach to me, mate of the *Eryr*. Nothing will move me from my purposes. To please you and the good Lady of Gêst, I have consented to convey your brother's child and the French maiden to Vannes. I should think that was enough for Dhu ap Rhys to bargain, to cumber himself with womankind, when he would be at his own work; but I have said it, son of Harlech.'

'Whist! Whist! You babbling dolt. You are wasting time, you sea rover,' interrupted the Lady of Gêst.

'On my soul! I am out of patience with Ap Dafydd,' persisted Dhu. 'Who would not be in my place? The furies take the fellow!'

'Whist! Whist! Dhu. Cold—be cold!' said the Dewines, holding up her finger, and looking sternly in his face. 'No passion, lest the evil eye be turned upon you. Take care from fixing the evil eye through impolitic anger. People pine under the evil eye into wasting death. It makes men, like you rovers of the sea, tame as a sick girl, aye sick in spirit, and unable to say, "God bless you!" Didst thou never hear of the slain by the evil eye? Beware the light touches thee not with its emerald flash. Thou hast seen the little snake creep stealthily from its damp cell in wary involutions, and fascinate the bird that would fain fly, but, in place of effecting its intention, flutter nearer and nearer to the poisonous fangs that doom it to destruction. Such is the power of the evil eye. Shall I turn it upon you, my son? No, no, Dhu: be cool. Husband thy anger. Ap Dafydd has been a good friend to thee. Visit it not on him.'

'The evil eye, Lady of Gêst! St Cyric keep it from me! I will be cool, good mother—I will be cool. What you require of me, that will I do. The son of Harlech shall have no cause to complain. I will keep my word—only keep the evil eye from me!'

The Dewines saw she had struck the right chord of a spirit dauntless and fearless before men, but abject under the apprehension of supernatural power, to which physical resistance was a thread of gossamer.

'Listen to me, pirate chief. I have seen the evil eye at my bidding look through the dark midnight, the dead sea to human vision, when all around was starless. I have seen that eye descend upon the topmast of a devoted vessel, and dance and reel there as the bark rode over the foaming furrows. Then a wild shriek has struck on the ear through the rayless night. After that eye had undulated, as the vessel rose and sank upon the ocean abysses, all was hushed, save the hiss of the curling wave over the bubblings of the drowning, as they sank in the boiling waters. Aye, rovers of the sea, you may look scared— but it is true! Hast thou never seen the evil eye upon the mast-head, Dhu? I have seen it there, when taken for the *corpi santi*. It lured my enemy to destruction under the sign of security.'

'Hold, good mother. For the love of heaven speak no more of these things!' cried Dhu. 'It makes my blood creep. I will keep my word. I have said it.'

'That is all right, my brave boy. You will do wisely to abide by the words of the Lady of Gêst. Hark ye! Remember, Dhu, the evil eye can penetrate through everything—even through the black sea of nothing, where the forms of things are unknown, and over which the stars never twinkle and the suns have all gone out. There, even there, the evil eye can penetrate. Do you hear that, Dhu? The Lady of Gêst has power to turn it aside from all brave spirits like thine, my bold boy, whom it delights me to serve.'

'Well, well, good mother, I am thine—thine as ever. Ap Dafydd is squeamish—more nice than wise, methinks, to wade to the middle of the stream and not to proceed further. It is of little consequence. Vengeance on the Keeper of Harlech is secured to myself. The satisfaction to others is no concern of mine. With me vengeance is virtue.'

Kynfin Tudor remained silent. Things must take their own course, thought he. Soon his brain was busily occupied with his poor mother, the daughter of Harlech, and *la petite* Jacqueline. Must he leave his beloved parent once more desolate, and not even restore to her the joy of her heart before he departed? A thousand thoughts flashed across his mind, till he became bewildered.

Ap Maelgwyn, who was sitting near, watched with newly awakened interest all that was passing. Dhu looked more composed, while the Lady of Gêst appeared as if she expected the son of Harlech had still something to impart.

'Well, son of Harlech, are you satisfied?' inquired she; 'we know what is best for you, far better than you do yourself. I know what you think, you think it strange I should have decided upon a plan to take the daughter of Harlech from her country. It must be so; destiny decrees it. Kynfin Tudor, it is necessary you should take her to Brittany, and present her to the Earl of Richmond. Before a score of years have run out their hours, he will mount England's throne. You will have the daughter of Harlech restored to her inheritance; you will have your country emancipated from the thraldom which it now endures. If so, take her to the Earl of Richmond. Let Jasper of Hatfield be present. She must then plead for her country and herself—she must make him promise that when he reigns over England's smiling land, he will sign a charter for the freedom of your country, and restore her inheritance. You know how deeply the Earls of Pembroke and Richmond are indebted to you. Had it not been for you, they would long since have been mouldering into their mother earth. You must do as I tell you. If the daughter of Harlech is like her noble grandfather, she will not be faint-hearted; the love of her country, and the desire to bring about the great work which her grandsire begun, will prompt her. Now, son of Harlech, forget not my message to Henry of Richmond: tell him these are the prophetic words of the Lady of Gêst—

'King of England reign will he—
He shall a Seventh Henry be—
Full of health, wealth, peace and plenty,
Years above the number twenty!

Speak out boldly what I have related to you. He will laugh; let him laugh—heed him not—lest you be as great a fool as he.'

As she concluded these words with great emphasis, she strode up to the window, and immediately turned again, exclaiming, in her usual high tone—

'Out on us—out on us—why it is break of day!' She

whisked round the apartment, and struck many of the sleeping men upon the back with her matted switch, shouting in their ears—'Rise, you sluggards! Will you snore here till the sun sets? Up, you heavy slumberers.'

She then took Kynfin aside; they conversed together in a low whisper, occasionally broken by a sharp high word from the witch, either to silence the busy jabbering of the men, or to impress some command upon the troubled and confused Kynfin, who began to grow faint from fasting and fatigue.

'Methinks, Ap Dafydd, you are sick in body as well as soul,' said she, in hurried accents, on perceiving that he not only changed colour but trembled. 'Get food between your lips, man, you need it; you have a hard day's work before you.'

Kynfin obeyed, not ill pleased to be released from her incessant talking. Taking his place by Roderike, they exchanged looks not without meaning, and then did ample justice to the viands which had been placed smoking before them.

'Gam, you must accompany the mate of the *Eryr*,' said the Lady of Gêst, approaching the table; 'you have a sister at Harlech—at her house my important business must be transacted. Remember, you see the old man as soon as you touch the shore; waste not your moments upon the waves; make all speed to reach the Cwm in good time. Summon those brave mountaineers; give the directions you already know. Impress upon them, Kynfin Tudor, that they must keep the castle till the *Eryr* is out of sight. After that let them fly to their hills again, and hide themselves from the light of day. A diligent search is certain to be made; and if not cautious, their heads will pay the penalty for your offences. That would, indeed, bring down sorrow upon the daughter of Harlech. Therefore be cautious, be politic.'

Kynfin set out shortly afterwards upon his hazardous mission, in company with Gam. Upon reaching the cottage at Harlech, they were told that Rowland was in the town. He was quickly summoned into their presence.

Rowland had never seen his young master since that memorable day when the family of Ap Jevan took their departure from the fortress. His joy knew no bounds; he wrung his hands, and looked in Kynfin's face, uttering expressions of delight, at beholding again the son of his old master. When he spoke of his little mistress, the daughter of Harlech, of her love for her people, of her beauty, of her endurance under all her cruel persecutions—the tears came into the old man's eyes. He declared she had been the only being in the castle that ever gladdened his sight.

Kynfin Tudor was pressed for time; he disclosed the conspiracy. The old man at first was embarrassed, and shrank from the treachery which it devolved upon him to execute; nevertheless for the love of his little mistress, and the fear of the terrible woman of Gêst, he consented, with a few exceptions, to play the part which had been assigned to him.

Not recognised by anyone, Kynfin passed through the town of Harlech on his way to the Cwm, and was soon on the threshold of Cader y Cil. There he flew to embrace his mother, and to pour into her ear a few words of consolation. He promised that when he returned her 'wyres bach' should be the first to throw herself into her arms, and cheer her last days by her cheerful presence.

The unhappy parent wept bitterly, while Kynfin, placing his kerchief to his eyes, wrung the faithful domestic by the hand, and once more quitted his wild dwelling in the Cwm for the shores of Brittany.

CHAPTER IX

A Vain Intercession—Unexpected Intelligence—The Saxon Lover— A Resolve of Friendship

'BE not angry with me, my uncle, listen to me,' said Jacqueline, in a tone of distress, sinking upon her knees at the same moment before Sir Gilbert; 'you are going to seize the smugglers, you have said that King Edward will have them all executed without trial. Kynfin Tudor, one of them, saved my father and myself from a watery grave. I implore you to intercede for his life. He is a good and honourable man, unlike the rest of that lawless race. It was from misfortune, not choice, that he joined them. Let my words touch your heart; spare the life of Kynfin Tudor, else I shall never more be happy.'

'My sword! do my eyes deceive me; *ma petite* Jacqueline, the simple French maiden, pleading in this earnest way, and upon her knees too, for a worthless cut-throat, a vile piratical scoundrel,' vociferated the keeper in a voice mingled with surprise and indignation. 'I intercede for that dangerous rebel, the first mate on the smuggler's hark, the colleague of that daredevil, Dhu ap Rhys, the scourge of our shores! I intercede for him, after going such lengths to secure the villain and his cunning accomplices! I intercede for him, after representing his atrocities to our royal master! My sword! little mistress, you know not what you ask. Honourable indeed! Pray who told you

272

that this notorious smuggler was honourable? I suppose he told you so himself, the lying bandit. You were fool enough to believe him, simple-hearted child that you are. I will enlighten you. That man was once in better circumstances. He is the son of a Welsh chief, the more disgrace to him. He ran away from his home eight years ago, and joined the lawless crew. Had it not been for him, Dhu ap Rhys would never have set foot upon these shores. Such is the individual for whom you would have me intercede. I see the colour come and go upon your cheeks. You may well blush, pleading for such a man.'

Jacqueline had risen from her knees, and stood pale and trembling before her angry uncle.

'No, uncle, I do not blush for what I have done,' said Jacqueline, with a quivering lip. 'You refuse me my petition, you wrong Kynfin Tudor; I know more of his history than you do. He is to be pitied, not censured. Should his blood be shed and it comes home to you, remember you refused me the boon I pleaded upon my knees.'

'Mistress Jacqueline, you are not yourself. How comes it that you are so familiar with the smuggler's history? A pretty pass things are come to. A young lady to be mistress of such a man's secrets. I don't understand it. On my sword! mistress Jacqueline, this affair must be looked into, you are under our charge. I shall not be satisfied, unless an explanation is offered.'

Jacqueline coloured deeply, and said:—

'No, Sir Gilbert, you have not granted me my petition, therefore I will give you no explanation.' She immediately left the apartment.

'Upon my sword! we don't know what women are, till they are tried,' muttered Sir Gilbert. 'These foreigners to boot, are always more difficult to deal with than the daughters of our own land. Who would have thought it of that simple-looking maiden? Beshrew me! it looks bad. I must leave the affair, I see, for her ladyship to unravel. The devil keep me from meddling with womankind.'

'Well, Jacqueline, I can see, by your disappointed face that your pleading has been of no avail,' said Gladys, as the French maiden joined her in the hall. 'I cannot say I am disappointed; I never indulged a solitary hope of your success.'

'My uncle is very cruel,' repeated Jacqueline, bitterly; 'I only hope and pray that the smugglers may escape from his grasp, aye, all of them.'

'I hope they may,' repeated Gladys, solemnly. 'I cannot think what my uncle is about that I have not heard from him again. This suspense is most painful.'

'It is indeed,' repeated Jacqueline. 'If possible, it is worse for me than you. Should he perish, I shall always feel that I brought him to his end. I was the innocent cause of his joining that lawless company.'

'Be comforted, Jacqueline; let us hope the best,' said Gladys, affectionately. 'You know that Dhu ap Rhys has always outwitted his pursuers. We only hear one side of the question; they may yet escape.'

'Santa Maria! grant it,' repeated the French maiden, fervently, while owing to her late excitement she felt so ill that she was obliged to retire from the room.

Some hours after Gladys had been sitting with her, and as she was retiring from the upper gallery on the way to her own chamber, her steps were arrested by the words:—

'Can I speak with you, meistres bach?' Thus muttered old Rowland from behind one of the pillars. 'I have been watching long for you.'

'Certainly,' replied the maiden, looking inquiringly round to see from whence the voice proceeded; 'speak on, yet be careful what you say.'

'Ie yn wir,' said the aged man, suddenly standing before her, 'we cannot be too cautious. It would be death, if the Saxons should overhear us,' continued he in a whisper, anxiously glancing from side to side. 'My words are for the daughter of Harlech's ears and none else.'

'Follow me, then,' said the captive; 'in my chamber no one can disturb us.' They left the gallery together.

Having entered the apartment, the old domestic immediately closed the door, and then stood at a respectful distance.

'Kynfin ap Dafydd will be here tonight, to set the daughter of Harlech free,' were Rowland's startling words.

Gladys stood before him almost petrified. 'What, Rowland, tonight?—tonight?' she repeated.

'Ie yn wir, meistres bach, you and the French maiden are to be in the chapel at half an hour after midnight. All the apparel you wish to take, place upon this table. I will see to its being conveyed away.'

'Mistress Jacqueline to accompany me? Suppose she should not consent, then where are we to go to?' inquired Gladys, eagerly. 'It would not be safe to take her to the Cwm.'

'They will take you away in the smuggler's bark, to Brittany,' said Rowland; 'but Kynfin ap Dafydd will tell you all when you see him. Mistress Jacqueline must not refuse; her life and your own depend upon it. You must break it to her when the family have retired to rest, and whatever you do, meistres bach, be in the chapel at half an hour after midnight.'

An indescribable sensation of delight flowed through every

vein of the child of the mountains. 'I am no longer to be a captive—no longer a partaker of the Saxon bread! I am to be set free! Free!' In the midst of her excitement, a shadow passed across her brow, and looking up anxiously at the old man, she exclaimed:—

'But, Rowland, tell me. Why am I to go to France and not to the Cwm, into the arms of my dear, my own dear grandmother, who is so unhappy about me?'

'Ap Dafydd will set your heart at rest,' replied Rowland, preparing to leave the room. 'There sounds the great gong for prayers. Dyd! Dyd! That gong will not sound again till the dreadful deed is done,' muttered the old man to himself as he closed the door, while an involuntary shudder shook his frame.

Gladys looked up fondly at the good Father Nutze, for she soon afterwards entered the chapel, and then knelt down to tell her beads. But her heart beat so quickly that she could not collect her thoughts. When should she kneel again in that holy sanctuary? When again hear the sound of the good priest's voice? Till then, she did not know how dear he was to her; how often he had been kind and sympathising, when everyone else had been cold towards her. How often he had softened her heart when evil passions rebelled within her bosom. She was going to be free—to be launched upon the world! She would no longer have his protection; yet how much more she would need it. She gazed upon his face again, and then bent her head upon her bosom, while the tears gushed into her eyes. So long and earnestly did she pray that when she arose from her knees, she was surprised to find all had left the chapel, save one individual, who had been kneeling by her side, and that was Ethelred Conyers. A thrill vibrated through her frame, and she slowly glided past him into an anti-chamber, the windows of which looked over the sea. There she had been in the habit of spending many of her hours. The moon was shining full into the room, and as she approached the well-known casement, the noble Saxon youth was standing by her side.

'Gladys, we have not met before, today,' said he, in a soft tone.

'No, Ethelred Conyers, but that can be no reason why you should intrude upon me, even at my devotions.'

'Gladys, would you deny the despised Saxon the privilege of having knelt by your side? To mingle my prayers with yours lessened my sorrow. Gladys, Gladys, be not cruel; you know not how miserable I am.'

The wretchedness of this appeal at length found an entrance to the maiden's heart. The thought that she would, perhaps, never see him again, never again hear his voice, bewildered her. Giddy and faint she tottered forward, and leaned for support upon the manly chest of the young Saxon, who drew his arm gently round her, and whispered—'Gladys, you will someday be mine!' Her tears trickled upon his hand. What a moment of happiness was that to him! He would not have exchanged the feeling for power, fame, or fortune's richest gift.

'Gladys, you will be mine,' he repeated, with extravagant joy—'and your people shall not despise me. I will devote my life, fortune, influence, all for them; I will adopt them as my people; my joy will be to make you happy; you shall indeed be happy. I will take you away from these dreary walls, and release you from your captivity: Gladys, you will be mine—promise that you will be mine?' He bent his head down and looked upon her face, pale as death, anxiously awaiting a reply.

'Ethelred,' said she in a hollow tone, 'why do you tempt me? You are more cruel to me than I have ever been to you—no link can ever bind us.'

'Say not so, Gladys; put aside those prejudices which you have imbibed from early childhood; none of your own country could be more devoted than I would be to you—none more solicitous and disinterested towards your people than I shall be.'

'Tempt me no further, Ethelred,' cried the maiden; then springing from his side and throwing her hands back, she buried them in her long raven tresses, with a convulsive grasp: 'No, Ethelred, we can never be anything to one another—never! The grand-daughter of the great Dafydd ap Jevan cannot, and will not give her troth to one of Saxon blood. The granddaughter of the great Dafydd ap Jevan cannot, and will not forfeit the love and respect of her people, by uniting her fate with that hated race, the Saxon, their common foe! These are bitter words, cruel words, you will say; would I could spare you, Ethelred—I cannot. Why, Ethelred, did you ever seek me? Why were my words unheeded? Weeks, months back, you knew it must end in making us both miserable. Leave me, Ethelred.'

'Gladys, I implore you to listen to me,' cried the young Saxon, in deep distress of mind.

'No, Ethelred, leave me,' said the daughter of Harlech, waving her hand, and turning away from him—'I command you to leave me. Go over the waters tonight; ask me not why—but go, Ethelred, go.'

'I cannot leave you in this cruel manner, Gladys, no,' replied Ethelred, once more approaching her with a look of anguish; 'at least, let us part friends.' He took her hand in his own, and pressed it passionately to his lips; he felt it trembling, and saw by the moon-beams that the tears glistened in her eyes.

'Farewell, Gladys,' said he, in a thick voice, from his emotion; 'curse not the Saxon, pray for him, for his days are embittered for ever. You will live with him, though he never sees your face; you will live with him, though he no more hears your voice; farewell.' He still lingered in silence.

'Go,' repeated the maiden, with trembling accents; 'leave Harlech to-night. The Virgin bless you, Ethelred—heaven protect you, go.' The doors closed upon his retreating outline. Gladys stood alone in the still chamber, listening to the only sound, the beating of her own heart.

From the casement she watched his tall figure move down the cliffs slowly and sadly, every now and then halting, and looking back at the castle. Soon afterwards he entered his little skiff, and was gliding over the waves—glancing ever and anon at the grey turrets, beneath which he left all dear to him. The unhappy Gladys still sat like a statue in the oriel, with tearful eyes riveted upon the dim ocean, fancying she saw, though she saw it not, the dark speck that had in reality become lost in the distance.

'They have been at supper some time, and inquiring for Mistress Gladys,' said old Rowland, suddenly putting his head in at the door; 'I told them you were with Mistress Jacqueline. Remember what you have to do, before half-an-hour after midnight.'

Gladys started upon her feet; took up the little lamp the old domestic had placed upon the table, and then remained standing a short time before her harp:—

'Must I part with thee, too?' said she, looking at it wistfully.

'Oh, why is it I am so sad, so very sad? Even when my freedom is at hand, the bright time for which I have so long looked, for which I have prayed amid tears and anguish, and now—strange, indeed, is the waywardness of the human heart!' She ran her fingers hastily over the strings, with the intention of playing a farewell melody, when a rich jewel left upon her finger attracted her attention. She raised her hand to the light, and having looked at it, cried, with newly-awakened grief—

'Ethelred, it is thy parting gift; why, why have you been so cruel to me?' She bent her head over her harp, and bathed the ring in her tears.

Once more old Rowland put his head in at the door. 'Meistres bach, are you still here? Sir Gilbert and his lady are just gone to their chamber.'

Not daring to trust herself alone again, Gladys immediately followed old Rowland, and gliding noiselessly through the long galleries soon reached the French maiden's chamber.

'Dear Jacqueline,' said she, approaching her couch, 'I have at last had a message from my uncle. I fear you will be startled when I tell you what the smugglers have arranged. Kynfin Tudor appeals to you, Jacqueline, and trusts that you will neither betray us nor object to his wishes. The smugglers leave the coast tonight. They are to take us with them to Vannes, to your father. Jacqueline, you will come with me, and set the captive maiden free, will you not?'

The French maiden's astonishment was depicted in her face; for some time she knew not how to act. Taking a part in a conspiracy against her own flesh and blood, would be dishonourable and unpardonable. She thought of her kind aunt, and how she would despise her. Her cousins, too, would heap censure upon her head; it would be most ungrateful. These thoughts passed away. Sir Gilbert rose to her imagination, her cruel, hard-hearted uncle, the persecutor of the poor Welsh, who had insulted her by his insinuations about the smugglers, had wronged Kynfin Tudor, and had refused to intercede for his life. How stood the matter at present? The smugglers were about to escape, before the revenue scheme could be put into execution. It was in her power to return a debt of gratitude to her preserver and her friend. He had appealed to her—How could she refuse?

After watching her companion's countenance for some time in silence, Gladys exclaimed:—

'Unless you accompany me, Jacqueline, I cannot go. It rests with you to set the captive free.'

The mountain child's history came vividly into Jacqueline's mind, as she replied:—

'Yes, Gladys, if the world condemns me, I will go.' Springing up from her couch, she threw her arms affectionately round her friend. 'Let us go and share each other's joys and sorrows, not caring what the world says, provided our own consciences do not become our accusers.'

CHAPTER X

A Pirate Puzzled—Witchcraft Influence—Preparation for a Deed of Death

WHEN twilight had overshadowed sea and land, the *Eryr* suddenly unmoored from beneath the red rock, or as best known in the country, beneath Graig Goch. Her sails proudly swelled to the breeze, and soon bore her out of the channel. Lightly and gracefully she bounded over the surge that curled gently to the breeze, awaiting the portentous hour which fast approached.

Upon her deck, her bold commander stood with more than usual fierceness depicted upon his countenance. He sometimes glanced towards the grey turrets of Harlech, but more frequently in the direction of the house of Gêst.

'Roderike, boy,' said he, moving towards the quarter-deck, where the second mate was standing.—'is it not strange that the son of Harlech is not yet in sight? Suppose he should turn traitor, carrying his own plans into execution, and desert our cause. Zookers! what a pretty condition we should be in. Hang the Pope in his robes, if I would not go back to the lady of Gêst, and plunge my dagger hilt deep in her blood. I would shout her dying knell to the tune that I struck, because she had betrayed me. Did you not mark that something passed between them before Ap Dafydd quitted the house? She takes good care to keep the mate of the *Eryr*'s secrets from me. I am more puzzled than ever, to discover why she takes so deep an interest in his family. You should have heard what she said before Ap Dafydd arrived last night. I have had my eyes opened. She declares she would never have turned her steps towards these shores, but for the daughter of Harlech; that if a hair of her head were injured, her curses should fall, sooner or later, on those who were the cause. She made me promise to take the child to Vannes, and to protect her on board the *Eryr* during the voyage. She threatened, if I heeded not her words, I should see her double-knotted handkerchief at the mast head, flapping more heavily in the gale than it ever flapped before. Then again, the threat of turning the evil eye upon one. You heard that threat, Roderike? It was enough to scare the devil, was it not? Her anxiety for the death of the old villain, the keeper, is not, I know, half as much on my account, as because he has been brutal to the daughter of Harlech. The child, she thinks, will not be safe in her own land. He will persecute her people to death, and make her miserable. She might have had more consideration for me, when she knows Sir Gilbert is my bitterest enemy. He is my bitterest enemy, though the lady of Gêst silences me whenever I would make it manifest. I will now tell you in confidence, Roderike. That man, from interested motives, persuaded my father to turn my mother and myself houseless upon the wide world. Had it not been for the good Earl of Warwick, I should have begged my bread from door to door. Sometime after that my mother was poisoned, through the instigation of a lady of rank; Sir Gilbert was her tool. He committed the crime, for which service she procured him the keepership of Harlech. It was he who made every effort to get me hanged, and upbraided me when I was in irons. He told me his revenge was sweet, because I had revealed to Warwick his sordid villainy. That is the man, Roderike, whose life I crave to take, and I will take it too. Methinks I have good cause for anxiety. The mate of the *Eryr* is still not in sight. The Lady of Gêst professes much solicitude for me. What care I for her professions, if she only take up another's cause, and leave me to fight my own battle?'

'You do the Lady of Gêst injustice,' answered Roderike. 'She will never forsake you, Ap Rhys, however much she may interest herself in Ap Dafydd. As to her mysteries, they are a part of her constitution. Methinks Kynfin Tudor has a tincture of it himself, and for that she likes him the better, and encourages him in nursing it.'

'You are right there, boy. The son of Harlech has become a great favourite of late with her,' replied Dhu, sarcastically.

The next moment he paced the deck with a more forbidding expression of visage than before.

'Sail ahoy! Sail ahoy!' cried Roderike, suddenly turning to address his companion. 'There, Dhu, there's our boat like a living waterfowl skimming over the waves. Yn enw'r Brenhin! see how she spreads her wings, and with what speed she scuds before the wind. Did you ever see a prettier sight? Now, Dhu, your fears were groundless. The mate of the *Eryr* will be at his post in less than half an hour.'

'So far, all well,' replied Dhu. Immediately going aft, and shouting at the top of his voice, 'Sail ahoy! Sail ahoy! Heave to, lads, Ap Dafydd is in sight.'

'About ship, about ship, look ahead, boys!' resounded over the deck.

'Soon as the mate comes aboard, tell him I am below,' said Ap Rhys authoritatively, and instantly disappeared from the deck.

'Hollo there, Ap Maelgwyn, is that you?' shouted Gam at the moment the boat ran alongside. 'Does the skipper think us late? The sharks! we have had a tough day on it, I can tell you, not a mouthful between our lips since we parted this morning. I am as hungry as a wolf.'

'Go, and make the best of your time then,' said Roderike, as the man came aboard. 'You will soon have something else to do, my man. Your day's work has not yet begun.' Then turning to his fellow-mate, he continued:—

'Ap Rhys has been in a terrible way, wondering what had become of you. Has all gone well?'

'Yes,' said Kynfin Tudor, with a wild and harassed expression of countenance. The moment afterwards they were in the presence of their commander.

'I am glad you are here, son of Harlech. I hope you have been successful, and that the old man did not give you much trouble?' said Dhu.

'I had to work him up to it,' replied Ap Dafydd. 'At first he objected strongly to take a part where so much was required of him. He has consented to all except taking the life of Black Donald, the porter. There, Dhu, the old man was right, and I rejoice at it. Instead of the poison, he will give him an ample portion of the intoxicating powder. That will serve our purpose just as well, and spare our consciences from a fouler deed.'

'Aha! I suppose that will reconcile you to it as well,' said Dhu, with a malicious smile. 'Does the good mother know that?'

'She does. I have hid nothing from her,' replied Kynfin, hurriedly, 'and she is pleased rather than displeased. As I came away, she bade me tell you that as you valued your own soul, and the souls on board your ship, not to forget your promise and her warning.'

'Confusion take her!' said Dhu, pettishly; 'she will have the last word, just like her. I want to know what you have arranged about the hour with the old man.'

'He is to let us in half an hour after midnight. Should things go wrong, the light in the south tower will be extinguished.'

'Good!' ejaculated Ap Rhys; 'and the maidens?'

'They are to be in the chapel,' resumed Ap Dafydd; 'but I think we have not much time to spare. Had I not better go and look after the boats? We must take two that I may bring the maidens off at once, and leave you and your men to follow at your own time.'

'Zookers! does the hour indeed steal on so rapidly?' said Dhu, taking his dagger from his belt, and holding it up to the light. 'Aye, it will do the deed,' muttered he, with a fierce look, relapsing into satisfaction.

Ap Dafydd and Ap Maelgwyn turned away and hastily mounted to the deck.

'Roderike,' said Kynfin, in a low, earnest tone, 'your heart's blood is young. Let not that man lead you astray. By the memory of your mother, by the love of your sister, fly the decks of the *Eryr*.'

Roderike looked up in surprise, but was instantly hurried away by Dhu, who was shouting to him to come aft.

Soon afterwards Ap Rhys leaped into one of the boats and said:—'Let every man be well armed, and keep his wits about him.'

No sooner had they taken their places than Dhu inquired of Ap Dafydd if he had met any of the young masters of Cricceath in the bay. Upon Kynfin answering in the negative, he continued:—

'We had a visit from one of them, and the fellow had the

impudence to come close alongside. I wonder what he was after at this time of night. No doubt going to report us.'

'That's nothing new for him, captain. He goes over every day to Harlech Castle,' rejoined Maurice, the lad who had accompanied them to take care of the boats. 'The people say on our side that he goes to see his lady-love.'

'Yn enw'r Brenhin! heart and soul! lad, you do mean Mistress Stacey? They say on it at Harlech that she is going to wed that soft jellyfish of a man Master Henry Stourton.'

'Mistress Stacey is not the only young lady there,' answered the boy, with a knowing nod. 'It is not for me to say which is the favourite.'

The son of Harlech turned round and fixed his restless eye upon the youth, but asked no question.

'Heart and soul! I hope it is not the little French maiden,' continued Gam, 'or our plans will be upset a bit, I guess. She will set her face against coming with us. Yn enw goodness! what are we to do, then?'

'Take her by force,' said Dhu ap Rhys. 'It will never do to leave her behind, after she has been let into our secrets. No, zookers! if it will. Besides the Dewines said we must take both or neither of the maidens. What says the mate of the *Eryr*? He won't quit the castle walls without his brother's child, or I am mistaken.'

'Singe a Jew's beard! who would have thought of our captain and our mate turning gallants,' said one of the men, an Englishman, 'and our "*Eryr* bach" to be laden with fair damsels for a cargo? The friars! this is a new kick up: is it not, lads? I wonder how we rough 'uns will like it.'

Jokes passed between the men till their mirth became clamorous.

'Hold your peace, rascals!' shouted Dhu, angrily. 'Let spirits, men, or maidens be my cargo, I exact the respect due to a captain. Now listen to what I have to say to you before these maidens come aboard. They must be treated respectfully by every man of us. It is not only my command, but that of the Dewines; and he who dares to disobey shall swing at the yardarm as sure as I am captain of the *Eryr* and the Dewines is the Lady of Gêst.'

These words were followed by a silence ultimately broken by an exclamation from little Maurice:— 'See yonder, captain, what is that tire upon the hilts?'

Every head was instantly turned to where a broad gleam of red light streamed across the waters, and was increasing at every stroke of the oar.

'It is the signal from the Cwm,' said Ap Dafydd, 'All is right.'

A few more strikes of the oar ran them up among the breakers just below the castle rocks, when the men all leaped ashore.

'Remain here a few minutes,' said Ap Dafydd, hurriedly, laying his hand upon Ap Rhys. 'Let me go first,' and he bounded up the cliff with the spring of a wild goat.

'Rowland, is the way clear?' asked the son of Harlech, in a hoarse voice.

'Ap Dafydd is welcome,' replied the old man.

'And the maidens, are they both in the chapel?'

'The son of Harlech has only to seek for them, and he will find them,' once more answered the domestic. 'Tarry not: call up your men.'

In an instant Kynfin sprang forward to the edge of the cliff and gave a shrill whistle, when he was again at the portal, on his way to the chapel.

'I am come at length to set you free, Gladys, my child,' cried the familiar voice of Kynfin Tudor, as he entered the holy sanctuary, and fondly folded the daughter of Harlech in his arms. To Jacqueline he extended his hand, and drew her near to him. The movement was followed by a few hurried whispers, and all three left the chapel together. A rush of many footsteps fell upon their ears. Kynfin, with blanched cheeks and a distracted air, drew them back.

'What is that?' inquired the maidens, clinging to him in terror.

No reply was given. With fearful rapidity their conductor hurried them out of the castle and down the cliffs. Ap Dafydd took them by turns in his arms, and carried them into the boat. The next moment they were steering their course to the *Eryr*.

Dhu, in the meanwhile, with his accomplices, followed old Rowland to Sir Gilbert's chamber, and the alarm was given.

'Master, master,' cried the old man at his door, 'the fires are on the hills—the freebooters and mountaineers are making havoc amongst your cattle.'

'Rouse the garrison, Rowland—let the dogs loose,' shouted the Keeper, starting upon his feet, and hastily putting on his garments.

'Zookers! rouse the garrison!—let the dogs loose! Hoary-headed knave! you are caught like a lion in the toils,' muttered Dhu to himself, as he stood waiting impatiently for his victim, a few paces distant from the door.

The door was soon open. Sir Gilbert, with his usual impetuosity, rushed towards the stairs, muttering as he went:—

'Rowland, you fool, where the devil are you? I believe the fellow has gone to sleep again.'

Dhu ap Rhys followed close upon Sir Gilbert. Scarcely had the Keeper reached the top of the stairs, when the pirate placed his hand upon his shoulder and arrested his steps. Sir Gilbert turning round, he seized him by the throat, half undressed as he was, and dragged him down the staircase, at the bottom of which his men, with lighted torches, awaited his return.

'Miscreant!' cried the rover, looking full and fiercely into the face of the affrighted man, 'dost thou know me? Look at me, thou sordid villain. I am Thomas Nevil, the bastard of Fauconbridge. I have started into life to take sweet vengeance—to have the blood of my old enemy—to show no mercy to him who never showed mercy to another. This, too, will be a lesson to thy son and his posterity. It will teach him and them not to interfere, as thou hast done, with smugglers and pirates—men honester than thyself or thine ever will be— men who have received more wrong from the crown than the crown ever received from them. You may look pale, poltroon as you are. The evil deeds you have visited upon me and mine are now about to be avenged. Your teeth may chatter. You shall have no more time to make your peace with heaven than you would give others, when you caught them.'

The keeper was speechless, petrified, before the terrible pirate who stood over him, looking more than commonly fierce before a foe. The victim's hair was erect, his eyes staring, his knees knocking convulsively together—the true sign, the very picture of abject misery, of petty tyranny caught in its own toils. He raised his hands in a supplicating attitude. Dhu, with a contemptuous laugh, replied by plunging the dagger into his heart.

'The world has a good riddance of you,' repeated Dhu, disentangling himself from the hold of the dying man, whose unconscious grasp he flung off, and fell heavily to the earth. There, contemplating for a moment the deed he had achieved, Dhu exclaimed—

'It is all over;'—addressing his men in a voice of savage fierceness,—'Now then, men, now is the time; unbolt the gates—let in the mountaineers!'

A piercing shriek was heard. Lady Stacey, in her white robes, fled at the same moment across the gallery at the stair foot. Again fearful cries resounded through the building, and Mistress Maud added her shrieks to those of her distracted mother. With these cries ringing in his ears, the pirate chief received the men from the Cwm.

'Now, lads,' cried he, 'plunder is the game; carry off all the arms. Keep the fortress manfully for the sake of the grand-daughter of Dafydd ap Jevan, till the *Eryr* is out of sight; then flee to the mountains my brave boys, and let the enemy be kept at bay, if they attempt to run you to cover. Success attend you all, is the wish of the sea rover, who is grateful, deeply so, to the brave men in the Cwm for their assistance.'

Wrought up to a fearful state of excitement, Dhu, passing the great gateway, gave a shout of triumph, and in a few minutes more was upon the waves, plying the oar himself, to gain as speedily as possible, the white decks of the *Eryr* bach. No sooner had that object been attained, than loud shouts of savage rejoicings arose on board, creating in the breasts of Gladys and Jacqueline a terror they had never before known. Clasped in each other's arms, they remained close together in a small cabin, scarcely daring to give utterance to the secret misgivings of their trembling hearts.

CHAPTER XI

Disappointment—The Catastrophe Disclosed—Vow of Vengeance—The Sick Pilot—A Weird Woman's Hold— The Spirit-Fire

Two hours after the mountaineers had quitted the castle with its stupefied garrison, Edward Stacey and young Stourton arrived, with additional revenue officials, to be in readiness, according to arrangement, for the decisive attack upon the smugglers on the following day.

The consternation which awaited them upon entering the walls may be imagined. The gates stood open; no porter was at his post. The first fearful spectacle that greeted their astonished gaze was the guardian mastiff lying dead across the threshold.

'Holy Virgin!' ejaculated young Stacey—'Henry, something dreadful must have happened. What can this mean?'

Not a sound was heard, not a figure moved across the court. Throwing the reins over his horse's neck, the young man hurried forward in breathless haste, and entered the deserted hall. Passing from room to room, the disorder and devastation which he encountered at every step, infused fresh terror into his mind. It was not till he had gained the gallery that the blood wholly forsook his cheeks—his eyes seemed ready to start from his head. Low sobs, stifled screams, and the sight of blood-stained garments appeared before him.

'Holy Father! Holy Virgin!' cried he, supporting himself against the wall. Henry Stourton, who had followed close upon his footsteps, also drew back. In a few minutes more, with terror-stricken faces, they were stooping over the gory remains of Sir Gilbert.

So perilous was the state of the country at this period that property became precarious, life hazardous, and plunder, rapine, and murder, were included among venial crimes, by virtue of sanctuary.[13]

Lady Stacey and Mistress Maud were both standing near the spot, the latter wringing her hands and weeping. The bereaved widow fixed her eyes upon the face of her son, but did not speak. She appeared not to recognise him, but stood like one petrified, pointing towards the murdered man.

'Mother! Mother!' cried young Stacey in a voice of agony, 'who has been guilty of these horrible deeds? Who has robbed me of my father? Who has committed this devastation in my home? Why will you not speak to me, mother? Oh, speak to your son,' continued he, approaching her, and addressing her in an anxious tone of entreaty. He now became more and more alarmed at her singular conduct. In vain he endeavoured to comfort her, or restore her to reason. She was immediately removed from the sad scene to her own apartment. Sir Gilbert's remains were quickly conveyed from the gallery to a room in one of the towers.

Some hours had elapsed—young Stacey inquiring in great

---

[13] Sir John Wynne, in his History of the Gwyder Family, adduced melancholy facts of the most flagrant crimes committed during the existing factions between the houses of York and Lancaster.—*The Beauties of Wales*, by the Rev. J. Evans.

agitation, of his sister, the cause of the scene which he had witnessed, she replied—

'I can scarcely tell you: our artful cousin and the hateful Welsh girl—it was they, I know, who delivered us into the hands of the villains: both have disappeared, and left not a vestige of themselves behind. Imagine, Edward, their consenting to be carried away by a brutal set of smugglers. I never had a good opinion of my cousin—artful, treacherous, ungrateful creature! I wish she had never been brought over here.'

'You may be doing her injustice, Maud,' observed her brother; 'the ruffians may have carried the girls off by force. I cannot think she would be guilty of the charge you make out—no, Maud, we will hope it is not so.'

'You will know some day, Edward, how much you are mistaken. You are not aware what things have been going on of late. Jacqueline has been behaving strangely. We all think, independently of her gratitude to the smuggler who preserved her, there was something more between them. You should have seen the distress she was in from the time the revenue officials came down. It was but yesterday morning she was pleading on her knees before my father for this Kynfin Tudor. He refused to grant her petition, and she turned white with passion, and kept her room all the day afterwards. Edward, the more I think of it, the more I feel convinced that she it was who let them into the castle, and warned them of your intentions. Thus they had time to escape. All this was done out of the spirit of revenge on her part.'

'What! Have all the smugglers gone?' asked Edward, with impatience.

'Somebody said so. That horrible murderer was chased in

his vessel by the cutters in the bay, but he escaped them. I wish, Edward, you had listened to the warnings not to meddle with them and that terrible woman of Gêst. It would have been better for us all. My poor father! I wish he had never come here among savages! We shall all be murdered. We shall never escape from the land alive. Let us go, brother—let us go from this barbarous land.'

Maud again wrung her hands in despair, and wept bitterly.

'My father shall be revenged,' said the young master of Harlech in a determined tone. 'I swear by all that is holy he shall be revenged. You say, and old Griff will say, that vile daughter of Satan had a finger in the outrage. My vengeance shall commence with her. I will burn her at the stake, with all who have participated in the murder. They shall suffer.'

'Don't be violent, brother. I entreat you to have nothing to do with them. If you do, you will be murdered too,' cried Mistress Maud in her terror.

'Better that we should all be murdered, than my vengeance should not be visited upon the assassins!' retorted Edward, fearfully excited, and with a firm, undaunted mien.

'Come, come, Edward, you had better compose yourself,' said Henry Stourton, soothingly. 'We will do all we can, at the same time being careful not to outstep the boundary of prudence, and make matters worse.'

'Don't provoke me, Henry. What I have said I intend to put into execution,' answered young Stacey, savagely. Neither the tears of his sister, nor the calm entreaty of his kinsman, could in any way divert him from his revengeful determination.

Appalling was the gloom impending at this time over the castle. Upon every visage terror was more or less depicted. Even the returned guardsmen moved from post to post with a nervousness and apprehension, as if they dreaded Sir Gilbert's spirit would appear to them. None after sunset would venture to cross the gallery where he fell. They spoke in whispers; and the slightest noise, sounding through the rooms or vacant galleries, instantly blanched every cheek. To behold such a melancholy change in a few short hours, was, no doubt, sufficiently trying. The aspect of things had generally changed. The blazing faggots no longer crackled on the hearth; the harp no longer sounded in the hall; the doors creaked, unclosed, upon their hinges. All was desolate and forsaken. Vermin, as if eager and excited by the scent of blood, came out from their lurking holes, and slowly passed along the haunted gallery or crept across the apartments, while all other living creatures bore marks of terror and sadness too heavy to notice matters of trivial importance.

Had Gladys and Jacqueline seen the destruction which the smugglers and mountaineers had left behind, their hearts would have sunk. Fortunately this trial was spared them, though other trials still awaited them.

Before Sir Gilbert was interred in the castle chapel, Henry Stourton, in compliance with his cousin's wish, sought means to ascertain the particulars of the recent catastrophe. From some of the men in Harlech, who had changed with the times, and now called themselves warm partisans of Edward of York, he discovered that the mountaineers had kept the castle in their hands for six hours; and that there had been evidently an understanding between them and the smuggler Dhu ap Rhys, who took the life of the Keeper with his own hand, and let them into the castle. By various other details mentioned, Henry Stourton came to the conclusion that the main object of both smugglers and mountaineers was to obtain the liberty of the Welsh maiden and the life of the unfortunate Keeper. Not perfectly satisfied on this point, he inquired for Griff, the pilot, and told one of the men to go and fetch him, not mentioning who it was who wished to see him.

'Yn enw goodness, Master Henry, you no hear the Dewines has caught old Griff by the leg,' replied the man, with a look of mingled horror and surprise. 'He has no been well this long while, and has been abed for the last four days. He takes on it so, he says he knows the Dewines has done for him, and all because he let his tongue loose upon matters belonging to her. I no think he see you: no, indeed, truth, Master Henry, it is no use you going.'

'Hold, you knave—I will go,' replied Henry, impatiently. 'Where does the man live? Take me there at once. And tell me, man—I have but one more question to ask—did Griff give the smugglers any warning of our proceedings against them?'

'Well, indeed, truth, Master Henry, I think yes. You see old Griff (his wife tell me) he feel the wind[14] in his head this long while. I no know all; but I think he feared the Dewines in his heart. Some people say he tell you, Master Henry, about the Dewines, and no could sleep for vexing on it.'

'That is not answering my question. I know the fellow is as much afraid of that foul lady of Gêst as he is of the devil. What I want to know is, if he gave the smugglers information of what we had got in store for them. Can't you speak plain?'

'Well, Master Henry, have a little patience and I will tell you. To make his peace with the Dewines, he go and speak to the smugglers. I see him go across every day, and I see him

---

[14] Any malady the Welsh call wind.

one night in Dhu ap Rhys's boat, and he has been in bed ever since.'

After descending a steep path, they came suddenly upon the pilot's cottage, and Henry Stourton immediately gave a loud knock upon the door, adding, as he did so, 'We will see if we can't get admittance.'

A woman soon appeared at the entrance, and asked them in a very uncivil tone what they wanted.

'I hear your old man is ill,' replied the young Englishman. 'I have come to see him.'

The woman looked at him for a few minutes, and then shaking her head sullenly, she answered, with much severity of tone—

'Ymaith â thi y Sais cas![15] My man will no see you—no;' and instantly she slammed the door in his face, and secured it by a strong bolt inside.

'Well, indeed, truth, Master Henry, I feared it would be on it this way,' observed his conductor, looking very ill at ease, and moving away from the door.

'Nonsense, man: you don't suppose I am to be treated in this way by an old hag. Don't you be sneaking off. Wait a few minutes, and see if I am not standing face to face with the old pilot very quickly.'

After repeating these words, Henry got upon a large stone close to the window and shouted to the top of his voice that if she did not let him in immediately, he would go and fetch the King's men from the castle, and seize upon them and their goods.

This threat had the desired effect. The poor woman, with a

---

[15] Get you gone, you hateful Saxon.

terrified countenance, opened the door, and once more appeared before them.

'My old man is very sick,' said she apologetically, 'too sick to see anyone. It makes him worse. Have pity on us, Saxon. I am sick in my heart about him.'

'I shall not detain him long, my good woman,' replied Henry, softened by the wretched appearance of the object before him. 'Griff and I are old acquaintances,' continued he, following close upon the woman's heels, till they reached a small, dark closet, partitioned off from the sitting-room by a few rude planks.

'Well, old pilot, I have come to have a look at you,' said Henry Stourton, drawing near to his bedside. 'On my sword! I am grieved to find you so ill.'

'That's a foul, hellish lie!' cried the pilot, starting straight up in his bed, and glaring, with extended eyeballs, upon his visitor. 'What brings you here—to laugh at me? See you, Saxon, what you helped to do for me—you hateful Saxon, son of a Saxon—curse your tongue—it sounds like rushing water in my ears! Why did you not think on what I said? My words have come true.'

Young Stourton started back in amazement, and turned pale. The glare of old Griff's eyes was appalling—fire literally appearing to flash from beneath his shaggy brow; this, with his drawn nostrils and sunken cheeks, changed his whole appearance to such a degree that in the sick man before him the old pilot was scarcely recognised.

'Look at me, Master Henry, look at me,' continued old Griff, in a strange and unnatural tone. 'Do you know the once merry old man, the sharp old pilot, who learned so much English, and always said a kind word for them foreigners?

What has he come to now? The Dewines's curse is upon him. O Duw anwyl!—you, you, Saxon, have been the cause of it—Go away with you, Master Henry. The wind is in my head burning, burning like fire itself. The Dewines! The Dewines! I have been a fool, I have been a madman; curses on you, you Saxon—and the Dewines will curse you. She will wash your head, with her broom, and drive her pitchfork into your shoulder, as she has into mine. Go, you Saxon, son of a Saxon—I see her mark upon you. There it is—take him away, my old woman—take him away. I am burning here, I am suffocating. Or' anwyl!—send him away.'

The frantic voice of the delirious man ceased; he fell back upon his bed exhausted; yet his arm remained raised, and his finger still pointed at Henry Stourton, who stood wondering in silence at the old pilot's ominous words. An involuntary shudder crept over his frame. Once more glancing at the sick man, a prey to superstition, he hastily quitted the cottage, feeling that no information could be obtained there.

Silently and sorrowfully he retraced his steps to the castle, and immediately repaired to his cousin's apartment.

'What have you done, Henry?' cried he, in an anxious tone.

'Our suspicions have been confirmed,' replied young Stourton; 'the freebooters and smugglers were in league together.' He then entered into all the facts which had been revealed to him; and the moment he had ceased speaking, Edward Stacey rose from his seat: 'Henry,' said he, taking his sword from its scabbard, 'my father will be buried tomorrow—I thirst for revenge. The smugglers are beyond our reach, the mountaineers are not. On them I will wreak my vengeance—those murderous villains—by heaven! I will give them no quarter, men, women or children. They shall pay the penalty of this outrage. We will make a regular massacre of them; the revenue officials will assist us.'

'This is unlike my son,' said Father Nutze, placing his hand softly upon young Stacey's shoulder; 'I told your father that no good would come by detaining the innocent child from her home. Recollect, Edward, that the Saxons unmercifully persecute the children of the soil. Fault is at your doors as well as at the freebooter's; let the affair pass over. Strictly avoid crossing the path of these wild men of the land. Heed my words that it may go well with you, my son.'

Young Stacey shook off his hand impatiently: 'No, reverend father, the cry of vengeance rises from the dead. I shall listen to no other call,' said he, passionately. 'Don't insinuate to me that what my father did was wrong. What injury have we done the mountaineers that you should place such an injury on a footing with theirs towards us? Why, Father Nutze, you know very well that, from the time we came into the country, we have been persecuted by those marauders; you irritate me by talking in this way.'

'Edward,' said Father Nutze, in a stern tone, 'your manner and words pain me. I will not attempt to argue with you; but oblige me by putting off your cruel intention for the present. Time will restore you to reason, and you will act differently.'

'Never,' replied the young Master of Harlech; 'my father's blood shall be avenged, let what may happen.'

Henry Stourton had been suddenly called from the room during this conversation, and now returned with a visible change in the expression of his countenance.

'Has anything happened?' inquired Father Nutze.

'Yes,' replied Henry, 'a fresh misfortune; a messenger has just arrived from Caernarvonshire with the intelligence that the revenue officials have been laying siege to the house of Gêst. The witch has escaped, and some of the assailants have been drowned in the vaults. All seems to be going against us.'

'How did it happen?' inquired young Stacey; 'I cannot understand how they could have been drowned.'

'They broke first into the vaults under her dwelling: the door being forced, they entered a passage, long and narrow; here they were furiously attacked by two mastiffs, and before they had proceeded beyond the termination of the passage, while they were combating the dogs, they were overwhelmed by a torrent of water rushing in upon them from the rear, which drove them further into the vaults. These being soon full, the water flowing impetuously along the passage to find its level, they all perished.'

Father Nutze crossed himself devoutly. The young Master of Harlech looked at his cousin in mute astonishment: to Henry Stourton, the pilot's prophetic accents came ringing in the ears. Not a word more was spoken for some minutes, as if each present felt too confused in mind to suggest or propose any specific course of action.

Ill news seldom arrives without company. The vengeance of the Dewines for the attack upon her dwelling had ended in the destruction of the attacking party, the servants of the crown, not of the castle.

Stephen and Tyrrel Conyers a day or two afterwards, came to Harlech in consternation, with tidings of the serious destruction of the property of the late keeper, and of their own.

'I do not understand you, I am confused,' cried young Stacey, with an expression of perplexity. 'Do you say the witch of Gêst has been destroying our property in

Caernarvonshire? I thought she had taken her departure, how is this, Stephen?'

'It is true she has fled the country, but she has left a fire-spirit behind her. It was water the witch used against the revenue officers, she has now punished us with fire. She has raised a spirit of hell against us. Cottages have been consumed; stacks and barns are burning even now. The Morfa is wasted, ruin is upon everything. The cattle, sheep, and lambs, upon your sheep-walk are destroyed. The fire-spirit has poisoned the grass, poisoned the air, all that eat herbage there die.'

'The holy Virgin protect us! You cannot really mean fire, a spirit-fire!' cried Henry Stourton, with a ghastly hue passing over his features. 'How do you know that it was the witch?'

'It is the witch, she was seen on the night the smugglers quitted the bay, standing on a rock in the middle of the Morfa Bychan sands, with a pale blue torch in her hand. Afterwards she was observed tracking her course in the direction of your lands and setting the marsh on fire. Every night since then it is to be seen. This spirit-fire is like a blue flame. Where its track is marked out, the judgment of the Dewines is consummated. It moves sometimes slow, sometimes quick. Tyrrel and I were there last night. We saw the ricks and barns flame up, as if kindled by lightning, and the grass wither beneath. Our curiosity was so great that we tried to catch it with our hands. It did not burn. Water will not quench it, yet it consumes our property. If you call to it very loudly it vanishes away, then returns. You must come and see it, Henry, that pale, blue, flickering flame hovering like a ghost over the wasted land. It shuns the sun's light, doubtless because it comes from the father of evil. The witch of Gêst holds a charm against the Saxons, several of our ricks and barns, and many of yours, are burned. Methinks it is a pity, Stacey, that we quarrelled with the ruler of the sea and land. The country people are in great trouble. Many are ruined, are homeless, and curse the Saxons for having crossed the path of the terrible woman of Gêst.'

Father Nutze, who was standing near, placed his finger to his breast and repeated an ave. Henry Stourton and the master of Harlech were silent, both thinking how the pilot's words were verified, and secretly regretting that they had turned a deaf ear to his warning. Despite his better knowledge, Stacey began to feel that there might after all, be something in the influence of certain mortals with invisible agencies. He thought of the witch of Endor, of the incantations of which he had read and heard, of the extent of the popular belief in all ages in such visitations, and was half persuaded, notwithstanding his late disbelief in them, that they might have some foundation in truth.

'Good Father Nutze,' said he, 'this is a mysterious affair. Do you think it possible that terrible woman can effect such wonders at her will? You who are one of the holy order will perhaps enlighten us upon what foundation we are to credit such agencies. I confess it shakes our reason.'

'We cannot question it, my son, there are supernatural agencies. The only difficulty is to define between the true and the false. It is better to believe too much than too little on all such questions, in order to be safe. As to the medium, it may be either man or woman. I take it we find woman employed early in tempting man to eat forbidden fruit, and why may she not become the actor in scenes of mischief again? The belief that time-consecrated opinions are always sound opinions, my son, is just. I believe this fearful woman of Gêst may be satanically endowed.'

After giving this opinion, to which all present paid great deference, the priest was silent. His lips, however, moved. He was reciting prayers inaudibly: while all present seemed occupied with the jeopardy of their existing position, rather than any inclination to look into the secret cause of their troubles.

Young Stacey, after an interval of silence, again mentally reiterated his determination to take vengeance upon the people in the Cwm, to whom he ascribed all the evils that had befallen his family. He did not, as before, express his resolution, but it became the main fixture in his mind. He dreaded lest the holy man should again interfere. In secret he laid down a plan of operations, it must be allowed more the result of angry inexperience than wisdom. He was not more dilatory in proceeding to action than the necessity of the circumstances required.

CHAPTER XII

Age and Sorrow—The Refugee— An Assault Defeated— Death in the Cottage

'Och, och, Katherine, my good Katherine, I never thought I should live to see this dark day,' ejaculated the unhappy and forlorn widow of the great Dafydd ap Jevan. 'My husband has gone before me to the abode of the dead, the home appointed for all living. My children have forsaken me. Now anwyl! anwyl! for our cause my poor people are plunged into danger. The son of their old chief is not here to help them. Ow, ow, Katherine bach, I am weary, I am weary of my life.'

The old lady was seated in her high-backed chair in the chimney corner, when these mournful accents escaped her lips. Katherine had just informed her of young Stacey's anger, and his cruel intention of attacking the people in the Cwm, and giving them no quarter.

For the last few hours Howel had been engaged in turning over huge pieces of stone and wood across the footpath leading to the retreat. Of late it had become much worn and trodden, and the old man was apprehensive lest the way to their rocky abode should be tracked.

'Come near to me, Howel, I want to speak to you,' said Mistress Tudor, in a weak voice, the moment he appeared in the doorway. 'I am sick at heart about the good people in the

Cwm. I have been thinking how I can help them. I know, Howel, that it is dark and foggy tonight, the time is urgent; you tell me the Saxons may be here tomorrow. Go down the glen and tell the people that Ap Jevan's widow has enough room at Cader y Cil for many of their wives and children. Let all those who are weak and infirm come to me, and we'll give them shelter. They shall remain till the storm has passed over. They will be safe here from the cruel bloodhounds. It will make the widow of Dafydd ap Jevan happy in knowing that they are secure. Katherine will get ready accommodations for them.'

The old sentinel listened attentively to the commands of his mistress. The moment her voice had ceased, he crossed the apartment, and reaching down an old jerkin that had once seen better days, and fastening it securely round his person, he prepared to leave Cader y Cil to execute his mistress's command. He was detained a few minutes by Katherine, who would not let him go without a mug of warm ale to support his strength, and prevent his old bones from catching cold, for it was growing late. A little black terrier that fondled and jumped about his legs, followed close at his master's heels, and was his only companion on his nocturnal route through the wild and rocky glen of Cwm Bychan.

In every hut Howel entered, he found the inmates in a state of consternation. Many were on the point of setting out from their habitations, others were preparing to do the same, and some of the cottages were entirely abandoned.

With joy the women received the message from the relict of their noble chief. Touched by feelings of gratitude, they clasped their infants in their arms, and hastily gathering together a few articles of clothing, prepared to set out in a body, with the worthy old sentinel for their leader. Their hearts full of anxiety, they parted from their husbands, fathers, and brothers. When the name of Saxon passed from lip to lip, the children clung in terror to their mothers.

The young men, and all those who were able to exert themselves, collected their arms, and devised plans to defeat the common foe. It was universally agreed that filing up to the heights would insure their own safety and place them in a position to inflict fearful injury upon their unsuspecting enemy.

As soon as the old men, women, and children, were safely lodged within the strong walls of Cader y Cil, some of the mountaineers who had accompanied their wives, at Howel's request, blocked up the outer entrance with huge pieces of broken rock, in a manner that would elude a scrutinizing eye. Meanwhile Howel secured the inner door, by throwing oaken beams across, sustained with stones and earth.

'Katherine, my old girl,' said Howel, upon the completion of his work, 'I think we are now in a position to defy every Saxon in Wales. We have only to keep order in the house, and to be careful of the provisions; for we don't know what these Saxon dogs are after. They may prowl about the glen for some time. We dare not leave these walls by night or day, for none of us, I think, would like to fall into their jaws, so Katherine bach, this is our position.'

'I will do my best with the provisions,' replied Katherine; 'should all beside come to want, I will take care that our good mistress shall not.'

'That's right, my old girl,' resumed Howel; 'and now, Katherine, I have a little bit of news to tell you; Sir Gilbert was buried yesterday, and all the Harlech folks were present

at the funeral. They had a dinner given them in the court of
the castle.'

'O'r Tad anwyl!' ejaculated Katherine, holding up her
hands in astonishment; 'and these are your Harlech men?
Well, in truth, I am glad our old chief has not lived to see this
day.'

'That's not all, Katherine,' interrupted Howel; 'young
Stacey made a speech to the men, and told them that we
fellows in the Cwm were a set of lawless murderers, that we
did evil in the sight of the saints, and that he would pay them
well if they would help him, in the name of the King, to
exterminate them from the land. Our friend Owen Lloyd told
me this; he is afraid, for the sake of gold, they will go against
us.'

'Ow, ow!' gasped Katherine, 'wfft iddynt!' in expression of
her contempt; 'our men of Harlech, our countrymen to turn
against us, and the widow of their dead chief!—It cannot be
true.—Don't tell my mistress, Howel, for she is already sick
in body and soul. I fear soon she will be taken from us. She
grieves now more than ever. Ow, ow, I feel in my heart for
her.'

'Indeed, truth, I am sorry too, Katherine bach,' replied
Howel, pensively, and shortly afterwards he turned away, to
perform some duty which he had omitted.

At an early hour on the following morning, Harlech was in
commotion. Groups of people, with anxious countenances,
stood in different parts of the town, conversing in low voices,
and a small party of men slowly proceeded to the castle. Many
pointed at them, and condemned them for the part they had
taken, and children ran from all quarters, and followed them
with clamorous voices. An hour after the sun was on the tops

of the distant hills, a stiff breeze drove in the advancing tide
far upon the shore. That sound alone had fallen upon the ear,
before the party issued from the castle, and proceeded on their
way to Cwm Bychan. Edward Stacey and his kinsman Henry
Stourton were mounted on two strong nags, and headed a
body of well-armed men. The young master of Harlech was
mortified upon discovering that scarcely half those who had
been in the castle on the previous day, had made their
appearance. Enquiries were circulated, but no satisfactory
reply could be obtained as to the cause of their absence. This
incident damped the spirits of their young leader, and Henry
Stourton's secret forebodings increased. Neither Englishmen
nor Welshmen exchanged a word, but proceeded on their way
in silence.

The morning was beautifully clear, the high wind had
driven every cloud out of the horizon, and for the first mile or
two, the deep blue ocean lay spread out before them, an
emblem of peace. Here and there a fishing-boat tossing on the
edge of the surf, attracted the eye. Soon the party turned their
horses' heads towards the ascent to the glen. Their anxiety
increased rapidly, on meeting with no human creature, and
finding every cottage deserted.

'Set them all on fire!' cried Edward Stacey, in a
commanding tone. 'I will have every one of them razed to the
ground! The cowardly rascals, they have taken to their heels.
Is not this provoking? It is evident they have been informed
of our intentions; we shall discover them soon.'

The crackling flames, and the lurid sparks rising in all
directions, terrified the horses. Edward Stacey, in as cheerful
a tone as he could assume, called aloud:—

'Come along, my men, the cottages will burn without our

watching them; we must be off in the chase of these miserable savages.'

'I have just been questioning some of the Harlech men,' said Henry Stourton, trotting up to the side of his kinsman. 'I believe there is treachery among them; no, not one of the rascals will give a straightforward answer. Edward, warnings have been given to us; we turn a deaf ear to them all; I wish we were out of the glen.'

'Confound you, and the devil take them!' replied the master of Harlech, bitterly; 'for heaven's sake, Henry, don't hamper me with your forebodings. On my sword, if you are not growing as cowardly and superstitious as any of these Welsh fools.'

As they continued travelling up the glen, the track became more rough and dangerous. The Englishmen found it difficult to keep up at all with their excited young leader, who at times was so abstracted that he did not know if his party were close upon his heels, or how much he was in advance of them, Henry Stourton, however, by continually shouting, prevented any from being left entirely behind.

Upon a turn in the road, they came suddenly in sight of a large building, standing out in bold relief upon an eminence.

'There is their meeting place,' cried young Stacey; 'I should not wonder if the scoundrels have concealed themselves within its walls!'

'Not unlikely,' rejoined his kinsman; 'but they are, no doubt, prepared for us, and will keep us at bay; we ought to be careful.'

'Well, Sir Circumspect, let it be so,' replied Edward; 'but as sure as I live, we will make a bonfire of them all. Should they attempt to escape, give them no quarter.'

The young leader leaped from his horse, and, having called to his men, prepared immediately to scale the mountain's side.

After a fatiguing ascent, they reached the edifice. To their mortification, when the rude doors were thrown open, no living creature was there.

Some swore, some laughed, while young Stacey could not conceal his annoyance.

'Well, Master Edward, what will you do now?' inquired one of the Welshmen, winking at some of his companions, and remarking in his own tongue what a fool the fellow had made of himself.

'Send you, you insolent knave, over yonder precipice,' retorted the master of Harlech, greatly irritated at the manner and tone of the speaker.

'Gently, Edward,' said Henry Stourton, 'you gain nothing by these hasty words; did you not say, you wished the building to be set on fire?'

'Set on fire, yes, with the devil's own fire,' cried Edward, passionately, 'and then let us be off. Forward, forward!'

Scarcely had they regained the foot of the eminence, when the building was in a mass of flame, rising and curling with the gust of wind which swept down the mountain's side.

'We shall leave a trace behind us, I guess,' cried Edward, with an exulting laugh, as he remounted his horse, and looked up at the burning edifice. 'Henry, what fools we have been; why, there are the bloodhounds!' continued he, suddenly changing his voice, and placing his hand across his forehead with a distrustful look. 'On my sword, I think I am losing my senses. If we had only thought of them, what trouble we might have saved ourselves,' and the next moment he was shouting to his men;—

'Let the bloodhounds loose!—Let the bloodhounds loose! All be upon the watch, while those swiftest of foot shall receive a double gratuity.'

For a few minutes all were in confusion, arranging themselves according to the orders of their young leader. Meanwhile, unfettered from their chains, the ferocious hounds gave tongue, and soon were in full cry up the glen, their voices echoing and re-echoing among the rocks. This had the effect of cheering the drooping hearts of the pursuers, their excitement every instant increasing. Hallooing and yelling, they kept up at a good pace in the direction of the dogs, that continued on their way till they reached the spot under Carreg y Saeth, and there they stopped. They then ran back, and holding their heads high in the air, bayed and bayed again; once more retracing their steps, they appeared puzzled which way to take.

Edward Stacey, Henry Stourton, and those most swift of foot now came up in breathless haste to the spot. Scarcely had they time to look around them, when the yell of their exulting enemy reached their ears, accompanied by showers of huge stones, hurled down with frightful velocity from the heights above. So deadly were they in effect that many of the unfortunate men were instantaneously crushed to death.

The confusion of sounds was deafening. Yells of terror, shouts of triumph, the loud yelpings of the bloodhounds, again off upon the scent, all combined to make the most terrific discord.

Springing aside from a falling stone, Edward Stacey lost his balance and fell backwards; while Henry Stourton, at that moment seeing his danger, was in the act of rushing to his assistance, when he was thrown violently to the earth, where he lay half concealed by one of the destructive rocky missiles.

The cry of agony and of distress brought those men who had just come up in the rear to their assistance. At the peril of their own lives, they succeeded in gaining possession of the wounded man, and carrying him out of the reach of the enemy. In horror they gazed upon their mutilated companions; and no sooner had they arranged themselves beyond the reach of the stones than showers of arrows flew amongst them, and compelled them to fly in self-defence, bearing along with them their wounded comrades. Their young leader, who had been stunned by a flying stone, could give them no directions. Henry Stourton, from loss of blood, remained at that moment insensible. In this condition the Englishmen fled down the glen, leaving the bloodhounds alone to combat with the exulting mountaineers.

Scarcely had the retreating Saxons disappeared from sight, when those sanguinary animals, after a long, circuitous range, rushed in full cry upon the summit, from whence the Welshmen had committed so much havoc.

'Now, lads, courage!' cried two or three of the bold leaders; and all turned round to face the furious beasts. 'Let us do for these savage hounds as we have done for the cruel Saxons, their masters.'

In an instant every man was ready with his spear and battleaxe, and a fierce struggle ensued. Some of the men were torn by the dogs before they could dash out their brains and hurl their carcasses over the precipice.

When the last of the pack was thrown down the craggy height, whirling in mid-air, a loud cry of delight burst from every lip. Their shouts re-echoed among the rocks. 'Our mothers, children, and our wives are safe! We have done for them! Let the Saxons or the bloodhounds appear again in the

Cwm. They shall never escape. We will teach them the laws of our own land, these base invaders. They boasted they would destroy us to a man. What have they got by it?'

Expressions such as these passed from lip to lip. But none descended from the heights before they had knelt down and offered up thanksgivings.

Shortly after, those whose wives and children were concealed among the distant hills separated from their companions, hastened to them, and communicated the glad tidings. Meanwhile the rest of the men repaired to Cader y Cil. No sooner had they reached the spot than with another wild shout of rejoicing they tore away the large stones from the doorway, and parents and children, husbands and wives, were soon locked in each other's embrace. Many wept for joy. Others danced about with uncontrollable delight.

'Wi! Wi! Wi! Our fathers have driven away the Saxons and have frightened them out of the glen,' cried the infant voices, in tones of glee. 'The blood of the dogs is sprinkled on the rocks. Wi! Wi! Wi!'

Mistress Tudor received the intelligence with uplifted hands, and a beam of pleasure passed over her wan features.

All endeavoured to cheer and comfort the widow of the great champion of Merioneth by assuring her that the daughter of Harlech would soon be restored to them; and that, while they could wield a battleaxe, no Saxon should again enter the Cwm. Their chieftain's granddaughter should be safe, and remain with her to the end of her days. They had said it.

This night of rejoicing in Cader y Cil was a striking contrast to the scenes that were taking place at the same time within the walls of Harlech castle. Henry Stourton had been brought home in a precarious state. One of his legs was broken, and he was terribly bruised. At this fresh calamity Mistress Maud was well-nigh distracted. She was a constant attendant upon him, and wept over him incessantly. Young Stacey soon recovered from the blow, deeply distressed about his cousin. He now blamed himself bitterly for having acted contrary to the wishes of his family.

Every hour the invalid grew worse. 'Is old Griff, the pilot, dead?' he asked many times in the course of the day. At last, when the news arrived that the old pilot was gone, and the whole of Harlech town were persuaded that the Dewines had taken him, Henry Stourton raised his head and uttered a bitter cry.

'Oh! Maud! Maud!' said he, 'forgive me for all my past unkindness to you: forgive me for taking the part of the captive maiden, and causing you so much uneasiness: forgive me, Maud, I shall soon follow old Griff. He told me that the mark of that terrible woman of the bay was upon me—that this evil day would come. Can you see it? He said it was here on my shoulder. The mark of that terrible witch of Gêst. Where is Edward? Maud, make him promise that he will never more raise his hand against anyone in this land. Make him promise.'

In vain did Mistress Maud attempt to soothe the sick man. In vain did Edward promise to do as he was requested. Still Henry raved on, repeating the same words over and over again.

After many hours, the larger portion of the time delirious, and passed in groans and agony, he with his expiring breath apostrophised the Dewines and old Griff, the pilot, until his accents were no longer audible.

CHAPTER XIII

A Pirate Bark—The Sea Rover— Unexpected results— Maiden Attractions

THE sun had almost set before the maidens ventured to leave their cabin, when Roland, who had been upon the watch, hastily advanced to show them into that of the chief. As they entered, the bold, fierce, yet handsome commander, Dhu ap Rhys, rose and bowed courteously. Kynfin Tudor, who was present on their entrance, hastily drew near, and having spoken kindly to Jacqueline, passed on to greet his brother's child, with that warmth of manner which was peculiar to his character.

'My Gladys bach!' said he, 'how earnestly I have longed for this moment!' The wild expression of his countenance was softened, as looking upon her features, he there traced a likeness to her mother. 'I only regret, my dear Gladys, that we are not in our mountain-home by the side of your grandmother; let us hope that the day when we shall be there is not far off.'

'We will hope so! It lightens my heart,' replied Gladys, returning the pressure of her uncle's hand; and taking a seat by his side, she continued in her usual soft tone:—

'Uncle Kynfin, when I look at you my thoughts are carried back to the old time in the Cwm. I was then quite a child, yet I seem to remember your features. When we return to Cader

317

y Cil, I trust you will never again leave us, but remain there
to increase our happiness.'

'Your words, Gladys bach, find an echo in my heart,'
replied Ap Dafydd. At the same moment, looking across the
table, and becoming aware that Dhu's eyes were riveted upon
the beautiful face of his niece, in an instant an involuntary
shudder crept over his frame, and he instinctively drew his
charge nearer to him.

Gladys saw by the expression of his countenance that
something of a painful nature had crossed his mind. In a
moment she changed the subject, by asking:—

'Shall we be long in sailing to Vannes? I hope not!'

'It depends upon wind and weather, if I may venture to
answer that question,' said Ap Rhys, anxious to attract the
maiden's attention. 'I fear by your last sentence, the sea has
no charm for you?'

'No charm, oh yes it has!' murmured Gladys. The azure
waters of Cardigan bay rose at once to her imagination, with
the room from whence she had so frequently looked down
upon them with feelings of enthusiastic admiration.

From a child she had loved the ocean. The weary days of
her captivity had been cheered by its proximity to her place
of restraint. Recalling that favourite room, her thoughts rushed
into another channel. There Ethelred had lately stood, her head
had rested upon his bosom, there she had felt his lips upon her
cheek, and marked the beating of his heart, his anxious
expression of countenance, his voice of anguish.

'Oh, Ethelred,' thought she, 'I saw your boat a dark speck,
gliding in the moonbeams, bearing you away from me, it may
be for ever, perhaps it is best that it should be so—better that
we should meet no more.'

These painful reflections, so fresh in her memory, passed across her mind, while the conversation was engrossed by the momentary remarks of a messenger from the deck, repeating the position of the ship on her passage. Dhu ap Rhys having answered the bearer of the report, was awaiting a reply. He did not repeat his question, but could not help observing the varying colour upon her cheek. He felt at that moment a respect for her which he had never before known, and wondered what could be the nature of the feelings thus written in her face.

Jacqueline and Ap Dafydd were talking of bygone things, until the time when refreshments were usually served. Ap Maelgwyn then came into the cabin and was introduced to the maidens.

Gladys felt the awkwardness of their situation more than the French maiden, who was of that happy disposition which soon reconciles itself to circumstances. Gladys, though particularly fascinating in manner, was reserved and dignified, and by her carriage demanded respect from all. She instinctively shrank from a close communication with any of the rovers, seeking the privacy of her own cabin, whenever an opportunity occurred of her being able to remain apart.

After the ladies had retired, Dhu sat a long time deeply absorbed in thought. Upon Ap Maelgwyn asking him why he was so unusually silent, he gave the following unguarded reply:—

'Why, yonker, I have been thinking how many beauties I have seen at the English and French courts. None of them could rival that daughter of Harlech. One ought to be proud of having such a girl on board. Zookers! had I known what was in store for me, do you think I would have raised any objection to the request of the Lady of Gêst? I was told she was a child, a little mountain colt; imagine, Roderike, my surprise!'

Ap Dafydd, who was sitting near, started up, his face was pale, his hand shook, as he hastily took up the chart he was examining, and went on deck.

'An odd fellow is that,' said Dhu, as the door closed upon the mate of the *Eryr*. 'I should like to know what harm I have done in admiring his beautiful niece. Did you ever see such lovely eyes, Roderike? I cannot get the girl out of my head.'

'Well, for my part, captain, I thought you were proof against all womankind,' said Roderike, laughing. 'If the great rover of the seas gets his heart turned by a girl, we may look for some prodigious change of wind in another quarter.'

'If she steals my heart, that is no reason why she should change the nature of the rover of the seas.'

'I cannot agree there,' remarked Roderike; 'the capturing of your heart would alone imperceptibly work a change.'

'Zookers! in that case the pirate-chief is in jeopardy,' cried Dhu, pledging his companion to drink the health of the daughter of Harlech.

The subject was continued with greater animation.

'What is this I hear?' said Kynfin Tudor, suddenly appearing before Dhu, pale as an apparition. 'You are desecrating my niece, by letting her be the subject of low conversation. The maiden is blood of my blood, and I will not bear it. Have you so soon forgotten your promise to the Lady of Gêst? I have not—Beware how you trifle with her or with me, Dhu!'

Ap Rhys coloured to his temples, and before he could make any reply, the mate of the *Eryr* was again at his watch.

'Zookers! Roderike, there's mettle for you,' ejaculated Dhu; 'how his Welsh blood boils. Did you ever come across a fellow so susceptible of affront, when in connection with his own family? He is an odd composition, soft as marrow, hard as flint. All the years he has been with me I cannot make him out, I defy the devil to make him out either. On my word, he had no occasion to come down upon me in this style. One would think I had committed a crime.'

'Captain,' said Ap Maelgwyn gently, 'upon considering, I think we have said enough to kindle Ap Dafydd. It is not likely he would calmly listen to our comments upon his niece. We are apt to forget, Dhu, that since we have become lawless rovers we should not attempt to aspire above our sphere.'

'Confound you, what do you mean by these insinuations? aspiring indeed! I have blood to boast of, as well as the son of Harlech. Is he not a rover as well as we?'

'I grant that, Thomas Nevil, but not by free will,' replied Roderike.

Dhu started, 'Who told you that?' said he.

'I shall not answer your question,' replied his companion; 'at the same time, I will not conceal from you that I am in possession of the secret between you and Ap Dafydd. When you recall the fearful scene that he has witnessed on board your vessel, and the intercourse which has passed between you, can Dhu Ap Rhys wonder that the son of Harlech is deeply solicitous about his brother's child, the heiress of the house of Einion? She has been placed by the Dewines under your charge, Dhu. The circumstance in her relation you already know. Neglect not the command of the good mother of Gêst. In such a case your reign over the sea is at an end. Ap Dafydd's feelings must be regarded. Swear not, bastard of Fauconbridge. It is the least sacrifice you can make for the injury you have done him, poor fellow. Has he not borne with you when it was almost beyond nature to do so?'

Dhu's brow was clouded and a superficial laugh escaped his lips, as he repeated:—

'I thought the son of Harlech was more honourable than to betray me. I had thought his lips were sealed upon that subject.'

'The son of Harlech's lips are sealed,' replied Ap Maelgwyn; 'it was not he who revealed the dark shadows of Thomas Nevil's character.'

'Roderike I will not bear this from you or any man,' retorted Dhu, with an angry gesture; 'let all look to themselves, and not pick holes in others; I don't understand this change in you, Roderike. Since you have been told my secret, it is but fair you should give up the author of the revelation. The Lady of Gêst must have been the tale-bearer.'

'I cannot satisfy you on that point,' answered the youthful Ap Maelgwyn; then striding across the cabin, he took down his cap from the place where it hung, with the intention of going upon deck.

'Stay, hot-brained yonker! You shall not quit me in this way,' cried Dhu, rising to detain him: 'Tell me, Roderike, has the Lady of Gêst played me false or not? Is it as I have always said that she is seeking my ruin under a hypocritical mask?'

'You wrong the Dewines, grossly wrong her,' said Ap Maelgwyn; 'if ever you perish under her hand, Dhu, it will rise from your own delinquencies, not from her malice.'

'Cursed be the day that my path was crossed by her,' repeated Dhu, bitterly; 'it is revolting to my soul to be under her thraldom; what do I profit by it? Drop after drop of poison is let fall into my cup. With regard to the daughter of Harlech, I consider I have been deceived; she led me to suppose that the maiden I was to take charge of to Vannes, was a character totally opposite to the lovely daughter of Harlech. She blinded me when she extracted the promise—therefore, I do not consider it sacred.'

'Dhu, put not such a construction on a matter so serious. If you break your parole, I shall tremble for the consequences.'

'I did not say I would break it; I merely remarked that I do not consider the promise sacred—while I curse the woman heartily for having deceived me.'

'Curse her not, Dhu; I never met with one so ungrateful. The Lady of Gêst has been a sincere friend to you; I believe at this moment she would go barefoot to the Holy Land to serve the fierce rover of the seas. How ill is she requited.'

'Hold, yonker, I may use what language I please, without being controlled by you; I will not be trampled upon in this way. I care neither for you nor Ap Dafydd. I will do as I have done before, if I see fit—I will defy the Lady of Gêst.'

At the sound of approaching footsteps, Dhu half turned his head, and asked who was there?—the next moment Gam stood composedly facing his master.

'I would speak a few words on it, Captain,' said he; 'the wind has veered round to a foul quarter, and looks on very squally.'

'The mate of the *Eryr* is in command of the course; go to him,' said Dhu, impatiently. Gam still lingered as if he were not satisfied. 'You lubberly knave, what makes you stand there? Be off, did you not hear me?'

'Aye, aye, captain, don't be on it so hasty. I think indeed, truth, you like very good to hear that Maurice has seen a sail from the mizen.'

'A sail. Zookers!—is it so?' exclaimed Dhu, and his countenance immediately brightened.

'Sail it is!' said Gam, proudly, at the same time eyeing his companions with curiosity beaming from the corners of his eyes, as he slowly went up the companion, muttering—

'Boil the fishes, head and all! Indeed truth, the wind blows in a very foul quarter. Our captain is not himself—I hear-ed him speak of the Dewines. Dyn anwyl! If he say a bad word for her, the sea waters will do more for him than wash his beard, quite certain. What's in the wind I no like, no. The son of Harlech, too, looks on it very sick. How is that—when the maidens, with their bright faces, are aboard?'

'The impertinent rascal! I thought he was about to question us upon the subject of our discourse,' said Dhu, the moment the door had closed upon the retreating form of Gam. 'Do you think he overheard anything?'

'I rather fancy not; your warm encomiums upon the good Lady of Gêst would have told upon the man's face,' replied Roderike, ironically.

'She has a strange influence over all my men: this I consider a great misfortune,' said Dhu; 'mind, Roderike, what I say— take every precaution that the good Lady of Gêst's mandate is kept from them. Should this sail turn out to be a Spanish merchant ship, I intend to capture her.'

'Capture her, Dhu, when the Dewines has forbidden it during the time the maidens honour the *Eryr* with their company. Take care, Dhu, how you trifle with her, lest your reign upon the seas come to an untimely end. The son of Harlech has also warned you.'

'Confound you, Roderike!—driving round the headland— I never knew you so provoking. You have tried my patience terribly tonight; however, my passion is over, and I bear you no malice; yonker, here is my hand.' Shortly afterwards he quitted the cabin.

Chapter XIV

The Rover's Resolve—Novel Situation—Attentions Undesired— The Broken Promise—A Vow

'How mighty is the strength of female fascination! How wonderful its influence: never till now have I repented of the past, never until the present hour has Thomas Nevil wished that he was not what he is. On my soul I cannot part with the fair daughter of Harlech, the new morning-star of my existence, the spell upon my heart! Cost what it may, the hour of her departure shall be delayed from day to day. I shall come under your severe censure, son of Harlech—let it be so. Mate of the *Eryr*, thou art yet in my power, and thou feelest it. Let the good Lady of Gêst imagine that she can visit upon me her curse, turn the evil eye upon me, and bring me to an untimely end. Vain illusion! Mere superstition! Some say as much—but is it so in reality? Thomas Nevil has stepped upon the stage to play a new scene. He will astonish them and all the world. When has he ever undertaken to act a part and been unsuccessful? The mate of the *Eryr* will place every obstacle in my way. As payment, fresh drops of bitterness shall be infused into his cup. I may yet trifle with him, and he may trifle too with the whole world—but not, son of Harlech, with the fierce rover of the seas!'

Dhu was sitting at the stern of his vessel, with a rich slashed jerkin thrown across his shoulder, and a cap in his hand, when he was roused from these dangerous reflections by the sudden appearance of old Rowland with the Welsh harp.

'Captain of the *Eryr*,' said he, 'the maidens are coming upon deck. The heat in the cabin below is become oppressive. I wish the harp to be a surprise to the daughter of Harlech. She does not know that it is on board. Where shall I place it?'

With a look of pleasure, Ap Rhys instantly fixed upon the most eligible place, and bade him go and fetch the silken cushions, which the cabin boy would give him.

The sun was shining with unbearable effulgency, and making the waters glow beneath, till they outshone burning gold. His beams were reflected back across the deck of the *Eryr*, dazzling the lawless crew, who were lounging about or reposing. A few were listening to the well-spun yarns, at intervals causing them boisterous merriment. The moment Kynfin Tudor and the maidens appeared upon the deck, every eye was diverted and the revelry hushed. Ap Dafydd was observed standing by the larboard bulwark, in conversation with his niece; Ap Maelgywn, at a little distance, was amusing the French girl with remarks on the quaint jokes of the men; while Dhu was pacing the deck on the starboard side with an air of apparent indifference. He then joined the group, and with a thoughtful expression said:—

'I am afraid the ladies have been inconvenienced by the heat below. It strikes me, if I may be allowed to judge, that here they are not much better off. Under a low awning methinks they would find it cooler. Are you not of that opinion, Ap Dafydd?'

'I did not think about it,' replied the mate of the *Eryr*, and, taking his niece by the hand, he conducted her to the place now shaded with a sail.

The cushions from the cabin were placed so that they might be in a cool situation. The sails hung back from the yards: the wind dying away increased the heat. Dhu managed to obtain a seat near the daughter of Harlech, and now appeared to sit with a temper perfectly calm. A few minutes had scarcely elapsed when old Rowland came from behind the awning. Taking the cover off the harp, he placed it at his mistress's feet.

'My harp!' ejaculated Gladys, with a radiant expression of feature. 'Who ventured to bring that from the castle?'

'The daughter of Harlech had left her tears upon the instrument. They told the old man at the castle that she would be sick at heart without it.' So reported the faithful domestic.

'It was most kind of you, Rowland,' said Gladys, and immediately extended her hand to the aged attendant as a token of her gratitude.

The colour mounted into her cheeks, increasing by contrast the brilliancy of her eyes. Her whole expression became animated. Her slender fingers lay upon the strings of the instrument. Unconscious of her beauty, and almost forgetting in whose presence she sat, she struck up one of her own sweet melodies, the air undulating with its enchanting notes.

Dhu sat with his eyes fixed upon her in silent admiration. If he had thought her beautiful before, what were his feelings now?

Kynfin Tudor regarded her with intense delight. His heart glowed with affection towards her. How widely different were the feelings prompting the admiration of these two men. Those of Kynfin seemed to say:— 'Thou art blood of my blood. I am indeed proud of thee. Could thy luckless parents but have rested their eyes upon thee! Alas, that was denied them. Bitter trials, too, have been thine. Child of my beloved Aliano, thou hast been a legacy bequeathed to me. I was to be an adopted father to thee; yet ask thyself, Kynfin Tudor, if thy duty in keeping her steps from harm led her into this vessel—into the presence of men of blood—of those who can mould themselves into any form they please—of those who deceive men older and more experienced than thyself. Yet how could I act otherwise? The Lady of Gêst would have it so. She told me she had bound the man by a solemn promise, and she knew I might trust him. My heart misgives me. Will he keep his promise?' He directed his eyes to those of Dhu's for an answer, and it was a negative. 'Heaven protect thee, my child! Come what may, if I am powerless in thy behalf, mayest thou see what the mate of the *Eryr* cannot reveal! Ill-fated as I am, a bondman to a man of crime!' Kynfin averted his face at these reflections, sitting silently, but before the soft tones of the harp had ceased, his place was vacated.

'Where is my uncle?' inquired Gladys, anxiously looking round.

'The mate of the *Eryr* never neglects his duty,' said Dhu ap Rhys in a low, deep-toned voice. 'Let me in treat you not to be alarmed, Mistress Gladys. You have others who will protect you and take a deep interest in your welfare.'

The voice fell upon her ear gratefully, for it said a good word for her uncle. Gladys immediately turned her eyes upon the speaker, and for the first time ventured to glance openly at his features.

The far-famed rover was sitting at her feet, well and even handsomely attired. His brown hair was thrown back, waving from his temples, and discovered a broad and lofty brow, with penetrating eyes. Every feature was good. His flowing beard and moustache did not, in the character he assumed, add any fierceness of expression to his features. Thus Nevil conversed with the daughter of Harlech in the character of a polished courtier rather than a pirate commander.

'Mistress Gladys has a soul for music,' said Dhu ap Rhys. 'I am passionately fond of sweet sounds. What can soothe the spirit more? It always opens a way into my heart, when nothing else penetrates to its recesses. The pathos of your strains has softened me. It has made me feel how base I am. Will Mistress Gladys pity and not despise me? You, fair lady, know not what it is to have a conscience that is ever smiting you. Dhu ap Rhys, would that he was not what he is!'

'If these are your sentiments, why do you not change?' replied Gladys, calmly. 'It is never ineffectual to atone for past evils by performing good in future.'

'I am afraid that is beyond hope. How much easier it is to promise oneself to act than to act in reality. Had I someone to sympathize with me—some kind spirit to direct me—I might be able to surmount the barrier of evil, and become a better, a happier man. I am now an outcast from society—a wanderer upon the face of the earth. Who will regard?—who will trust a rover of the seas?'

'When we diverge from the path of duty, we are our own enemies. We forfeit the love and esteem of others. That should be remembered before we wander from it,' said Gladys, turning her eyes from his gaze.

'You too cruelly judge me, daughter of Harlech. You cruelly judge your uncle too. Did you know the circumstances which caused us to quit the path of duty, your censure would have been withheld.'

Gladys coloured at her uncle being classed with the pirate.

'I would not intentionally be severe,' she quickly replied. 'I only think, if you would return to the right path, it would lead you to happiness. You appear craving to be happy. My uncle is not happy. I hope, when he returns to our mountain home, that at least his mind will be at rest. My poor uncle, I shall always try to give him comfort.' She added, in a low tone, 'I cannot bear to see him unhappy.'

'I envy him,' said Dhu, passionately. 'Had I only one person in the world who would take such an interest in me, that would smile upon me, I should be a different man. It would make a dark soul bright, a sad heart joyful. Mistress Gladys, it would be bliss indeed.'

Gladys rose with a dignified air. 'Where are our companions?' said she—'my uncle?'

'I am afraid I have unintentionally offended you,' said Dhu, also rising. 'The isolation of my own heart makes me sensitive. You touched a tender chord, Mistress Gladys: forgive me.'

The daughter of Harlech was embarrassed. She inquired hurriedly if he knew where her uncle was. She did not like the manner of the pirate chief, she scarcely knew why.

'On duty,' replied Dhu, endeavouring to detain her by asking simple questions about the harp.

'On duty,' repeated Gladys, with an air of disappointment.

'Kynfin Tudor is on duty,' said the rover, looking anxiously in her face. 'Why do you doubt me? Why are you in such a hurry to leave this cool shade?'

The maiden drew back, and as she did so a step from behind attracted her attention.

'Kynfin Tudor is not on duty,' said a voice in a stern, reprimanding tone; and the next instant the son of Harlech stood facing the rover. Their eyes met.

It was Dhu's turn to look embarrassed.

'I thought you were on duty,' said he; 'but since that is not the case, I suppose that duty devolves on me, and I am neglecting it.'

As he finished the sentence, he bowed courteously and quitted the spot.

The captain of the *Eryr* bit his lips, as he proceeded on his way towards his post. 'Confusion take the fellow he shall pay dearly for this!'

Little Maurice, who was a great favourite with the crew, at this instant passed near the commander, and was immediately stopped.

'Hold, you rascal! Where is the sail you saw the other night? You were dreaming at the masthead.'

'No, captain, no,' replied the boy, reddening. 'I seed the white sails as clear as a herring. Indeed, truth, I was not dreaming. She was gone in the morning.'

'Well, you little numskull, you need not look frightened. Tell me, did you see her ahead or astern of us?' continued Dhu, impatiently.

'Ahead of us, to the starboard,' replied the boy, moving a step or two away, as if he dreaded a blow upon the head.

'Enough, you little fool! Go away to your duty. Recollect, when you spy another sail from the masthead, that you call someone to scan it besides, before you report to your commander.'

'Yn enw Tâd! captain, don't be hard on the lad,' said Gam, coming up, good naturedly, to defend the little favourite, whose face betrayed great alarm. 'I am quite certain the lad did see a sail ahead. You forget, captain, that night was more than squally. I think on it, anyhow, that ship got a little more seawater than she liked. Dyn anwyl! Why, if we had not worked hard, and the Dewines was on our side, we should have been nicely high and dry, or squag'd down at the bottom of the Scilly rocks, indeed, truth.'

'You jabbering knave! If you think the vessel in question is gone to old Beelzebub, I don't. Since you are certain the boy was not mistaken, we will change the course of the *Eryr* and go in search of her.'

'Dyn anwyl!' once more ejaculated Gam, 'what will the maidens and the mate say to that?'

'You incorrigible rascal! How dare you volunteer a remark! The pirate chief is master of his own ship. Attend to orders, or a noose at the yardarm shall serve your turn!'

'The shades eat me! Maurice, fy ngwas bach i (my little fellow), I never seed it on this way afore—never. Our captain is in a fury of a temper. His mammy spoiled him, I'll be bound, be his mammy who she may,' said Gam, the moment he got beyond hearing.

'Lorks! Taffy, man, bubbles and surf! Who is his mammy, do you think?' interrupted one of the seamen who had caught Gam's last sentence. 'I thinks I know. Lend your ear, man: I will tell you. I don't want that little devil chick to get wind of it. No, by Davy Jones!' and the man having drained off a cup of liquor, which he held to his lips, fell back sprawling upon the sails.

'Gowning, you are drunk, man,' said Gam, looking down upon his companion with an air of disgust 'What do you make so much noise for, yn enw y goodness? The captain will hear you.'

'Bubbles and surf! nonsense, man. Would you not like to know who the skipper's mammy is?'

The seaman immediately seized Gam by the arm, and whispered in his ear—'The Dewines! The Dewines, to be sure, man.'

'Ffol gwirion! The sharks!' cried Gam, turning up his eyes with a look of astonishment. 'Gowning, never say that again. If our captain hears you talk in that way, you will be dangled up at the yard-arm—quite certain—quite certain.' And with these words upon his lips, Gam, with a thoughtful expression, moved away, leaving his companion to quaff deeper from the bowl.

The daughter of Harlech and the pirate chief met once more before the evening closed in, but not a word was exchanged. Dhu looked thoughtful; while Gladys and her uncle appeared more than ever devoted to one another. Dhu watched with jealousy Ap Dafydd stroking back the long black tresses from off her brow. He envied every word or smile that was lavished by her upon his mate. Refreshments were served upon deck. Long after the moon had risen, Kynfin Tudor and his charge sat conversing together. That evening, that memorable evening, the secret of his love for her mother was divulged, and the daughter of Harlech's sympathy and affection were increased tenfold.

A short time after the ladies had retired to rest, Ap Dafydd prepared to take his watch. The transparency of the cool atmosphere was delicious, after the day's heat. The stars shone with peculiar brilliancy, and equally brilliant was their reflection in the calm waters beneath. The son of Harlech bent over the bulwarks of the vessel, thought of his niece, and felt for the moment that he was happy. It was only for a moment: suddenly, raising his eyes to the spangled heavens, and discovering the north star, he became aware that the ship had changed her course.

'Thomas Nevil!' cried he, striking his hands on his forehead, while a rush of blood went to his heart. He staggered backward, caught one of the shrouds for support, then leaned once more against the bulwark, and breathed heavily.

The commander of the *Eryr* was below, carrying on an urgent conversation with the youthful Ap Maelgwyn. Their attention was suddenly drawn to the entrance of the son of Harlech.

'Dhu ap Rhys,' said he, placing his hand upon the table, with fearful excitement, 'I demand an explanation: is it by your orders that the ship has changed her course?'

'Yes, by the orders of the pirate chief,' said Dhu, with an undaunted air, 'and he prohibits anyone on board from interfering with his will.'

Kynfin Tudor's lips quivered, the pupil of his eyes dilated, and he looked steadily into the face of the rover.

'Dhu,' said he, in a hoarse voice, 'you have broken your parole; the Dewines's curse will rest upon thee—St Cyric save us!' The next moment he was gone.

'The saints in heaven protect my Aliano's child!' cried Kynfin Tudor, falling on his knees upon the deck, and extending his hands towards heaven. 'Visit not my sins upon her innocent head. I have been guilty of many offences; I am guilty in bringing her here. Yet let it not be my hand that causes the destruction of my poor Aliano's child. Spare her, heaven! spare her!' The son of Harlech bent his head till it rested on the deck, and he groaned deeply. In that attitude he remained for some time. When he again paced the deck, his step was steady and his thoughts clear.

'Thomas Nevil,' he muttered, between his clenched teeth, 'I call upon the numberless stars to witness my vow that should you injure a hair of the head of my niece, or gain the affections of the child, the last scion of the house of Einion, my hand shall send your demon spirit into eternity!'

CHAPTER XV

An Altered Course—Female Alarms— A Strange Sail—The Conflict

SEVERAL eventful days passed away on board the *Eryr*, now ploughing her course across the Atlantic, leaving Vannes far to the eastward. The son of Harlech shrank from revealing to his niece the rover's artful manoeuvre, and the violation of his word. He knew if he were questioned, it was not in his power to give a clear answer; and he dreaded the alarm that it would cause. Sooner or later would the explanation of all arrive.

Again Kynfin Tudor's face wore that peculiar wild look it had occasionally worn before. It was well he did not know how frequently Dhu sought an opportunity to pour his insinuating words into the ear of his unsuspecting and inexperienced niece. Fortunately Gladys, with her pure, noble mind, and engaged affections, treated him with reserve, and an indifference which could not hide from the rover that the progress he made to attain his object was slow and uncertain. Still he continued that progress with cautious steps, and did not despair. To be piqued by the haughty beauty, only increased his passion. Every hour she became in his idea more necessary to him; but his perseverance he determined should be rewarded. He would gain her affections, set her uncle at defiance, and make her his bride: 'Yes, she shall be the queen of the *Eryr*,' thought he—'the wealth that I have for years

accumulated shall be hers; she shall be my beautiful bride—
she shall rule the fierce rover of the seas, and his proud *Eryr
bach!*' He never thought of quitting his ship's deck, even for
the object of his affection—that would have been too great a
sacrifice! From boyhood, Dhu had been passionately fond of
the ocean; his pride and his love for his ship being intense.

One evening, speaking of his wild life, Gladys casually
remarked that though she acknowledged it was a life of
excitement, it was not an innocent life; therefore it was to be
regretted he did not quit the *Eryr*, and return to the path of
duty.

'Do not be so cruel, Mistress Gladys, as to ask me to part
from my *Eryr*,' cried Dhu. 'The rover of the seas and his *Eryr*
are one. In all my wild sorrows I feel that my ship alone is a
part of myself. It sympathizes with me. We bound over the
waves together; we share the summer's sun and the winter's
storms; we drink in the balmy summer air, and set our teeth
to the biting winds of the frozen north. Say a kind word for
my *Eryr*, Mistress Gladys. I would value a word in her praise
from you, if but one, and only one!'

Dhu spoke so pleadingly, so enthusiastically, yet naturally,
that his words found an echo in the heart of the mountain
maiden. She smiled upon the rover, and humoured him in his
request.

Dhu's heart bounded within him. He had discovered a
secret. He knew how to vibrate a chord in the maiden's soul.

'Bless you, Mistress Gladys, bless you!' said he, as she
repeated a sentence in favour of his ship, and leaning over her
harp to help her to string her instrument, he said rather
hurriedly, while his face glowed with animation:— 'Does it
give you no pleasure to make others happy, Mistress Gladys?'

The maiden looked up with surprise, and repeated—
'Pleasure to make others happy, most certainly. Why should
you question it? We should be selfish indeed if we took no
interest in our fellow-creatures.'

'Then, Mistress Gladys, you have made me supremely
happy.'

Kynfin Tudor was standing at a short distance, and Gladys's
eye fell upon him. 'Would I could make him happy,' cried she
with an earnestness that startled the rover. 'I cannot think what
has come over him. He is so changed within the last few days.
He evades all my questions, and looks wretched.'

'Mistress Gladys,' said the rover, with an air of
disappointment, 'you are a stranger to your uncle. I have lived
with him for years in close intercourse, and find that Kynfin
Tudor's happiness consists in being unhappy.'

'The pirate chief is mistaken. He cannot read the human heart
as I can,' replied the maiden, seriously. 'His face did not look
as it does now, when we sat together last week under the
shadow of the sail, while moonbeams played upon the waters.
Something must have happened. Old Rowland, too, is changed.
Jacqueline and myself were remarking it this morning. Will
Dhu Ap Rhys oblige me by solving the mystery?'

'I am not aware of any mystery,' replied Dhu, endeavouring
to look calm.

'Dhu ap Rhys,' said she, turning her full, dark blue eyes
upon him, and looking as if she doubted his veracity—'since
you cannot solve the mystery, you will perhaps tell me why
we have not reached Vannes before now? I ask you as a
favour, tell me candidly the reason.'

Dhu felt the appeal too urgent to be refused. He could not
lower himself in her eyes by repeating a falsehood. He must

reveal the truth, whether it would be to his advantage or not. Kynfin Tudor stood no longer opposite—they were alone. The moment had arrived, and the fierce pirate trembled.

Once more Gladys repeated the question. He fixed his penetrating eyes upon her, and replied in passionate accents:—

'It is because the rover has been loath to part with the fair daughter of Harlech. The *Eryr*, even the *Eryr*, would fail to cheer his soul without her presence, the star of his existence, the loadstone of his heart. Do not despise me, Mistress Gladys, do not be angry; it is you who have robbed me of my peace, and made me feel that the world, aye life itself, would be a blank without you.'

'Peace!' cried Gladys, with a look of terror. 'This is a presumption I did not look for. This is an infringement upon fair conduct, of which I did not think Dhu ap Rhys capable. Rover of the seas, I command you to take me back to Vannes. I call upon you, on your honour as a man, to deliver up those who have, in full confidence of its integrity, placed themselves under your protection.'

'Gladys, daughter of Harlech,' said Dhu, taking hold of her outstretched hands and pressing them between his own, 'ask me to take my life's blood, rather than deprive me of the star of my existence. I cannot live without you, I cannot part from you. You must, you shall be mine.'

The cry which broke from Gladys brought Kynfin Tudor to the spot. In an instant she had thrown herself into his arms, and was sobbing upon his breast.

The pirate chief was standing by, his arms were folded, and a determined expression sat upon his countenance, which became of ghastly paleness.

'Monster!' cried Kynfin Tudor, with a ferocious glance towards him. 'What has he said to thee, my child? repeat it to me, word for word. Has he insulted thee? If so, by heaven he shall suffer.'

'I have told her what you were afraid to tell her, Ap Dafydd,' said Dhu calmly; 'that the commander of the *Eryr*, for the present, has no intention of going to Vannes. I have not insulted the maiden. I have too much respect for your niece, mate of the *Eryr*.'

'Take me away,' said Gladys, in a hollow whisper; 'why did you not tell me this before? Why did you bring me from the castle, to be still a captive—worse, far worse, in a pirate vessel?'

'You may well blame me; spare not your uncle. He is deserving of your censure. Yet, God knows his heart, he did not do it willingly. Dhu, who reigns supreme upon the decks of the *Eryr*; it is he has broken his solemn promise. We are at his mercy.'

Gladys would not tell her uncle what Dhu had confessed to her. She dreaded lest the consequences might prove fatal to him; and without the protection of her uncle, how soon would her fate be sealed. Dhu's words passed continually across her mind like a frightful dream. She was glad to retire to Jacqueline and their cabin. There, upon her narrow bed, she turned her head to the boards of the vessel against which the waves rippled, and wept in secret bitterness.

On the following morning, at sunrise, the captain of the *Eryr* was on the watch. The expression of his face had changed, it did not look like that of the rover of the seas. He had caught a glimpse of the maiden's face, before she passed into her cabin. Even his heart was touched. Unprincipled as he was, his love for Gladys was sincere. He grieved that he should cause her a tear, and would have given worlds to have thrown himself at her feet and confessed his sorrow. His steps were often bent to the same spot, where, on the previous evening, the scene of perturbation had taken place. The harp was still there. The past rose vividly to his imagination. Again and again, he asked himself if he should ever gain that heart, dearer to him than life. His passion had been unreturned, she even seemed to have an aversion to him. Must his bright visions then fade away, as if they had never been? No; he would rather die than give up his treasure. With feelings of desperation, he turned to pace the deck again, when his reflections were broken by a youthful voice from the mizzen top:—

'Look ahead, Gam—look ahead, I won't tell you this time what I see, or I shall be called a fool—a dreaming boy.'

Both the seaman and the pirate chief looked up, and saw little Maurice aloft, scanning, with half-closed eyes round the rosy horizon.

'Sail ahoy!—sail ahoy!' shouted others of the crew. Dhu, appeared more eager than any of them, as if glad of the excitement.

'Well, yonker, what do you think of her?' said the pirate, addressing Ap Maelgwyn, who, to get a sight had hastened up the shrouds, and then descended upon deck.

'I should say she is a heavy-laden Spanish merchantman,' replied Roderike. 'We are gaining fast upon her.'

This opinion soon became general, and that she was bound for the Spanish coast.

For some time, Dhu stood with his eyes riveted upon the strange ship. At length, with a look of eagerness, he exclaimed:—

'She is ours. This time she shall not escape me. Hurrah my lads! Hurrah for the plunder! Show them your teeth, boys! Double your courage! The safety of the maidens, too, will be at stake. Keep that in mind.'

Ap Maelgwyn, placed his hand upon Dhu's shoulder, and asked him in a gentle tone if he would give him a few minutes' attention.

'What is it you want, Roderike?' said he, with so strange an expression that the youthful mate, starting back, exclaimed:—

'Dhu, I wish you would be more composed, be not so hasty in your decision. You will be sorry for it if you do not mind. Have some consideration for the maidens, captain.'

'I have great consideration for them,' replied Dhu, bitterly. 'Beware how you speak to me, boy. I am in no humour to argue. I will have my own way. I must have excitement; better be in danger, better perish, than endure the burning within. Roderike, don't cast your ominous warnings in my teeth. Listen to me—she hates me. She despises me, and I have frightened her, and made her wretched.'

They were standing in the cabin, and the rover, approaching the table, filled up a goblet of aqua vita, raised it to his lips, and drank it off. He was again on the point of filling it, when Ap Maelgwyn drew his hand away, and in a gentle and soothing tone, said:—

'Don't Dhu, don't, the maiden does not hate you; you are going the way to make her do so. Be calm, Dhu, things may take a better turn. The pirate chief has never before been faint-hearted.'

Ap Rhys pushed the glass from him, and then asked in a thick voice, if he knew how she was.

'I have no doubt she is all right this morning,' replied Roderike. 'I have not heard. It is yet early.'

'Yonker, it is dreadfully hot here, I must go again upon deck,' said the rover, with a nervous, restless movement of the limbs.

'Stay and have a little breakfast first,' said ap Maelgwyn, persuasively. 'Once more, I entreat you to have nothing to do with the capture of this merchantman.'

'I forbid you mentioning the subject again,' said Dhu, hastily. 'It will be excitement, Roderike, and excitement will keep me alive.' He turned his eyes suddenly in the direction of the cabin door and continued:—

'There goes Rowland, ask him how she is.' The account being favourable, Dhu appeared more composed, and went upon deck without having touched a morsel of the viands which Roderike had placed on a plate before him.

The whole of that day the rover paced the deck; he seemed scarcely aware of the heavy rain that was pouring down incessantly. A thick mist covered the ocean, and the desired prize was no longer visible: there was sorrowful stillness over all. Kynfin Tudor moved about like a spectre—not a face showed a gleam of cheerfulness from stern to stern. On the deck of the *Eryr*, Dhu contrasted every hour that passed with those which had been spent in the society of the daughter of Harlech, on the previous day. The moments he had enjoyed, and the anguish and disappointment at the total overthrow of his hopes—these were all revived again and again.

The rain seemed likely to continue. Ap Rhys, after giving his orders, retired to his cabin to take some repose; but the rover could not sleep, his brain was too busily at work. At an early hour the following morning, he was aware that someone had entered his cabin, and almost immediately felt a hand placed upon his shoulder.

'Who have we here?' cried Dhu. Looking up, he beheld the diminutive figure of Maurice standing by him.

'Captain! brave captain!' cried he, 'I have come to tell you that the Spanish ship is in sight, the breeze has sprung up, and the *Eryr* feels her helm.'

'Are you sure, you little numskull, that you have not been dreaming again at the masthead?' cried Dhu, bounding upon his feet. On Maurice assuring him that the merchant ship stood as large as life upon the waters, he patted the boy upon the head, and bade him go and bid the mate call all hands to quarters.

Dhu himself appeared, with a more excited look than on the previous day, and shouted at the top of his voice—

'All hands up to quarters! Hurrah, my lads! hurrah! We shall have her now, there's no mistake in the matter. Courage, my boys!'

The tumult and confusion were increasing every instant. With intense anxiety Dhu watched the progress of the heavy-laden Spanish ship. They were gaining upon her; and now she approached so near that Dhu's deep-toned voice was heard, shouting through the trumpet—

'What ship's that?'

'The Dona Teresa,' was the reply.

'Whither is she bound?' inquired the rover; and before he had received an answer, the *Eryr* proudly rode over the waves to windward. Again she neared the merchantman, and could almost look into her decks. Never did the *Eryr* appear to such advantage. This set the Spaniards in amaze; they began to speculate upon what was her object.

'Ap Maelgwyn,' said Dhu, suddenly taking his eyes from the exciting scene, 'are the maidens in the cabin?' Upon the answer being in the affirmative, he continued, 'I must go to them for a few minutes: keep the *Eryr* steady on this tack, till I return. Give my orders to Ap Dafydd.'

With a trembling hand Dhu raised his cap from his brow, and entered the cabin. The maidens were seated side by side: the face of the daughter of Harlech was concealed among her long tresses, upon the shoulder of her friend. The rover stood before her 'ere she knew he was in the cabin.

'Mistress Gladys,' cried he, bending upon his knees before her, 'we may never meet again. I have come to ask your forgiveness—I have come to bid you farewell. The rover's heart is broken, and he will receive his death-wound with a cry of joy.'

With a look of sorrow on sorrow the maiden raised her eyes, and fixed them upon the changed object before her. She did not speak, nor attempt to withdraw her hand from the warm pressure between the rover's burning palms.

'Say you forgive,' repeated Dhu, with a still wilder gesture: 'let these words comfort my dying hour—say it, Gladys!'

The daughter of Harlech tried to articulate, but the words died away upon her lips. Yet he could read the meaning in her eyes. Dhu started instantaneously upon his feet, and, waving his hand as he quitted the cabin, repeated—

'Bless thee, Gladys, daughter of Harlech—farewell!' and he was again upon the deck.

The *Eryr*'s course was now a determined one; and the Spaniards felt there was no alternative but to fight.

Dhu's voice sounded above every other, giving his peremptory commands; and when the words came—

'Luff man, luff! Lay her aboard!'—the vessels ran alongside, and were soon locked together. The fearful savage cries rending the air, caused a thrill of terror through the maidens' bosoms; they sank upon their knees and cried to heaven, in the deepest alarm. The turmoil on deck overhead became fearful; every sound and renewed shout infused fresh terror into their hearts, and they became completely paralysed.

Kynfin Tudor, notwithstanding his aversion to blood, and anxiety for his niece, with that of his own personal safety on her account, rushed into the midst of the combat, and fought with a courage worthy of the son of the renowned chieftain of Harlech. His sword caused more havoc that day than it did at the memorable battle of Wakefield.

There were far more Spaniards on board the enemy than they had supposed, and the conflict soon became more fierce, and prolonged in consequence. Already the decks were strewed with the dead, yet the clashing of arms did not cease.

Dhu in the midst of the carnage, engaged hand to hand with the captain of the merchantman. The latter had fallen upon him with the utmost fury, but the rover was too well experienced in personal combat for his adversary. His dexterous hand soon laid his antagonist at his feet. Then it was his danger became more imminent. The Spaniards seeing their captain fall, rushed in a body upon Ap Rhys, who kept them at bay with surprising coolness and courage.

The son of Harlech, shortly after seeing Dhu wounded, and the great peril he was in, forgetting at the time all the injury the rover had done him, rushed forward to his assistance, placed himself between the Spaniards and his commander, while the latter almost immediately afterwards fell wounded at his feet.

Ap Maelgwyn, Gam, and several of the seamen hastened to the spot and bore away the renowned rover of the seas, whose reign over the *Eryr* was at an end for ever.

END OF VOL. II

VOL. III

CHAPTER I

A Tragic Scene—The Pirate's Bequest

THE commander of the *Eryr* was no more seen upon the deck.
The soft melodies of the harp no longer floated upon the
waters. Deep gloom was over all. In a cabin below the water
line, a small lamp cast a glimmering light across the narrow
cabin, and its ray rested upon the pale face of the daughter of
Harlech. She was sitting by the bedside of the wounded chief.

'Gladys are you there?' murmured a weak voice from the
narrow couch.

The maiden instantly rose and leaned over the prostrate
man. 'Does Dhu ap Rhys want anything?' said she in a tone
of sympathy. 'Your lips are parched, let me give you
something to moisten them.'

'No, Mistress Gladys, no.' He felt for her hand. When he
had placed it in his own, he remained perfectly still, save that
the palpitation of his heart was more audible.

The rover was fast sinking from his wounds. The pain he
endured was excruciating, yet no murmur escaped his lips. He
felt there was no hope of his recovery. That did not seem to
distress him. The only anxiety he appeared to feel was, lest
the daughter of Harlech should leave him, and the last hours
of his fast ebbing life be passed without her presence.

So heart-rending had been his appeal that even Kynfin
Tudor wavered, notwithstanding an impulse to reject his
prayer. Yet was not the rover expiring? Should living hate

leave the world resting still on the heads of the departed? Should it not die with them? The dauntless Dhu ap Rhys, who only a day or two before had trod the deck of the vessel in high health and in the full vigour of manhood, was now but a melancholy wreck of humanity. The maiden's distaste and even dread, was now changed to pity and sympathy, when Kynfin Tudor wavered, it was Gladys's entreaty that fell upon his ear, and made him finally yield to the dying man's petition.

Kynfin's mind was in confusion. He left his niece to attend upon the prostrate man, and took upon himself the new duty of a commander on the blood-stained deck.

He well knew the rover must die. The secret between them would then be at rest. His own emancipation was at hand, and his beloved charge would be safe. This was cheering, yet he was not cheered. With Dhu he had passed six years, and now he was about to part with him for ever. He did not rejoice in his death; yet he felt that there was cause to be thankful for recent events. He was on the eve of parting with the comrade of his own wild sea life. Was this strange? Was it inconsistent? It might be so, but the shades of Thomas Nevil's character did not at that moment appear of so dark a hue as certain redeeming points that arose in Kynfin's benevolent and forgiving heart, and suggested the question. 'If he has wronged me, have I not also wronged him?' Ap Maelgwyn had told him of the rover's pure love for his niece. He thought of his own love for Aliano. Why had he no sympathy for Dhu? He who knew how hard it was to resist temptation, why had he been so uncharitable when he himself had fallen short in so many duties which would be pleasing in the sight of heaven? He knew the rover must die. He therefore could not, and would not blame the pirate chief; but he blamed himself that he should have listened to the Lady of Gêst, and have placed the fair daughter of Harlech on the deck of a rover's ship.

Voices of distress broke in upon these saddening meditations, for he stood among the slain upon the still sanguinary deck. Looking in the direction from whence the voice proceeded, little Maurice approached wringing his hands. He had been stooping over the almost lifeless body of Gam.

'Oh, mate of the *Eryr*!' cried he with the uncontrollable grief of a child. 'I must lose my best friend, my true good hearted Gam, who never said one unkind word to me. Ochan! Ochan! he says he cannot live for the Dewines's curse is upon us. He has seen her knotted handkerchief at the mast-head; and I too have heard its heavy sound, flap, flap, like a wet sail upon the yards, we all know what it bodes that our ship shall never see another summer sun! I am sick at heart, mate of the *Eryr*, very sick.'

The words of the boy knocked loudly at the heart of Kynfin Tudor. They struck the chord of his sympathy in repeating— 'I am sick at heart, very sick.' Soon afterwards in kind tones, he administered words of comfort to the broken-hearted lad.

'Come, come, Maurice bach, you must cheer up,' said he, 'we will have Gam taken below and see what can be done. The other men also shall be attended to.'

The vessels remained lashed side by side. The Spaniards had been massacred to a man. It was a fearful sight. The son of Harlech, sensitive as he was, shrunk not from performing his melancholy task, and attended to the wounded. The dead were thrown overboard, and the decks washed. Those who expired subsequently were committed to the waves with an unhallowed prayer, the bubbles rising as they, without a dirge, sank in the deep water. Kynfin sent the Spanish merchantman adrift, after securing what was most valuable on board. He soon restored order. When the early dawn shone upon the rover's pride the next day, no tragic spectacle was there to shock the eye. Silently the vessel glided on her course towards the French coast.

Ap Maelgwyn had been slightly, and many others of the crew, severely wounded. The maidens, like ministering angels, attended to the wants of the sufferers, and did all in their power to alleviate their miseries.

The first night after the contest, the leave-taking of Gam with his comrades was touching. When the good-hearted seaman breathed his last, his little favourite, the life of the decks, was inconsolable. The gentle voice of the maidens could not comfort him. The kind persuasions of the mate and second mate to abate his grief were of no avail. The boy shook his head, and fixing his eyes upon Kynfin Tudor, the tears rolled faster and faster, saying, though his lips repeated it not.

'The Dewines, the Dewines! I am sick at heart, mate of the *Eryr,* very sick!'

The son of Harlech stood alone upon the solitary deck, watching for the third time since the fatal day, the last faint glimmer of the evening upon the ocean. The vessel scarcely moved; the wind sighed mournfully through the rigging, and the monotonous flap, flap, of the sails against the mast, sounded ominously, and made him ready to start even at his own shadow.

The monotony was at length broken by a wild distracted cry from the cabin below. The names of the Lady of Gêst, and the daughter of Harlech vibrated on the ear. Louder and louder became the cry. Ap Dafydd hastened to the bedside of the wounded rover. He was sitting up with outstretched hands, and eyeballs glaring. His gentle nurse had started from his side, and was standing at a distance, burying her face in her hands that she might conceal from her affrighted vision the frantic gesture of the pirate, whose voice still resounded through the cabin.

'Gladys! Gladys! I cannot part with thee. Thou hast cursed me, Lady of Gêst! Thou hast cursed me, false woman! There was a *corpi santi* sent by thee on the masthead yesternight. I saw the livid fire, forky and fierce, come and depart, now thou hast set my soul in a flame. Thou hast made my brain boil. Why didst thou tempt me? Didst bring me joy only to dash it from my lips? Why didst thou do this, false woman? Thou sayest that I deserve it, that it is retribution, ha, ha, false woman! Thou once proclaimedest the rover of the seas more to thee than all the world, and yet thou hast cursed me. My last hour is at hand. I cannot die. Hell with its torments is open before me, I cannot die. The cry of blood sounds in my ears. O, that I could wash the stains off my hands. I cannot die. Angel of hope console me! But one hour's reprieve more that I may make my peace with heaven. I cannot die yet!'

A loud shriek followed this wretched appeal, and he lay back upon his couch exhausted and insensible.

The anguish of his heart had struck deeply into the spirits of all on board. Every face bore traces of grief. They listened to the quick breathing of the dying man with anxiety.

When he had returned to consciousness, his delirium was gone. The violent trembling of his frame had subsided. He was restless, and appeared as if he wished to articulate, brightening as man sometimes does before his vision is darkened for ever.

'Kynfin Tudor, where art thou?' he exclaimed as his eyes fell upon the distressed features of his mate. He held out his hand and said: 'Forgive me, I am going my last long journey, at least let me make my peace with you. I have injured you. You know how wrong I have acted towards you, who have been my best friend; your hand prevented me from committing a crime that would have called louder upon my conscience than any of the evil deeds of which I have been guilty. I am grateful for your having spared me remorse for that crime, I am grateful to you for permitting your brother's child to administer succour to me in my last moments. It is with sincere penitence of spirit I now ask you to forgive me for the past. Oh! could my life but be spent over again!'

For a few minutes the dying man was silent; upon being raised up he revived, and looking eagerly round he continued: 'Mate of the *Eryr*, I need not warn you not to follow longer a life similar to mine. Hear my last request. Let my ashes and those of my proud *Eryr* both moulder together, burn her, burn her with the rover's remains—let her be his winding sheet.'

His voice grew thick, his eyes once more wandered round the cabin. They fell at last upon the daughter of Harlech, who was standing by weeping bitterly.

'Come to me, come to me, Gladys! Let me once more hear your voice before we part for ever. Let me look upon you, look my last! Alas I cannot see your features—the—light— bring the light!'

The maiden took the rover's hand and looked sadly in his face, but his sight was obscured. He could only lay her hand upon his heart before his head fell back, and his voice was heard no more.

CHAPTER II

A Foreign Land—The Conflagration— The Cabin-Boy—A Daughter's Sorrow

THE sun was sinking into the western waves, when from the cross trees of the *Eryr* the French coast appeared in sight. It was the dead of night before the good ship approached Vannes. The boats were lowered, and the mate of the rover's bark with the ladies were seated in their places in the stern sheets. Old Rowland and little Maurice with four of the seamen composed the boats' crew, Maelgwyn and the rest of the seamen in the vessel being to follow as soon as they had placed the combustibles in the proper situation to execute the last singular wish of their late daring commander.

The moon was shining bright; not a ripple disturbed the waters that reposed calm as sleeping infancy. The steady strokes of the oar that drew their skiff nearer and nearer to the land were alone audible, that land they had so long desired to reach. The daughter of Harlech was sad at heart; her feelings were widely opposed to those of her light-hearted companion. The latter was naturally diverted from the late melancholy train of events, and the reflections they were calculated to inspire, by the pleasure she experienced at once more beholding her own country, and her father Louis Agustine, and anticipating further the joy of soon being clasped in his arms. Gladys could only return the pressure of her little friend's hand; she had not a smile at her command; she could not frame an expression of sympathy in unison with her friend's feelings; she sat bending over the skiff, with her eyes fixed upon the glassy waters, buried in her own painful reflections. The late events were uppermost and with the rover appeared constantly before her vision, while her ears still resounded with the dying cry of the departed:—'Gladys, Gladys, I cannot part with thee!' She had no affection for the unfortunate pirate, that was impossible; but she was not so insensible to pity as not to feel when circumstances had made her recollect his deep regard for her, if she had no regard for him. With her gentle and benevolent heart, her memory could not so soon be faithless to his look of gratitude for the office she had rendered him, or to his look of sorrow when she attempted to leave his side. She could not forget his entreaty for her prayers, any more than the heart-rending supplications of a great sinner. The last hour before his spirit departed, the moments before delirium came on, when he earnestly thanked her for her kindness, and the anguish he had exhibited when he felt the hour was come to part with her for ever, were all too fresh in her memory not to affect her spirits. In his winding sheet, too, he haunted her imagination. She had never before seen death. She reflected that she had been the cause of his dissolution, and the extorting tears from every eye in the ship, for even the cold-blooded pirates wept on the death of their commander. These thoughts troubled her so much that when she set her foot upon the land no sign of pleasure, no expression of thankfulness, escaped her lips. Kynfin Tudor, and Jacqueline on the other hand, in earnest conversation, showed unmistaken marks of delight as they proceeded towards the landing place, which was close to the garden of Louis Agustine's residence. Gladys did not seem to heed her companions, in her abstraction appearing scarcely to know that she had left a foot print upon the sand, they had arrived before the gate of the Frenchman's garden. There her reverie was broken by an exclamation of delight from Jacqueline, who seemed all happiness; and bounding on before them, was quickly out of sight.

Kynfin felt a singular sensation overtake him as he conducted his beloved charge up the well-remembered path from the water side. When he reached the garden, his first impulse was to fold her in his arms and pronounce upon her a fervent blessing. Gladys warmly returned this testimony of his affection. Soon afterwards her restless eyes wandered in the direction of the rover's ship, where so many eventful days had just been passed. She had bid the vessel farewell, and prepared to see the flames consume it.

The ship was even now on fire; soon the whole horizon was illuminated, and the ashes of the rover were mingled with the glowing embers of the bark in which he had rode the waters so long, and signalized himself by so many daring exploits. A faint cry broke from Gladys's lips as she exclaimed:

'Oh, my uncle! see! O see! The rover and his proud *Eryr* bark are consuming together!' Her voice dropped into a whisper, and she stood supported in her uncle's arms, for some time gazing upon the flames. They rose higher and higher, their lurid light reflected in the sleeping waters of the bay, at once giving a fiery look to the land and sea around. It was a painful sight. Even Kynfin Tudor's frame trembled, with that of his more fragile companion. She did not attempt to dry the tears which she had shed, much less to conceal her agitation.

The party found Agustine unfortunately from home, and although it was a great disappointment to the French maiden at not finding her father upon her return to her native country, she was so unselfish that she concealed her disappointment in order to exert herself in making her guests comfortable. She cheered Gladys, using the most affectionate and sympathizing terms; to Kynfin she made remarks on the happy time she had spent with him in that home during the days of her childhood, which she styled a new era in her existence.

Jacqueline was distressed soon afterwards at hearing that her father was not likely to return to Vannes, having been for the preceding three months resident in the Duke's household at Rennes.

'What can he be doing there?' thought Jacqueline. He had so frequently said to her that he would strictly avoid taking any situation under the existing government, and that the vacillating potentates of the day, were never to be trusted. 'One day,' said he, 'you may be their favourite, the next their slave, their greatest friend or bitterest foe!' Jacqueline wished her father had not gone to Rennes, and she only longed the more to see him that she might express her fears.

'*Ma petite* Jacqueline must not distress herself,' said Ap Dafydd one evening when he happened to overhear her communicating her fears to Gladys. 'If we can only learn your father's intentions, and be sure that this report of his acceptance of a post is true, we will lose no time in conducting you to Rennes, where your parent will soon embrace you. All have their disappointments; I have just come from visiting an old friend of mine in the town, one of my countrymen, I find the Earls of Pembroke and Richmond reside no longer in the neighbourhood of Vannes, so we shall have to go and seek them.'

Ap Dafydd looked anxiously towards his niece as he finished the sentence; he had only a short time before been buoying up her hopes that their mission would soon be fulfilled, and the disturbance which he feared her flight and that of the smugglers had caused in the neighbourhood of Harlech, would ere this have subsided, and consequently nothing would prevent their speedy return to the Cwm.

Gladys was startled at her uncle's words, and a shade of disappointment passed over her brow. A moment before she had been picturing to herself a happy meeting with her grandmother, the pleasure of again scrambling over her native hills, the plunging her feet into the mountain streams, and more than all the joy of being free and independent; words she did not yet feel in their old and true meaning.

'Where are they gone to?' said she with eagerness, 'surely, uncle, they have not yet left Brittany?'

'They have not left the dukedom,' replied Kynfin Tudor soothingly, 'I hope we shall not be long in discovering their new quarters. It is but recently that they have taken their departure from Vannes. The whole of France appears to be in an unsettled state, this I learn through the partisans of the different factions. The old Duke is more than ever governed by his favourites; but what is more surprising than anything else, the Earls of Pembroke and Richmond are in high favour with his Grace. They say they have been to visit him at his palace. This intelligence is difficult to comprehend. I know the minister Landais, who is still in power, has been their greatest enemy from their arrival in this country. I warned Jasper of Hatfield to beware; Jasper has so good a heart that he can never think ill of others till too late. I hope he may not fall a victim to Landais's machinations.'

'I saw the minister several times formerly, he was with my uncle,' observed Jacqueline, 'I never liked his appearance; there was something particularly forbidding about the expression of his features, and his mean, spare form, deep sunken eyes, hook nose, and swarthy complexion, his restless shuffling gait, and that peculiar sinister sneer when he was addressed upon any topic that did not happen to meet with his approval. That man is my aversion. If he were my father, I don't think I could have one particle of love for him.'

'I have good reason to remember his ill countenance,' replied Kynfin thoughtfully. 'I have kept my eyes upon him, and watched the working of his evil features for an hour at a time. He will ruin himself someday. There is folly in his knavery, more than beseems villains of long practice. No one abuses reason with impunity, *ma chère petite*. The time of reaction will come with Landais, too, for he rushes of late too heedlessly into wine. There is much policy in becoming a successful knave, and in keeping the system long flourishing lies the art of great and heroic villainy. Methinks the minister is a small professor after all, for he plays on the Duke's enfeebled faculties.'

'I am delighted your opinion of Landais bears out what my inexperience surmises. I wonder how it is that we dislike some people because we do dislike them. When I was a little girl I recollect meeting the minister with my father, when a sudden terror seized me lest he should take hold of my hand or kiss me; I hastily stole away with this impression upon my mind. It was an instinctive feeling of his real character, I often regret my father made his acquaintance.'

'We will not recall those times, *ma petite*,' resumed Kynfin on observing the colour come and go upon her cheek, 'you and I know too much already of the Duke and his deceitful satellites ever to wish to mention their names, much less to have any communication with them.'

'It is that which makes me so unhappy about my father,' replied the French girl sorrowfully, 'I would rather he had nothing to do with individuals so unprincipled, and void of good feeling.'

'Let us hope, *ma petite*, that affairs will improve, when we reach Rennes. I think a visit there is the alternative,' said Ap Dafydd looking at his young companions with a paternal expression. 'The journey will be tedious.'

'I do not object to the journey,' replied Gladys, 'I rather think it would be more agreeable than otherwise, I was thinking of old Rowland. He has friends not many leagues from here; but what is to become of little Maurice who I have promised should return with us to the Cwm.'

'He had better accompany Ap Maelgwyn to Wales, and join us afterwards. I have been speaking to him upon the subject. Ap Maelgwyn leaves tomorrow, he told me he would be here this evening to bid you farewell. We can, perhaps, come to an arrangement about the lad with him.'

'Poor little Maurice is so fond of you, I fear he will be disappointed,' rejoined Gladys, looking up into her uncle's face pleadingly.

'We shall soon meet him in Wales, I hope, meantime our movements are uncertain, so that we cannot do better than embrace this opportunity. Ap Maelgwyn will take every care of him.'

'I am convinced of that,' said Gladys, and nothing more passed.

They had not seen Roderick since they parted upon the deck of the *Eryr*. The moment he entered the apartment Gladys turned pale. He brought back to her painful recollections.

As the maidens extended their hands to the young mate,

there was a great contrast between the carriage of the two girls. Jacqueline was confused; the colour, it is true, might have appeared deeper in hue upon her cheeks by the side of the pale features of the daughter of Harlech. Without accounting for such an appearance, they were visibly of a more rosy tinge than they had been a little before. Kynfin, observing it, remained for some minutes deeply thoughtful.

Ap Maelgwyn consented to look after the little favourite of the quarter deck. When he took his departure, his leave-taking with Jacqueline was different, and apparently more touching than with his other friends.

Some time had elapsed since their arrival at Vannes, and yet no intelligence had reached them from Monsieur Agustine. This increased Jacqueline's anxiety, and Ap Dafydd at length determined upon starting for the capital.

The change of scene, and the novelty of the journey revived the drooping spirits of the maidens, and kept them from many painful reflections.

The son of Harlech, their only protector, watched the varying expressions upon their countenances with a pleasure new and strange. By the death of the unfortunate rover, a load had been removed from his heart; now they were recovering from the late painful scenes in which they had been involved, he felt happier than he had done for a long time before. His fair legacy and his anxiety for her welfare, almost wholly engrossed his attention; both were still uppermost, though it was true his cares were lessened.

When they reached Rennes, Kynfin despatched a messenger to the palace, to inquire for Louis Agustine. The reply was that he had been sent by his Grace, to the Duke of Orleans upon urgent business, and was daily expected back.

Jacqueline was cheered by this information, but she soon grew impatient again. Time swept on, and her father did not make his appearance.

Kynfin Tudor, too, became uneasy on her account. At length, he went himself to the palace, and upon making inquiries, learned with horror that Louis Agustine and all his escort had that morning been discovered murdered in the forest. They had also been robbed of important papers belonging to the Duke. The intelligence had thrown all in the palace into consternation.

This was a fresh trial to Kynfin, who sickened at the thought of breaking the melancholy news to the poor orphan.

The two girls were seated in the window watching his return. The moment he entered the apartment, they sprang to him, one on each side. The expression of his face alarmed them, and both, in more eager tones than usual, inquired what had happened.

'Jacqueline, my little Jacqueline, Heaven comfort thee,' murmured Ap Dafydd, sinking into a chair, and drawing her near him. 'I have not brought you cheering news, would to heaven I had been able to do so! What shall I relate to you of your father that will least wound your affectionate heart, my Jacqueline bach?'

'If he is ill, oh! do take me to him!' cried she, bursting into a fit of extravagant grief. 'Take me to him this moment! Do not keep me in suspense—let me hear the worst!' cried the unhappy Jacqueline, with fearful apprehension in her countenance.

Gladys stood by her side, and entreated her to be comforted. The sorrow thus visited upon her friend, seemed at once to restore the daughter of Harlech to her former self. Her own grief became hushed. She could now only think of, and sympathize in, the distress of one who had given up so much for her, and was so true-hearted and affectionate in her nature.

'Your father has been ill, Jacqueline,' said Kynfin, not wishing to be too sudden in his disclosure of the melancholy intelligence in its more violent aspect.

'Let me go, how far off is he? How long shall we be in travelling to him? For the love of the Virgin take me at once!'

'Calm yourself, my dear Jacqueline, I am grieved to tell you he is so ill that we cannot arrive in time to see him alive.'

'Let us go, let us go, I must see my dear father—my dear, dear father!'

'Jacqueline bach, you must bear up against this trial; you must be prepared for the worst—your father is no more!'

The poor, grief-stricken girl fell into the arms of Gladys, and was borne in a state of insensibility to her apartment, which, for several days, she was unable to leave, until which time, the manner in which he met his end was not communicated to her.

CHAPTER III

An Unexpected Friend—Courtier Baseness—The Prophecy— The Royal Pledge

'BY my troth, Kynfin Tudor!' ejaculated the Earl of Pembroke, as he quitted the side of a *distingué* looking Frenchman, who was pacing up and down with him before an antiquated château, situated amid rich scenery a few leagues from Rennes. 'Kynfin Tudor, can it be possible? This is an unexpected pleasure!' Jasper of Hatfield hastily advanced, and wrung the hand of his kinsman with the same generous warmth as in bygone days.

'I hope all has gone well with you for the long period since we parted, my good kinsman,' continued the Earl. 'Let me assure you that I am delighted to see you with us once more.'

The son of Harlech's countenance brightened at the sight of his old friend, and for a few minutes he could scarcely speak from emotion.

'Good Jasper of Hatfield,' at length he exclaimed, 'your kind greeting touches my heart. I cannot find language to express my joy at seeing you. I only wish that our meeting had been in our own country, and not in this land of our exile.'

'Ah, my good kinsman, I fear that day is farther off than ever,' replied the Earl, putting on a more serious expression of feature. 'I have almost ceased to hope that my native shores will ever greet my eyes.'

'There are many hearts in Wales that would be heavy with sorrow, did they think so,' replied Kynfin.

'Indeed!' slowly repeated the Earl, 'I should have thought 'ere this that the Yorkist's long and glorious success had destroyed the last hope in every British heart for the house of Lancaster.'

'No,' said Ap Dafydd, eagerly, 'there are many who still live upon the hope that a glorious day for Lancaster is gleaming in the distance, and that an evil one for the House of Marche is not far off.'

'This is dangerous language,' observed the Earl, looking anxiously round, 'Kynfin, you must be cautious.' The Earl placed his arm within that of his kinsman, and turned down a walk leading to a more secluded spot. 'The Frenchman you saw in company with me just now was Lord Lescun, a great favourite as you may recollect with his Grace the Duke. I see, his lordship has gone to join the party in the pavilion. We can continue our discourse uninterrupted.'

'Times are changed,' observed Ap Dafydd, 'since I took my departure from the shores of Brittany; you were not then in very good odour with his Grace, now, I understand, he loads you with attentions. I hope Jasper of Hatfield feels his ground, and acts accordingly.'

Pembroke smiled. 'Ah! Kynfin, wary as ever. I missed you sadly after you left, and frequently longed to have you near that you might aid me in my troubles. The anxiety I have since suffered has been great, yet, my good kinsman, you see the exiled nobles have hitherto escaped the fangs of their enemies.'

'The Virgin's name be praised that they have,' said Ap

Dafydd, gravely. Shortly afterwards he made enquiries for young Richmond.

'His health has not been strong,' answered the Earl, 'but his change of residence has been beneficial to him. The Duke permitted us to quit Vannes for a season. Young de Montfort has given us the use of his château. Thus Kynfin you will perceive that we are not destitute of friends even in banishment.'

'It does my heart great good to hear it,' responded Ap Dafydd, 'I hope the Earl of Richmond has not been much indisposed.'

'Not seriously, no, but he has been harassed. His indisposition is more of mind than body. Last winter ill reports from England were in circulation here. Now we have arrived at that point, I will breathe the secret to you. The ground we tread upon here is not smooth, and we find it a difficult task to walk without stumbling. We are at present in the Duke's favour, it is true, but that arises from interested motives; *entre nous,* he is anxious to form an alliance between my nephew and his fair cousin, Claudine de Montfort. We imagine that Peter Landais, his minister, who is a base hypocrite, does not approve of these proceedings, nor does Lord Lescun. The latter has promulgated a report that his Grace purposes paying his respects to us almost immediately. He, you know, is not a more exalted character, unless by birth, than his friend Landais. Under these circumstances, the Lancastrian nobles cannot feel easy in mind.'

'It is to be lamented that the Duke has such characters contaminating his court,' remarked Kynfin, 'the truth cannot reach his ears. They dupe their master even more than they oppress his subjects.'

'It is indeed to be lamented,' repeated Pembroke. 'Lescun has a more fashionable air than Landais, confident, well-looking, having all the vices of the court in which he was bred, that of Fontainebleau. He is not of a petty state like Landais, narrow, and pretending in proportion to their insignificance. Gay, vicious, dishonest, and given to play, Lescun hangs upon Landais without any tie of friendship beyond that of his own pecuniary advantage, and a sympathy grounded in a similarity of nature; thus, I have not the dread of Lescun that I have of Landais.'

'He may not be quite as dangerous,' replied Kynfin, 'but we must recollect that he is a pliant instrument, or rather a partner in the schemes of the minister. To him he is useful at all times, from possessing those talents, and that experience in moral degradation which are of such effect, when certain orders of statesmen endeavour, after concocting depraved schemes, to find instruments for effecting them. A friend of mine at Vannes, was speaking of Lescun to me the other day. He said Lescun had sold all his estates, with which he could well make away, to pay the debts of his profligacy, and getting the proceeds, he thought better of his chance honesty, and lost every sous of the money at play. He is of good family, which he has degraded; was the heir of a fine fortune he has squandered, and is now the lackey of a base born adventurer, in whose knavery he partakes, partly from congenial feelings with those destitute of honour, and partly from pecuniary necessity; as you Jasper of Hatfield have already observed.

'Both he and Landais are blots upon the Dukedom of Brittany, having made their court to the Duke's confidence by all the bye-ways which lead in an opposite direction to the temple of honour.'

'I must again warn you to be cautious,' said Pembroke.

'See, Lord Lescun and the rest of the party are approaching.' Shortly afterwards they were joined by them. Henry of Richmond expressed more delight in seeing his old friend, than he had ever evinced on any former occasion, for his nature was cold.

The young Earl was so much changed that Kynfin scarcely recognized him. He had settled from youth into manhood, and from a ruddy healthy looking boy, had become in appearance a sallow foreigner. For some moments he stood looking upon him with surprise.

'You see in me a greater change than I do in you, Kynfin Tudor,' said the Earl of Richmond, laughing at his earnest scrutiny.

As they were sitting in one of the saloons of the castle a sudden arrival took place at the gates, and young De Montfort's cheerful voice was heard as he was ushered into their presence. He was in his hunting attire, and to all appearance an open-hearted, generous young man, overflowing with animal spirits.

'I have come to insist upon our noble Earl of Pembroke joining us in the chase tomorrow,' said the youth with an animated expression of feature. 'What, are you here?' continued he, bowing coolly to Lord Lescun. Then immediately taking his place by the side of Jasper of Hatfield, the conversation was carried on between themselves.

Kynfin, meanwhile, sat silently watching the expression of the countenances of the strangers around. He saw that Lord Lescun's bow, upon this occasion, was even colder than that of young De Montfort, as they recognized each other. Shortly after, he became aware that he himself had become an object of attention to the wily courtier, whose lowering brow was the harbinger of mischief contemplating in some quarter, of that he felt fully convinced. He was relieved in mind when he arose to take his departure.

As soon as he was gone the conversation became more general, and young De Montfort inquired if they knew the particulars of Louis Agustine's assassination.

'No,' said the Earl of Pembroke, Kynfin looked eagerly towards the speaker.

'*Mon Dieu*! was there ever such a monster to be found in the annals of history as the French monarch,' resumed De Montfort, with a shrug and a gesture of horror. 'That man is a disgrace to his country—to humanity. The foul perpetrator of that assassination was no other than Louis himself. I have been told from good authority, he had, by his spies, discovered that a clandestine correspondence was going on between our Duke and the Duke of Orleans. Hearing that the Duke's ambassador was passing through the neighbourhood where he happened to be at the moment, he and several nobles of his train disguised themselves in the garb of bandits, and falling upon the unfortunate secretary, robbed him of his papers, and plunged a dagger into his heart, slaughtering the rest of the party in pure wantonness. There is a royal example for his subjects! With such a monarch to command, can we wonder at the frequent disturbances and ill feelings extant in unhappy France!'

Kynfin questioned De Montfort regarding the affairs of Louis Agustine, relating the friendless position of his unhappy daughter.

De Montfort was touched by the simple tale, as were the exiled Earls. They felt deeply indebted to the unfortunate Frenchman. He had been to them a sincere follower from the time their kinsman had quitted them at Vannes. They promised to intercede with the Duke on behalf of the orphan Jacqueline.

The Duke being expected the following day, the chase was deferred to the next but one. When De Montfort took his departure, he expressed a wish that the Welsh chieftain's son would accompany his august kinsman. After some hesitation Kynfin consented.

These trifling interruptions of his plans made Kynfin more than usually impatient. When morning came, and he knew the Duke and his suit would be at the château in a few hours, he hailed the visit with very little pleasure.

At the appointed hour, the Duke Francis and his gay retinue appeared before the gate of the château. He was received by the noble Earls with the greatest courtesy. The Duke introduced them to his favourite, the lively and attractive Antoinette de Magnelais, Lady of Villequier, with several other distinguished ladies of the court. Peter Landais and Lord Lescun were in attendance. Before he was well aware of the circumstances, Ap Dafydd found himself standing face to face with the very man who was at the head of the conspiracy against the noble exiles upon their first arrival in the country. The conspiracy was directly in disobedience of the mandate which the Duke had issued, respecting the treatment of the Lancastrian nobles. Landais had seen it signed, sealed, and delivered. Yet had he the boldness to keep up a correspondence, under anonymous names, with Edward of England. He had attempted a deed that had it been discovered, would have raised the executioner's axe over his head. He had escaped, and none besides the conspirators knew his secret, save Kynfin Tudor, who had now suddenly risen like an apparition before him, and threw back the blood from his face.

Landais grasped Lord Lescun's arm with nervous

irritability, and turned away to traverse a walk in a contrary direction to that taken by the rest of the party.

'Lescun,' said he, 'your fears are too true, that is the very man. What has brought him here but to betray me? He knows the exiled nobles are now in favour, that Louis Agustine is dead; and that it is at present his own time. Had we not better arrest, and have him taken off in a quiet way for the murder of those two unfortunate men, who have ever since he quitted the country been missing? We can manage it without a trial, and without his Grace knowing of the matter.'

'*Certes*! if it can be so managed without a trial, and that our own deeds are not to be canvassed. We must remember that young De Montfort favours the English exiles, and will adopt the part of their friend and relative. I know that to be certain.'

'I shall not have peace till I have that man out of the power of doing me a mischief,' replied the minister, with a still more embarrassed look. 'I never closed my eyes last night thinking of the fellow. He must be put out of the way.'

'*Parbleu!* the matter must be well considered,' said Lord Lescun, with a shrug of the shoulder, casting up his eyes.

'We must speak to Albert Agustine, and Jean de Groits, and hear what they say,' resumed the minister, repassing at the same time to join the august party, now but a little in advance of them.

The Earl of Pembroke and Kynfin were in earnest conversation with Lady Antoinette, when Lord Lescun joined them. She did not conceal her annoyance at his intrusion. The names of Louis Agustine and his daughter caught his ear, and he began speculating upon what turn the matter might take. Kynfin, he thought, had probably some design. He was a shrewd man, and was beginning already to work his way. Lord

Lescun therefore turned to study the looks of all three. He thought in the man they dreaded, there was more than an embarrassed expression; there was a look that augured the contemplation of ill.

Kynfin Tudor was thankful when the Duke left the gates of the château. He did not like either the expression of Landais's visage, any more than that of Lord Lescun, or the conduct of either towards himself. With a presentiment of evil, he took the earliest opportunity of relating his history and of introducing the subject of his mission to Jasper of Hatfield.

Pembroke was deeply interested in Ap Dafydd's narration; and did not conceal his impatience to see the daughter of Harlech, his fair kinswoman, whose escape from the fortress, had caused so much disturbance in North Wales, gently chiding Ap Dafydd for not having mentioned the circumstance before.

'I don't think you can put off going to the chase tomorrow,' resumed the Earl thoughtfully. 'I told De Montfort you were a famous marksman, and would teach them all to use the crossbow. He will be grievously disappointed if you are not of the party.'

Kynfin was disappointed. Something seemed to whisper within 'go not to the chase' yet he retired to rest, slept calmly, and the morning with its bright sun shining in gloriously at his casement, tempted him from his slumbers to venture among the huntsmen, scampering through the forest, and over the plain. It was an exciting scene. It reminded him of his early happy days; yet his thoughts were not in France. To please the Earl of Pembroke he did wonderful execution with the crossbow. This called forth universal admiration, and he became a marked individual. Albert Agustine and Jean de

Groits, two of the conspirators, Kynfin soon singled out amongst the hunting party. Once as the latter stood near him, he observed him draw the cap over his face, peering from the corners of his sharp dark eyes at the same time.

As they were returning, Ap Dafydd finding himself alone with the Earl of Pembroke, expressed his fears that Landais had a design against him. The Earl in amazement inquired upon what ground he was apprehensive of such a thing.

'You cannot have forgotten that I was the discoverer of the conspiracy against your lives, I have met with some of the very men who contemplated that deed. The sight of me disturbs their conscience, I am not safe in Brittany. If the Earl of Pembroke will allow me, I will bring the daughter of Harlech here, and present her to you at once. It will cause me deep regret to part so soon from my revered friend, but I must for the sake of my beloved charge, the precious heiress of our line, hasten from a country where I am surrounded by dangers.'

'You may be alarming yourself unnecessarily,' replied Pembroke in a tone of sympathy, 'now we are in high favour with his Grace, and have a staunch friend in De Montfort. You are safe under my roof, my good kinsman, you must not be in a hurry to leave us. Look to the bright side of the horizon.'

'The bright side,' repeated Ap Dafydd gravely, 'Jasper of Hatfield, I have not known a bright side to anything belonging to me for long, long years. I could not feel safe under your roof, I am too well aware of my danger. My soul is heavy, when I think by one imprudent step I may bring fresh trouble upon my niece. Heaven knows she has suffered enough already, do not I pray you urge me to remain.'

Pembroke knew Kynfin Tudor too well to attempt further to divert him from his purpose. Shortly after, his companion turned his horse's head towards the village where the daughter of Harlech and her friends were remaining during Kynfin's absence at the château.

At an early hour the following morning, Kynfin and the young ladies appeared before the gates of the exiled noble's princely residence. It was a sunny, happy-looking day. As they entered the gardens the air was perfumed by flowers and shrubs. The repose that reigned over all, found a sweet welcome in the eyes of the daughter of Harlech. Her first impulse was to turn away from the mansion, and saunter over the broad walks which she did with a pleasure she had not felt for a long time before.

'We seem to have been transported to a land of enchantment,' said she, addressing her companion. Her eyes wandered from the blooming flowers at her feet, to the rich foliage of the forest trees that stood in bold relief against the dark blue sky. 'It is beautiful! I will no longer say, Jacqueline, that your country is not beautiful!' many applauding words escaped her lips as she wandered along, and new beauties at every turn attracted her attention.

But the spell of enchantment was soon broken by the sound of voices. Her uncle immediately introduced her to the noble exiles.

The young Earl of Richmond hastily gathered a few choice flowers, and arranging them into bouquets, presented one to each of the maidens with a courteous smile. The kind and open address of Jasper of Hatfield at once placed them at their ease. The daughter of Harlech was soon in earnest conversation with the old friend of her family. His name had been familiar to her from childhood, and she looked in his face with feelings of reverence.

After rambling about the garden, and conversing upon the state of their unhappy country, they retired to the shade of the pavilion, where they partook of refreshments. Pembroke was delighted with his fair kinswoman, and with the candour and appropriateness of her language. Her beauty and fascinating manners rendered her particularly attractive, and he regretted to her that her stay would be so short.

As the shadows of evening lengthened upon the grassy sward, Ap Dafydd became anxious to bring their visit to a conclusion. He therefore asked the Earl of Pembroke, if he had mentioned to his nephew the subject of which he had talked the day before.

'Yes, Kynfin, my uncle amused me last night by relating some of your adventures,' rejoined the Earl of Richmond, 'I understand you have a prophetic message for me from a singular woman in your remote land. To be honest, I am curious to know what it is?'

'It is from a staunch friend to the house of Lancaster,' said Ap Dafydd, 'we look upon her in our land as a prophetess. She bade me speak to you these words:

"King of England reign will he,
He shall a seventh Henry be;
Full of health, wealth, peace and plenty,
Years above the number twenty."'

'What folly!' ejaculated Richmond with an incredulous smile, 'bah! I never expect to see England's shores again, much less mount her throne!'

'He will laugh, let him, for that day will come. Caesar believed not the soothsayer, yet his words came true. Tell him so. These are tantamount to the words of the Lady of Gêst,' said the son of Harlech, looking earnestly at young Richmond, and then at Gladys.

'And the daughter of Harlech has a petition to present,' said Gladys with a deep blush suffusing her cheeks, suddenly falling upon her knees before the astonished Henry of Richmond.

'Henry, future King of England,' cried she, 'you who are blood of our blood, you who have felt our oppression, you who have witnessed tears shed in secret for our daily wrongs, I implore you to promise that when the day comes, which will come, you, in mercy, will issue a charter to emancipate our people from that painful Saxon yoke, a yoke loathsome to every noble true-born Cambrian heart. Oh, let it be your pleasure to restore our country's freedom, to give back to our bards their privileges, to bring joy to our hearths, and smiles upon our mountain land!'

The young Earl looked down upon his fair supplicant, somewhat embarrassed by her beautiful eyes and gentle tones. He would have raised her from her supplicating position, but Gladys continued:—

'I have yet another request to make, which did I not solicit I should incur the good Lady of Gêst's displeasure. It is on behalf of my family, and myself. Henry, future King of England, when the bright day dawns upon you, restore us to the home of our ancestors—give me back my inheritance?'

Young Richmond looked still more embarrassed, and made no reply.

'Henry,' cried the Earl of Pembroke, 'why do you hesitate? Should the prophetic words of the good Lady of Gêst come true, surely you would be too delighted to emancipate the good people in the land of your birth, and make our fair kinswoman the Lady Keeper of the bold fortress of Harlech, the key of North Wales?'

'Did I place as much faith in this prophecy as you do, my good uncle, I should have been more prompt in my reply;' said the young Earl, 'by affecting to grant this request, I feel I shall be only raising hopes which will never be realized.'

'I plead in the event of the prophecy being fulfilled,' said Gladys, with an air of disappointment and yet a more eager expression.

'It shall then be as you wish, my fair kinswoman,' said the young Earl. Standing and retiring to a writing table, he then drew up a document pledging himself to that effect. The moment he presented it to Gladys he said:—

'Should ever I support England's crown, present this paper to the royal Henry, fair daughter of Harlech, I herein promise you shall be restored to your inheritance, and that you shall be the bearer of a charter to the good people in Wales, which shall break the chain of Saxon bondage and once more restore happiness to the land of our forefathers.'

CHAPTER IV

Female Loneliness—A Tale of Horror

To return for a moment to the native mountains of the fair Gladys. The winter which followed the smugglers' escape from the bay was particularly severe, and most so in the vicinity of Cwm Bychan, where all was cheerless and dreary beyond example. As Jevan's relict sat silent and sad in the chimney corner, withered in frame and broken in spirit, she shrunk from the keen mountain blast that penetrated into every nook and corner of her dwelling. No tidings had reached her from France. For some time she lived in daily expectation of seeing the beloved wanderers return, but they came not, and at last she grew weary of listening and watching. Howel and his wife were growing old with their mistress, the voice of youth was wanting to rouse and comfort their declining spirits, and to bring back cheerfulness to their hearth, that cheerfulness which had so long forsaken it.

In the dim twilight, Katherine sat spinning before the window, while her mistress with folded hands and closed eyes rocked herself to and fro in her armchair.

'What is that?' cried she, suddenly starting at a slight noise outside in the court.

'Only Howel,' replied Katherine, 'bringing in peat from the stack.' The good wife with her ever ready attention, at once hastened to meet the old man in order to relieve him of his burden.

'What now, Howel bach—I see by your face something has gone wrong. What is it?'

'Aye, sure, always something going wrong,' he replied shaking his head mournfully. With a heavy tread, entering the house he took out his handkerchief, wiped his bald head, and gave a deep sigh.

Katherine surveyed him with a look of alarm mingled with surprise, enquiring eagerly if anything had befallen the son of Harlech or their beloved little mistress.

'No, Katherine bach, only the old work over again. These cursed Saxons one way or another are always bringing trouble upon us wherever they root themselves. Yn enw'r Brenhin! there is no end to it. Why cannot they rest contented to remain in their own country, and leave us to our mountain land in peace. Here they come not like the fairies, but black devils as they are, thus planting themselves in our soil, taking our land from us, throwing us into prison and hanging us as if we were dogs of the earth? Who can wonder at the change you see come over our faces. Who can wonder at our heads growing white and our backs becoming bent before the time, when we live out our days in suffering and dread? What is it, I ask, do we simply demand of our Saxon neighbours? Justice and fair dealing, both of which they deny us. What then ought they to expect at our hands? Nine times out of ten you will find that after they have goaded us like oxen and we have become furious, we make the guilty or innocent party suffer for our offences. See you, Katherine, the sin rests on the heads of those Saxon villains. They excite us to do evil, and I will say it, and will say it again, let the foulest, darkest curse be upon their heads!'

Katherine held her breath between amazement and fear. 'What can you mean, Howel?' said she, 'something very

dreadful must have happened to make you speak in this way—
this cruel way.'

'Aye, sure, something dreadful has indeed happened, but it
is a long sad story, Katherine bach. What will my old girl say
when she hears it, the blood will creep from her face and the
cold come upon her heart. Our countrymen have been
murdering two young Saxons on the opposite shore, and we
are all in terrible alarm lest government should take up the
matter, and in return visit upon us greater misery than before.'

'O'r Tad Anwyl! I am sorry in my heart to hear such
dreadful news. Our people been murdering the Saxons,'
ejaculated Katherine, turning deadly pale and shaking
violently. 'Pobl Anwyl! as if we had not trouble and sorrow
enough already in the land, this is indeed ugly news. Let us
go, Howel, to our mistress, you must tell us all about it.'

Howel followed his wife as he was bid into the inner room.

A brief explanation was necessary before relating the
particulars of the sanguinary catastrophe, which had happened
only a few days before in the immediate neighbourhood of
Cricceath.

To give a translation of Howel's version of the tragedy,
would convey but an imperfect knowledge of the
circumstances. It is better to leave him to continue his
narrative, accompanied by those gesticulations and varied
tones of voice peculiar to himself, and to take the statement
fresh from the lips of Stephen Conyers, who at the same
moment as Howel had crossed the bay and was now entering
the gates of Harlech. Having traversed a gallery and two or
three half furnished rooms, Conyers had just been shown into
a small apartment well lighted by a blazing hearth, on one side
of which sat Edward Stacey, and his sister on the other.

'Stephen Conyers! What! out in such weather as this!' ejaculated the young Warden as he advanced to greet the visitor, 'you must be the bearer of some startling intelligence methinks, or surely you would never have ventured across the bay on such a night.'

'You conjecture right, my friend, but, as of old, I am the messenger of evil. The news I have to communicate is startling enough as you will find, if you have not already been made acquainted with it.'

'To what do you allude?' exclaimed Edward Stacey and his sister in the same breath. 'I leave the castle walls so seldom now,' continued the Warden. 'How should I hear?'

'Tell us, Stephen, what is the calamity?' added Mistress Maud, at intervals clasping her hands together, and waiting with nervous trepidation for a reply.

'I think, Mistress Maud, you must have heard me or my brother speak of Mary Dunston,' said Stephen Conyers, drawing his chair nearer the fire, and patting the dogs to keep them quiet. 'She has been one of the most prominent actors in a tragedy, for the worst termination of which you must be prepared,' then addressing himself to Edward Stacey more directly, he commenced:—

'You must know something of our compatriot, Dunston, who for so many years has been a resident in the country. He holds an office under government. No doubt you have met him frequently at the county meetings.'

'Ah! Yes; I know whom you mean, what of him? He is always getting into rows with those confounded brutes of Welshmen, there is nothing new in that.'

'It is more than a row this time, my friend, I am puzzled where to commence,' replied Stephen with a slight hesitation in his speech, 'not knowing how much and how little you are acquainted with the folks on our side. Do you recollect anything relative to John ap Owen some months back? I mean that fine good looking fellow one occasionally met rambling over the country, whose father owns the property which joins Plas Hên, where Dunston resides.'

'Yes, I remember hearing something about him; was he not sent a prisoner to Carnarvon Castle for some offence against an Englishman? I was away at the time, but still I can recall the circumstance, though none of the separate facts. To tell the truth, I care so little about these Welsh rascals, and find so little interest in the country that I never take the trouble to acquaint myself with anything that is going on. I abominate the whole race, were I King of England I would extirpate every living man of them from the soil. By foul or fair means I would contrive to do it.'

'Hold, Stacey, my good fellow, whenever you get upon this subject you are too severe. Preserve your censure for the present. What I am about to communicate, will convince you that however much the Welsh may be in error, we English are by no means immaculate. I can foresee the Saxons will have to quit the country altogether, if they do not act with more complacency towards their neighbours. We are cutting our own throats, as the vulgar phrase goes, and all because we have the evil spirit of persecution ingrained in our veins. We would fain make the nobles of the land here, our slaves. We trample upon them whenever we find the opportunity. This cannot last: the wronged seek to be avengers.'

'Enough, enough! The old story over again. I shall quarrel with you, Stephen, as I did with your brother, if you persist in shielding these treacherous savages,' interrupted Edward Stacey with great petulance of manner.

'No, Stacey, we will not quarrel. It is not worth making a breach between us,' replied his companion with a placid look of good temper; he was too good tempered, Stacey at least thought as much, and was only the more provoked.

Mistress Maud who was secretly longing to know what had occurred in relation to Mary Dunston, began to feel apprehensive lest Stephen after what had been said, should not again broach the subject.

'Edward,' said she, 'I think it is a pity you do not disguise your antipathy to the Welsh. If you consider for a moment, it is unreasonable in us to expect others who have not the same feeling we have to be of the same opinion. Pray reserve your vindictive epithets for my ears only, we never disagree upon that subject. Do not argue any more, Edward, I want to hear the particulars. Come, Stephen, you have kept us long enough in the dark—do proceed.'

'I was speaking of John ap Owen. To go on with the story, I must first tell you that the young man, more than a year ago, fell in love with Mary Dunston. She accepted his addresses, and they were engaged to be married. To make all clear, you will understand that Dunston is an overbearing man. He had been encroaching upon his neighbour's land ever since his arrival. Owen it seems would have remonstrated with him, but the family being on good terms, and expecting the alliance to take place between his son and Mary Dunston, he never complained of the injustice of his Saxon neighbour. From month to month this went on. It happened that for some reason the wedding was put off, much to Mistress Mary's regret. A short time after, a young Englishman, named Hilbardi, a connection of the family, came on a visit to Dunston. After he had been staying there some time, he succeeded in stealing Mary's affection from Ap Owen, and did not rest until he had prevailed upon her to break off her engagement with John. He, poor fellow, you may suppose was much cut up at Mistress Mary's inconstancy, and fearfully jealous of the man who had surreptitiously robbed him of her affections. He therefore took the first opportunity of encountering Hilbardi, and of remonstrating with him upon his unhandsome conduct, and high words arose between them.

'Hilbardi used the most insulting language towards Ap Owen. He called him an ill-tempered cub and other abusive names, threatening to kick him as he would kick a dog, for his impertinence in seeking an interview with Mistress Mary after she had pledged him her troth. He taunted Ap Owen till the Welshman's indignation and rage knew no bounds. "Kick me as you would a dog!" cried he, "hold, you Saxon coxcomb, I will soon see if the cub as you call me, can't trample you under his feet, and make you curl like a skulking snake, or a writhing worm." Ap Owen then flung himself upon his rival, and inflicted such desperate wounds upon him that Hilbardi was some weeks before he recovered. Dunston took up his kinsman's cause with great violence. In a few days Ap Owen was arrested and sent in irons to Carnarvon Castle, to await his trial. The disgrace of John's imprisonment was felt by every member of his family, too keenly to be passed over. His mother took it so much to heart that she was seized with a fever of which she died. Owen, at the change which had been thus wrought in his household, became broken hearted, and felt deep hatred towards Dunston. The land which had so unjustly been taken from him he now demanded back; but Dunston treated his demand with contempt, and refused to give it up. By every means Owen tried to obtain his right, but his efforts proved of no avail. With a man like Dunston, who has so much weight in the country, there could be no successful resistance. Dunston set watches on his land boundary, and Owen's men were frequently assaulted. From day to day a petty warfare was carried on between the parties. Owen became so changed in person that his friends could scarcely recognize him. If he could only have had justice for his son, he would have been reconciled to all his other calamities; but of that there was no hope, for Dunston had declared Owen should remain in chains to the end of his days, on no other food but prison fare, and he had interest enough with the venal Saxon magistrates to carry out his threats. Thus matters stood for little more than a week after the marriage of Hilbardi and Mistress Mary had been announced as to take place, and their friends were invited to Plas Hên, where festivities had been going on for several days previous to the nuptial feast.

'Owen all this time had shut himself up in his house, and was never seen out by daylight, occasionally he had been observed prowling about Dunston's premises at midnight. His eyes were bloodshot for want of sleep, he was observed to be so restless that he could remain only a few minutes in a place; he muttered indistinctly to himself, his cheeks became blanched, and his friends distressed at his appearance, grew alarmed lest he should lose his reason. I observed the poor fellow looking the wreck of what he once had been, having become a miserable object. On Wednesday, early on the wedding day, the company were collected in the hall, waiting with impatience for the bride and bridegroom. Time passed rapidly, but neither bride nor bridegroom appeared. The party assembled looked at each other in amazement, and at last some of their friends went to seek them and find out the cause. The bride's chamber had not been visited by the inmates of the house before they proceeded thither. They knocked, all was still, and they obtained no reply. The door was forced, and to their horror they found the bride weltering in her blood. Her body was cold, which showed she had been murdered some hours before during the night. Those present were paralysed with fear, and incapable of proceeding farther—where was the bridegroom? They hastened to his newly furnished dwelling, and arrived just in time to meet a terrified domestic who had just before discovered Hilbardi's room had been entered by the window, and his throat cut most probably in his sleep. What consternation followed you may imagine, the house of rejoicing was turned into a house of mourning. Dunston appeared, of all the party, the most collected. With a terrific oath he vowed vengeance on Owen to whom he rightly attributed the horrible atrocity. The bridegroom's friends as well as those of the lifeless bride set themselves immediately to discover where the murderer, whom they did not doubt to be Owen, had secreted himself. They found the doors and windows of his house all thrown open, but he was nowhere to be seen, and this confirmed their suspicions. The common report was that he had taken to the wild fastnesses and rocks among the highest mountains in a state of madness.'

'What a category of horrors!' exclaimed Edward Stacey, looking at Stephen with an expression well suited to his words. 'I am convinced you have been partial in your narration, these accursed Welsh are more to blame then you would wish us to believe.'

Stephen shook his head. 'No, Edward, I have endeavoured to give you the particulars as faithfully as possible. Do not let us get into further argument. You are as free to hold your opinions as I to hold mine. See, your sister looks as pale as, a ghost. Do you feel ill, Mistress Maud?'

'Ill! to listen to all the horrors you have related is enough to take the blood out of my cheeks, and make me feel ill indeed. How can you be so calm, Stephen? To take the life of two innocent young persons is very shocking to our common humanity. I trust they will make the assassin pay the penalty of his offence.'

'He has paid it, and more than paid it already,' replied Stephen.

'Do not say another word upon the subject, or I shall feel as provoked with you as with my brother,' responded Maud hastily, 'from this time, Edward, I hope you will not leave the castle gates without your strong bowmen in attendance. How often I have said we were surrounded by perils—perils that we know not of. We must keep this truly horrible affair from my poor mother, it would only increase her nervous feelings, and make her still more unhappy.'

'How does Mistress Conyers support these trying times?' enquired Edward Stacey after a long pause, 'at present you appear in a worse neighbourhood than we are.'

'My mother is a stout-hearted woman, who troubles herself little about reports or anyone's affairs save her own. To look to those immediately around her, she considers is her duty and she never neglects that duty. Of course, she was shocked as we all are to hear of the murder, but I do not think it has caused her any alarm for her personal security.'

'Well it is,' said Edward, 'she can be so reconciled to living in this cursed country.'

'For my part, I envy her composure,' observed Mistress

Maud. 'Have you heard, Stephen, of your brother lately?'

'What Ethelred, no; but I expect by this time he has left England.'

'What an infatuation was his love for Gladys, I verily believe were the girl to place to his lips a cup of poison, aye, were he sinking under its effects, he would still maintain she was innocent.'

'He is much changed since he became acquainted with her. Well, we must acknowledge that in point of beauty she far exceeds anyone we ever beheld here; you say she was artful and haughty, I fear those were her failings. Do you suppose she will ever venture again into the country?'

'The son of Harlech would venture anything, and his accomplice would venture anything. Under the guidance and control of two such notorious characters, surely we may ask what is there we may not expect from Gladys?'

'How severe you are, Mistress Maud. Had Ethelred heard you make that speech, he would never have forgiven you. But women I have always thought more tenacious, more bitter, more unforgiving towards their sex than we men are towards ours.'

Mistress Maud drew herself up with affected dignity.

'You need not have made so rude a speech, Stephen, but it is like you, from a boy you were always free enough in giving an opinion.'

The announcement of the evening's repast put an end to further litigation.

CHAPTER IV

Homeward-bound—A Disguise—
The Pursuit and Deliverance

WITH feelings of mingled grief, joy and apprehension the son of Harlech, in company with his niece, took his departure from the city of Rennes. For the first few hours Gladys could not restrain her tears, parting with Jacqueline and leaving her in deep sorrow was a severe trial. She felt occasional consolation whenever the thought flashed across her mind that every mile she travelled by land, and every league by sea, brought her nearer to her beloved grandmother. The freedom of her wild native home, it seemed to her spirit joyous to anticipate.

The delicious mountain air and the perfume of the wild heather were more attractive to her than the rich garlands of France, and the odours of its delightful gardens. In her enthusiasm, she spoke of the far off future, the happy daydream when the Red Rose banner was to float once more over the battlements of Harlech. Then would she welcome little Jacqueline again, her warm-hearted, lively friend, to the home of her ancestors. They should once more stand side by side, watching the billows rise and fall over the azure waters of Cardigan Bay.

These illusions of hope were cheering, for they were but illusions. Yet Kynfin warmly sympathized with his niece, praying earnestly to himself that nothing might again overshadow the bright perspective. For he who had his presentiments of evil from his experience of the fallacies of hope, now anticipated cheeringly the future. A mere chimera of the brain might picture a reverse, but before a few days were over, they would be safe out of France. Encouraging this hope, he avoided communicating his apprehensions to his niece; why should he do so, when things seemed wholly in their favour? The travellers were on their way to St Malo, and from that place they proposed setting sail for England. Upon their second day's journey they stopped at a village for the night, taking up their rest at a small auberge. During the evening as they were sitting by the hearth, several men entered, rudely demanding a night's lodging.

The rough voice and malign looks of the strangers made Gladys shrink close to the side of her uncle, when casting her eyes upon his face she was startled by the paleness of his look. Upon the entrance of the strangers, her uncle had looked up, and his eyes were met by the thin figure of Jean de Groits. He became spellbound; a rapid dialogue passed between their hostess and the men. Jean de Groits kept his eyes fixed upon Gladys. At length, upon the innkeeper assuring them she could give them no accommodation, they hurried away. As the door closed after them, they left the apartment much more silent than it had been before they arrived, and yet without apparent cause.

'Why do you look so pale, dear uncle?' said Gladys in an anxious tone of voice. 'Do you know any of those ill-looking men?' Kynfin's eyes were riveted upon the door, he did not seem to be aware that his niece was addressing him.

'Tell me, uncle, answer me,' she persisted pressing his hand and looking more eagerly in his face, 'your manner alarms me!'

'We must start early, very, very early in the morning,' replied her uncle abstractedly. 'Why am I continually visited with misfortune? My Gladys, my child! Heaven grant that whatever evil befalls us, we may not be separated, with thee I could bear anything, but to be separated would be painful, horrible!' He clasped his arms round his ward and looked at her with intense anxiety written on his features.

'What is it you apprehend?' said Gladys anxiously enquiring.

'Those men, I am convinced, have no good intention towards us. By daybreak we must start, and endeavour to divert them into a false track. Go to rest, my child. I will call thee in good time.'

It was with reluctance Gladys obeyed. The moment Ap Dafydd found himself alone, for the other guests had retired before, he set at work to outplot his pursuers. He and his niece must take a circuitous route to be safe, and if a village dress for each could be obtained, the disguise might aid to prevent detection. He cast his eyes round the apartment and saw standing in a corner an oaken chest, which had every appearance of containing linen, perhaps the family wardrobe. He lifted the lid, and within was a variety of rustic clothing. He hastily selected the outer garments he desired, placing a purse with money in lieu of the goods he extracted, and closed the chest. He then occupied himself in making preparations for a quick departure.

The dogs were barking, and not a soul was moving in the village. The aurora was still faint when Kynfin Tudor and the daughter of Harlech stole out of the auberge and mounted their mules without noise. Before the sun had appeared bodily on the horizon they were several miles from the spot, having, for the sake of security, struck off into a bye-road.

They breathed more freely as they lengthened their distance from their late resting place. The freshness of the morning air seemed to cheer Gladys. She was scarcely able to suppress a smile, when the daylight discovered to her the new character and costume they had assumed.

'Uncle, methinks we are so completely disguised our friends would hardly recognize us, much less our enemies, if Jasper of Hatfield could only see us, he would smile indeed; but if he knew of the danger that necessitated our disguise how deeply would he grieve!'

'If any unforeseen event separates us, remember, my child, fly to him,' said Kynfin Tudor with his old harassed expression of feature. 'Let us not be too sanguine, should our pursuers come upon our track, they may question us: answer only in monosyllables. Recollect to be upon your guard; lose not your self-possession. Everything will depend upon its preservation.'

They continued some way further without the smallest interruption. At length they reached the outskirts of a forest, and their route laying directly through it, they proceeded until they came to a spot where several roads met. There they were compelled to wait till some peasant or traveller appeared to give them the information of which they stood in need. While thus waiting, a party of horsemen riding by, eyed them for a moment and passed on.

'Thank God! the Virgin's name be praised!' ejaculated Ap Dafydd. 'They have not recognized us.' Gladys looked at her uncle with a smile of pleasure. They discovered the right road, and hastened forward with more cheerfulness than they had exhibited for some time before. How soon were they to be undeceived in their hope of security! Scarcely had they ridden above a league, when the tramp of horsemen in the distance fell upon their ears. Gladys with a foreboding of evil, felt her heart sink within her.

'Oh, uncle!' cried she, in a low tone, 'my heart misgives me, it must be our enemies who are coming.' Too quickly they rode up abreast. In a commanding tone they asked if some English travellers had been seen upon the road, Jean de Groits turning to scrutinise Gladys from head to foot. In an instant he saw that the colour faded upon her cheek. Peering closer into her face he began questioning her roughly, and throwing his head back laughed aloud.

'Ah! ha! *ma chère amie, la belle Anglaise* who knelt at the shrine in the cathedral at Rennes could not disguise herself, even in a village dress, from the eyes of Jean de Groits. How could he forget her lovely eyes, and sweet voice in a day's time, no, not even in a lifetime?' Again Jean de Groits laughed, and giving a sign to his men they fell upon Ap Dafydd, seizing his arms before he had time to draw his sword. Had he made resistance, it would have been in vain, for they were eight or ten to one. They took him prisoner in the name of the Duke. It was the work of a moment. Gladys, speechless with horror, stretched out her arms towards her uncle, whom they immediately dragged away, and he was already disappearing in the distance. Jean de Groits was standing by her side staring rudely in her face, and giving his orders to two men in whose care he left her.

'Do you hear, take *la belle Anglaise* to Simon Bonne, the forester. Tell him and his wife to take every care of her, till I come. Get her off the highway as soon as possible. Do you hear? Disobey orders at your peril.' When Jean de Groits turned to remount his horse, Gladys shrieked aloud and implored him to let her go with her uncle and share his prison. Groits only laughed louder, made yet more extravagant encomiums upon her beauty, and immediately galloped off after Kynfin.

Bereaved of hope and painfully alive to her position, she could sustain herself no longer. She shrieked and fell forward from her mule insensible.

How long she remained in that unconscious state she was not aware. On recovering and opening her eyes, she found herself sitting by the roadside, partly supported by her rough companions, whose long beards and ill looks almost made her relapse into the same insensible state as before.

'*Allons, allons, ma belle Anglaise,*' was shouted in her ears, 'if we don't go directly it will grow dark. We shall lose ourselves in the forest.' Gladys was upon her knees in a moment.

'Have pity on me! Oh have pity on me!' cried she. 'Do not take me to the forester's. If you are fathers, for the love you bear your children have pity on me. In mercy, have pity on me, and let me go to my uncle.'

Her entreaties were of no avail, the men only shook their heads with a dogged expression of face, and began to tighten the girths of their horses for immediate departure.

With a sickened heart, the daughter of Harlech turned away from her companions. She knelt under the shadow of the large forest trees, forlorn and in danger, and her soul found utterance in prayer. She had still her God to go to. He would not forsake her, and in him she would put her trust. The sacred words were quickly repeated in her vernacular tongue. Those who were in charge of her, ruffians as they were, stood aloof for a moment, hesitating to disturb her. Meanwhile, a sudden confusion of sounds fell from a distance upon their ears. Her companions ran across the road shouting at the top of their voices:—

'*Hommes de guerre! Anglais, Anglais, hommes de guerre!*' drawing their animals on one side, and standing ready to let them pass.

With a bewildered expression Gladys listened to the tramp of the soldiers. She instinctively shrank from their rude gaze, vulgar exclamations and surprise at finding such a pretty lass in the forest. She looked in vain for some kind face, feeling the necessity of throwing herself upon their mercy. Greatly embarrassed, she at length saw that there was a party of horsemen in the rear, and resolved to await their arrival ere she made known her captive condition. On them her fate depended, and with a beating heart she awaited their nearer approach. What language could express her astonishment when directing her eager gaze towards the horsemen, it rested upon the features of the young Saxon, Ethelred Conyers. So sudden, and so unexpected was the discovery that it paralyzed her for a moment. She could neither move nor cry out. Ethelred, engaged in conversation, had passed on without observing that a maiden was by the roadside. She was aware that he had not seen her—too keenly aware that he was leaving her to her fate unwittingly. Her uncle would be murdered, there would be no one to tell Jasper of Hatfield of his danger, and her misery would be complete. Her feeling was like a frightful nightmare, from which she could not escape, while conscious of her situation. In vain she tried to articulate—in vain she attempted to move, she could only fix her sight upon Ethelred's retreating form, and wring her hands.

'*Allons, allons, ma belle Anglaise,*' sounded once more upon her ears. One of the men caught hold of her to lift her upon the mule. This incident had the magical effect of restoring her presence of mind. In one frantic bound, she freed herself from his grasp. Darting up the road with the fleetness of a deer, she shrieked aloud: 'Ethelred! Ethelred!' His name echoed through the still forest. Exhausted by the effort, she sank upon her knees, covering her face with her hands.

She had torn off her village maiden's cap. Her long black tresses once more flowed over her shoulders in their natural luxuriance. Her wild cry of distress, had, in the interim, caught Ethelred Conyers's ear. He recognized her voice, and turning his charger round, galloped up to the spot from whence the sound proceeded, attended by several of his troopers.

'Gladys, the captive maiden! my own Gladys!' cried the young Saxon, springing from his horse to her side. The next moment she was locked in his arms. In a few hurried sentences she told her melancholy tale, and with frantic eagerness repeated her apprehensions for her uncle's safety, and her anxiety to be taken to the Earl of Pembroke, who would befriend them. Ethelred promised to do all in his power to help her; begged her to be comforted, and sympathized in her distress in the tenderest and most delicate manner.

The ruffians with whom she had been left in charge, demanded the maiden with angry gestures. Taking no notice of their demand, Ethelred only thought of the urgency of going forward, and ordering his bugle-men to sound the call, quickly brought all his troop to his side, in a moment, the captors of Gladys were arrested. Gladys was then placed upon her palfrey, and the whole escort moved back on their way to the capital.

By what Gladys heard Jean de Groits say, she knew they were taking her uncle back to Rennes. It was indeed a comfort to feel that she was following in his footsteps, with a friend and protector by her side who would take her to the exiled nobles. He promised to prevail upon his general, who was acquainted with the Duke of Brittany to intercede for her uncle's life. The daughter of Harlech was bewildered, she looked again and again upon the young Saxon's face, and listened to his deep tones with feelings which it would be impossible to describe. The terror and excitement which she had undergone the last few hours, began to tell upon her constitution. She was seized with a violent attack of fever. Repeatedly clasping her hands to her head, she complained of pain, to the great alarm of her companion. On reaching Fougères, where the troops quartered for the night, Ethelred prevailed upon Gladys to remain, and to lessen her anxiety assured her he would send off messengers that night to acquaint the exiled Earls of Kynfin Tudor's danger. With increased anxiety, the young Saxon lifted the daughter of Harlech from the palfrey, and carried her to her chamber. The moment he had given her in charge of the hostess, he proceeded in search of the most skilful surgeon he could discover in the town.

Upon his return, he found the object of his solicitude was worse. The whole of the night she was delirious. The young Saxon was the only friend near, and he would not quit her side. Every hour he was bathing her temples, administering draughts, and listening to her incoherences, which revealed to him the painful state of her mind for some time before. She called upon her uncle, demanded if they had murdered him— then upon the Earl of Pembroke to save him. In the tenderest accents; she repeated his own name, imploring him not to leave her in the forest. With frantic gestures and changed expression, she would then call upon the rover, and in horror exclaim:—

'I saw the rover die! I saw the rover die! I saw him in his winding sheet and it was I, I!—who did it—I! I.'

She remained in this distressing state for several days. The young Saxon was unremitting in his attentions. He had a full sense of the danger in which she lay. The thought of losing her had rendered her doubly dear to him. He felt intense anxiety, and aware of his responsibility, sent for Jacqueline.

The fever at length abated. It was after a very calm sleep of some length that Gladys opened her eyes and became for the first time aware that the young Saxon was by her bedside. She seemed at first trying to collect her scattered thoughts. Then she closed her eyes, and a blush suffused her cheek. She had heard Ethelred's deep toned voice repeating solemnly, 'Thank God, thank God, Gladys, you are better!' That voice thrilled through her frame, she could not speak, but she felt that it was a moment of happiness.

CHAPTER VI

Statesmen Perplexed—The Prisoner Relieved—A Confession

'*PAQUES Dieu!* who would envy our position?' said Lord Lescun, walking slowly up and down the apartment with a measured step, and stroking his chin thoughtfully.

'All would have gone right if Jean de Groits had not been so intolerable a fool,' replied the Prime Minister with an angry frown. 'He disobeyed my orders by bringing the caitiff here, instead of taking him to Vitre. The knave has the impudence to say I never gave him such orders.'

'Was it correctly reported to me that Monsieur Agustine's daughter had been to *la belle* Antoinette, about this Kynfin Tudor?' inquired Lord Lescun with some anxiety.

'*Certes*! that is the provoking thing!' replied Landais. 'The little wench will perhaps reveal all that we are anxious to keep in obscurity. There is a report, too, that the men were not murdered by the pirates.'

'*Diable*! Landais, I think you had better get quit of this affair as soon as you can.'

'If I could,' said Landais shrugging his shoulders and turning red and livid alternately.

'Set your head to work and hush it up,' replied Lord Lescun. 'I am in no way inclined to be soused out of office, and have the headsman's axe suspended over me.'

'*Parbleu*! nor I neither,' muttered Landais looking more like a thief than a Prime Minister, '*certes*! I wish I could get the fellow taken off by poison. I am a born idiot not to have had him settled in the forest. That failure was as much yours as mine.'

'You will be your own executioner some of these days if you escape from this dilemma,' observed his companion sarcastically, 'this fellow is a near relative of the English nobles. Now they are in favour with the Duke, supposing you had murdered him or poisoned him, you would have seen, Landais, what you would have got by it. You would have taken a step overboard—you would have gone headlong down a precipice. Young de Montfort has been with his Grace today. He carried a message from the exiled nobles.'

'The Earl of Pembroke is expected tomorrow, that's more,' said the Minister, 'General Stanley who is now quartered in the town with the English troops, has been this afternoon to pay his respects to his Grace. I was present and heard him speaking of the prisoner, but chiefly about the maiden, they have all taken her part violently.'

'It was they who rescued her in the forest,' said Lord Lescun. 'That part of the affair was ill-managed.'

'I know it was,' said the Minister laying his hand flat upon the table, 'that was Jean de Groit's fault, not mine. My orders were to take her at once to St Malo and ship her off to England.'

'Aha,' said Lord Lescun, reproachfully, 'you ought to have known your man better. I gave you credit, Landais, for being more wary. The poor girl is dying of a fever brought on from terror. Claudine de Montfort has taken Mademoiselle Agustine down to Fougères today. Considering all things it will go very awkwardly with our little scheme. If Kynfin Tudor did not betray us before, he will do so now. We have provoked him, and we must be prepared for the result. We must swear boldly that it is false from beginning to end, and keep the Duke in the dark. We have done it a thousand times. If we can get his Grace to ourselves, without De Montfort, I have no fear. For my part, I would rather have that young Hotspur put out of the way than any man in the dukedom. But for him the exiled nobles would not have been in favour. *Certes*! I feel a presentiment that fellow, that spy upon us, has taken up the prisoner's cause already.'

'Mention him not—I hate the name of the prisoner,' said Landais, his cowardly heart sinking within him, and seeing, in imagination, Kynfin Tudor's stern eye fixed upon him. 'You know, Lescun, I had a horrible dream last night; I thought the Welshman destroyed me by pinching my flesh off my bones. Suppose we uphold our false statement, and he brings up witnesses against us. What then?'

'It is too long ago—too long ago! I don't feel the apprehension you do,' said Lord Lescun. '*Pâques Dieu*! Landais, you must not grow chicken-hearted. You drew me into the affair, and you must clear me. I wish you had left the fellow alone. Did you hear that the prisoner had been ill? They thought he would have died last night.'

'No; but I wish he would die,' ejaculated the Minister, clasping his hands together in perplexity. 'I wish he would die, I should feel in Paradise. Who told you that he had been ill?'

'It is an *on dit* all over the palace,' said Lescun, 'everybody talks of the prisoner, and the unfortunate girl who was nearly frightened to death in the forest. Everyone whispers, too, that it was Landais did it.'

'*Sacré*!' ejaculated the Minister with a nervous twitching in his face, and both hands grasping his hair.

'Landais, sleep not tonight. Remember you have to make a plausible defence. Draw it up with care before the morning,' said Lord Lescun. Then, he added, with a sarcastic smile, 'I think I need not remind you of that.' The wily colleagues separated.

From the time Kynfin Tudor had been torn away from his beloved charge, no food had passed his lips. He sat alone in the gloomy prison, where he had been placed, grief-stricken and stupefied. He spoke not a word, he made no sign; he passed the night and day in the same silent absent attitude. To himself what had occurred seemed a dreary blank, a bewildering and hideous dream. Years afterwards he recurred to that event with a shudder. Landais had issued orders that no one should be admitted to the prisoner. Ethelred had been sent by Gladys with cheering messages to her uncle. He was resolved not to return without first having executed her wishes. He addressed himself to Claudine de Montfort, who took a deep interest in the history of Gladys, and through her influence succeeded in obtaining the Duke's permission.

Kynfin Tudor started on hearing himself addressed by his own name. When Ethelred told him that Gladys, the daughter of Harlech, had sent him, he cried:

'Oh, bring her to me! my Gladys, my child!'

It was all he could say. In a moment his limbs tottered under him, and before his visitor was aware, exhausted with want of food and sorrow, he fell upon the floor. It was some time before he could be brought to himself. This alarmed the young Saxon who would not leave him till he was restored. In some degree he succeeded in comforting him, by relating every particular with regard to his niece, which had occurred since she parted from him. He assured Kynfin he had many friends, and that he would, in all probability, be released in a few days.

This was unexpected to Ap Dafydd; who, with an eager ear, listened to every word. Still no expression of joy, nor thankfulness escaped his lips. He remained like a statue, except that tears rolled down his cheeks, the personification of the deepest misery.

The young Saxon was moved. Gladys had told him so much about her uncle that interested him. He now rested his eyes upon Kynfin's features, with feelings of much emotion. After many persuasions he prevailed upon him to take nourishment. It was for Gladys's sake he did so, and for Gladys's sake he wrung the young Saxon's hand, and blessed him for having saved his niece from the base and licentious De Groits, a man thoroughly despised in the town of Vannes, and wherever else he was known.

When Ethelred rose to take his departure, the prisoner was calmer. He sent affectionate messages by him to his niece.

As the Saxon rode out of Rennes on his return to Fougères, the Earl of Pembroke and his nephew, accompanied by young De Montfort, arrived at the palace. They were received cordially by the Duke. The prisoner's case was discussed; Landais and Lescun were ordered to be in attendance. Claudine de Montfort and *la belle* Antoinette were already present. They were speaking to young De Montfort and the Earl of Richmond, about the daughter of Harlech, and *la petite* Jacqueline, when the arch-minister and his companion in intrigue entered the state room.

'How oddly the Minister looks. He is either white with passion or fear,' said De Montfort in a whisper. 'I wish my

uncle's eyes were opened in regard to these two officials—
shall I not say knaves! It is astonishing what an influence they
have over him. What a plausible tale that fellow Landais is
already framing, and Lescun at his elbow to sustain him.'

'Well, brother,' said Claudine, laughing, 'it is of little
importance to us what they have to say for themselves,
provided the prisoner is released. During this discussion, I
think we may as well go into the garden. I dislike those men
so much; their very voices are unpleasant.'

La belle Antoinette assured her that no one could have a
greater aversion to them than herself. Accordingly they
sauntered over the broad walks, and sat among the delicious
shade, listening to the refreshing play of the fountains,
forgetting, though but for a time, the wily minister, his
colleague, and the prisoner.

Henry of Richmond was becoming daily more attached to
the gentle and amiable Claudine. The Duke was so anxious
for the alliance that at this period he would have done
anything to oblige the English nobles. He did not, therefore,
disguise his annoyance that any one belonging to them should
have sustained injury within his Dukedom. In the presence of
Pembroke, he did not spare either the Minister or Lord
Lescun. He concluded by giving peremptory orders that
Kynfin should be released forthwith, and that when it was the
prisoner's pleasure to leave the country, he should have an
escort to any of the sea ports from where he wished to embark
for England.

The joyful intelligence was conveyed by Pembroke to the
party in the garden. Claudine de Montfort was full of
expressions of delight. She could only think how many would
be made happy by this concession of the Duke. Jacqueline had

told her, in confidence, the private history of the prisoner and his niece. She had avowed her sympathy with Gladys. The sweet saddened eyes of the daughter of Harlech were before her, and she longed to be the bearer of the happy result of the application to the Duke. She immediately expressed a wish to young Richmond, to visit the invalid before she quitted Brittany.

Pembroke went in person to receive Kynfin upon his pardon being declared.

He was shocked at the change that so short an imprisonment had wrought in his appearance. He was not yet convalescent. He was, for some days, too ill to be removed from Rennes. Good Jasper of Hatfield never left his couch. Meanwhile Gladys daily gained strength. Ethelred and Jacqueline were her companions. Thus strangely had circumstances once more brought them together. The time passed under the grey old battlements of Harlech, and the events which occurred there often became the subject of conversation. Explanations were given respecting the sudden departure of the two friends with the smugglers. Jacqueline related to Ethelred the rover's death, and the circumstances which were its attendants. Thus terminated any surmises in the mind of Ethelred, which might have arisen from her exclamations in her delirium, when the fever attacked her. He felt that the trials which she had undergone endeared her to him the more. Such a position was a dangerous one for Gladys, and might possibly sow the seeds of future sorrow; yet how could she escape from it. She was conscious her affections were becoming fixed. She could not drive the young Saxon from her heart, as she had done when at Harlech from her presence. He had rescued her uncle, and saved herself from a cruel fate. He had even nursed her in an illness when she had no other friend near. She glanced at his countenance when unobserved. She listened to his voice, and afterwards asked her trembling heart if she ought not to be grateful? Her heart seemed to reply in terms that raised a species of rebellion in her mind, since it had made her question whether her people would not despise her, if she united herself to one Saxon born, however deeply indebted to him. Then she reflected in a way more agreeable and flattering to her prepossessions that consisted in a union with him—if she could explain all the circumstances which rendered that the truth, they would not permit her to sacrifice herself to gratify their traditional predilections. Then would her grandfather's noble and patriotic spirit flash across her mind, and make her blush at her selfish thoughts. Ought she to consider anything a sacrifice too great when so many were concerned? Then her heart prompted the desire and wish—'Ethelred, Ethelred, would that you were not a Saxon!'

With these conflicting feelings she sat looking out of the window down a long avenue of poplars, listening to the rustling of the leaves. Suddenly flowers were placed in her hand, and the youth who occupied her thoughts was standing close to her with a melancholy expression of countenance.

'Gladys,' said he, 'our troops must leave Rennes in a day or two. I must soon leave you. Our last leave taking was at Harlech. I need not say how much we have both suffered since that time. Let me not leave you with those cruel words unrecalled. Say that you do not despise me still, because I am a Saxon?'

'Ethelred, how is it possible I could despise you?' said Gladys, turning very pale, and looking him full in the face, from a sudden anxious fear which seized her at the thought of parting with him.

'Say, Gladys, that our hearts are united, you know and feel that we cannot live and be happy separated from each other. When ill, and I thought you would be taken from me, you cannot have suffered as I suffered, my mental agony was more than I could have borne, had it not been supported by the hope of being the instrument of your restoration. Only tell me, Gladys, that our hearts are united, the declaration will, I know, make us both happy. It rests with you to make us both so.'

'Ethelred, in mercy, spare me! Say not that it rests with me alone,' she replied, greatly agitated. 'My heart is wholly yours. That fact I will not conceal. It will beat for none other, till the grave closes over me. Here I must stop. I am going back to my people. Are you not aware that we can never be united, because I cannot remove the cruel barrier? Would to heaven it were in my power! Ethelred, do not blame, pity me. To part with you now is sorrow, bitterness! But we must part. Never again shall I hear your voice, never again will my eyes rest upon features so dear to me, aye, dearer to me than all the world besides. I own it, though many of my sex would disguise such an acknowledgment, and pine in misery under the secret. You are the object of my dearest affection. I must say no more, I have said too much.' Here she threw her arms round the young Saxon's neck, and wept bitterly.

'You have said it, Gladys, you have said all I asked, your heart is mine—mine for ever! It is enough,' cried Ethelred, 'that confession is enough,' pressing her passionately to his heart. 'We only part to meet again. Your people shall not sacrifice your happiness to their prejudices; no, by heaven! I will break down every barrier, I will come for you amid your native wilds—I will make you my bride. None shall censure you, my pure-hearted, affectionate Gladys.'

Again the Saxon folded her in his arms. He kissed away the tears which bedewed her cheeks. He repeated in her ear a thousand tender expressions; he comforted her with future hope, nor did he leave her side until putting back her long dark disordered tresses, he looked into her soul-speaking eyes, and brought back a smile upon her lips.

Kynfin Tudor was expected that evening. The young Saxon left the presence of his lady-love, only to hurry into the court, mount his horse, and with a light heart, gallop off on the road to Rennes, to meet and conduct the uncle to the side of his beloved charge.

CHAPTER VII

The Departed—Ocean Reflections— Homeward-bound—The Maternal Reception

ONCE more Kynfin Tudor sat by the side of the daughter of Harlech. Once more he listened to her gentle voice, but he read with feelings of new anxiety, traces of more than usual sorrow in her countenance. The Earl of Pembroke and Richmond, Claudine De Montfort, and her brother, had all accompanied Ap Dafydd to Fougères. They had just left, bearing away *la petite* Jacqueline from the side of her friend; but the son of Harlech was quick in perception, and guessed that was not the only cause from whence her heart was sad. They were on the eve of their departure. The Saxon lingered still in their company, and the maiden's eyes were often fixed upon his features. Kynfin observed all this, and his heart misgave him. The seaman's remarks in the boat respecting the Master of Cricceath on the night previous to the attack upon the fortress, flashed across his mind. Little Maurice's words recurred. 'It is not for me to say who is the favourite.'

Just as the sun had risen, the Duke's escort stood ready to conduct the fair daughter of Cambria and her uncle to the port of St Malo. With what different feelings did they again set out upon their return. Gladys was silent, she spoke no more of Harlech's proud battlements, and Jacqueline, she looked forward no more to the happy greeting which awaited her in the Cwm. She even averted her eyes from her uncle's face, that kind careworn face. Gladys's heart was troubled. She had now more soul engrossing cares, stronger ties upon her affection. She had parted with Ethelred. Her meditations were upon his cherished words. Her vision could descry nothing but his open and generous countenance, and fine and manly form. She dreamed of a different future than ever she had dreamed of before.

Ap Dafydd's forebodings increased on observing the taciturnity of his niece. He did not question her being changed in some degree, he knew how she had been weakened by illness. He was ready to make allowance for her, since she had told him how deeply thankful she was that he was restored to her. He knew that her anxiety had been great during his imprisonment, and when he felt her head was nestled upon his bosom, he endeavoured to persuade himself that he was satisfied although he was not so in reality.

Upon entering the town of St Malo, they immediately went on board a vessel which was to set sail in a few hours for England.

It was a lovely evening in June, twilight was drawing its mysterious veil over the land. The tall white buildings in the port rose up against the dark blue sky, and were again reflected with the varied forms of the shipping in the watery mirror beneath.

Gladys stood upon the deck; her eyes being riveted upon the calm, beautiful scene. The sight of the vessels and the ocean, brought back to her memory the *Eryr*, the rover, and her uncle's sufferings. She recalled his anxiety for her when she was in Ap Rhys's power; and while such thoughts were passing through her mind, she chanced to look up in his face.

Then it was her conscience smote her. How cruel had she been to him, since he had been so recently restored to her; how cold towards him. She had, she imagined, shut herself out from his sympathy. How changed he must think her. She felt she was herself changed. She had grown selfish, she began to despise herself. She did not feel the same regard towards her country as she had once done. These reflections made her heart ache. She would soon be by her grandmother's side, who would fold her wyres bach in her arms; her wyres bach would not be the same she had once folded there. This brought another pang to her heart. She would now be free to wander again over her native wilds, why did she not experience greater pleasure at the prospect? The answer made her heart sick. The young Saxon was the cause of all this dissatisfaction. Kynfin Tudor fancying her little hand shook while he held it, looking tenderly into her face, said:—

'Gladys, my child, what is it that troubles you? Why is your brow overshadowed? You do not regret to leave the French coast, for your feet will so soon tread the heather of your own native wilds, you will be free from peril, free from care and sorrow. No longer a captive partaking of the Saxon's bread, but free to wander among your rocks and glens. You will soon be again on the threshold of your mountain home, cheering the last days of your unhappy grandmother. Will not this elevate your spirits, my dear Gladys? Surely these thoughts will bring back that voice which has been so taciturn for the last two or three days. My heart feels vacant without your conversation. What distresses you, my child, repose your sorrow in him who loves you with the devotion of a parent.'

Gladys could not attempt to answer these questions, because she could not answer them. She entreated forgiveness.

When Ap Dafydd and his niece landed in England, the country was politically quiet. Edward, the handsome young Earl of Marche, the warlike hero of former years, had now degenerated into a luxurious debauchee, fond of revelry and wine. Surrounded by dissipated courtiers, he was too pleased to accept overtures from the French monarch, rather than enter the field in behalf of the rights of his country. Louis, the unprincipled and wily King of France, was well aware of the weak point of his opponent. He kept Edward at play as a child plays with a soulless kitten, and the English monarch became the dupe of his secret designs. The mysterious death of the Duke of Clarence was another topic that excited the popular indignation, sowing in secret the seeds of contention. A brighter day for Lancaster was dawning, the Red Rose banner was soon to float again over England. Many hearts that had been mourning for years were to be made glad. These were thoughts which occupied Ap Dafydd, when he drew the daughter of Harlech's hand within his own, and they knelt together upon the seashore, to offer up a prayer of thanksgiving for their safe return to the land of their forefathers. But their feet were not to linger in England. Rocky Cambria, their own peculiar country, was still in the distance. They hurried on from post to post with increasing impatience, till they reached the desired spot.

If memory often turns the past to pain, how often does it bring back bright and happy days. The daughter of Harlech stood once more among her mountains, knee-deep in blooming heather, once more fanned by the balmy breeze, listening to the well-known sounds of the roaring torrent, the bleating of the mountain sheep, and the cry of the solitary bittern, memory brought back departed pleasures on the spot where they had been enjoyed, to be enjoyed once more. She was no longer a captive. She was free, in the land of her childhood, that appeared to her enraptured eyes more lovely than ever. In her delight, even the young Saxon had for a time little share in her thoughts. With a smile upon her face, in glad and eager accents she recalled the visions of the past, and her days of innocent childhood, happy days, which she had a thousand times recalled during her captivity, to cheer many dreary hours. She looked upon the mountain's rugged side, she watched the torrent leaping madly down the precipitous crags, and pressed her foot upon the velvet mosses of the soil with new feelings. So pure, so refined, so holy are the feelings of nature. Those feelings prompted her to sink upon her knees in gratitude to Him that had framed the noble scenery around her, had watched over her welfare, supported her through her passed trials, and was now restoring her to her home. Why had she ever thought that her lot was hard? Why had she ever doubted that His mercies would be continued, and that He would refuse to give her comfort and support in the trials which awaited her? She would no longer be ungrateful, but would lay her cares open before Him, reposing her burden upon Him, resigned to let Him do with her as seemed good in His sight. Contentment and happiness, she felt, might still be her portion.

Kynfin Tudor, standing at a little distance from where the maiden was kneeling, with his eyes transfixed upon her beautiful countenance, felt his heart glow with reverence and affection. He rejoiced that smiles had returned, that her joyous voice once more greeted his ear, and that the Saxon, and young De Montfort with his flattery, had not, after all, either changed or spoiled his niece, as his secret forebodings had apprehended. The child was now restored to her mountains, and her innocent face remained the same.

It was a moment of unspeakable pleasure to the son of Harlech to have fulfilled his promised duty thus far. A load of solicitude was removed from his heart. Gladys was the same as she had ever been. It was to him renewed pleasure to hear her accents as of old, and to watch her innocent delight, as they journeyed on over moorlands, and through wild and shadowy glens. Ap Dafydd's feelings were still more exalted, on witnessing the ecstasy of the daughter of Harlech when they entered their own beloved pass, and saw the smoke rising from the massive walls of Cader y Cil, when they first burst upon their view. With a cry of joy Gladys exclaimed:

'There! there is my old mountain home! There are the dear old rocks, the lake, the woods, all as when I left them in my early days! Oh! my home! My dear, wild, wild home! This is happiness!'

Kynfin Tudor could not take his eyes from the excited face of his niece. The brilliancy of colour upon her cheeks, her entire countenance was irradiated with an expression which he had never observed upon it before. His regard for his charge was measureless. She was the sole hope of his ancient house, and she loved her people. Her actions seemed to him a thousand times dearer, better, more precious than to any other individual. It was not wonderful that such were his feelings, and that Gladys brought smiles into her uncle's careworn face. The scene at that moment was ever afterwards present to his memory.

As the daughter of Harlech drew near Cader y Cil, her joy was suddenly damped by the apprehension that her grandmother might have passed into the grave, and her voice might not greet her return. The feeling engendered impatience. She now hurried forward with uncontrollable eagerness. At length the barking of the dogs fell upon her ear, and old Howel's familiar voice sounded from the inner court. The doors were thrown open. Gladys saw and heard nothing more, for hasting over the well-remembered threshold, she sought the old chimney corner, and threw herself into the arms of her delighted grandmother, who pressed her fondly to her bosom, and wept and smiled alternately unconscious what she did.

'O fy nghalon anwyl! My firstborn's child!' sobbed the old lady, at last overcome with joy. 'Let me look into your face, let me look into your blue eyes! Yes—yes! It is my own wyres bach! my firstborn's child! I have lived to see this day; she has come—come at last! Her joyous voice, her bright and happy face, her light step, so long desired will again cheer the lone walls of Cader y Cil, and restore joy to a bereaved and forlorn widow.'

The kind tones of her grandmother, her dim hazel eyes beaming with love and affection upon her, made Gladys's heart overflow with delight, and she did not attempt to withdraw herself from her embrace. Katherine and Howel stood waiting to give her welcome, and were all impatience to have a smile, a greeting from their meistres bach. Still she knelt before her grandmother, with her arms thrown round her neck, her eyes fixed upon her face, and whispering assurances that her wyres bach would never again leave her.

Ap Dafydd stood in the background. He would not interrupt a scene which he looked upon as sacred. His heart, nevertheless, was full of emotion. He yearned to clasp his aged mother in his arms. The widow of Ap Jevan was the first to break the spell:

'Where is your uncle, my wyres bach? Where is my son, my poor Kynfin?'

She had no time to repeat her inquiries. The son of Harlech was in his mother's embrace; and with a cheerful voice, and a brighter look than he had worn for a long season asked her if he had not kept his promise, namely, that her wyres bach should be the first to throw herself into her arms.

CHAPTER VIII

The Welcome—A Bard—An Unexpected Interview—Love Sacrifice

THE moment the mountaineers heard of the arrival of the daughter of Harlech, an 'adlais o lawenydd'[16] resounded throughout the glen. Matrons and maidens, stout men and aged, all hastened to Cader y Cil to bring their offerings of welcome to the granddaughter of their valiant chieftain, the great Dafydd. Soon were the rude court and gateway strewed with grouse, hares, partridges, honey, fish, eggs, and numberless other trifling gifts; humble offerings of humble, yet attached souls, all were laid promiscuously at the feet of their meistres bach.

Gladys, her heart overflowing with gratitude, returned their affectionate greetings. It was both a touching and unexpected scene to the fair daughter of Cambria. So many joyous countenances gazing upon her face. So many kneeling at her feet, and kissing her garments; so many clamorous voices eager in expressing their joy, while on all sides infant voices joined in the concert:

'O Riau! O Ferch Harlech! Meistres bach anwyl hawddgar croeso, croeso, i dy wlad a'th gartref etto!'

The heart of Gladys now smote her that she should ever have felt the slightest indifference towards her tribe, that she should

---

[16] An echo of gladness.

have looked upon them as a barrier to her happiness. They were her devoted good and faithful people, they had suffered without a murmur on her account; and she now beheld them kneeling at her feet in extravagant joy at her return, all blessing their chieftain's grand-daughter. It was a moment of intense delight. With a sweet and benevolent smile upon her face, she stood in the midst of them, lifting up her voice and committing them to the care of the Creator, calling on Him to reward them, and bless them for their devotion to the grandchild of their lamented chief. The tears chased each other down her cheeks. Earnestly and fervently she prayed that the stream of joy now flowing through her heart, might ever continue to carry sweet waters. Never might it be embittered more.

The men of the Cwm, their wives and children regarded the scene with reverence and delight. The child that had been stolen from her rocky nest, and kept as an hostage on their account, in the hands of the Saxons, had, at last, been restored to them. She that, in former years, had been the sunbeam in the glen, seen at every hearth with her light step and beaming face, now stood there to greet their delighted vision. It was true, the wyres bach was no longer a child, but the intelligent and lustrous eyes were the same. Some said the peculiar gentle tones of voice were the same, and that her complacent and winning address brought their meistres bach as she was in her childhood fresh to their recollections.

They could scarcely tear themselves away from her presence. They talked over the years that were past, and reminded her of little circumstances connected with herself, revealing to her without any formal profession, how deeply in word and thought she was idolized by her people. The brave men of the Cwm, no longer, able to restrain their feelings, addressed her as follows:

'O meistres bach anwyl! May you never be taken away from us. May St David and all the saints bless thee, and make thy home a home of peace! May thy bright face ever cheer us, and the sound of thy footsteps bring joy to our hearths. We will protect thee, daughter of Harlech, heiress of great Einion race, we will protect thee. No Saxon shall molest thee here, who stole thee from thy nest, and horned our dwellings, and destroyed our meeting-house shall never again set foot in the Cwm. The blood of their savage dogs have been sprinkled upon the rocks. They shall never again set foot in the glen. Yea, yea! We have said it, daughter of Harlech! We have said it, no Saxon shall molest thee here! Our clubs and our battleaxes shall keep the enemy at bay. Yea, yea! The daughter of Harlech shall roam where she pleaseth over the wild hills, or down the glen, she will be safe. The daughter of Harlech may bathe her feet in the mountain stream, and none shall intrude upon her solitude. She may pour forth her songs, she may repose in the heather on the mountain's side, and be lulled by the rushing waters, no stranger shall come near her. The daughter of Harlech may sail over the lake, and scale the crags, and upon the heights may dance with glee; she may kneel before her God, who has guided her path from infancy, and has now restored her to her people in safety and in health; none shall trespass on her solemn worship. We have said it, Meistres bach anwyl! We have said it! The brave men of the Cwm have said it!'

This day was an era in Gladys's life. When the excitement was over, and she found herself alone in her chamber, she no longer fanned her secret passion by recalling the words, the accent and the features of the young Saxon, who she felt was now for ever and ever shut out from her. With a smile of calmness and resignation, and a gentle step, she approached her narrow bed, and kneeling down beside it, sought what her soul hungered for, comfort and consolation, before she retired to rest.

The son of Harlech, present at the affecting scene in the morning, had also been heartily welcomed by the good people of the Glen. With earnest entreaties, they begged him to remain, and be their chief as his father had been before him. They assured him that with their meistres bach, he would spread a halo around the Cwm, and make every heart happy.

Ap Dafydd was distressed on hearing from the mountaineers of young Stacey's devastation in the glen. He evinced great interest at their account of the deadly attack upon the Saxons, who had never since been seen in the neighbourhood of the Cwm. They told him how the revenue men had been destroyed in the vaults below the house of Gêst; how the Dewines had consumed Sir Gilbert's property by a spirit-fire, and she had never been seen since the smugglers had quitted the shores. Young Stacey, it appeared, was disliked in the vicinity of Harlech, although he had ceased to interfere with the people of the soil. Lady Stacey, and Mistress Maud had lately left the castle. Its young master it was expected would be married in a few weeks.

Kynfin's information from Howel, whom he met in his wanderings at a little distance from their dwelling, was to a similar effect.

'Do you know how they are going on at Harlech?' inquired Ap Dafydd. 'I hear young Stacey is still at the castle.'

'Ow! Ow! (an expression of sorrow) I am sorry to say he is,' replied Howel, 'the people in Harlech will tell you that he is a hard master. Since the death of the old keeper, there has been a greater gloom than ever over the town. No Welshman is allowed to set foot within the castle walls. No one passes out of the gateway without a bodyguard. Indeed truth, I never like to go near the place. To think of the change since my dear old master was there, it makes my heart sick. Ow, ow, whether there will be a merry laugh, and a happy face in the old town of Harlech again, St David only knows. These are sad times, son of Harlech, sad times! I fear my failing sight will never see a change for the better.'

'I did not expect such desponding words from you, Howel, now the daughter of Harlech has been restored to the Cwm,' said Kynfin, a little reproachfully.

'O'r anwyl! son of Harlech, you take it in another way, I was not speaking of the Cwm,' replied the old man, and a ray of pleasure passed over his shrivelled face. 'Indeed truth, there is a change for the better in the Cwm. We all feel that the daughter of Harlech is like the sun in the heaven, throwing light upon every step and every face near to her. O diolch! They are happy days for us in the Cwm. The prayer of an old man will ever be that we may be blessed by a continuation of them.'

Ap Dafydd appeared to have excited this remark purposely, in order that he might witness the pleasure in the old man's face upon his niece being mentioned.

'Well, Howel, let us hope since we have lived to see the joyful change in the Cwm that you will also live to see that day when the Red dragon banner[17] floats once more upon our old fortress. That will be a change for the better.'

---

[17] Urthyr, King Arthur's father, was surnamed Pendragon by Merlin or Merddin, a great bard and prophet, who likened him to a dragon's head, that at the time of his nativity appeared in the heavens, at the corner of a blazing star. Other historians assert that from his wisdom and subtlety he was so called. Be it as it may, his son, the first Christian monarch of Britain, bore upon his helm a red dragon, and from hence it became the national arms of the Cambro-Britons.

'Dyn anwyl! do you think that day will ever come, son of Harlech?'

'The Dewines has said it!' replied Ap Dafydd.

'The Dewines has said it,' repeated the old man, 'young Master Stacey will be driven out of the land; our mistress, the daughter of Harlech, and you, Ap Dafydd, will go home to Harlech Castle,' said the domestic, jumping at the happy conclusion. 'Did she say that?'

'She did.'

'O diolch! O moliant! If I live to see that day, I shall close my eyes with joy, and drop into my grave with a light heart.'

'May it be so,' resumed the son of Harlech, 'meanwhile, Howel, is the family of Conyers still at Cricceath?'

'Mistress Conyers and her two sons are there, but the young master is not,' replied the domestic, a little startled at the sudden question. 'They seldom come over on this side now. There was a quarrel between young Stacey and the son of Cricceath, who, the country people say, took the part of the Dewines, the smugglers, and the maidens, and greatly provoked him. There have been a great many things said besides that,' said Howel, hesitatingly.

'Speak on,' said Ap Dafydd.

'Well, indeed truth, I should be sorry to hide anything from the son of Harlech. They say that the young Master Ethelred was much at the castle before the maidens were carried away by the smuggler's vessel. His eyes rested constantly upon the daughter of Harlech, his manner, and words were always gentle and kind to her.' Howel looked up at his master with an expression of great anxiety and distress, and then continued:

'I should not like to think, son of Harlech, that our

chieftain's wyres bach, had given her heart to the Saxon, although they say the young gentleman is breaking his heart after her! It looks like it, for shortly after your departure, he was missing from the country. Ow, ow, I hope the attachment is only on his side.'

Kynfin made no reply, but moved away with a thoughtful air. Tempted by the freshness of the evening, he continued his walk for several miles, until he arrived at a spot from whence the towers of Harlech were visible in the far off distance. His heart yearned after his old home. He stood for some time leaning against a rock, his cap shading his eyes, which were fixed upon the beloved object that engrossed all his thoughts. The smoke was ascending from a few scattered cottages, nestled among the rocks in the little valley below. The atmosphere was brilliantly clear, and so tranquil that the children calling to one another below, could be distinctly heard across the glen. The son of Harlech had not been long in that attitude, when soft strains of music fell upon his ear, and looking over the cliff, he recognized beneath, the honoured bard of the Cwm, formerly an inmate of Harlech Castle. His attention was immediately riveted by the sweet sounds which were vocally accompanied by the following strain:—[18]

'Ah me! that Harlech's ancient towers should be in Saxon thrall.
Great Einion's race, my master dear, driven from their ancient hall,
While Howel's harp must silent be, nor tell the wrongs they bore,
Until oppression drove them far, far from their native shore.
                                        Ochan! Ochan!

---

[18]   These stanzas the author was favoured with by a friend.

My harp is hush'd! Though dear to me the memory of his kind,
Our noble chief who died, and left a spotless name behind,
Dared I but strike the chords again, not Taliesin's lyre,
Should ask revenge more loud and deep from Cambria's son or sire.
Ochan! Ochan!

Ye mountains where the blue skies rest, that are so dear to me,
When on your summits shall I meet our glorious ancestry?
And rear the song as bards of old, when Cambria free and wild,
Danced with the stars of Heaven along, like a joy-drunken child.
Ochan! Ochan!

Where Modred sleeps, near Snowdon's brow, where on his cloud-
    capp'd crest
Old Idris gazed upon the heavens, and long'd to be at rest,
By Mona's shore, or Bala's wave, or deep Llyn Idwal's gloom—
Oh! Woe! Woe! Woe! I nothing see, but sorrow and a tomb!
Ochan! Ochan!

I'll strike my harp, no, never more, while Harlech's towers to me,
Their silent story tell so true of Cambria's destiny,
There is no joy for Music's son in notes that from today
Can only tell of our lost chief, and glory past away!
Ochan! Ochan!'

When the voice ceased, the son of Harlech brushed away the
tears from his eyes, for the words had sunk deep into his heart.
He hastened down to the revered minstrel, and with a greeting
on both sides cordial, yet saddened by recollection, they
conversed upon the misfortunes which overshadowed their
country. The son of song, his hand resting motionless upon

his harp, sighed over the fate of their unhappy bards. From the reign of Edward the First to the Wars of the Roses, this distinguished order of men, or all who escaped the massacre by Edward, struck their harps by stealth, and taught the art of soul-thrilling harmony to their children down to the Wars of the Roses. Still their profession, though of ancient date, was prohibited from holding its cleras and eisteddfods. Every privilege had been withheld, and they had become enslaved in the land of their pristine glory. They could no longer inspire the Cambrian hearts with sentiments of patriotism, enliven hospitality, kindle a love of freedom, or awaken a thirst for glory. Their harps had too long been hushed, and compelled by despotic laws to remain in obscurity, they bemoaned in secret their own fall. With sadder hearts than the rest of their countrymen, throughout mourning Cambria, they grieved the death of song, as well as of their land's liberty, but they grieved in vain.

After imparting their regrets that hope seemed to withdraw its cheering beams from their future path, Kynfin turned his steps homewards. Evening was closing in, all around was sombre, and in unison with the melancholy which hung over his spirits, until late even to the noon of night.

Months passed in uninterrupted peace and enjoyment within the old walls of Cader y Cil. The widow of Ap Jevan talked cheerfully, and even smiled. Kynfin looked happier than he ever had done since his return to Harlech after his brother's death. Old Katherine Howel and little Maurice, who had now joined the household, had all a look of contentment in their faces. Gladys, though at times thoughtful, the colour slightly fading upon her cheeks, appeared cheerful and contented with the rest. Almost daily her light form glided through the glen, either on a mission of mercy, or to convey a message to someone or other of the tribe. Varying her way by scrambling over the heights or skimming over the lake, sometimes with her beloved uncle in company, and sometimes alone. The independent life has its charms. She experienced moments of pure, and innocent enjoyment; but they were too frequently superseded by intervals of poignant grief, not less so for being concealed. With all its strugglings, moments will come when human nature confessing its weakness in spite of itself, throws down the supports which have for a time sustained it against intruding passions, and bares itself to the blast. Thus it seemed with Gladys, many months having passed away since the young Saxon had told her he would come to her wild land, and claim her for his bride. It was not that she wished him to come, and claim her for his bride. She had long resigned herself to the belief that she must never unite her fate with his. Nor was it that she wished ever to see the young Saxon, because she dreaded her own weak heart, and its betrayal of her secret to her people. It was the apprehension that he might be in danger. She persuaded herself it was that alone which made her anxiety increase daily. She felt more than ever that as the love she had for him could never be destroyed, it would be in vain to attempt wholly to eradicate a passion so deeply rooted.

The heart of the daughter of Harlech was oppressed with these reflections, when she turned her steps towards the rude carved chapel in the rock. There visiting the tomb of her mother, she could weep in secret; while at that sacred spot, she imagined she saw the noble form of her grandfather appear before her. She had seen him kneeling in that vault with his hoary locks and sorrow-stricken face, breathing a prayer for her his wyres bach, the last descendant of his noble house. Many were the prayers he had offered up for her, the possessor as he was of so many virtues, the sufferer from so many trials, and yet inflexible in the path of duty. She reflected that he had been left her as an example, as well as her own pure and exemplary mother. She prayed earnestly that she might follow in their footsteps. When she rose from her knees and quitted the sanctuary, she felt her heart glowing with fresh resolution to go boldly on upon the path which they had trodden. She then turned to wend her way up the rocky pass. The winter winds had swept over the land and departed. The snow had melted away even from the tops of the mountains. The bright warm sun of a spring morning tempted her, upon this occasion, to wander farther than was usual from her home, and at every step her heart grew lighter. The rocks, woods, leaping cataracts, and distant ocean, all lay before her in their variety, and to her heart seemed ministering angels. They spread an atmosphere of beauty around her. They appeared to mingle with herself, and infuse comfort into her soul. The air seemed redolent of new life, and the colours of land and sea, tree and herb, to her looked deeper and richer than they ever did before. This arose from her feeling that happiness had been so long absent. With glowing cheek and beaming face, she scaled the giddy heights, and felt unwonted activity. She bathed her feet in the sparkling waters, and she revelled in the scenery of the romantic and beautiful land of her fathers, as none but those who feel and love nature can do. Suddenly she reflected that the sun was beginning to be low in the horizon, limited by the waters of her native bay. She retraced her steps homewards. After continuing for some time, she was startled by Ethelred's voice among the rocks repeating her name.

Before she could observe from what quarter the sound came, she was in the arms of the young Saxon. Neither could speak for some time. Gladys could only perceive that he was present, safe, and that she had laid her head upon his breast. She had not the power, the strength, perhaps not the inclination, to tear herself away from him. Still less, could she, at that moment break to him intelligence which would cause him immeasurable bitterness under the pangs of disappointment. She did not at the instant of this sudden meeting, pass it across her mind. She welcomed him only with tears of joy, secretly thanking heaven he was safe, and invoking a blessing upon his head. Resolutions and duty all gave way for one short moment, a moment as sweet to Gladys as stolen water, but its sweetness was as evanescent as it had been overcoming to her nature.

The young Saxon pressed her to his heart, and both becoming more collected, he in a few hurried sentences, explained the reason of his long absence; informed her he had been immured in a French prison, and then described the anxiety he had suffered upon her account.

'Let us not dwell upon past miseries, my dear Gladys,' cried Ethelred, 'I am again at your side, I am come to claim you for my bride. Henceforth our joys and our sorrows shall be shared together, none shall interfere with our happiness—none shall check the sympathy of our glowing hearts.'

The wan moon had already peered above the crags, and still the maiden hesitated to tell the Saxon that they must meet no more, and that she could never be his bride. He had undergone many hardships since they parted, and she could read suffering in his face. This softened her heart the more towards him, whenever she attempted to relate her real position, and the cruel truth. The words died upon her lips, unable longer to control her grief, and she wept bitterly a flood of tears upon his bosom.

'Why do you weep so, my Gladys?' said Ethelred, looking tenderly in her face. He then became alarmed at the thought that her people might have influenced her during his absence. 'Gladys, you have not forgotten what passed between us in the little room that looked into the long poplar avenue at Fougères? Those cherished words on which I placed implicit faith, which afterwards cheered the dark and dismal hours of my imprisonment. Do not overshadow the joy of this moment by repeating your former scruples. I am determined nothing shall stand between us to prevent our union. I am ready to combat, to support, to meet any difficulty or danger to make you my bride. Do not weep so, Gladys, speak to me, make not my heart more desolate, than it has long been. Cheer me with a word of comfort. I will overleap every difficulty, and bear you away as my own bride.'

Gladys heaved a deep sigh. The little chapel in the rock, her mother, her grandfather, her resolution, all flashed across her mind, as coming to lend her aid at this trying hour. At last, with a resigned expression on her face, considerable agitation, and in deep pathetic accents, she replied:—

'Ethelred, my own weak heart would yield, my own weak heart would respond to all your wishes, but there is a sacred agency that rises within to restrain me. My former fears that you, Ethelred, tried to persuade me were childish superstitions, infant prejudices, I have come to my country and my people to learn, are too well grounded realities, too clearly pointing out the sacrifice required of me. A stranger in this land, you cannot enter into the feelings of our people here;

their prejudices, superstitions, or whatever you may consider them, are time honoured. In me the people see the granddaughter of their chieftain, and the last in the direct line of our noble house. In me they centre all their hopes. They are all devoted to me, children, property, lives! Their hearths are made happy by my presence. They regard a Saxon with undying hatred. I repeat they are devoted to me, and have showered down their benedictions upon my head, and given me such a reception as will remain indelibly imprinted upon my memory. Is it not a sacred duty to respond to them? Is it not a duty to give up myself to preserve their traditions, when such a sacrifice renders them happy? It is a hard task, but it must be borne for their gratification, and to escape the reprobation I should incur by a contrary action. The granddaughter of Dafydd Ap Jevan dares not bring down censure upon herself, reprobation upon her family, and sorrow and disappointment upon her people. She will do this by uniting herself to a Saxon. No, Ethelred, I have said it before, and have felt it long, the same chain cannot bind us that binds others. Would to heaven, Ethelred, that you were not a Saxon. It is a bitter fate that we must part, and for ever.'

'Gladys, this cannot, shall not be!' cried the youth with a frantic gesture, his frame trembling with the agitation. 'All you say may be true, still you shall be mine! Gladys you will not desert me, you cannot. You must still be mine!'

'In mercy listen to me!' replied the maiden in her anguish of soul. 'Do not increase my sorrow by inculcating vain hopes. There is no hope—hope is dead for us! Do not beguile me from the law of duty. I must obey that law. I have made a solemn vow upon the tomb of my mother that I would not forsake it. I cannot break that vow. Let me entreat you,

Ethelred, my dear Ethelred, to bear up against this trial, for my sake to do so. My heart will remain with you, my prayers will ever be offered up for you. I will be the bride of no other. Ethelred, for my sake be calm!' continued Gladys, kneeling by the side of the young Saxon, who had flung himself on the earth.

The disappointment was so sudden, so great. His expectations were so unexpectedly dashed to pieces that the effect for the moment almost deprived him of his reason. He groaned deeply, and then the bold and manly young Saxon wept like a child. Gladys tried in vain to console him, her tears fell upon him. It was in vain, he would not be consoled. She looked into his face to second her earnest entreaty, but he placed his hands before his eyes.

'No, Gladys, no; take those eyes away from me. They set my soul on fire. We must part, and for ever! Oh, Gladys! After all that has passed, do not desert me. What have I done that I should be visited with a sorrow that will bring me to an early grave?' Gladys threw her arms round his neck, and again and again implored him to be calm, and to bear up against his grief.

The young Saxon only uttered the bitter cry:—

'Gladys! Gladys! Do not desert me, you will have your people to comfort you. I shall be desolate and broken-hearted. Gladys, open your heart, I implore it of you!'

A bugle horn sounded from the Cwm. Gladys started up in alarm.

'Ethelred, I must go, they are calling me. We must part!'

Ethelred rose from the ground dejected, still weeping like a child. He clasped Gladys in his arms fondly, passionately. 'You will then desert me—we must part and for ever!'

'For ever!' repeated the maiden in a tone and gesture as agonized as his own, 'it must be so!'

The dogs at this instant from Cader y Cil, suddenly appeared over the rock, and were barking furiously at the stranger.

'Ethelred! for the love of heaven, fly!' cried Gladys, with a terrified voice, 'no Saxon is safe in the glen.'

'Say, Gladys, that you will not desert me once more,' persisted Ethelred in a hollow distracted voice, 'O God! Gladys, will not you give me one hope? Cruel, heartless girl!'

'Alas! Ethelred, there is none!' cried the maiden, in an agony at his delay, 'fly, fly! dear Ethelred, fly!'

'Without a hope, without a ray of comfort, deserted, forsaken, and broken-hearted!' cried the Saxon, and he pushed her from him. Then snatching her in his arms again, he hugged her to his breast. At last, with an exclamation of frantic despair, he tore himself away, and bounding over the rocks, was lost to her for ever. Mechanically, Gladys turned her steps towards home.

She had not gone far, when she trembled so violently that she was compelled to sit down. Her struggle had been severe. She had forgotten herself in Ethelred's grief, and re-action had ensued.

The night was calm and clear. The moon and the stars were looking down upon the daughter of Harlech who had forgotten the hour. She did not notice that it was night. Her absence alarmed the family of the Cwm. Kynfin Tudor, after searching for her in great anxiety, found her kneeling amongst the heath. Her face was concealed in her long hair, and her heart almost breaking, sought vent in tears.

'My Gladys bach, my child!' cried her uncle in alarm, sitting down upon a stone, and taking her upon his knee.

'What has happened? What can it be that has thrown yon into this distress? Tell me, you alarm me, hide nothing from your uncle, who is open to sympathy, confide your sorrow in me, my child, my Gladys bach.'

'I am miserable, very miserable,' cried the wretched girl, 'I have parted with him for ever! Despise me, uncle, I cannot help it. Ethelred, the young Saxon, has been the idol of my heart, and will ever be my heart's idol. I have parted from him for ever! I have left him broken-hearted. He says I have deserted him, he to whom I owe so much, says I am cruel and heartless. O uncle! my burden is heavy! I crave your sympathy. I am miserable, and he is miserable. I have parted with him for ever!'

The cries which followed this hurried confession, fell upon Kynfin's ear with serious misgivings for the future happiness of his charge. He was somewhat prepared for it, yet when the truth was revealed, he was speechless. He thought of his brother's clandestine marriage with Aliano, of the early impressions of his father, and his strong objections to any of his family forming an alliance with the Saxon race, Aliano's anxiety that her child should not know that her mother was one of that race, his own love for her; and the sorrow that had been visited upon himself and his family, since his brother had opposed his father's wishes. In the case before him, it would be many degrees worse. The last of their noble house would bring a Saxon lord and master to rule over their people. There would be nothing but dissension, nothing but sorrow in reserve for Gladys, his beloved niece.

During this pause, Gladys became more calm, but her calmness was unnatural, it was more painful than her suffering.

'Do not reveal my secret, dear uncle,' she resumed, placing

her hands on her beating temples, and looking eagerly into his face. 'Do not let the good people of the Cwm know that their chieftain's wyres bach ever loved a Saxon. I have given him up; I shall never see him again, never. Bitter is the trial, bitter indeed. None can read my heart, none shall ever read it or know what are my sufferings. O, uncle! if there was no God in heaven, I could not support it! But you will promise to keep my secret.'

'Gladys bach, my beloved child!' ejaculated her uncle, pressing her cheek to his, and stroking his hand down her long black hair, in his own peculiarly tender and affectionate manner. 'The spirit that prompted you to take this unselfish noble step, will support and bless you. You will have your reward, you will never be forsaken by Him. I grieve for you, my child. I deeply sympathize with you, yet I rejoice that you should have done what you have done. Great as is the sacrifice at the moment, you will never have to repent of it. Your conscience, Gladys, will not be a torment to you; mine has been a torment to me. A peaceful conscience will alone secure that happiness which we all crave after. My Gladys bach, be comforted. Your people and your family are here to love and devote themselves to you. Happiness is still in reserve for you.'

'Ethelred has none to comfort him, no people to care for him,' replied Gladys, with a bitter expression of grief. 'Uncle, if you would go to him and whisper comfort to his sorrowing heart, as you do to mine, and bring me word that he was more calm, more resigned, I should be happier. He seeks comfort— he merits it. He is wretched.'

Kynfin Tudor went over on the following day to Cricceath Castle. What passed between him and Ethelred did not transpire, but Gladys seemed more satisfied after the result of his visit was made known to her.

CHAPTER IX

Woman-hating—Love's Straggles— Maternal Solicitude—Fraternal Regard

'Tyrrel, was not that Kynfin, the son of Harlech I saw here today? I could not be mistaken. His face is one that on being seen engraves itself deeply on the memory,' said Mistress Conyers, addressing her youngest son who was standing in the hall adjusting some of the lances along the wall which had become deranged from their stand.

'Yes, mother, it was he, and a very pretty time the fellow remained closeted with Ethelred.'

'With Ethelred! Oh, that reminds me he has not yet made his appearance this morning. How is that?'

'Evil genii have been at work, mother, torturing his spirit, inflicting wounds upon his heart, and overshadowing his path with the gloom of their ugly faces.'

'What do you mean, Tyrrel?'

'Had you seen Ethelred this morning, you would not have been less discerning than myself, you would have discovered that such was the fact.'

'Do not speak perpetual enigmas. Why puzzle me—let me hear the fact, as you designate it.'

'The fact, mother! Why, it is the fact that men are the greatest simpletons on earth to trouble their heads, or fret their hearts about women. I am monstrously glad I am not a woman. To support the responsibility devolving upon them is to me something fearful. It would annihilate me—crush me to the earth. A pretty climax the world is worked up to: the root of mischief that transpires of every startling thing which takes place, only dig for it, and you are sure to find it is a woman. I could prove it to you in ninety out of a hundred instances; aye, as clear as that sad affair in relation to poor Mistress Mary Dunston. From Gladys of Harlech to the witch of Gêst, women are all alike. Their special mission, their ruling passion seems, in my humble opinion, to be to make tools of men, and turn the world upside down. We men are complimented as the lords of the creation. Lords of the creation, indeed! Why, the upholding such an idea is a gross fallacy. You women govern us all. Mother, you shall see if ever I suffer myself to be caught by a girl. If I am, I will go at once and drown myself.' While concluding the sentence, Tyrrel grinned, half laughed, and shrugged his shoulders, partly in earnest, and partly in jest.

'Come, Tyrrel, be serious altogether for once in your life; ramble no more from the subject. I am curious to hear what you have to say respecting Ethelred.'

'Well, honoured mother, as you look so anxious, I will come to the point. Yesterday, Ethelred went across into Merionethshire, setting out in high spirits. He has returned an altered man. It is no secret, for you know already that the poor fellow has been a woman's slave for years. I have strong suspicions that this Gladys of Harlech, this little queen and liege lady of his heart, has been playing him false. You are aware, mother, that they met in France, and were much in each other's company. The attachment between them grew stronger. Ethelred had reason to hope she would share his destiny: from what I gathered from himself I imagined they were betrothed. All I can add is that if my suspicion proves true, she has ill-treated Ethelred, my noble, generous hearted brother. If so, I know not where my indignation will terminate. I shall feel infuriated against the wench. I shall hate the jilt after what has passed between herself and my brother; such conduct cannot be palliated—it is cruelty, baseness. Yet, I sometimes feel this can hardly be the case. My very suspicion puzzles me. How, too, could any woman withstand that fascination, that warmth of affection interwoven in Ethelred's temperament. To my fancy, mother, there is no cavalier in the country, who in heart, appearance, and address, can outdo him. A princess might be proud of an alliance with one so truly noble in person, so generous in heart. Had you possessed two such sons as Ethelred, my dear mother, it would have been more than your due. This accounts for my being such an odd looking ugly pigmy. Ethelred has stolen all the good looks, and fine traits of character designed in part for others of his family. No matter, I do not believe it causes either Stephen or myself a single jealousy, or cows our spirits. If he were not our superior we should not feel the pride we now honestly feel in him. There is a pleasure in surveying him at times from head to foot, and mentally pronouncing, my noble brother! You know, mother, you are proud of him?'

Mistress Conyers laughed, while Tyrrel, after musing a few minutes, continued:

'Honestly speaking, mother, it will be a pity, indeed, if this maiden has made a fool of him. Will it not?'

'Yes, more than that, but we will hope it is not so,' replied Mistress Conyers, with a more thoughtful expression.

'No, mother, it is hardly possible either when I think of the poor captive of Harlech with her beautiful eyes resting on the Master of Cricceath, as I have observed them cast so stealthily. I feel sure she never could shut her heart against him. I must give my suspicion to the winds, and fancy my brain turned, for I am left in a maze.'

'Strange events come to pass, the origin of which cannot be given. I hope, in this case, the conclusion you have come to will be correct. I own that I, too, am puzzled.'

'That coincides with my views. Wherever a woman is concerned, more wise heads than ours have been puzzled to unriddle matters of a similar nature. Fair bewitchers and witches of all lands, spare me from your snares! Once more let me tell you, mother, if ever I am caught by them, I will go and free myself by a spring over the Castle cliff into the sea.'

He again shrugged up his shoulders, and made the hall echo with one of his irresistible comic laughs. Then with an odd expression of countenance, peculiar to himself, he leaped over all the furniture which came in his way, and hurried out of the hall.

Mistress Conyers sat musing for a few minutes, then rose with a thoughtful expression of feature yet glowing with maternal solicitude, and hastened to Ethelred's apartment. Without knocking for admittance, she, at once, opened the door, and stepped softly up to the sad and silent occupant. He was sitting with his back to the door by which she entered. His hand resting upon the table supported his head.

'What is it vexes your spirit, Ethelred?' said his mother in a low anxious tone of voice, leaning over him, and placing her hand gently upon his shoulder. 'Not having seen you today, and hearing of an interview having taken place between the son of Harlech and yourself, an unusual circumstance, I am come to learn what it all means, and why I find you thus cast down. You cause me fresh anxiety. Impart to your mother what is casting such a gloom over your spirit.' She felt his frame quivering under her outstretched hand, but he did not reply.

'Ethelred, tell me what brought the Welsh chief's son here. Hath Mistress Gladys ought to do with your distress, hath the maiden inflicted a thorn in your flesh? If so, the Virgin may forgive her, I never can. Heartless, indeed, must the woman be to bring trouble upon you. She is not worthy of your love, Ethelred.'

'Hold, mother, recall what you have said, not a shadow of censure must be cast upon Gladys, my noble and guileless Gladys. You have wronged her, and probed afresh the wounds in my afflicted heart.'

His head which had been partly raised, in giving utterance to these words, sunk heavily upon his arm still trembling with emotion. The anguish depicted in the face, touched the mother's heart as he raised it to meet hers. For a few minutes, she stood beside the object of her solicitude in silence, and then said:—

'Furthest of all things is it from your mother's wish to probe your wounds already too deep, but keep me not in the dark my dear Ethelred. I would fain share your trouble. I would sympathise with you, and not impute to Mistress Gladys that which is not her just due. I would not willingly wrong anyone. The bitterness I expressed towards the maiden, arose from my suspecting that one whom I love so dearly as yourself had been wronged by her.'

She then took Ethelred's hand and pressed it tenderly, repeating as if he were a child again, 'Tell me all, my beloved boy, I am your mother.'

After a slight hesitation, he imparted what had passed between himself and the object of his affection. During the recital, both mother and son felt overcome, and the interview was extremely painful; but she seemed to Ethelred a counsellor in whom he could confide, to whom he could unburden his feelings, and having her, he stood no longer solitary in his grief.

Although he had lost all hope of obtaining Gladys for his partner through life, he experienced, at intervals, a melancholy pleasure in speaking of her virtues, and convincing his mother, that hard as that which her lips had sealed was for him to support, she had acted with the noblest intentions. To be reconciled to his fate, as the son of Harlech had told him, was a part of his duty. He now felt the force of that advice, and determined to abide by it. He endeavoured also to persuade himself and his family that he was getting over his disappointment. He began to attend to the Castle Keep, and became again one among the home circle. All this would have augured well, but that a glance at his changed appearance told a different tale. His muscular frame appeared to be wasting away, and his visage was marked with a stamp above his years. Tyrrel, above all, lamented the contrast which had taken place. He watched his brother with inward misgivings, and would have vowed vengeance openly against the woman who had worked so much mischief, but that he felt by such an act he would cause his brother new pain. In private, he told his mother again and again that his views with regard to the female sex were confirmed.

'You shall one day see, mother, how "truth will force its way in spite of all obstacles" says Cato the wise or Catwg, as our neighbours the Cambro-Britons call him. You shall see and someday agree with me, in asserting that the pseudo-lords of the creation are nothing more nor less than the fools of the earth and the tools of women, the evil genii that inhabit it.'

'Methinks, considering I am a woman there is a want of civility in your speeches to your mother, Master Tyrrel,' said Mistress Conyers laughing. 'How comes it you disparage women, and indulge odd fancies in your head of men and things. I must warn you against encouraging such a propensity: maybe it will bring you into trouble in years to come.'

'Not a bit of it, mother, I purpose running through the world without so much as soiling the tips of my fingers with human miseries, or troubling my head with human evils. I will live within myself, like a snail in his shell. When I see a storm threatening, I will draw myself in and not show my horns again until I am sure it has burst or passed away. Above all, I will draw back into my shell rather than come in contact with a woman, if I stay in until I starve.'

'Surely, in your present excited state you forget that I am a woman, or you would never recapitulate these incivilities to a mother.'

'No, honoured mother, I do not forget that, but I consider you an exception. There is no woman in the world like you. There are exceptions in all things you know, from the race of men down to the rules in grammar.'

'At all times I have thought you an odd boy, Tyrrel. Today, methinks there is something in you more strange than ever. You speak in bitterness not in joke. You share an earnestness amid all unlike yourself. Recollect those who rail the most against the opposite sex, often get caught at last. How I shall laugh, when I see the self-confident little snail entangled in the meshes from which he so strenuously seeks to escape. The mischief makers, as you choose to think us women, will be the more on the alert to catch the hater of the sex, and they have caught wiser and older heads, my dear Tyrrel.'

'Nonsense, mother, there is no fear of their entrapping your son, Tyrrel, with his ugly phiz, saying nothing about his strong will to resist their wiles.'

'How serious you look, child, there is no bringing a smile upon your face. You speak feelingly, too, upon the matter, as if perchance your words belied you, and you had already experienced the torture caused by their incantations.'

'Not I, but you see in your more favoured son, in person, that melancholy spectacle. You are right in saying I am not myself today. I have been with Ethelred, and am unhappy about him. Who can look upon his altered face, his wasted frame, and listen to him trying to be gay, when the canker worm, we know, is at its meal, without feeling for him? I have great bitterness towards Gladys. It is absurd to make excuses for her conduct. It is all sophistry, superstition and nonsense; there is no extenuation whatever for her; it is as much as I can do to keep my tongue from uttering a volley of invectives against her.'

'Hush, for Ethelred's sake be softened towards her.'

'Oh, mother, how can I be softened? Ethelred is labouring under an infatuation. Mark the change she has wrought in him. You must feel for him, and think of Gladys as I do. Why disguise it? Would she could see the havoc she has made. Surely it would touch her heart.'

His face generally full of life and animation, gradually became overcast. When his eyes encountered those of his mother they oftentimes swam in tears. The attachment of the brothers was like that of Saul and Jonathan in Holy Writ.

CHAPTER X

The Troubled Heart—A Painful Position—An Old Relationship

IT was past midnight. The inmates of Cader y Cil had long been in the arms of sleep, save Gladys; from whose chamber-light dim ghost-like shadows were cast upon the overhanging rocks opposite her window. The unhappy girl felt a weight oppress her heart, and her brain burn with fever. Finding she could not sleep, she moved softly and silently up and down the apartment; but her gait was languid, as of one who sought and could find rest nowhere.

One moment she stood at her casement looking out upon a wilderness of rocks, which rose in shapeless masses darkening against the deep blue sky studded with a thousand stars. Then again she resumed her movement to and fro. Her eye at times resting upon a piece of furniture, or on some valued heirloom or long remembered gift. But, in reality, rocks, furniture, heirlooms or gifts, were viewed alike with a vacant indifference. She saw nothing, in reality, save the young Saxon's face—his figure came uppermost to her vision, only to recall her conviction that he was lost to her for ever. At intervals she sunk upon her knees, and struggling with her feelings would fain have prayed; but the weight upon her heart paralysed the utterance of an oraison. Every feeling, every thought, was concentrated in the one great sorrow, and she had to support it destitute of the aid she would gladly have craved.

The darkness of the night passed away. The dawn arose; but it brought no sunshine to her heart. On the contrary, it carried the conviction that the painful ordeal was again to be sustained of wearing a cheerful appearance when her heart was breaking, in order to disguise the secret from her family. She deemed the dawn unwelcome as it drew near. Unwonted weariness oppressed her, rendering the task of concealment still more onerous. It is difficult to struggle with a sinking heart. She sought her grandmother's apartment soon after the day opened, and prepared for her the morning repast.

She attended to her little wants, and listened to her whims and fancies with patient sweetness. She strove hard to be cheerful, and cautiously averted her tell-tale countenance when Katherine or Howel appeared in her presence. From day to day she lived in dread lest with their ever watchful eyes they should discover her secret; however improbable such a discovery might be, the consciousness of the possibility made it painful to her mind.

One evening as she was sitting with her grandmother and uncle, wearied by the constant stress laid upon her feelings, she had retired to a distant corner of the room, in the hopes of a few quiet moments; but had scarcely hid her face in her kerchief, and closed her eyes, when her grandmother missing her, exclaimed:

'Is Gladys there? How quiet she is—come child, I want to hear your cheerful voice. What is the matter with my wyres bach?'

The old lady held out her hand to receive her. Gladys came and seated herself by the old lady's side.

'I like to feel you near me. I love to know you are safe. Let me look at you, child. What has made you quiet so long? I have not been cheered by the sound of your voice for the whole day.'

She then caught Gladys by the hand, drew her close to herself, and with her aged eyes began scrutinizing her countenance more minutely.

'I cannot see if there is ought there which bespeaks a troubled heart,' said the old lady, impatiently; 'but your hand trembles. What is the matter, Gladys? I fear something ails the child.'

'I do not feel well,' replied the trembling girl; 'I have not felt well for some days,' she then cast an imploring look at her uncle, while her heart fluttered lest the betrayal of her secret was about to take place.

'Not well, my Gladys; why did you not say so before? Perchance the mountain air is too bracing for thee after living so long in the valley,' said the venerable dame with an expression of anxiety. 'You must not stay out so late of an evening. My Gladys not well—not well,' she repeated. 'It distresses me to hear it. I hope she is not growing weary of this wild spot, and it is that which affects her health and spirits.'

'Oh, no,' exclaimed Gladys, 'my mountain home is as dear to me as ever.'

'Then what is it, my wyres bach? These little fingers are still trembling—something must be the matter.'

'Methinks, mother, a little change would do her good,' said Kynfin, drawing near and endeavouring to divert the old lady from further scrutiny. 'My uncle, Grono, is anxious I should go and see him before he is numbered with his forefathers. He also expressed a wish that Gladys might accompany me. Let her go, we shall not be long away.'

'How dreary I shall again be without you,' ejaculated the old lady, neither expressing a negative nor an affirmative to Kynfin's proposal.

Folding her hands together, with a blank expression upon her features, she sat for a few minutes in profound silence. At length she resumed.

'I fear I grow selfish and exacting in my declining years. I would not willingly part with you for an hour. How then can I be reconciled to be separated from you for days, perhaps weeks?'

'You would do that to restore her to health, mother. Gladys is not well. Change of scene would do her good. You will consent to let her come with me for her own sake. Will you not let her come?'

'And is my Gladys really not well—it pains me,' murmured the grandmother. 'If it is change of air she really needs, I must consent; but it will be a weary watch till she returns.'

'The time will soon pass away,' observed Gladys, kissing her grandmother affectionately, and feeling, in some degree, relieved at the thought of a respite from her painful position.

The necessary arrangements were shortly after made for their departure. When Kynfin Tudor and his niece were about to set off, Katherine Howel and little Morris hastened forward to wish them a safe journey, and with native pathos, repeated:

'Brysiwch yn ol, brysiwch yn ol (make haste back).'

Katherine unable to control her feelings, with tears in her eyes, affectionately embraced the knees of the daughter of Harlech, while she sat upon her horse again re-iterating:

'Meistres bach anwyl brysiwch yn ol, brysiwch yn ol!'

With the voice of their faithful attendants still sounding in their ears, our travellers left the Cwm, and commenced their ride without an escort over the hills. Gladys, in the fullness of her heart, could not refrain from expressing her gratitude to her uncle for his consideration in removing her from home for a time.

'I rejoice to be alone with you, dear uncle, it soothes me to feel no concealment between us is required. The cause of my sorrow is in your possession, and from past experience I know you will bear with me, and help to cheer me when my weak heart is oppressed. I wish, uncle, I had both a stronger heart and a stronger will, I could then bear my trials better. I need the aid of Heaven, but I have no power to ask it. Is it not strange I cannot pray, and yet I can feel the only hope which supports me, is my trust in God. My faith is in Him alone, but it slumbers in the darkness of my soul. I feel that in years to come I shall not regret what I have done; but, oh how great is the cost!'

'I know it, and feel for you, Gladys darling. May God support you. It is well you put your trust in Him, who alone can give you that which you need. All earthly consolations fail—they pass away like the mist upon the hills. I have learned by long experience that we must look to no other source for comfort.'

'Yes, uncle, but would I could pray,' ejaculated Gladys, with a look of sorrow. 'This makes my trial more hard to bear. Why is my heart so dead? Why do my lips refuse to supplicate, when it would bring me comfort? Am I forsaken by Him? I sometimes question it.'

'No, Gladys, you must wait His time. Prayer will return to your heart. Rest assured God is near at hand both to comfort and support you. Wait His time.'

Gladys relapsed into silence. Throughout the journey she

was less communicative than she had ever been before, though none had more of her confidence than her uncle, and none could be more considerate and affectionate than he was towards her.

On their arrival at the venerable chieftain's domain, a spot from early associations rendered dear to Gladys, they were conducted at once into Grono's presence. The old man had nearly reached a century in years, yet Kynfin who had not seen him for a long time, thought him little changed.

As they approached, the veteran warrior was sitting upright in his chair, with the same contented and benevolent expression upon his features as of old. The same silky hair fell over his shoulders, white as the driven snow. The same clear complexion, with his furrowed cheeks streaked with rose colour like a summer apple, imparting at that time of life an unusual lustre to his eyes. In conclusion, the Welsh chief was a picture of old age under its most pleasing and cheerful aspect.

The moment Grono recognized Kynfin, and was introduced to Gladys, his mild blue eyes were immediately raised to her face, greeting her with an expression of joy. Kynfin felt interested as he stood watching the aged man, examining the features of his lovely young kinswoman. Grono's heart was swelling with pride, and when he bowed his head in order to listen more attentively to the tones of her voice, tears bedewed his cheeks. Kynfin guessed what was passing in his mind. In the lifetime of Tudor and Aliano, they had been his special favourites. In the presence of their child, the past did not return without many painful recollections.

'Thy dear mother's soft-toned voice, yes, just like that of Aliano,' murmured the old man. Then taking her hand, he placed it on his shrivelled palms, and felt her slender fingers, repeating,

'And those little fingers too, thy mother's over again, my Gladys bach. This was kind of you, Kynfin, thus bringing her to see me. In these disturbed times, I hardly hoped my request would have been granted. I thought, perchance, Mistress Tudor would have raised objections to her taking the journey, merely to see an old man on the brink of his grave. Yes, it was kind of you both, permitting her to come. The sight of you, and the sound of your voices, my children, warms that of the old man. You are welcome, right welcome to the house, where many of your renowned ancestors have lived and died, loyal to their prince, and faithful to their country. Honour shall be shown to my young kinswomen, such as that to which she is entitled; waiting women shall be in attendance. While she is my guest, all that she can desire shall be hers. Let me hope in becoming acquainted with this forest district so famed for affording refuge to our princes in time of danger, and under the shadow of our sacred hill, the temple of our bards, her young heart will rejoice. I am proud of my country, proud of my ancestors. Ah, Kynfin is smiling at my enthusiasm,' concluded the old man, for an instant averting his eye from his young companion's face. After a short pause, with renewed warmth of manner, and an encouraging tone of voice, he again resumed:—

'Now, let me hear from your own lips, my Gladys, what the old man above all desires to hear that though you have been a partaker of the Saxon Yorkists' bread, you have not been corrupted by them that you are still a Lancastrian in heart, and regard these Yorkists our oppressors and scourgers, with a patriotic hatred as it should be. Say that, my child, and it will act as a cordial to comfort the old man's heart when it is winter time with him.'

'I think, honoured Sir, I can faithfully say so,' replied Gladys impressively, Sir Gilbert, and her imprisonment at Harlech Castle being only present in her mind. 'My sojourn with the Saxons did not efface what must be engraved on every true Cambrian's heart—bitterness towards their oppressors.'

'Thou art a noble daughter of Wales!' cried old Grono, patting her fondly on the head. 'Like thy patriotic grandsire, a true Einion in heart. Our bondage under the Yorkists' reign has been a hard trial. It has re-kindled tenfold our hatred towards the common foe. God and all the saints in the calendar protect us, my children. These are hard times for our beloved Cambria.'

The veteran soldier spoke with more bitterness of feeling than he was ever known to do before.

Grono's dwelling, it will be remembered, was in the centre of the hills. It was surrounded by woods, torrents, and crags. Snowdon, or Yr Wyddfa, best known by that name, to which Grono had already alluded, stood preeminent in grandeur, amongst the conspicuous mountain range so famed for its beauty.

Gladys had passed a week in this romantic district. Her innate love for her native scenery made her appreciate it even in her sorrow. She now wandered alone among the wilds. For the first time, after her trial and parting with Ethelred, upon the crags of Yr Wyddfa, she found utterance in prayer. She afterwards appeared calm and more resigned. Would all might have terminated here.

In better spirits than usual, she one day set out upon a

ramble, tracking her way by the banks of a torrent, leading through the Snowdon forest. She continued her route deep in thought. Pausing on one occasion to gaze with renewed pleasure on the ever-varying scenery, she descried a diminutive youth on the opposite side of the stream, making his way through the brushwood. A few minutes afterwards, he sprang across a wooden bridge, and stood with a knotty staff in his hand, on the path before her. In an instant, she recognized Tyrrel Conyers.

'Mistress Gladys,' said he, 'I heard you were in these parts. I left the castle this morning with the intention of seeking you. I am fortunate in having encountered the object of my search.' He paused and surveyed his companion, who was startled at his sudden appearance. After a slight hesitation in his speech, he continued:—

'I crave your pardon for thus intruding upon your solitude, and for the plain language I am about to use. The emergency of the case prompts it. I come to tell you that through your cruel and unaccountable conduct, cheerfulness has disappeared from our hearth. My brother is sadly changed, you would not know him. Listen to me, Mistress Gladys, if ever a man had a regard for woman, it is Ethelred who feels a regard for you. How have you requited him?' He stood as if expecting a reply. Again he resumed: 'Cannot I soften your heart towards him? Cannot I persuade you to recall your cruel decision? Let me entreat you to send me back to my brother with the glad tidings? Let me be that joyful messenger, and the past shall be forgotten?'

Gladys stood supporting herself, pale and trembling by leaning against the bough of a tree. Tyrrel thought he saw her lips move, but could hear no sound.

'Gladys,' repeated he, drawing closer to her, and looking in her face, then taking her hand, 'do you hear me, Ethelred is very ill, we fear his health.'

Still Gladys remained silent.

Again Tyrrel repeated her name, and became more earnest in manner. 'Have you no heart; do you shut out hope when you know what you have done? I implore you to listen to my appeal on behalf of my brother. Be no longer indifferent to one whom you may say from boyhood, has been faithful and devoted to you. Let me go and tell Ethelred you recall all your cruel words. Let me tell him, Gladys,' he lowered his voice— 'you will be his wife!'

Tyrrel once more scrutinized her face. It was expressive of deep emotion. There was a ray of hope at least, he fancied he saw it.

'Yes, yes,' continued he, 'I knew your heart would reproach you when you heard what sorrow you had brought upon Ethelred. I knew you would relent. Speak, only whisper the words. Speak, Mistress Gladys?'

The colour mounted to her cheek, and faded away. She looked the picture of mute despair. Her companion could not comprehend her feelings.

'Mistress Gladys, why do you hesitate?' said Tyrrel half angrily, 'it rests alone with you to restore Ethelred to health.'

She withdrew her hand, and shook her head mournfully. At the same time, so strange an expression passed over her features that Tyrrel was puzzled. He eyed her for a moment in silence, secretly hoping he was gaining ground. Once more he was resolved to see what his persuasions could do. In a kinder tone than he had before assumed, he continued:—

'Gladys, you are deceiving yourself. You know you cannot

be insensible to Ethelred's manly affection, you cannot really undervalue his love. Think of him, Gladys, and how deeply and sincerely he cares for you. If you would not like me to convey the message I crave, let me only go and tell him you will see him again. Tomorrow, shall I say tomorrow in this spot? Shall I?'

'No! No! No!' cried Gladys, in a firm determined tone of voice, but a wild and agonized expression of feature. 'I cannot, Master Tyrrel, I cannot. Leave me; you might have spared me this,' she covered her face with her hands, and pressed against the tree more strongly for support.

'Spare you, and is this your only reply to my intercession on behalf of my brother?' repeated Tyrrel, standing aloof while he surveyed her with a look of indignation. 'What is your heart made of, lady? Those who have no mercy for others can expect none themselves. I have said that through your cruelty Ethelred has become changed, so much changed you would scarcely know him. I have told you he is ill that we have anxious fears for his health. Will nothing touch your heart? Mistress Gladys, I would understand, if I could, what all this unfeelingness means? You cannot regard my brother. Do not endeavour to make me believe you do. Your country's superstitions and bigoted doctrines destroy the finer sentiments and natural good feelings of your heart. There is some other cause beyond that you have given for your cruel conduct, I can see it written in your countenance. Before I leave you, daughter of Harlech, before I return to my brother, without one word of solace from you, suffer me to impress upon your mind that you alone are answerable for what you have done. As surely as I fling my staff into yonder torrent, may you meet with your reward.' Tyrrel then with an appearance of suppressed anger, whirled his staff over the precipice, into the foaming eddy beneath.

Gladys saw his face flushed with passion, she heard his retreating steps as he bounded across the bridge. His angry and ominous words were still ringing in her ears, till they seemed to press upon her brain, and her ideas became confused.

'Ethelred is ill, I am answerable for what I have done,' were the only words she felt she comprehended, or was able to articulate. With a strange effort, she straggled forward in the direction where she had seen the staff fall, until she reached the brink of the rocks overhanging the torrent: looking down into the roaring cataract beneath, she again repeated Tyrrel's parting words, for they came pressing upon her brain, until the objects before her seemed to swim in wild confusion. Scarcely conscious of what she did, she wrung her hands, and called aloud on Ethelred.

At the same instant her foot slipped, and staggering forward, her fate appeared inevitable in the foaming torrent beneath, when her uncle fortunately came up at the moment, and arrested her footsteps.

'Gladys,' cried he, in a voice of terror, clasping her in his powerful arms, 'how you have indeed terrified me, what were you about to do, my Gladys bach?'

'I do not know, uncle,' said she looking vacantly in his face. 'Ethelred is ill. Oh this weight that presses on my heart!' and before Kynfin was well aware of what had occurred to place her in her existing situation, she sighed deeply, and became suddenly insensible.

It was a considerable time before Kynfin could restore her to consciousness. His own alarm was great upon seeing his beloved ward so near falling over the precipice; but he had witnessed Tyrrel Conyers's menacing movement in taking leave of Gladys, and guessing the youth's communication could only be of a painful nature, had hurried forward more rapidly in time to prevent a fatal accident to her whom he loved and esteemed beyond all others in the world, the centre of his family hopes, and the beloved of its dependants, although overshadowed for a time.

Gladys, under her weak state of health, experienced from Tyrrel's unfortunate interview a severe shock to a frame already too much weakened. For some days she lay almost lifeless from exhaustion. Sometimes stupor seemed to overpower her; so that apprehensions were entertained lest her reason should suffer. Kynfin began, at length, to question himself as to whether he were acting right in permitting his brother's child to sacrifice her feelings, and cast a blight upon her existence for the sake of her people. The sacrifice in itself was laudable, but was it required of her, under the painful circumstances then existing? He began to doubt where he had not before doubted. Gladys might lose her reason, which to him was a terrible thought. Were her parents in existence would they have acted in persuading her as he had done? Would they have witnessed her sufferings without seeking to ameliorate them? With such a nature as Gladys possessed, he knew there was little hope of her affections ever undergoing change. The deep-rooted affection she bore towards the Saxon would only slumber in her heart, and cause her secret sorrow throughout life. Hers would thus become a dreary future; how could he live and see one so beloved in the flower of her youth, bowed and broken in spirit, when it might be in his power to remove the evil? It would be an everlasting reproach on his conscience; he therefore determined he would henceforth seek to reconcile his people to the granddaughter of their late chief forming an alliance with the Saxon. The time had arrived that the sufferings of his ward should cease, under the absorbing wish that she should be restored to happiness, all former scruples which had appeared insuperable barriers being cleared away.

From over-anxiety about the health and future welfare of his niece, Kynfin could not rest. He frequently, during the night, entered Gladys's chamber: the same chamber which had been appropriated to her mother during the time she had partaken of Grono's hospitality. While he sat by her bedside, the well-remembered objects in the room recalled the past back too vividly to his imagination. Aliano as he had first seen her in the freshness of youth, rose uppermost in his mental vision, and the memory of the past troubled his spirit. Then Tudor followed with his manly carriage and open countenance reminding him of happy days never to return. Gladys meanwhile was buried in slumber.

From this visionary scene, he turned to look upon the face in which he traced the delicate features of her mother. There were, too, the same intelligent eyes and noble frankness of expression so peculiar in the father. In her they lived again. How doubly dear then Gladys was to him.

Since he had become the guardian of his niece, how often had he been a melancholy witness of her trials, some of which he might have averted. He thought of Dhu ap Rhys, and the painful events which had transpired on board the *Eryr*. The rover's passion for Gladys, his own terror, remorse, and the agonising feelings he had experienced during the time she was in the power of his dangerous comrade the pirate. He could only feel with an involuntary shudder how thankful he was those trials were over. Still trouble remained, his heart was not at ease, nor could it be otherwise, until peace was restored to the self-denying and noble-minded girl, in whom the greater share of his thoughts and love were concentrated. Again his former resolutions to bring about her union with the Saxon occupied his thoughts. In the excitement of the moment, he repeated not to himself, but aloud almost unconsciously:—

'Yes, heaven will aid us. Happiness shall be secured to her through the medium of her uncle.'

His words awoke the sleeping girl.

'What was my uncle saying?' said she, endeavouring to rouse herself.

'That I will be a witness no longer of your sufferings. They shall cease. Gladys, my child, I am about to seek some means to reconcile our people to your union with Ethelred the Saxon, who we all know to be a worthy scion of the great House of Conyers. I doubt if the sacrifice be required of you. By constant prayer, I feel confident good will come of this foreign alliance, and not evil as we apprehended. Be comforted, therefore, let me no longer see upon you the face of sorrow.'

Gladys looked very earnestly in Kynfin's face. A moment afterwards she covered her eyes with her hands as if to collect her thoughts, and then replied:—

'Your words, dear uncle, have startled me, they seem to have roused me to a sense of my real position. I have been so occupied with the intensity of my own sorrow that the thought never occurred to me before, that by fretting and giving way to my grief, I was causing my dear uncle to feel great anxiety and pain. Pray forgive me! Do not I entreat you, out of kindness of heart, and sympathy for me in my distress, allow yourself to act contrary to your sense of what is right. Often I have deemed my trial greater than I could support, and have murmured too frequently. Do not now be pained about me. I feel the extreme of my suffering is past, the strong feeling of opposition is fast bending to my lot. You must not, my dear uncle, deceive yourself in your over-anxiety for my happiness. Lead me not from the path of duty, which, in the words of my noble grandfather, is the only sure path which can conduct us to unalloyed happiness. Let me beg of you not to despair, on account of my present depression, or suppose I shall never have more strength of mind than I have hitherto shown. Give me time. We all know the severest trials can be surmounted if we only possess the will. It is the will we lack. Let my dear uncle rather than hold out hope, where there is no hope, aid me by prayer that my will may be to do my duty, not reluctantly nor with a stubborn heart, but with a free and cheerful spirit.'

'In giving utterance to your pure sentiments, my dear Gladys you cast me in the shade, and I stand reproved,' said Kynfin in a voice almost choked with emotion. 'God bless you, my noble child, and may He reward you for this truly great deed, from which no temptation is able to seduce you.'

'No, uncle, withhold your praise. Let me not deceive you. Do not commend me where there is no commendation due. You do not really know how weak I am. I tremble when I think how nearly I have yielded to my own desires. Twice, nay thrice I have been upon the point of breaking my determination, and many times would I have recalled my parting words to Ethelred. Again, and again I have wished the noble deed, as you term it, unsaid, undone. See, my dear uncle, how your love for me blinds you to my faults. I only need succour as an infant needs succour. Let me then again entreat you not to lead me astray, lest I should at last fall. Rather aid and encourage me to work out my mission as required of me. The idol must be banished from my heart. It is demanded, and sacred must that demand be.' A slight tremor passed over her frame while she continued:—

'For the future, I must strive to have no interest of my own. My country and my people must be my all. I must have no concern but to make you all happy in the Cwm. This must be my prayer, and it ought to bring me peace, for we are sent into the world to live for others, not ourselves. Let us remember, too, how the Lady of Gêst prophesied that a happy day is dawning for our dear Cambria, and that I have been appointed to take a part in that emancipation of our country which is to bring joy to our people. Will not their joy be my joy? Ought I to despair of happiness, when I think of the exalted task? Rather should it be a stimulus to cheer me on till the day comes, and then when it does come, shall I not once more feel the glow of true happiness warm and cheer my heart?'

In giving utterance to the last sentence, unbidden tears stood in her eyes, though when her gaze encountered Kynfin, her face was irradiated with a smile.

Weeks elapsed. The visit to Grono was drawing nigh to a close, and Gladys appeared cheerful. With her peculiar gentle, and attentive manner towards those declining in years, she could not fail to win the old man's heart. He was as loath to part with her as he had been to separate from her mother in days too long departed.

On the eve of their departure, the venerable chieftain called Gladys to him.

'Gladys!' said he, 'you must accept from me these parting gifts. They are the greatest treasures I possess.' Between his shrivelled fingers he held the brilliant cross, which had been presented to him by Henry's Consort, Queen Margaret, in token of her gratitude for his protection and hospitality.

'This, my child,' said he, 'you will value for its original owner's sake, our unhappy, unfortunate, Queen Margaret of Anjou. I rejoice to have an opportunity of placing the gift in your hands. Never part with it.' He then took from a casket, which was resting on his knee, an armlet made of Adder stones, or rather Druids' beads, so well-known in Wales by the name of gleinian y nadroedd. He drew near her, and fastened it upon her left arm, saying, as Kynfin thought, in an ominous tone:

'There are stormy days yet to come before the sun dawns upon our oppressed Cambria, you need a talisman, my sweet kinswoman. Wear it on your left arm, and do not forget the donor, the aged Grono, whose eyes have been gladdened by a sight of the noble daughter of Harlech, the last descendant of the great tribe of Einion.'

CHAPTER XI

A Royal Decease—Courtier Intrigues— Exiles Unexpectedly Emancipated

'Son of Harlech, the tyrant is dead! Edward of York is dead! The cruel and incontinent Edward is dead!' Thus cried the men of the Cwm, who had assembled before the walls of Cader y Cil with the joyful intelligence.

The children shouted on all sides: 'Wi! Wi! Wi! The tyrant is dead! The king of the pale rose is dead!'

The widow of Ap Jevan clasped her hands together with an expression of great thankfulness. Kynfin Tudor's features brightened. The venerable Howel shook upon his chair, muttering incessantly: 'O diolch! O moliant!'(expressions of thankfulness).

The monarch had died suddenly at the age of forty-two, the slave of pleasure, destitute of any sentiment of humanity; rapacious, vindictive, sagacious, bold, perfidious, and brutal. It was rumoured that he died of poison, or by some other foul means. He was fortunate without any claim on the score of merit, or any reason, but that it was his destiny. The heir of York was yet but an infant. The general feeling was that the house of Lancaster would again struggle for England's disputed crown. Great excitement appeared throughout North and South Wales. Letters were privately despatched to the Earl of Richmond, who was still in Brittany. In reply, the Earl expressed great unwillingness to hazard an attempt to obtain the crown of England while the brutal Richard of Gloucester had influence in the realm. Things, were thus in suspense when a melancholy event took place in England. The Prince of Wales and his infant brother were murdered in the Tower of London. Whispers were heard on all sides that the Protector Richard was the perpetrator of the atrocious deed. Soon afterwards, by artful and insidious means, the Duke of Gloucester got himself crowned King of England, with the title of Richard the Third. This bold and daring proceeding caused division and discontent throughout both England and Wales. Letters were again sent from the adherents of Lancaster, in Cambria, to the Earl of Richmond, entreating him to make a descent, and free the land from Saxon bondage. He was flesh of their flesh, blood of their blood, and in the country of his nativity, everyone was ready to receive him with open arms.

The Countess of Richmond hearing of the great zeal evinced on the part of the Welsh towards her son became alarmed. With maternal anxiety, she sent repeated messengers to him, earnestly entreating him to take no step towards gaining the crown. A fatality had marked the arms of the Red Rose, and Richard of Gloucester was a determined foe, much to be dreaded both in the field and cabinet.

For some months, no decided step was taken. Henry of Richmond, however, was extremely gratified to find he would be heartily welcomed, and in particular be warmly remembered by the good people of Wales. He humoured them by forming plans for the future, in case of a fortunate concatenation of circumstances. The words of the Lady of Gêst flashed across his mind, and with the good Jasper of

Hatfield, he would frequently turn the conversation to that singular prediction communicated by Kynfin Tudor from the prophetess. Jasper would, at times, jestingly say:

'Well, Henry, before you take the precipitous step, you must send and consult Kynfin Tudor and the good Lady of Gêst, or as she is better known in the country, by the title of "the Dewines".'

The Dewines had followed Richard of Gloucester through all the passages of his life, she had often haunted his footsteps. He now sat on England's throne, and was in the zenith of his ambition. She had shifted her abode from the Welsh bay, and repeatedly the words 'fratricide, regicide, murderer of the innocent,' sounded mysteriously through the galleries of Windsor. Sometimes, in sepulchral tones, the sounds seemed to come from behind the tapestry. Richard was superstitious, and dreaded to encounter the witch. While he feared, he sought every means to destroy her. It was in vain, for she always eluded his emissaries. Some thought that she, herself, had taken King Edward's life. The royal household were terrified at her name, so that this ginger woman was not only the terror of the palace, but she was reported to haunt Windsor forest. One day she encountered Richard of Gloucester alone, separated from the rest of his hunting party. She boldly told him he was not safe upon his throne, which owned another master. He, therefore, became doubly anxious to cut off the Earl of Richmond, the last hope of Lancaster. He endeavoured, by bribery, to prevail upon the Duke of Brittany to deliver him up. Duke Francis was not inclined to enter into negotiations with one so unscrupulous in evil.

'I have made no agreement with the new King of England. It is my intention to favour the young Earl.'

These were the startling words of the vacillating old man. A short time before, he had been bitter against the exiles. The desired alliance between the fair Claudine de Montfort and Henry of Richmond was at an end. The artful Landais, who had regained his former position, revenged himself upon the exiled nobles, and remained their secret enemy. But he was surprised, almost as much as Richard of England, at his august master's sudden resolution to befriend Richmond. Landais, therefore, sought the first opportunity of opposing him.

'I should wish to know what are your Grace's intentions,' said Landais, drawing himself up to the side of the imbecile duke, and shouting in his ear. 'I cannot see any point whatever to be gained, now the unfortunate Claudine de Montfort is no more. You have no desire of bestowing the Princess Anne upon the Earl of Richmond. Will your Grace tell me what is your motive, for I am puzzled.'

'Peter, Peter, speak not so fast, nor so loud,' said the old man, with a nervous shaking of the head. 'My object I will endeavour to explain if thou wilt give me time. If we can only secure the crown of England to Henry of Richmond, he will restore to me his earldom, to which, thou already knowest, I have pretensions—that is my object.'

Landais rose, and walking across the room, appeared to be much surprised. The artful treasurer was at his old game. He had to play two parts; one to administer to his own avarice, and the other to dupe his master.

'That will be no easy point to carry, your Grace,' said Landais. 'I am afraid you will only get into trouble by intermeddling with these foreigners.'

'Peter! Peter! Bear with an old man. Thwart me not in this matter. It may be my weakness, but I have a particular wish that my rights should be restored to me. I have promised the Earl of Richmond that I will raise troops and aid him to the full extent of my power—look to it!'

Landais stroked his chin, looked thoughtful, and added that he should be sorry to thwart his Grace, since it was his particular wish. He advised him to consider the matter well before he touched a point so difficult to manage.

At this time Landais was carrying on a clandestine negotiation with Richard, whose bribes were irresistible, and Duke Francis was deceived. No orders were given to raise the troops his Grace had particularized. Meanwhile, the young Earl, received kindly at the palace, was led to suppose that preparations were in progress, not only in his own country, but in Brittany, to enable him to contest the crown of England. Henry was in high spirits at the turn affairs had taken. In the presence of his Grace in the Cathedral at Rennes, he made a solemn declaration that he would espouse the Princess Elizabeth, the eldest daughter of Edward of York; and thus he considered himself on the eve of success, and the fulfilment of the Dewines of Gêst's prophecy.

In this fancied security, with these flattering prospects before him, the Earl of Richmond suddenly discovered, by letters from his friends in England, who were kept as spies at King Richard's court, that treachery was at work against him.

'This is Landais!' exclaimed Henry much chagrined. 'He is at the bottom of all the mischief.'

'It would have been better had we more strictly attended to Kynfin Tudor's warnings in regard to Landais,' said the Earl of Pembroke '"Never sleep while you are in the presence of that man, Jasper of Hatfield," were almost the last words Kynfin addressed to me.'

'Would I were safe and sound over the borders of the dukedom,' said Henry with much vehemence.

'I would recommend your seeking assistance immediately from the youthful Charles of France,' said the Earl of Pembroke, 'obtain a passport from him, and you may get over the borders.'

'That is easier said than executed,' replied Henry, 'but we will do what we can towards that object. It would be worth a king's ransom to outwit that contemptible smooth-faced Landais. Suppose we send Kit Urswick. He is an energetic fellow, and will do anything to serve us?'

Shortly after this conversation, Christopher Urswick was despatched to the King of France, and returned with wonderful speed bearing the desired passport. The anxiety the exiled nobles felt during his absence was great; and they were almost as much embarrassed when the passport arrived. How were they to escape from the dukedom, under the surveillance which scarcely permitted them to quit their own residence for a mile, without some of Landais's spies being at their heels. Fortunately an occurrence took place which they eagerly embraced. The Duke of Brittany had been a great invalid for some time, but was now convalescent.

'Now, Henry, is your time,' said the Earl of Pembroke, 'all the English nobles and their suite of gentlemen, shall accompany me to pay court to the old Duke, and address to him Our congratulations upon his recovery. This will divert the attention of our own countrymen, and with them, that of Landais's spies.'

'If you do that, we shall not escape together,' said Richmond, with an air of disappointment.

'That is of no consequence, do not trouble your head about

me, Henry,' said Jasper of Hatfield. 'It is your safety that we must consider. Let us manage the affair as it would be done, if our worthy kinsman, Kynfin Tudor, were here. You may take five as an escort. Disguise yourselves as merchants, be careful not to betray yourselves, and stop nowhere until the borders of the Dukedom are passed.'

The Earl of Pembroke and his suite having quitted Vannes for the Duke's palace, as thus arranged, and the Earl of Richmond having made all the preparations necessary, he set off with his companions upon their adventurous journey. Soon after quitting Vannes, they left the high road, and took their way across the country. They were fortunate enough to attain the borders in safety. They were so closely followed by the minister's spies that not an hour after they had reached Anjou, their pursuers appeared upon the borders.

Henry of Richmond was received with great courtesy by the youthful monarch of France. The disquietude of his court at that period, prevented Charles from giving the fugitive Earl immediate assistance, but protection to his person was freely bestowed. He remained in perfect security, therefore, until the Earl of Oxford, who was already known to be a warm partisan of the House of Lancaster, was released from the castle of Ham, in Picardy, and hastened to join Henry, in order to offer him his services.

CHAPTER XII

An Unexpected Interview— The War-cry Raised—A Tyrant Dethroned—The Prophetess

Two years had elapsed after the welcome intelligence had been brought to the Cwm of King Edward's demise. The weather at that time was sultry. Late one fine day, Gladys and her uncle had strolled down the glen. The owls were hooting in the woods, the martin cats were answering one another from rock to rock, and the sheep and goats were browsing amongst the heather. It was a calm and soft evening. The tints upon the mountains were more than usually lovely. The reflections in the lake slept in beauty, and the purple bloom upon the heath, in all its rich profusion, was wafted on the breeze, and heightened the attraction of the hour.

The harassed expression commonly seen in Kynfin Tudor's countenance was gone, leaving no trace behind, and in its place there was a placid look of content on his features. Gladys's soft voice was pouring into his ear one of the adventures of her childhood, recalled by the locality. The reference to her early years brought a more than usually animated expression into her countenance, a momentary expression of something like happiness, that made Kynfin Tudor's heart more at ease than usual. He knew how much his charge had suffered, how often she had wept in secret over her sorrows, he who had witnessed her resignation to her position, and duty, knew as well how to rejoice in her smiles, and to be thankful that peace was once more restored to her bosom.

He had been her monitor and comforter before, he had now become everything to her, and she to him, a devoted parent to a dutiful child. Kynfin Tudor was naturally well endowed in mind, and possessed a refined taste. His spirit was no longer disquieted by sorrow and misfortune. He began to develop more and more its better qualities. The eccentricities and wildnesses of his earlier life, seemed to have given way to more consistent views and more matured action. In the sight of Gladys, Aliano's gift, he seemed to take a new character, still strictly performing the duty which had devolved upon him of being a father to the orphan. He had never felt anything approaching real happiness until now, when all his past turbulence of spirit was subdued. With his arms around the slender form of his beloved charge, they continued their walk till they drew near some cottages, to which Gladys was bound, intending to pay a visit to a poor woman, one of her people who was in ill health. At the cottage door she was about to enter, two horsemen had halted, apparently making inquiries. Kynfin wondered who the strangers could be, and what could have brought them there, when Dafydd Ap Thomas, the friend of his younger days, seeing him approach, suddenly sprang from his horse, and shook him by the hand.

'Kynfin Tudor,' said he, 'I am in search of you, I come with intelligence in which we are particularly interested, all, at least, who have aided Lancaster to escape from the hands of his enemies; all such will rejoice to hear that Henry of

Richmond has landed at Milford Haven, and that the cause of the Red Rose may again prosper. Henry is on his march by North Wales to Shrewsbury. Sir Walter Herbert has allowed him to pass unmolested; Rhys Ap Thomas, and John Savage, have already joined him with their men. Here is a letter from the Earl to yourself. I have spread the news far and wide, and every heart in Cambria is rejoicing. Our friends are preparing to join the good cause once more. He who is blood of our blood, flesh of our flesh, the child of our soil. Hure! Hure! Shall we not support him?'

Ap Dafydd's pleasure knew no bounds. With the true spirit of his race again kindling in his bosom, the loud war-cry of his Cambrian fathers broke from his lips. This cry was taken up by every man in the Cwm. Loud were the echoes which rebounded from rock to rock. One happy scene of rejoicing and confusion intermingled together alike new and unexpected, was witnessed on every side.

'Rhyddid am byth! (Freedom for ever!) Hure! Hure! Lancaster for ever! Down with the Saxon Kings! No more tyrants! No more Saxon encroachments! No more cruel enactments against our bards. Hure! Hure! One of our soil, one of our blood. The Red Dragon banner will again float over old Cambria! Hure! Hure!' Such were the words passed from lip to lip with an excitement arising almost to madness.

Kynfin Tudor addressed his brave countrymen, and then gave orders that every man should furbish up his arms, and be ready to march with him at break of day, to join their prospective sovereign, who had conveyed to him that especial request.

As they retraced their steps to Cader y Cil, Gladys exhibited unwonted feelings of joy and apprehension, hope and anxiety.

In secret, she had worked the Red Dragon banner, upon a ground of green and white silk,[19] in anticipation of the present event. She mentioned the subject to her uncle, and expressed a wish that he would take the banner to the Earl of Richmond, with her petition that he would display it before his army on the battlefield against the Yorkists.

Kynfin was at a loss to express the surprise and admiration he felt on this revelation of her patriotism. He pressed his beloved ward to his heart, and craved a blessing upon her head.

This demonstration of her uncle's affection drove the banner from her mind, her thoughts at once turned to him, her stay and support, who was leaving her to go to the field; to rekindle those Wars of the Roses, the narrative of which had appalled her childish mind, and the recollections of which were still fraught with terror. She could not refrain from expressing her fears. Kynfin reminded her of the prophetic words of the Dewines, and cheered her by picturing their return to the home of their forefathers, when the gates of old Harlech would be thrown open to receive them, and they should once more stand upon the battlements that overlooked the broad waters of their favourite bay, repeating once more:—

'This is my home, the home of my forefathers. I am restored to my inheritance.'

Before the sun had gilded the mountain tops, the daughter of Harlech stood upon one of the heights, watching her uncle and the men of the Cwm winding their way through the pass.

---

[19] 'Henry VII, sensibly appealing to that union of local attachment, innate honour, and perhaps prejudice, which constitutes what is called "nationality", displayed a red dragon upon a standard of green and white silk at Bosworth.'—*W. L. Cambro-Briton.*

Their wild war cry echoed, and re-echoed among the rooks. She waved her handkerchief, and breathed a prayer for their return. They were soon over the hills on their march, halting not many miles from the little town of Dolgelley, awaiting there Henry of Richmond's arrival.

The Earl made his appearance at the head of a large body of men. Ap Dafydd's delight was unbounded, at beholding unexpectedly his old friend Jasper of Hatfield. Expressions of lively satisfaction were exchanged on their again meeting in their own country. The Earl reminded Kynfin of circumstances in which Henry and himself had both been concerned in connection with him. He assured Kynfin they should ever feel how much they were indebted to him, particularly in the instances when their assassination was contemplated in France, and in Pembrokeshire, and when they would, but for him, have fallen victims to the cruel monarch of England. The Earl further informed his kinsman that they had met with many misfortunes in Brittany after his departure.

The Red Dragon banner with a message from Gladys, was presented on the following morning to the Earl of Richmond. He received it with grateful acknowledgments, and proceeded on his march, full of hope, and in high heroic spirit. He recited to Kynfin by what means he himself had escaped from Brittany, and the various difficulties he had encountered before he could prevail upon the youthful monarch of France to lend him military aid during his first advance. Notwithstanding the secret encouragement he had received by communication from England, and the confidence he particularly placed in the hearts of his Cambrian friends an additional force was necessary, before he could undertake his bold enterprise.

'I have been in a state of great anxiety, son of Harlech,' said the Earl, 'after I embarked from the French coast, I had many misgivings before I landed, but now the die is cast. I begin to feel my strength. I am in my native land. I behold my followers increasing. I hear loud acclamations on our line of march, "Long live King Henry, God bless him!" I begin to feel, Ap Dafydd, that the prophetic words of your Lady of Gêst will yet be fulfilled. I shall not forget my promise to the fair daughter of Harlech if I succeed. Remember she is to come herself to receive the gift. She must grace my court with her presence on that occasion.'

After a rapid and fatiguing march, Henry with his native adherents and French auxiliaries reached Shrewsbury.

Henry's anxiety was greatly relieved by the courtesy shown to him by the inhabitants. He was received by Sir George Talbot, and the young Earl of Shrewsbury his ward, who joined him there with two thousand men.

During his short stay in the town, Henry received the intelligence that his stepfather Lord Stanley, and his brother Sir William were levying troops to oppose him. This greatly embarrassed and annoyed him. Upon drawing near Atherstone, he became undeceived. Bent upon knowing the truth, he obtained a secret conference with Lord Stanley by the aid of Kynfin Tudor, and was assured by his stepfather that he had no real intention of deserting his cause, though obliged to dissimulate on account of young Lord Strange, who was unfortunately in King Richard's power, dreading lest the monarch should wreak his vengeance upon his son.

The Earl now advanced towards Lichfield. There were several excellent officers in his army, expectations became more sanguine, and his resolution stronger. Meanwhile, his

antagonist was in consternation. Richard had flattered himself
that it would be an easy thing to silence the invader. With a
confidential air, and the courage of self-reliance which he
possessed in a remarkable manner, he prepared his strength
for the field. Upon receiving the information of his opponent's
accumulating success; of Sir Walter Herbert's infidelity, as
well as that Richmond was on full march to Lichfield, he
became more alarmed. His apprehensions increased upon
finding that many of his officers were going over to the other
side. Rumours reached him that Lord Stanley and his brother
were wavering, and that treachery might be expected in that
quarter.

With disappointment, resentment, and apprehension, King
Richard hastily marched to Leicester. Henry hearing of the
King's movement abandoned his first design of marching on
the metropolis, and determined to go and give the King a
meeting in the field. It was a bold resolution. Richard prided
himself upon his military skill. He was considered an excellent
soldier. He had born down everything in his way till now, and
wore the crown of England, in itself a tower of strength.

Henry had only the hope of overcoming in the field by the
justice of his cause. The tide of fortune might turn against one
so much abhorred by the nation and by humanity, the
perpetrator of deeds the most daring, treacherous, and cruel
that stain the pages of England's distinguished annals. What
if his enemy were more powerful in men at arms, and bore the
charm of kingship, his cause was bad, his diadem was sullied.
What if his courage were fearless and his hand dexterous at
the sword, he who has truth and justice on his side might hope
to vanquish the most formidable enemy. Thrice is he armed
who has a just quarrel. A kingdom for a prize! Was there to be

cold hesitation? 'Let apprehension go to the winds!' Such were the reflections of Richmond while the moment of the impending conflict drew near.

The hostile forces approached Market Bosworth, a town of Leicestershire. The forces of Richmond numbered a little more than six thousand, those of Richard were nearly double that number. But the Earl of Richmond was well aware of the intended treachery of Lord Stanley, who posted himself near Atherstone, a spot from which he might join either side as the tide of fortune turned. Richard was not unaware of his intention, but concealed his apprehensions.

When the day awoke, on the 22nd of August, 1485, Henry of Richmond placed his army in array, the van under the Earl of Oxford, the wings under Sir George Talbot and Sir John Savage. Henry, with Jasper, Earl of Pembroke, placed himself in the centre. Kynfin took post at the Earl's side. The van of Richard's army was conducted by the Duke of Norfolk, the King himself commanded the centre.

The experienced generals in the army of Richmond would not have compensated for the greater number in that of the king's, had not the followers of Lord Stanley been neutralized. Henry of Richmond and the Earl of Oxford encouraged their forces before the engagement took place. The animated speech which Henry delivered to them, was received with shouts that spoke the zealous feelings of the adherents to his cause, particularly the brave Welshmen.

Richard's mind was in a state of great anxiety respecting the fidelity of the Stanleys. In silence he watched their approach, and saw them draw up their forces and place themselves in a position that awakened fresh suspicion.

'Why do they post themselves so far apart,' cried he with a

look of perplexity and annoyance. Turning to one of his attendants, he exclaimed with an air of authority:—

'Command the Stanleys to march, and join the rest of our army immediately! No delay—remember!' Shortly afterwards he withdrew to a little distance from his attendants, and again turning his restless eyes in the direction of Atherstone, he once more repeated:— 'Why do they post themselves there? Serpents, slippery serpents, traitorously inclined; my secret misgivings have not been unfounded. Their treachery will turn the tide of fortune, base serpents!'

While occupied with these painful reflections, and every instant becoming more impatient for an answer, a tall, gaunt female figure stealthily approached him. Her long grey dishevelled hair was floating over her shoulders, which were covered with a dingy cloak. Fixing her large keen eyes upon the monarch's harsher visage, and with a contemptuous laugh, she exclaimed:—

'Thy mind is ill at ease, King Richard!—Ill at ease!'

The hump-backed monarch started at the words. Too well he recognized the voice, and shuddering, his eyes came in contact with those of his unwelcome visitor. Dark and silently he lifted his withered arm and motioned her away. Still she remained, stretching herself upwards as if to increase her stature, and making the most hideous grimaces, while pointing her skinny finger at the deformed monarch.

'Hag! perfidious hag!' cried Richard recovering himself instantly from his sudden fear, for such was his undaunted nature, 'dost thou come to greet me on the eve of deeds that will mark or mar my crown! Avaunt I say, woman! Avaunt to hell!'

'Ha! ha! Thou art pale, King Richard, aye pale. Thou wilt

soon be paler. Dickon, Dickon, thou art bought and sold—thy mind is ill at ease! Conscience! Conscience!' shrieked the wild woman with another of her hideous gestures.

'Leave me, woman! Conscience is the word only cowards use,' cried the King with a look of scorn and anger kindling in his features. 'Ho! the guard; the guard, I say.'

'Ha! ha!' laughed the Dewines. 'Dickon, I tell thee, thou art bought and sold! Hell calls for the fratricide, regicide, murderer of the innocent! The hour of retribution is at hand! Dickon, Dickon, thou art bought and sold! Glory for England! Glory for Cambria! The days of thy ambition are numbered— Dickon, Dickon, thou art bought and sold!'

This conversation was the work of a moment. The Lady of Gêst hurried away. Soldiers were coming up to the spot, and the messenger was approaching with the answer from Lord Stanley that 'he would come up as soon as it was convenient'.

'The devil have the slippery serpent!' ejaculated Richard with an angry frown. 'By the holy Virgin, I will send back the son headless to the father. Brackenbury hearest thou my command?' continued the King addressing that dependent, who had just come up. 'Lay the axe on Lord Strange's neck. Linger at your peril! Hell take the Stanleys. Snakes in the grass, traitors!'

A few minutes afterwards the Duke of Norfolk came up in haste to the King—

'Brackenbury has just informed me that your highness has issued a mandate for the execution of young Lord Strange. Is it politic on the eve of combat? Your highness's surmises may prove unfounded. Permit me to remind you, Sire, that neither Lord Strange nor his brother Sir William, have declared for Richmond.'

'That may be, Norfolk: yet their position declares for him. They are traitors—before God they are traitors!'

'Should it be their intention to remain neuter in the combat and join the victor, which please your highness is not unlikely, it will not avail to concern ourselves yet about their conduct,' said the Earl of Northumberland taking the side of the Duke of Norfolk. 'Our army far outnumbers that of Richmond. If Stanley prove a traitor, we have still Lord Strange in our power.'

'Recall the royal mandate, I beseech your highness!' once more urged the humane Norfolk, seeing that Richard wavered. He trembled lest the execution should take place before the reprieve could be sent to Brackenbury.

'So let it be—suspend the mandate: it is of little moment,' replied the King pettishly. 'I am right still, you will soon find that out. Stanley is a traitor!'

The kind-hearted Norfolk heard no more, but hastened to rescue the hope of Lancaster from the axe.

Richard was again alone; it was for the last time. The accents of the Dewines still haunted his mind. In vain he strove to shake off his horrible forebodings. With a sickening heart, he bent his steps to his tent. There while equipping himself for the field, with more than usual care, a glittering crown upon his helmet, his manner suddenly changed; with a determined and dauntless front, he seemed ready to hurl defiance at destiny itself. He mounted his charger, meditating still on the words of the strange woman, 'she prophesies ill—what if ill comes? It is, at least, left me to defy it.' He then rode to the field and took his station, the whole army having been previously drawn up in battle array by the Duke of Norfolk.

The archers of Richmond began the contest, and their salute was immediately returned with loss on both sides. The men-at-arms met hand to hand, and sanguinary was the combat, Richard the self-possessed and accomplished soldier, was ever where danger was most imminent, fighting with desperate courage for his crown and kingdom. Wrought up to frightful excitement, he penetrated even to the centre of Richmond's army, hurling down all who came across his path, officers and men alike; covered with dust and blood, rage and despair depicted in his countenance, 'Dickon, Dickon, thou art bought and sold,' seemed to rankle in his mind, and render every blow of his short, nervous arm more deadly in its effect. Like a ravening tiger, he continued to search for Richmond, 'where is he? Lucifer shields him from my vengeance,' cried the King, once more spurring his horse into the centre of his opponent's array.

Just at that moment, Lord Stanley seeing how the fortune of the day was leaning, marched rapidly along, and took up his position so as to strengthen the centre of Richmond's army, which Richard's fierce onset had caused to waver. This sudden movement confused the Duke of Norfolk's previous arrangement, and rendered any manoeuvre on his part wholly impracticable. He now saw the treason of the Stanleys fully displayed; and that the day was lost. He, too, had received a prophetic hint of the impending evil coming out of his tent early that morning. It was in a billet inscribed:—

'Jack of Norfolk, be not too bold,
For Dickon thy master is bought and sold!'

The lines were somewhat mysterious, he thought, and though he hastily flung them aside, they made a deep impression upon his mind. They did not, however, shake his faith towards the cause he embraced; and he was content to brave the consequences.

Richard continued to rage over the field, now shouting to his men to encourage them, now showing them their duty by his example, now calling like one bereft of his senses, 'Henry of Richmond, where is he? Let us dispute the crown hand to hand.' Striking down all who intercepted his progress, he slew Sir William Brandon, the Earl of Richmond's standard-bearer with one blow of his battleaxe. Sir John Cheney, he dismounted, still trying to open his way to the Earl of Richmond, who did not decline the hand to hand challenge. His friends, however, placed themselves before the Earl, and among the number was Kynfin Tudor, who more than once had previously taken up that post to resist the monarch's infuriated efforts. The followers of Lord Stanley were pressing in around the Earl of Richmond at that moment. Kynfin suddenly assailed by Richard, struck the monarch so violent a blow on the helmet that the back part of the axe penetrated his skull, and he fell to the ground. Kynfin could strike no second blow, nor was it necessary, the first had proved fatal. A hundred bills from Lord Stanley's newly arrived men, fell upon the fallen King, who was past feeling 'ere they reached him.

Kynfin had thus avenged the death of his father, who had expired under Richard's treacherous back-blow upon the field of Tewkesbury. The tyrant, guilty of so many crimes, was no more. When the battle was over, and night had restored peace to nature, Kynfin propped upon his knees, uncovered his head, and offered up a prayer of thanksgiving to heaven. Nor did

Henry of Richmond neglect the next morning to command that the Te Deum should be chanted by his army in gratitude for his success. Acclamations of joy burst from every lip, and the air was rent with the cry of 'Long live King Henry VII.' The sound was a grateful one to the Earl of Richmond. His nobles flocked around him, and throwing themselves at his feet, swore him fealty. Lord Stanley brought the crown, which Richard had worn throughout the engagement. It had been found on the field suspended upon a hawthorn bush. The crown was placed upon the Earl of Richmond's head, and again the cry was raised 'Long live King Henry VII!' From that moment, Henry wore the title throughout the British Isle, though only formally acknowledged the lawful King of England and Wales, sometime afterwards.

The casualties on the side of Richmond were not great in comparison with those of the enemy. Providence seemed to have watched over his forces. Sir William Brandon was the only chief of note who fell. The enemy left four thousand men on this memorable field. The Duke of Norfolk with the witch of Gêst's words upon his lips, was amongst the slain. The troops of the new monarch quitted the field of battle to take up their quarters at Leicester, with the mangled remains of King Richard besmeared with blood and dust. The body thrown across a horse, was borne with mock triumph to the town. The Dewines had prophesied that his crowned head would be brought low, and touch the pavement of one of his towns. In passing over one of the bridges in Leicester, it swung against a curb stone, and thus was her prophecy fulfilled. The banner of the Red Rose was now floating over England; and gleams of sunshine at last broke in upon rejoicing Cambria.

CHAPTER XIII

The Prophecy Fulfilled—
A Battlefield—The Weird's Warning—
A Crown Won

AT Leicester, heedless of everything around him in the locality, Kynfin Tudor went in search of his fellow-mate in the *Eryr*, his old friend Ap Maelgwyn. He had placed himself under Richmond's banner before Ap Dafydd had joined them with the brave men of Merioneth. Loud and happy congratulations were exchanged on their meeting. The prophecy made to them many years back in the house of Gêst, had now been fulfilled. They spoke of the past, and the present with pleasure, and glanced forward at the future with renewed hope. Men long depressed in circumstances by the late wars now began to look forward to an elevation to their pristine position. Ap Maelgwyn informed Kynfin that Henry of Richmond had already promised to create his uncle Rhys ap Thomas the Governor of Wales, and through that influence he hoped to be restored to his fortunes.

Ap Dafydd warmly sympathized with his friend in the happy prospects of his family, and rejoiced that one so worthy as Ap Thomas, should be promoted to that distinguished post. Ap Maelgwyn expressed a wish to go over and visit Bosworth Field again, and Kynfin consented to accompany him.

The day was warm, and even oppressive. After walking

over the silent field, where they were interring the dead, Kynfin and Ap Maelgwyn stretched themselves under the foliage of a wide-spreading oak, and contemplated the scene of the previous day's conflict, now no longer resounding with the clangour of arms. They had thrown the bridles over their horses' necks, and left them grazing hard by where they lay.

Kynfin was struck at the contrast the field presented to that of the day before. The warmth and fatigue almost lulled them asleep. They were suddenly aroused by a voice close at hand, and looking up, the Dewines was standing over them. She, at once, addressed Kynfin in a shrill voice:—

'Son of Harlech, what are you doing here, when—

'He, King of England, doth reign,
The seventh Harry of that name?'

'Remember the daughter of Harlech, Ap Dafydd. Go fetch the maiden from her mountain home. Take her to London city. Tarry not. Waste no more precious hours asleep in the sun. Go sluggard!'

'Good mother! I am ready to do as you wish,' replied Kynfin Tudor, with his eyes fixed upon her altered features. 'I must first acquaint my royal master with my intention.'

'Whist! whist! You buzzard, you blind beetle!' resumed the Dewines, with an angry frown, 'you go not back to Leicester. Gainsay me not, and you will do well. You too, Ap Maelgwyn, I have somewhat to say to you presently. Gainsay me not, and you too will do well.' She struck a strong matted switch of rank grass across the shoulders of each.

'I will be guided by what you say, good mother,' again

responded Kynfin. 'But what am I to do with the daughter of Harlech when I bring her to London? These are early times. It may be the King will be too much engaged to receive so soon, either the daughter of Harlech, or myself.'

'Ha! ha!' laughed the Lady of Gêst, contemptuously, 'why, infant, you must meet evils more than half way. There is time enough to talk about that, foolish child, blind beetle that thou art! Babble no longer, son of Harlech! Go, it is the Dewines that bids thee, and the Dewines will look upon the fair daughter of Harlech, and welcome her to the metropolis of England. What are you looking at me in that way for, Ap Dafydd? Have you forgotten the Lady of the creek of Borth that you stand hesitating there? Have you forgotten what she did in that remote corner of the land? Have you forgotten, son of Harlech, that it was she who foretold this day seven long years ago? Who told the crooked-backed King Richard, the regicide, the murderer of the innocent, that yesterday would be his last? Who warned Jack of Norfolk, mate of the *Eryr*?' continued she, lowering her voice to a sepulchral tone, and staring at them with her bloodshot eyes, 'have you forgotten who checked the bold commander of the *Eryr* in his course. Alack! alack! Had he not disobeyed me, poor boy! Poor boy! It would have been well for him, and for me. My heart was with him.'

Her frame trembled as she repeated the last words, and throwing her arms into the air with one frantic bound, rushed towards a thicket, and with unnatural cries, disappeared from their sight. Kynfin and Ap Maelgwyn looked at one another in mute astonishment. The spell was soon broken by the tramp of horse and cheerful voices. Soon after, Sir George Talbot, and a party of officers came up to review the field of combat.

The Earl of Oxford, and Rhys ap Thomas were of the party. The latter seeing his kinsman, immediately rode to the spot, and entered into conversation. The Earl of Oxford shook Kynfin warmly by the hand, spoke of the valiant chieftain of Harlech, and of the good cheer that he had partaken of under the hospitable roof of Cader y Cil. He inquired after the daughter of Harlech, declaring that she still lived in his memory. The enthusiastic child with her deep intelligent eyes, while clinging on her grandfather's neck, made a deep impression upon his mind. Kynfin and Ap Maelgwyn mounted their horses, and rode with the party in question across the field. None could refrain from congratulating themselves upon the late glorious victory, but lamenting the loss of so many brave soldiers and countrymen, who had perished in the cause of the White Rose. Lord Ferrers, Brackenbury, Ratcliff, Clarendon, the Duke of Norfolk, Sir William Conyers, these had been among the slain.

'Do you know what his Highness intends doing with the prisoners?' inquired Kynfin of the Earl of Oxford, as they rode off the battlefield together.

'For the present they are to be sent to the Tower,' replied the Earl. 'Henry thinks of leaving Leicester in a few days. I feel anxious to see how the good citizens of London will receive us. The King is perplexed to decide, under what title he shall lay claim to the crown. There being three from which to choose, makes it difficult to settle. Sometimes he thinks of retaining it by military election. I would not advise him to such a step. It would be hazardous. There is still an heir to the House of York.'

'The Earl of Warwick you mean, the son of the unfortunate Duke of Clarence?' replied Kynfin.

'The same. Sir Robert Willoughby was sent off this

morning to fetch the boy from Sheriff Hutton, in Yorkshire. He is to be placed in confinement in the Tower.'

Kynfin looked at his companion in surprise: 'What! is that by the royal Henry's command?' said he. 'The lad is not bright in his intellect I should have thought it hardly necessary.'

'For the present it is best to be cautious,' remarked the Earl. 'When Henry of Lancaster is firmly seated on his throne, these restrictions may be withdrawn.'

Kynfin became thoughtful, and after he had ridden with them above a mile, made an excuse for returning to Bosworth; and exchanging looks with Ap Maelgwyn they parted.

Henry of Richmond was received by the citizens of London with demonstrations of joy. Their rejoicings were greater upon his solemnly protesting that he would espouse Elizabeth of York. Thus the bloody Wars of the Roses, that had for years spread terror, devastation, and sorrow, throughout the land were at an end. England was to be blessed by a long peace. Ap Maelgwyn, who had followed in the royal train to London, through the interest of his renowned kinsman, Rhys ap Thomas, was made one of the royal equerries, and many more of his countrymen were favoured with similar honours. Henry felt peculiarly indebted to the zealous hearts in Cambria, and took every opportunity of evincing his gratitude towards them, seeming pleased to have them about his person. His first step was to promote to the dukedom of Bedford his valued kinsman, the good Earl of Pembroke, who had not only been a cheering companion to him in his exile, but had acted the part of a devoted parent and friend.

Mirth now filled the royal palaces and everyone felt that,

'The land from a tyrant was freed.'

Animation and joy were in every face, disunion had spread its wings and taken flight. Old friends embraced each other, and many talked over bygone scenes with varied emotion. Margaret of Richmond flew in haste to behold her beloved, her long absent son. With tears of gladness she welcomed and blessed him with all a mother's affection.

CHAPTER XIV

The Stranger—An Injunction Repeated—A Mysterious Interview

A THICK fog hung over the streets of London, and a chill wind crept through the crevices of the windows. Mysterious, or rather novel, sounds were heard from the apartment where Gladys and her uncle were sitting before a cheerful fire, reposing themselves after their fatiguing journey. The noises in the streets gradually abated, for the hour of midnight had arrived before the travellers thought of rising to separate for the night.

'Gladys, you are excited, and over fatigued,' said Kynfin Tudor, kissing her burning cheek. 'You must go to rest my child. We will resume the subject of our discourse tomorrow!'

'Not yet,' pleaded the maiden in no way disposed to forsake the blazing hearth, and her uncle's society, 'I am interested in all you have been relating. Tell me, uncle, when do you think the Dewines will pay us a visit?'

'The daughter of Harlech will not have occasion to repeat that question,' said a voice from the further end of the apartment, and the gaunt figure of the Lady of Gêst glided into the room, and slowly closed the door after her.

'The daughter of Harlech is welcome, thrice welcome,' continued the Dewines drawing near Gladys, who was still sitting at her uncle's feet. Placing her long bony hands crosswise over her head, the Dewines repeated several hurried sentences. 'The daughter of Harlech is welcome, thrice welcome to England, as well as to Wales. She is welcome on sea, as well as on land. The daughter of Harlech is always welcome again and again,' repeated this singular woman, fixing her eyes upon those of Gladys, and examining every feature with apparent interest.

'The daughter of Harlech is grateful to the Dewines for all that she has done in her behalf,' said Gladys, in one of her softest tones, extending her fair hand as an acknowledgment.

The strange woman looked into her eyes with a bewildered expression, and bowing her head, imprinted a kiss upon the fair hand, and instantly drew back.

Kynfin Tudor was a silent spectator, every instant becoming more and more absorbed in the scene. The query flashed across his mind, why the Dewines should concern herself so much about the welfare of Gladys. He had often asked himself the question? and it had long seemed to demand a reply. The Lady of Gêst's eyes were still fixed upon the object of her solicitude. She continued:

'Let me warn the fair daughter of Harlech ere she appears in the glittering halls of King Henry, to hold herself aloof from the vain Saxon maidens, and the gay courtiers. They are full of flattering words: she will do well to avoid them. Let her be firm to gain the charter. Let her look to the good Jasper of Hatfield, and the Earl of Oxford to befriend her. She must not look to King Henry VII, monarch of his name. The good heart of the Lancaster of old is already departing from the race. The cowardly misgiving soul already fears his throne is insecure, and that he must link himself to a Yorkist, the descendant of the deadly foe of his house. By that deed, the noble spirit of a Lancaster dies within him. Henry VII, monarch of that name, is no longer Henry of Richmond. His soul is narrow and avaricious. I knew he would show his true nature; I knew he would fling off the mask. It is well you have that parchment under his hand; that promise which I made you exact from him—that charter for Wales. Else it would be suspended for many a dreary year. He would sell it: he would sell you, and all Wales. He is a Judas—a Judas, he thinks only of the bag. Have you the writing safe, child of Cambria? Is it safe?'

'Yes!' repeated Gladys, as rising and drawing the precious document from the fold of her dress: she presented it to the weird sister of Gêst.

The Dewines held it between her skinny fingers to the light, and perused it with eager scrutiny. 'Good, good!' she repeated as she returned it. She then scanned the maiden once more from head to foot, with an admiring expression of feature, not without a cast of melancholy.

'Fair daughter of Harlech, granddaughter of Ap Jevan, I once more warn you, as soon as you move in King Henry's glittering halls to remember my injunction. Then, when you return to your mountain land, the hare will not follow in your footsteps, nor owl thrice hoot ominously over your head:

"Filthy and untoward fowl,
With broad head, and ominous howl,
With demure and solemn face—
Goblin of the feathered race!"'[20]

As the Dewines concluded, she moved away from Gladys, and looking at Kynfin Tudor, exclaimed:—

---

[20] Davyth Ap Gwilym.

'When I send for thee, tarry thou not. Farewell daughter of Harlech! Farewell!' The door then softly closed upon the retreating form of the prophetess of Gêst.

The moment she was gone, Gladys threw her arms around her uncle's neck, and looking in his face tried to read what was passing in his mind.

'Bless thee, my Gladys bach!' ejaculated Kynfin. 'I might have spared my anxiety. Few maidens would have looked upon that woman without an expression of terror; few would have given her so gentle a greeting as thou didst. You require no monitor, my blessed child. The Dewines is pleased.'

'She is a terrible woman to look upon, I acknowledge,' said Gladys, 'but we owe her much: I should have been sorry to hurt her feelings or cause her displeasure. This, too, is the woman the pirate chief so often called upon! This is the woman that spread such terror over the bay, and foretold that the red rose banner would again float over the battlements of Harlech. I have seen at last this prophetess of our land! She will ever live in my memory.'

When Gladys retired to her apartment, she experienced no superstitious feelings, no childish terrors. She calmly stretched herself upon her couch, and fell asleep, dreaming of the Dewines and King Henry's glittering halls.

'One of the royal household is waiting to be admitted,' said the hostess of the inn where they sojourned, addressing Kynfin Tudor, who immediately gave orders that the visitor should be introduced, and Ap Maelgwyn entered the apartment.

Gladys did not recognize the mate of the *Eryr* at the first glance, and the gay equerry in his court dress, bowed formally on his entrance. Ap Maelgwyn's frank laugh following the formality, revealed him under his disguise. Gladys welcomed him with a smile of real pleasure.

She had seen him but twice since they had parted at Vannes, and he had entrusted to her a secret of his heart. He would have lingered for some time, and chatted away to his old friend, but he remembered that he had come with a message from the Dewines, demanding as usual no delay. To Kynfin, he whispered a few hurried sentences, spoke his farewell, and then with Kynfin quitted the apartment, leaving Gladys in solitude.

Kynfin and his companion proceeded through a labyrinth of alleys and streets in breathless haste, until they readied a narrow dark court in the heart of the city. Ap Maelgwyn gave a loud whistle, and a youth immediately appeared with two horses ready equipped.

'Mount, Ap Dafydd,' cried Maelgwyn as he sprang upon the animal nearest to him. 'We have a long ride before us. The Lady of Gêst awaits us in Windsor forest, I fear we shall be after time: forward, therefore, with speed.' Without another word both put spurs to their horses, and kept up at a hard pace until they reached their destination.

'Softly, softly,' ejaculated Ap Maelgwyn, drawing in the reins. 'This I think was the oak, yes, I am sure of it; can you see her anywhere?'

'Whist! whist! you talk loud enough for the vulgar in Windsor palace kitchen,' cried the Dewines laying her matted switch across Ap Maelgwyn's shoulders, who had just dismounted and was patting the sides of his panting steed.

'Welcome, son of Harlech, you have done well,' continued the Lady of Gêst, turning to face the individual whom she had addressed. 'The Duke of Bedford has just ridden by; it is he who concerns thee and me. Thou must see his Grace this night, aye this very night, late as it is, Ap Dafydd; Ap Maelgwyn, that bird of gaudy plumage, must conduct thee to the castle,' continued the Dewines with a wild laugh, 'thou must gain access into the good Jasper of Hatfield's private apartments.'

'But, good mother,' rejoined Ap Maelgwyn, 'supposing the noble Duke refuses to be disturbed at so late an hour, what are we to do then?'

'Peace, you blind buzzard,' cried the Dewines in a sharp voice. 'Son of Harlech, I tell thee thou shalt stand in the august presence of his Grace the Duke of Bedford before the sand has run out the coming hour. He will greet thee with kindness and complaisant looks, delay not! The injunctions I have already given, remember them. Leave him not till an early day is fixed for the daughter of Harlech to be presented to Henry the Seventh of that name. Obtain the promise from his Grace that he and the Earl of Oxford shall be present. Speak boldly! Let your tongue be loose, guide it discreetly, fear nothing; now mount again, Son of Harlech, away! Let speed be thy motto. Remember a Saxon and a Yorkist still breathes within the walls of Harlech, the home of thy forefathers, the inheritance of the last of the house of Einion, the child of thy lamented brother, the fair Gladys. Speed! speed! Away! away!' were the words which followed the two horsemen as they started on the gallop through the forest, towards the keep of the royal castle towering above the surrounding oaks. Soon the lower battlements of Windsor were unbosomed amid the foliage, and under the Round Tower by a back portal they obtained admittance, and were winding their way through the dark passages and staircases towards the apartments of the Duke of Bedford.

On gaining the entrance of the Duke's suite of chambers, a page demanded their business.

'We would see the Duke of Bedford,' said Kynfin in a firm tone, 'I will take no denial.'

'It is late,' said the page, 'it is not usual for his Grace to be disturbed at this hour.'

'No matter, tell his Grace that the son of Harlech would speak with him.'

The sallow-looking boy eyed the intruders with the prying expression common among court servitors, and pointing to some seats nearby, immediately entered the private apartments of the Duke.

'His Grace will see you,' said the page on his return.

'I will remain here,' whispered Ap Maelgwyn.

Ap Dafydd moved after his conductor, who threw open several doors in succession, and ushered him into a costly apartment adorned with paintings and tapestry; at the further end of which sat Jasper of Hatfield, apparently engaged in perusing some documents which were upon the table before him. The moment he caught sight of Kynfin, he arose and advanced to meet him.

'Right glad am I to see you, my noble kinsman,' exclaimed the Duke, 'I have been looking for you many days past. Is the fair daughter of Harlech well, have you brought her to the metropolis?'

'I thank your Grace for your kind inquiries, she is well, I left her side but a few hours ago in London,' replied Ap Dafydd. 'That is as it should be,' answered the Duke, 'but we must have her within the old walls of Windsor to gladden our sight once more, her beaming face and look of intelligence have remained fresh in my memory since we parted in

Brittany; I am impatient to see her, I am anxious too that our Cambrian fair one should vie with the haughty Saxon beauties of the royal suit.'

Kynfin's countenance became more thoughtful: for some minutes he made no reply, and then with a little hesitation observed that it was on account of the daughter of Harlech that he sought the interview. 'It was the Dewines, the prophetess of Gêst who sent me hither at this unseasonable hour,' added Kynfin.

'What!' ejaculated the Duke with a look of surprise, 'has that strange woman left the remotest corner in Wales to share the rejoicings of the Red Rose party? Who is the Lady of Gêst, Kynfin? Was it not the Lady of Gêst,' continued the Duke placing his hand thoughtfully upon his brow, 'that warned King Richard on the field of Bosworth, an incident of which everyone is yet talking?'

'The same,' said Ap Dafydd, 'she has not been in Wales some years.'

The Duke silent for a moment continued:— 'If that is the case, the ghost or troubled spirit that report made wander about Windsor, Westminster, and the Tower, for several years past, must have been the Lady of Gêst. It is whispered that it was this woman who administered a draught to King Edward; Richard was in confederacy with her. She must be a most dangerous person. How is it, Kynfin, that you are in her secrets?'

Kynfin somewhat confused, gave as a reply:—

'It was because, good Jasper of Hatfield, your Grace I mean, she has been a sincere friend to the unfortunate Lancastrians, and those who have been deprived of their rights and were sufferers during the long reign of the implacable

Yorkists; I am deeply indebted to her, as are all of the Red Rose party. Let it please your Grace not to pass censure upon this singular and unaccountable creature. None know her history, save that she has received some marks of ignominy at the hands of the Yorkists: by them have her days been embittered. She is surely rather an object of sympathy than censure to every good Lancastrian.'

'By my troth then, the good Lady of Gêst shall not be censured by the Duke of Bedford,' replied the Duke, 'if she have suffered in such a cause, therefore, my worthy kinsman set your heart at ease. I am now quite ready to hear what is expected of me by this mysterious being, who you say has just sent you hither.'

'That your Grace will interest yourself in behalf of the daughter of Harlech, and fix an early day for her presentation to his highness, and that the Earl of Oxford and yourself be present at the time to urge the King to sign the charter, and break the yoke of our people without delay. We have a longing desire to go back to the home of our forefathers, carrying the glad tidings to the hearts, the many, the yearning hearts in Cambria.'

'Nothing will give me more pleasure than to interest myself in behalf of the fair daughter of Harlech, my sweet kinsman. But you must not be in a hurry to deprive us of her society, she shall be conveyed hither without delay. We will then, at a convenient moment, seek an interview with the royal Henry: do not think of fixing any very early period.'

'The Dewines bade me not return till an early day was named,' observed Ap Dafydd.

The Duke of Bedford looked somewhat disappointed, and replied:—

'If Kynfin it must be so, I will give you an answer in the morning. Perhaps, when we have you secure in the palace, you will think better of it; you must not carry from us the sweetest flower in Cambria, till we have at least inhaled some of its sweetness.'

CHAPTER XV

A Palatial Castle—Court Scenes— Royal Waverings—The Petition— Home Desires

THE daughter of Harlech, the enthusiastic maid of a wild mountain home, now stood within the palatial walls of Windsor. The Saxon beauties gazed upon the fair Cambrian with envious eyes, not untinctured with jealousy. Her elegant form appeared to great advantage in the fashionable costume of the court: it had been presented to her by Jasper of Hatfield, or, more correctly, the Duke of Bedford. The flowing robe and the pale blue satin petticoat richly embroidered, and chastely trimmed with costly point lace and silver knots, were strikingly attractive, and were particularly becoming to Gladys. She was greeted in the corridor on her way to the royal apartments by the Earl of Oxford, who had lately been installed Constable of the Tower. That warm-hearted courtier, with the peculiar charm of manner which attaches to high breeding, ever at ease with itself and others, entered into conversation with her. He reminded her of his visit to Cader y Cil, how she had alarmed him by dancing on a precipice, and had laughed at his apprehensions. He alluded to her known devotion to her rocky land when younger, and how she had stamped her little foot, telling him she hated a Saxon, but above all others the cruel Yorkists, bestowing wrathful words upon them for taking away her grandfather.

Gladys smiled at the enumeration of these trivial incidents in her early years, expressing surprise that he should have retained them in his memory; she added that she did not think years had much changed her predisposition, since she had the same wild inclination for roving over her native mountains, and felt the same pleasure at standing upon the brink of a precipice as she did when a child.

In animated conversation, the daughter of Harlech passed on through the crowd of gentlemen of the bedchamber and the royal household, who gazed with admiration upon the loveliness of the kinswoman of the Duke of Bedford. There was one eager face beyond the rest that bent forward to look upon her features, and then fell back against a pillar for support; his countenance assuming a pallid hue, his limbs in tremor. There seemed a weight of blood pressing upon his heart. He became insensible to all else passing around him; he saw only Gladys; he heard the music of her voice alone, and then placing his hands against his forehead, he stood with his face to the pillar, mute and motionless as a statue.

Well was it that the daughter of Harlech did not observe that face, nor encounter its gaze. Well was it that she was spared so sad a trial. She passed on, unconscious of the pang which she was inflicting upon a heart that was still as dear to her as ever.

She now entered the royal apartments, filled with more than their usual brilliancy of beauty and rank. She was received by the King and the Duke of Bedford with every demonstration of satisfaction and pleasure. The King introduced her to his mother, the amiable Countess Richmond, and to several other distinguished ladies of the court.

A grand entertainment was given at the palace the same evening, and several others succeeded. Gladys felt bewildered at the gay and glittering scenes around her.

Old courtiers and young thronged to lavish their attentions upon one so honoured by the King, and so lovely in person; crowding around her to glance at the daughter of Merioneth[21] whose beauty was without an equal at the court of King Henry. The Countess of Richmond distinguished herself by her kindness to the orphan in a strange land, and took her under her especial protection. The Duke of Bedford and the Earl of Oxford never ceased their attentions, and were ever at hand to help her in every difficulty that ignorance of etiquette might otherwise occasion.

A few days after the arrival of Gladys at the palace, King Henry demanded the presence of the daughter of Harlech and her uncle. This was a moment of considerable anxiety on her part, as she was introduced leaning upon the arm of the Duke of Bedford, and thus she passed on from room to room, as far as the King's private apartments. The Duke felt her hand tremble, and observed the colour rise upon her cheeks; with the same warm and generous heart he always displayed, he raised her spirit, assuring her that as long as he could befriend her she had nothing to fear. The charter she had exacted might cause some division in the cabinet, it was a question that would necessarily demand consideration; there would be delay before it was properly engrossed and signed, but all he assured her would be finally arranged to her satisfaction, the promise fulfilled, and her hopes realized.

After passing through several antechambers and

---

[21] The daughters of Merioneth were proverbial for their beauty, and are so to this day. The bards have been profuse in their panegyrics.

encountering many pages and sentinels, Kynfin Tudor had scarcely whispered a few words of comfort to Gladys, before they found themselves in the presence of his Highness. The monarch appeared, as they entered, to be engaged in some state matters with his stepfather Lord Stanley, the Earl of Derby, Willoughby, Lord Brooke, and Cheyney.

'We will defer this subject to a more convenient time,' said the King. Immediately afterwards Lord Brooke and Cheyney withdrew.

'Please, your Highness, I have brought the daughter of Harlech according to your command,' said the Duke of Bedford, advancing and leading the maiden by the hand towards the King who was sitting in state.

'I trow you have done well, worthy uncle,' answered the monarch, carrying an expression upon his features which did not exactly agree with his words. Kynfin Tudor's eyes were fixed upon the royal countenance, and the words of the Lady of Gêst came into his mind. 'Henry the Seventh, monarch of that name, is no longer Henry of Richmond, the heart of a Lancaster is departing from him.'

The King's face was overshadowed; it seemed an effort when he observed with a voice of assumed cheerfulness:—

'Welcome, fair daughter of Harlech, you have acted in accordance with my words delivered to you in the pavilion of the chateau in Brittany years ago, I requested you to come in person to claim my promise. Methinks, the fair maiden of Cambria is in some haste to be restored to her rights: it matters not, as it is your wish, we will this day install you as keeper of our castle of Harlech, the impregnable key of North Wales. With it we restore you the broad acres of your inheritance, which on the side of your mother we find have been accumulating to a large amount. May the fair heiress long enjoy her possessions, and be a comfort and blessing to her people. These are my sincere desires.'

Gladys threw herself upon her knees before the King, and with peculiar grace and propriety of language expressed her gratitude; but there hung still an anxious shade over her features; she felt a misgiving at her heart. The monarch's voice had ceased, and not a word about the promised charter had been spoken, no allusion was made to the scroll which she held in her hand. What would her castle and her broad acres be to her without the emancipation of her people? How could she ever return to them, without the document of which she had promised to be the bearer? She cast, at the same time, furtive glances at the Duke of Bedford and her uncle, feeling an overpowering anxiety and zeal in the good cause of her people. The injunctions of the prophetess, too, came sounding in her ears. She clasped her hands together, and in a tone of supplication entreated his Highness, not to be displeased with her for reminding him that in restoring her to her property, he was only fulfilling a part of the promise he had made to her on that memorable day in France, and she presented him with the paper containing the ciphered promise.

'Troth! fair daughter of Harlech, keeper of my stronghold, this had nigh escaped my memory,' said the King perusing the paper with apparent eagerness and curiosity. 'Our council must take this into consideration. Yes, yes, it is true our good people in Cambria have suffered deeply from the Saxon yoke. We will endeavour to restore them, as we have restored their fair pleader, to their just rights.'

Gladys looked earnestly in the King's face: she did not feel satisfied with the royal words or manner. Again the injunctions of the prophetess of Gêst flashed across her mind, she felt she must be firm, or the charter would remain suspended, and her people continue in bondage.

'Pardon me, please your Highness, but it may perchance have escaped your Highness's recollection that I was to be the bearer of the charter to my people, I cannot return home without it, I dare not meet my people, for they know of the royal promise of Henry of Richmond,' resumed Gladys, her voice sinking into a whisper, and a deep blush mantling her cheeks. 'Let me entreat your Highness to take the matter into your royal consideration without delay that my people may feast their eyes upon that charter with the great seal which is to free them from the Saxon yoke. The hearts in Cambria beat warm for their royal master; the hearts in Cambria will ever be devoted and grateful to their sovereign, one of their own soil, one of their flesh and blood.'

The gentle tones of the maiden, the charming expression of her countenance, and her graceful air, gained the hearts of all present in favour of her petition, and all more or less sympathized with the fair pleader.

'It is impossible your Highness can refuse such sweet tones of entreaty,' whispered the Duke of Bedford to his royal nephew. 'Release this flower of Cambria with a word of comfort.' The Countess of Richmond, also, spoke to the King in her favour, who replied to the fair petitioner:—

'In the presence of these present, composing a part of my court, I make my royal declaration that the charter shall be engrossed and signed with as little delay as possible,' replied the King, raising the beautiful petitioner from her knees, and placing a costly bracelet around her arm. 'In the interim,' continued the monarch, 'I hope she will continue to grace our court with her presence. It is further the royal wish that the fair keeper of Harlech should bestow her hand upon someone of the noble gentlemen in the royal household, methinks the fair keeper will require a helpmate to retain the strong walls of Harlech against our enemies, if any such again appear before them.'

The colour faded from the cheeks of Gladys, with a look of surprise and apprehension she replied:—

'May it please your Highness not to exact that wish, my uncle Kynfin will afford me all the aid I require in protecting the walls of Harlech: your Highness may be assured there will be no cause for complaint.'

'The fair keeper of Harlech must not rely upon her worthy uncle,' replied Henry. 'We have a post in reserve for him, his feats of archery in the wild woods of Brittany have made too deep an impression upon my memory to permit, in my present position, such skill to remain useless to the nation. We are about to establish a strong guard of archers near our person, I know of none so deserving or so well calculated to fill the distinguished office of their commander, as Kynfin Tudor. You will receive the appointment of their commander-in-chief very shortly.'

The nomination fell upon the ears of Kynfin and his niece like tidings of some great evil. The desired period of their restoration, for so long a time to the home of their ancestors, every plan of their future happiness to be shared together was thus abortive. No thoughts of separation seemed to have intruded upon their minds. The King's words, therefore, were painfully received by both.

'My fair kinswoman must not look so distressed,' said the sympathizing Duke of Bedford, taking Gladys by the hand

and leading her aside. 'Is your uncle's society so necessary to you that you cannot be happy without him, nor bestow your affections and hand upon a helpmate?'

'Your Grace is already aware that, till of late, my uncle's life has been darkened by trouble,' replied the maiden, 'and just as I am able to make his sad heart happy, inestimable parent as he has been to me, it will be a bitter and hard struggle for us to part. It is a sudden and unexpected mortification,' concluded Gladys with a trembling voice, while tears fell from her eyes. 'Do pray intercede for us my Lord Duke, do not let my uncle's brow be again overshadowed; the restoration to my rights will fail in making me happy when I know he is wretched.'

'The daughter of Harlech's happiness shall not be interfered with; the happy restoration to the home of her forefathers shall not, by my troth, be darkened so long as Jasper of Hatfield stands near the royal person,' exclaimed the old courtier with great warmth and animation, 'let us only have a little patience.' He sealed the pledge he had given by kissing her hand.

They were delayed in the King's household some time, on account of the charter not being completed. Gladys began to grow weary of the gay scene, she longed to be where her heart was, in Cambria, surrounded by her people, she grew impatient to stand upon the battlements of Harlech once more, and to see her beloved grandmother seated in the great hall of the castle again. She thought of her friend Jacqueline, and what happiness it would be to welcome her to her home. She felt isolated from her uncle and the quiet intercourse she loved: and became weary of King Henry's glittering halls, the fawning parasites of the court, the flattering insincerity of the courtiers, and the perpetual dissipation surrounding her. She longed to stand again knee-deep among the purple heather of her native hillsides, to listen to the browsing of the deer and the bleating of the sheep, the dashing of the cataracts or the roaring of the wind as it lifts the foam crested waves, and dashes them into spray among the rocks; she longed again to rest her eyes from the place of her repose upon the deep blue waters of her native bay.

CHAPTER XVI

The Sleeper Interrupted—A Midnight Adventure—The Confession

THE revelry in the royal banqueting halls had not ceased when Kynfin Tudor secretly withdrew to his chamber. He had passed a day of bustle and anxiety, and was weary like his niece, though the gay scenes of a court were not new to him as they were to her, for the palaces of Windsor, Westminster, and the Tower had long been familiar to him. He was satiated and fatigued, and threw himself upon his bed with a long drawn sigh. The lamp he had left upon the table flickered, giving symptoms of an expiring flame, and causing dark ghostly shadows in the remoter parts of the ample room in which he lay. His eyes were fixed upon the arras, till he fancied it moved, and the figures of its horsemen and men at arms seemed coming down from the walls and approaching his bed.

Soon afterwards sleep drew its curtain over his eyes, and he dropped into a heavy slumber. How long he had thus slumbered he was not aware, before he was aroused by a strange noise, from what quarter he could not divine. Starting up he beheld the bright beams of the moon shining in through his window, and discovered the gaunt figure of the prophetess of Gêst in the middle of the apartment. She approached him, and exclaimed:—

'Son of Harlech, you heavy slumberer, arise! Arise!' and with a gesture of impatience she continued, 'I will be here again quickly. Be ready for me!' She then disappeared behind the arras.

Startled as he was, Kynfin did not take long to prepare himself: and soon afterwards the Lady of Gêst reappeared with a lantern in her hand.

'What is it you want with me at this hour, good mother?' said Kynfin Tudor facing his mysterious visitor and telling her that he was ready.

'Whist! whist! babbler,' cried the Lady of Gêst in an undertone, beckoning him at the same time to follow her through a secret door behind the tapestry which she opened.

'Step softly, don't beat your foot like a clown,' muttered the Dewines, pursuing her way in haste through long galleries and cold cheerless-looking apartments till they reached a flight of steps. Pausing for a moment, and holding up a bunch of keys to the light she examined them, and found the one she sought. The moment she had unlocked the last door that intercepted their progress, she dashed the lantern passionately upon the ground and placed her foot upon the light. They now stood without the gates of the Castle of Windsor.

'Speed, speed,' cried the Dewines; speed was a favourite word of the Lady of Gêst. In this instance she repeated it with tenfold emphasis, suiting the action to the word, and hurrying on with such fearful strides that Kynfin, fleet of foot as he was, found it no easy task to keep up with her.

Where the Dewines was taking him, and what object she had in view he was wholly ignorant. A profound silence was observed the whole way, save when her companion lingered a little, and then she repeated the words 'speed! speed!' The forest of Windsor was entered, and Kynfin was led along a narrow unbeaten track, the Dewines looking occasionally behind her. The wind roared and whistled through the ancient oaks, the scattered clouds were driven along the heavens with whirlwind rapidity, now concealing, then revealing the moon's pale orb, now darkened partially, and then with fitful gleams, shining forth with redoubled brightness.

Kynfin's mind was busy thinking of his strange conductress, and how far she intended to lead him, when she suddenly stopped, and turning round, held out her arm at full length to impede his progress.

'Son of Harlech,' she cried, 'have you the papers which your brother's widow instructed to your charge?'

Ap Dafydd started at the question and replied:—

'No, good mother, I gave them to the King, and in the first instance he told the daughter of Harlech that she should claim her mother's estates; but now he has scruples on account of our not being able to prove the marriage, and he doubts if he can reserve them. The Duke of Bedford had words with him, and he was warm in the maiden's cause, while the countenance of the King was overshadowed.'

'The heart of a Lancaster is departing from him,' muttered the Dewines swinging her matted switch over her head, 'he doubts; and he doubts where there is no foundation. I knew it would be so, he is a miser, he loves money obtained by any means, he has the devil of avarice. He will keep back the estates if he can frame an excuse—you hear—dost thou heed me. The marriage must and shall be proved, aye, it shall be proved. The fair Saxon lily was lawfully wedded to that generous, and noble heart, handsome youth of Cambria.' With these words 'speed, speed,' she again rushed forward with greater impetuosity than before, nor did she halt till she reached a small low thatched cottage. Kynfin out of breath and quite bewildered, followed close to his mysterious companion, who ever and anon was cramming her fingers into her mouth, and making the most uncouth sounds close up against the window. Again and again, she repeated the noises.

At length a step was heard, the door was suddenly thrown open, and the moonbeams shone full upon a tall bony youth with a skin of sickly hue, and pale yellow lank hair falling over his unclad shoulders.

'Ha! ha! idiot!' shrieked the Dewines, on perceiving that he shrank back from the stranger. 'Does the spirit of the holy father yet inhabit its mouldering day-built tenement—no, boy? dolt!'

'No, yes, no, he is not dead yet,' stuttered the lad with fear and trembling, as not knowing scarcely what he was about, he stumbled over a stool in getting out of her way and then fell flat upon the floor.

'Timorous idiot! Heed him not, son of Harlech,' cried the Dewines, as Kynfin was about to render him assistance.

Then seizing her companion by the arm she drew him into a small side room, dimly lighted by a glimmering lamp suspended against the wall.

'Holy Father we are come,' cried the Dewines approaching a narrow bed. 'Behold the brother of Tudor Ap Dafydd, that noble, generous-hearted youth of Cambria.'

'Santa Maria! Holy mother have mercy on me, sin! sin! sin! sin!' muttered the monk, clasping his shrivelled hands together, not aware that anyone was present.

Again the prophetess of Gêst repeated the same words, this

time stooping over the bed and shouting them in his ear; the sick man then opened his eyes and with a strange expression looked her full in the face.

'Whither! whither!' cried he, 'bring the light and I will look upon his countenance.'

The lamp was then held up before Ap Dafydd, who had been pulled forward by the Dewines. The monk's eyes met his own.

'I would have seen thee years gone by, Kynfin son of the Harlech chief,' said the old man catching him by the hand, 'I have long had somewhat to say unto thee, I have not kept my promise to the Cambrian youth. It is too late, I am suffocating, I am dying.' A violent fit of coughing choked his utterance, and for some moments he appeared to be strangling.

The Lady of Gêst hastily quitted the room, and on her reappearance she had a bottle and, drinking horn in her hand.

'Holy Father take this,' she shouted in his ear holding the vessel to his lips, 'It will ease your throat, and do your stomach good.'

'Poison! poison!' muttered the monk shuddering violently and pushing the drinking horn from his lips. 'Woman, let not thy evil spirit disturb my last hour, thou mightest have spared thyself this crime. Sin! sin! sin!' and again his shrivelled hands and bony fingers were clasped together in the same attitude as before.

'Fool! Madman! Drivelling dotard!' vociferated the Lady of Gêst, drawing herself up erect, and dashing the cup of cordial to the further end of the room. 'Yes, madman, worse than madman, drivelling dotard! Foulest of sinners, it is thy last hour; thou mayest thank me that it did not come before; that thou wert not hung like a dog for the crimes that have been visited upon us, thou ungrateful wretch! thou wolf in sheep's clothing! thou demon of another world! Poison, indeed! Poison! when my object would have been ruined by it; ha! ha! thou ungrateful wretch!' With three strides across the room she then dashed through the doorway, slamming it behind her with such violence that the craggy cottage shook to its foundation.

If Kynfin Tudor's astonishment was great, he felt still more so the strangeness of his position. There he stood over the bed, with the lamp in his hand, listening to the groans of the sick monk. A thousand strange thoughts flashed across his mind. He endeavoured to rouse the old man to whatever promise he had to fulfil; for it was evident that promise was connected with his brother's marriage. It was all important that he should obtain it, but he still failed in his attempts. To give the sick man something seemed necessary, and Ap Dafydd turned himself to look for the lad, whom he had seen upon his first entrance, and immediately went in search of him.

Seated on an old trunk in the adjoining apartment, he discovered the youth fast asleep.

'Boy!' cried Kynfin, shaking him by the shoulders, 'I want you to give your master something, he is very ill?'

'Dying, yes dying, the woman said so,' muttered the youth, burying his knuckles in his hollow eyes, looking more asleep than awake, and more stupid than if he were wholly either.

'Come, come, rouse yourself,' said Ap Dafydd with some impatience, 'Have you nothing to give the Holy Father—does he not take something?'

'Yes—no—yes! Stop, this is what we give him when he is very bad,' replied the boy at last, staggering across the kitchen, and reaching down a bottle from a shelf; 'you must not give him too much.'

'Come yourself, you shall administer it to him, while I hold the light,' said Ap Dafydd, dragging the youth by force into the sick man's chamber. In a short time, the cordial was poured down the monk's throat, and he quickly began to revive, inquiring in a voice of terror, 'Is she there?'

'She is gone,' said Ap Dafydd, leaning over his bed. 'There is none here, but the son of the Welsh chief.'

'Listen to me, then, listen to me, my son!' cried the sick monk, clawing the bedclothes, and blinking with his red-shot eyes. 'It was I who married the handsome Cambrian youth to the fair lily of the court of King Henry VI. It was in this house they were united, in the presence of that woman, who aided them in everything. It is she who has been tormenting me many days past, for the clue of the document which affords evidence of their marriage. I would not give it her. I promised Tudor, son of the Welsh chief, I would, in case of his demise, place it in your hands, the hands of his brother. That promise I have neglected—it troubles me. It lies there in that trunk. Kynfin, brother of Tudor, you will find it, here is the key.'

'That is to the purpose,' ejaculated Ap Dafydd, 'but tell me, is that woman anyway connected with my brother's widow?'

'Yes!' cried the monk, drawing his hand over his face, 'her daughter was the foster-mother of thy brother's widow. Speak no more of the woman who brought thee here, she was Bridget of Windsor. It troubles my soul, sin! sin! sin! Oh, Santa Maria! Save my soul! Ease my soul in purgatory, sin, sin, sin!'

'Is there no one of the Holy brethren near, Father; would you not like to confess?' said Kynfin, concerned at the troubled state of the dying man, who continued clutching at the bedclothes, uttering deep groans, and appearing to grow weaker and weaker.

'Yes, Holy brother, come near me. Let me confess—let me confess before my soul is in purgatory. Holy brother, buy my sins, buy my sins!' cried the monk frantically clasping his hands, and looking towards Kynfin, whom in his distracted state, he now took for a brother of his order. 'It was I who delivered up the innocents. Why did I commit so foul a crime? Why, Bridget of Windsor, did I take thy innocent child, and sacrifice her to the young Lord of Fauconbridge, so tender in years as she was, and so beautiful. What expiation can I make for that? Another crime! worse—blood, I spilled blood! Excommunicate me not! Bridget's cries were ever sounding in my ears, Bridget's curses were suspended over me. I had no peace, she came to me and said if I would aid to save her grandson, Fauconbridge from the block, she would cease from haunting me with her curses. She would leave me to my remorse. I consented: Holy brother I consented, to deliver up a victim to the crown, my own sister's son in place of her grandson, Thomas Nevil, the child of Bridget's daughter. The girl I stole from the widow and gave to the gay young Lord of Fauconbridge. Santa Maria! forgive me. Holy saints, forgive me—sin! sin! sin! Purgatory! Eternity!' The dying monk's heart palpitated, then beat only at intervals, his jaw rose and fell, the death rattle came into his throat; and the still chamber was filled with that sound of death more loud than it usually waits upon expiring nature.

Kynfin contemplated the frightful spectacle like a statue. The monk's confession had startled him. A veil was drawn from before his eyes. The Dewines was the rover's grandmother; the foster mother of his Aliano had been her daughter. All the bygone words and actions which the Lady of Gêst had said and done so unaccountable in themselves, now came into his mind with their motives. He approached the trunk to which the monk had referred him, and raising the lid began to search for the desired paper. Packet after packet, endorsed with the name, 'Bridget of Windsor' attracted his attention. After he had secured the testimony of his brother's marriage, he leaned over the chest indulging his curiosity. He discovered that Bridget was the widow of a canon; that the rover's mother had fallen a victim to the Duchess of York, whose son, the Duke of Gloucester, had taken a prominent part in the mysterious circumstances connected with the history of the unfortunate girl. A correspondence between Sir Gilbert and the Duchess of York, also fell under Kynfin's eyes, revealing all the particulars of the keeper's baseness, and confirming Dhu's statement to Roderike on the night of the murder.

Ap Dafydd was employed in the perusal of these papers, when the Lady of Gêst suddenly re-appeared.

'Hold, hold! son of Harlech!' cried she in an angry tone, 'how darest thou read those papers? How darest thou go to that chest, thou vile meddler?'

'The monk bid me, good mother,' replied Kynfin, rising with some confusion from his knees.

'Have you the paper of your brother's marriage?' she inquired with impatience.

When Kynfin answered in the affirmative, she passed on towards the bed where the monk now reposed in death.

'Dead! dead!' she repeated, placing her palm upon his forehead, and lifting up his stiffening hands, 'give me a light!' cried the Lady of Gêst. Then she began to examine the body more minutely, repeating again, 'dead! dead! Paul Leewood, thy troubles are over in this world, but not in the next.'

Having satisfied herself that the monk was no more, she hurried towards the chest. Then with surprising activity, she tossed out its contents upon the floor, heaping upon them pile after pile of straw, litter, and every combustible she could find.

The son of Harlech watched her in silence, not conjecturing what her intention might be. On a sudden she snatched the lamp from his hand, and placed it in the miscellaneous heap. The straw immediately caught fire. The higher the flames rose, the more the prophetess of Gêst laughed. Twice and thrice she danced round the burning pile, filling the room with shrieks more like those of insanity than joy or sorrow. The smoke increased. She suddenly seized Ap Dafydd by the arm, and dragged him out of the chamber, through the kitchen into the open air, calling upon the yellow-haired youth to follow.

At a little distance from the cottage, they all three stood watching the progress of the flames, which had already begun to issue from the door and windows, and seize upon the thatched roof. The Dewines laughed, and shrieked alternately. The lank youth stood clinging to a tree for support, his teeth chattering, and limbs trembling, while the son of Harlech was astounded from being unable to comprehend events so singular as were thus suddenly presented to his attention.

CHAPTER XVII

The Charter Delivered—A Sacrifice Consummated—The Daughter of Harlech in Its Halls Again

IT was early when the daughter of Harlech arose from her couch, and offered up an earnest prayer of gratitude to heaven. That day the charter was to be delivered into her hands; from that day would date the emancipation of her fellow countrymen, and their equality with their Saxon invaders. They had groaned under the yoke for more than two centuries: they were now to be upon an equality of right, privilege, and law. What gladness, what shouts of joy would resound throughout her own rocky land at the intelligence! The hearts of Cambria would at length be made glad from north to south, from the west to the borders. Her heart overflowed with unutterable pleasure at the prospect; her conscience too was at rest. Hard as the struggle had been, she had fulfilled her duty, she had not forsaken the determination she had made in her early years: she was about to be rewarded, she was about to be restored to the home of her forefathers that had been desolated by the stranger. There, on that very spot, her uncle's and grandmother's hopes would meet fruition. Her people would be secured in their privileges on the same footing as the Saxons before the law: they would be happy, and she should enjoy the reflection of having been the instrument of so much good.

The King had commanded the presence of the daughter of Harlech at a fixed hour, as soon as the necessary legal forms were completed. Great interest was evinced on the occasion of the presentation of the charter; the old walls of Windsor were filled, every member of the royal household, and many distinguished visitors were desirous to witness the presentation of the document to the favoured fair one, whose love of her country had been so conspicuously displayed, and whose beauty had excited so much notoriety in a court, remarkable for the personal charms of the fair dames who paid homage to its queen.

Henry was sitting in regal pomp. The grand hall was crowded when the daughter of Harlech made her entrance at the side door, accompanied by the Countess of Richmond, and several distinguished ladies of the court. Lord Stanley and the Duke of Bedford, the Constable of the Tower and Kynfin Tudor were in her train.

At this time, Gladys had just entered her twenty-fifth year being in the prime of womanhood and beauty. Her attire was chaste, simple and elegant, she was more than beautiful; she looked all radiant. Some little defect indeed seemed wanting to set off her dazzling charms by contrast. Her carriage was simple yet dignified, but her simplicity and dignity were natural, owing nothing to artifice. Every eye was turned upon her, and every tongue involuntarily whispered its admiration.

After the king had greeted his fair kinswoman, and paid her merited compliments, with truly royal condescension, the charter was delivered into the hands of Lord Stanley, and he was commanded to read it. This he performed with a clear and audible utterance.

The maiden's eye never once wandered towards the gay

assemblage around her, nor even to the throne itself, but remained fixed upon the precious document, listening with attention to every word pronounced by the reader until the whole was concluded.

The king then demanded if she approved of what had been granted, and in reply expressing her satisfaction, his Highness immediately signed the document in her presence, and that of the courtiers at his side. Afterwards he presented it to her with a gracious smile and the following regal address:

'Take this charter, fair keeper of my fortress of Harlech, declare and proclaim it to my good people of Wales. May they live to enjoy the rights which have so long been withheld from them. Henceforth, England and Wales enjoy equal privileges. Impartial judgment shall be dealt to both without favour or affection. Heart and soul let England and Cambria be united. Such, fair Lady of Harlech, is my royal wish, and irrevocable decree.'

The maiden's heart overflowed—it was too full to do more than look her thanks. She uttered, indeed, a half intelligible sentence of acknowledgment. Overborne by delight she pressed the charter passionately to her lips, and then to her heart, forgetting for a moment how she was situated. It was only a momentary impulse. On a sudden, recollecting herself, she sank upon her knees before the monarch, and bending herself towards his footstool invoked a blessing upon his head. The monarch gently raised her up, and thanked her for the prayer she had uttered.

There was one in that gay attendant throng, who felt more interest, more admiration than all the rest, and it must be added the most acute pain, while he bore himself calmly. He took not his eyes a moment from the face of Gladys, and beheld joy gilding every feature at the all-absorbing wish of her heart being at last realized. But for him, there was no joy, although he rejoiced in her happiness. The gratification of her people stood before his; it was theirs, not his. The veil fell from before his eyes. The sacrifice made of her affection was necessary for the good of her people, and she had made it. The pure unselfish Gladys, whose heart was still his, if circumstances forbade the open acknowledgment, would, in future, appear to him that of a guardian angel, rather than of mortal love. She had told him that her heart should be his till death. That which she had said could not be unsaid, for he had now proved the determination and steadfastness of her character. With that knowledge, and a full reliance upon it, he must be satisfied she would never belong to another; that, at least, was a consolation, a proud consolation to his saddened heart. Again, he thought of her as of his guardian angel. He formed the resolution to devote himself to the service of her people and dependents, as well as herself. None should have cause to complain of the Saxon keeper of Cricceath, while his eyes could discern the ocean roll between him and the lofty turrets of Harlech.

Before the cold blasts of winter swept over the land, or the snow covered the mountain-top, the daughter of Harlech was on her journey home, there to carry glad tidings to the oppressed Welsh people. The Duke of Bedford and the Earl of Oxford escorted the fair keeper to her castle. Rhys Ap Thomas and other Welsh gentlemen were of her train.

Scarcely had they crossed the borders, when they were met by crowds of their countrymen, cap in hand, to behold the charter, and welcome their fair deliverer. 'Happy Cambria!' loud were the rejoicings which resounded from hill to valley, and valley to hill, throughout the emancipated land. Loud the echoes from rock to rock of 'happy Cambria, freed Cambria— Cambria for ever!' The Saxon yoke was no more, for Cambrian and Saxon were one; the old privileges of the people being given back to them. 'Cambria is free,' they shouted; one town and village taking the tidings from another. 'Cambria is as it was in the days of our forefathers. He who sits on England's throne is the child of our soil, of our own true blood. Cambria, thou art free! thou art free!'

From the aged to the infant, all who could lisp her name lifted up their voices to bless the peerless maid of Merioneth, to rejoice that the sun once more shone upon her hearth, and smiled again upon the dwelling of her grandsire, the brave Dafydd ap Jevan.

Her journey through the mountain land was slow, because it was a scene of rejoicing in which she was bound to participate with the people. On every height blazed a huge bonfire; over every monastery and homestead the Red Dragon banner floated in the breeze. It was a joyful sight for the emancipated people; again their native wilds breathed freedom. The tyrant cannot enslave nature, and those wilds were not more free than her people.

Great as the rejoicings were before the daughter of Harlech arrived upon the borders of Merioneth, there the welcome was still more enthusiastic. The brave men of the Cwm, bearing the Red Dragon banner, first hailed her with shouts of joy that rent the heavens. Indeed, it seemed more like madness than joy, and the blessings they invoked upon Gladys unlike any other blessing ever pronounced.

Their own mountain child, the sunbeam in the Cwm, their chieftain's wyres bach had returned filling every heart with delight. Always devoted to the granddaughter of their chief, they were now become so proud of her that they seemed as if they had no language to express their pride. Their feelings were sometimes stifled into silence, sometimes frantic in action without language, sometimes uttered in unmeaning sounds, and frequently only expressed by tears. Their hearts were overcome. With uncovered heads they bent before the fair heiress of the house of Einion, and blessed her. The devotional prayed in return for the favour bestowed upon them. The less reverential indulged in rioting and feasting.

Followed by increasing crowds of her countrymen, the daughter of Harlech continued on her way, riding upon a milk-white charger, abreast with the Duke of Bedford, and the governor of Wales; Kynfin Tudor and the Earl of Oxford following. Kynfin rode up to the side of his niece when the grey turrets of their home came first in sight to gladden their eyes together, to gaze upon the old walls, and again on the deep blue waters of the bay as of old.

At length they arrived at the castle gate, where deafening acclamations from the zealous hearts of Merioneth greeted them.

The feelings of Gladys could only be read on her countenance, or judged of in her own heart. Her people knelt before her in the manner of those times, and the simultaneous cry of joy which burst from every lip, as the fair keeper was presented with the keys of the castle, rent the air, and made the old walls vibrate with the sound.

Bewildered and overwhelmed with joy, Gladys again stood in the hall of her ancestors. There almost overcome by her sensations, she received the congratulations of the people. The first voice of her family which welcomed her upon the threshold of the apartments within the walls, was that of her grandmother, and the first merry laugh which fell upon her ear, was that of her friend Jacqueline. The last threw her arms around her neck, and whispered that the bride of Ap Maelgwyn had come to join her voice with the good people of Cambria, in welcoming Gladys to the home of her forefathers.

In the midst of these cheerful and noisy congratulations and rejoicings, there glided into the hall a female figure in a singular garb. It moved slowly up behind the daughter of Harlech. Strange accents, more strangely uttered, hushed every voice.

'Welcome! thrice welcome! daughter of Harlech to the home of thy ancestors. Welcome—thrice welcome to Wales, as well as to England! Welcome on sea and land! Where is the daughter of Harlech not welcome? Kneel, peerless maiden of this land, kneel, I command you!'

The daughter of Harlech obeyed; and as if by instinct all present followed her example. It was the prophetess of Gêst, who crossing her hands once more over the maiden's head, uttered some incomprehensible sentences, and instantly disappeared through the crowd.

The Red Dragon floated over Harlech; the smoke arose from the house of Gêst, and the daughter of the castle stood once more upon her favourite battlements, her devoted uncle and protector at her side, neither a captive, nor again overshadowed by the dark visions of the present or future. In the place of these gloomy visions, sweet whispers were heard from Gladys, 'This is my home! the home of my ancestors, the home of my warrior forefathers! All around me I have made happy; yes, dear uncle, and I am happy, well-nigh too happy for a mortal!'

A solitary boat is often seen floating in the moonlight upon the waves beneath the grey towers of the fortress. Before the sun has gilded the mountain tops, it has returned to its moorings, and the keeper of the bold rock of Cricceath is again at his post. Though the waves roll between him and Harlech, the souls of the respective keepers are in alliance. Their hearts work together, both supporting the claims of the children of the soil.

The bold keeper of Cricceath, and the fair keeper of Harlech, are thus not only the commanders of the two strong posts which protect the bay, but are equally guardians of the freedom—privileges of the noble spirits in Cambria.

THE END.

ABOUT HONNO

Honno Welsh Women's Press was set up in 1986 by a group of women who felt strongly that women in Wales needed wider opportunities to see their writing in print and to become involved in the publishing process. Our aim is to develop the writing talents of women in Wales, give them new and exciting opportunities to see their work published and often to give them their first 'break' as a writer. Honno is registered as a community co-operative. Any profit that Honno makes is invested in the publishing programme. Women from Wales and around the world have expressed their support for Honno. Each supporter has a vote at the Annual General Meeting. For more information and to buy our publications, please write to Honno at the address below, or visit our website: www.honno.co.uk

Honno, 14 Creative Units, Aberystwyth Arts Centre Aberystwyth, Ceredigion SY23 3GL

Honno Friends

We are very grateful for the support of the Honno Friends: Annette Ecuyene, Audrey Jones, Gwyneth Tyson Roberts, Jenny Sabine, Beryl Thomas.

For more information on how you can become a Honno Friend, see: http://www.honno.co.uk/friends.php